SUMMER
of the
WAXMAN

ENDORSEMENTS

Summer of the Waxman is a must-read. This book had me turning pages, and that's a rare thing for me. With strong characters, including a severely disabled man who is sure to win your heart, and a surprising ending, the story will stay with the reader for a long time. A book worth re-reading again and again.

—**Linda Wood Rondeau**, author/speaker, and Selah Award Winner.

Set in rural Kentucky, *Summer of the Waxman* highlights the impacts on human relationships of prejudice, unresolved anger, and human pride. As he tells us about a big-city cop who returns home, Brent Brantley illustrates how our past experiences don't have to define our future. I found myself constantly wondering what would happen next, as his wide array of unforgettable characters traveled through the novel to its dramatic conclusion. I recommend you join Deke, Cecil, and Rita on their eventful journey, a story underscored by God's love, grace, and the power of redemption.

—**Steven Rogers**, author of the award-winning novel *Into the Room*.

Brent Brantley weaves yet another tale of a surprising mystery filled with a budding romance. Also at the heart of the story is a curious man known as the Waxman. In a touching novel of redemption and unconditional love, the author shows how the least of us can love and forgive the worst of us—those of us who believe we are unscathed by sin.

—**Claire O'Sullivan**, *Romance Under Wraps*, and *Rules of Engagement*.

I was captured by the superior characterization and excellent pacing in this book. Absolutely loved the characters! Also, interesting twists and turns in a believable plot for a real page turner. I look forward to seeing Brent Brantley's future books and highly recommend *Summer of the Waxman*.

—**Dr. Mary Ann Kerl**, author and former journalist.

SUMMER

of the

WAXMAN

BRENT I. BRANTLEY

A Christian Company
ElkLakePublishingInc.com

COPYRIGHT NOTICE

Cover and Interior Design: Derinda Babcock, Deb Haggerty
Editor(s): Mel Hughes, Deb Haggerty
Author Represented By: WordWise Media Services

PUBLISHED BY: Elk Lake Publishing, Inc., 35 Dogwood Drive, Plymouth, MA 02360, 2023

Library Cataloging Data
Names: Brantley, Brent (Brent Brantley)
Summer of the Waxman / Brent Brantley
398 p. 23cm × 15cm (9in × 6 in.)
ISBN-13: 9798891340329 (paperback) | 9798891430336- (trade hardcover) | 9798891340343 (trade paperback) | 9798891340350 (e-book)
Key Words: Christian fiction, suspense, romance, mystery, deputy sheriff, faith journey

Library of Congress Control Number: 2023946769 Fiction

DEDICATION

Dedicated to my family and friends of Western Kentucky who match my love for this part of our country. The story, events, and characters are a figment of my imagination. However, the spiritual lessons are real.

ACKNOWLEDGMENTS

In appreciation of all those who encouraged, edited, mentored, and prayed for me: Deb, Mel, Derinda, Cristel, Rose, and my wife, Jeanette.

CHAPTER 1

"What the heck!"

The eerie creature raised his arms like a shield.

Deke Campbell braked hard and whipped the Jeep's wheel to the left, sending his patrol car squealing and sliding to a halt fifteen feet from the figure.

Pulse racing, taking slow, measured breaths, the deputy stared at the strange character. He'd never seen anything like it, except maybe in a horror movie.

The man's face was distorted with scars, waxen and stretched as if his flesh had melted. Below a prominent scarred nose, a lipless mouth formed a wide O, as wide as his red-rimmed eyes, which seemed sunken into their bony sockets.

Deke stepped from the Jeep and approached the man. "Uhh, you all right? Sorry if I startled you. That was a sharp curve, and you pretty much appeared out of nowhere."

The eyes held the lawman spellbound. Drooping flesh partially obscured one eye, giving the man a haunting appearance. Yet, the damage could not hide two dark sad pools. The eyes reflected a gentleness which seemed out of place with the rest of his hideous features.

The man blinked rapidly and stretched his face into what might have translated as a subdued smile.

He stretched out long pale fingers behind his head and tugged a cord that held his yellowed Panama hat suspended on his back. Deke noticed he was missing an ear. The other lay crumpled against his head like a boxer's cauliflower trophy after years of ring abuse.

Without a word, the man slid the hat over his sweat-stained bandana, lowered the brim over his face, then whirled and disappeared into the woods and brush.

"Hey, you sure you're okay?" Deke shouted.

Only bobbing brush remained where the man had entered the woods.

Deke returned to the Jeep, closed the door, and slumped back into his seat. He took a deep breath, thankful he had not wrecked. More grateful that he had not hit the man with the melted face. He hadn't expected this. He was more concerned about Amish buggies then horror flick characters showing up on the road.

A dark memory forced its way forward. Deke shoved it back into the past, shaking his head. He needed a distraction.

Grabbing his notepad, Deke jotted as many details as possible—the man's tattered bib overalls tucked into laced-up, lumberjack black boots, his gray work shirt, and his straw Panama hat. He also described the small olive-green bag that hung by a cloth strap over the man's shoulder to his waist and the small rock hammer suspended in a loop on the leg of his bib. He didn't need to describe the face. He'd never forget that image.

The deputy drew a deep breath from the breeze entering through the open window and passed a hand over his close-cropped dark hair. He absently patted his left shirt pocket. Empty. He needed a cigarette.

Deke sighed, donned his Ray-Bans, released the brake, and headed for the command center in the courthouse. He had plenty of time to analyze the event on his twenty-minute drive back to the courthouse that housed his law enforcement headquarters.

From the second-floor window of the county courthouse, Sheriff Tim Holloman watched his new deputy glide the mud-splattered Jeep into its parking place. Deke slid from the vehicle and retrieved a large black case and a flashlight from the rear seat. He slammed the door and walked a few steps before returning to the patrol car. Grabbing his uniform hat, he adjusted it on his head and looked toward Tim's window.

Before Tim could back out of sight, Deke caught him with his wide grin. When the deputy reached the steps to the courthouse, he paused, removed his hat with a sweeping flourish, and bowed.

Sheriff Holloman shook his head. "Clown." He chuckled and turned, startled to see his assistant standing in the doorway.

"Amanda, I told you to use the intercom. That's what it's for. I could have been busy—cleaning my gun, playing poker on my phone, or maybe sleeping!"

Amanda smiled as he moved to his desk, plopping his lanky frame into the chair. He cradled his head in his hands and leaned forward, elbows resting on his desk, and spoke with exaggerated sarcasm. "Now, pray tell, what do you want?"

"I beg your pardon, High Sheriff, but I thought better of using the intercom with your potential guest hovering over me."

Amanda's curly brown hair danced as she leaned forward. "It's your favorite public defender."

Tim leaned back in his chair, rolled his eyes toward the ceiling, and stretched his hands out.

"Why me, God?"

"Hush! Your Momma would have your tail for joking like that!"

"Who says I was joking? What does she want?"

Amanda waved a dismissive hand and turned to open the door. "I'll let her tell you. Shall I send her in?"

The sheriff nodded and lowered his voice. "Amanda, Campbell is on his way up. Keep him out. I don't want those two to meet. At least not yet."

Amanda gave him a wry smile. "Yes, that might be wise."

She'd no sooner left Tim's office than the petite public defender, Rita Courtney, stepped through the swinging gate attached to the front counter and strode toward the office door.

"The sheriff will see you ..." Ms. Courtney stepped past her before Amanda said, "... now." Amanda gave the sheriff a shrug and closed the door.

"Good afternoon, Counselor." Tim flashed a half-hearted smile.

She ignored his greeting. "You have not returned my calls."

"Ms. Courtney, I have been serving warrants all morning and am just now getting back to the office." He paused, rose from his chair, and signaled the woman to a seat opposite his desk. "Please."

She took a deep breath and lowered herself into the oversized office chair, which had seen better days. "Thank you."

Was she always this serious? He let her ramble, resorting to a strategy he had used in the past with people whose conversation he'd missed. "Meaning?"

Rita squinted and sat silent for a few seconds, then slowly spoke again with an edge to her voice. "You have not heard a word I said."

Tim shrugged and opened his hands in surrender. "Look, Ms. Courtney, I have had a full day, and I apologize that I am distracted by other issues."

The public defender spoke with measured calm. "Sheriff, I said I was just in the jail this morning meeting with my client, Bobby Page. Well, I should say my former client, but I am sure the judge will appoint me again to represent him."

The sheriff allowed himself a faint smile. "Bad Boy Bobbie. What has he gotten himself into this time? Come on now. You've represented him before—you know he's not in the running for deacon at the First Baptist Church."

Rita leaned forward. "What he has gotten himself into is not relevant. However, what has happened to him should be of concern to you."

"Go on."

"One of your deputies roughed him up last night."

Tim mentally reviewed the details he'd read of Bobby's arrest on the blotter. Who made the arrest? Ah. Right.

"I believe Mitchell Dust was working last night, but I have not seen a report. He's not the sort who would muss up his own hair, let alone someone else's."

At her raised eyebrow, he continued.

"Mitchell is not exactly a 'Dirty Harry.' No disrespect intended to Mitch, but he is fat, fifty, and he thinks everything is funny."

The attorney shook her head. "No, no. It was the new guy. From Chicago. Campbell, Deacon Campbell."

"Oh. Well, that's different." He hurried on. "Not that Deke is prone to that behavior, but he does have a somewhat, shall we say, unorthodox—"

The office door flew open.

Deke Campbell leaped into the office, holding his hat like a shield and thrusting his black steel flashlight into the air as he shouted, "Freedom!"

His grin dissolved when Tim nodded at the visitor's chair. The young lawyer clutched the chair, her body suspended about four inches above the cushion.

In a monotone voice, the sheriff made introductions. "Ms. Courtney, allow me to present Deke Campbell, a.k.a. 'Braveheart.' Deputy, this is one of our public defenders, Ms. Rita Courtney."

Wide-eyed, the woman stared at Deke, lowering herself back onto the chair as she nodded.

Tim couldn't dismiss the deputy now. She'd accuse them of concocting an alibi. The best approach was to trust that Deke knew the drill. He jerked his head to a high-backed wooden chair. "Have a seat, Deputy."

Amanda appeared in the open doorway, sending Deke a glare. "I was in the file room and didn't see him."

Tim cleared his throat. "That's fine, Amanda. Close the door, please."

Deke tugged the chair nearer to the imposing wooden desk. He smiled at Ms. Courtney and raised his eyebrows at Tim.

The sheriff cleared his throat again and chose his words carefully. "The counselor represents Robert Page, and I believe you arrested him last night or late afternoon. I haven't read the arrest report yet."

"Yes, Sheriff. I arrested him. Caught him stealing a FedEx package from a front porch on Cold Springs Road."

"Counselor Courtney says he sustained injuries from the arrest. I assume he gave you some problems?" Tim held little regard for telepathy but hoped the deputy was picking up his silent plea.

Deke glanced at the scowling woman and replaced his smile with a somber expression. "Well, I was on routine patrol and passed him walking down the road near the victim's house and saw the FedEx truck pulling out of the drive. When I was further down the road and out of his sight, I turned around and returned. I parked my patrol unit and walked over a little rise to see what he was up to."

Deke halted and looked at the lawyer. She folded her hands in her lap and crossed her legs.

Tim hurried the narrative along. "And?"

"I saw him walking down the drive with the FedEx box, looking back at the house. So, I double-timed it, jumped into my vehicle, and overtook the suspect on the road back to town. I called for him to stop over my loudspeaker." The deputy shrugged. "He chose not to stop and ran down the road. He looked back at me, threw the box in the ditch, and then cut over to the left side of the road. He realized that Jeeps are not high-performance vehicles, but they are still faster than the average man."

Ms. Courtney leaned forward. "So, how did you apprehend Mr. Page?"

Deke turned his dark eyes to the questioner and, with a twinkle and a smile, said, "I *adored* him."

The sheriff hung his head. Maybe he wouldn't say it.

"Excuse me?"

"I *adored* him. When he would not stop, I got right beside him as he ran and timed it to open my door behind him. The pursuit terminated by door plus blacktop."

Tim sighed as Rita sat up straight.

"You used your vehicle as a deadly weapon to strike my client in the back and knock him to the ground?"

"No, I used a non-lethal door to gain control of an escaping perpetrator."

"You could have severely injured him. He has abrasions all over his arms and face. That was undue force."

Color rose in Deke's face. "Counselor, the elderly woman who lived in the house where he stole that package was awaiting critical medications. A month earlier, she went into the emergency room in a diabetic coma because she had not received meds shipped to her. I suspect that Bad Boy Bobby had visited her before and taken her previous delivery. She was easy pickin's." His color receded, and Deke's voice softened. "I figured it better he had a little road rash for his efforts, and the widow received her delivery. I did not put it in evidence because she needed the meds. I did him a favor. If I had placed the drugs in evidence, Bobby might be facing manslaughter charges in addition to theft because she could have died if deprived of her meds."

The attorney's eyes widened again, but she set her chin and gave him a defiant glare.

Deke stood and stepped toward Rita. "Counselor, you may be indignant on behalf of your client. However, I tend to be more indignant for the victim, an old lady who depends on medications for her life."

The attorney's features softened. "I, I'm sorry about the lady. I did not know that."

Deke absently patted his shirt pocket, then broke the awkward silence.

SUMMER OF THE WAXMAN

"Are we through here? I need to put some evidence in the locker and grab a bite to eat. It takes regular sustenance to abuse criminals." The deputy gave Rita a curt nod.

Tim sighed. "Easy, easy. Let's try to understand each other's perspective."

Deke turned to leave. "Y'all have a nice afternoon." He closed the door, leaving both sheriff and lawyer staring at the heavy wooden door.

Ms. Courtney turned back to the sheriff, raising that eyebrow again.

Tim shrugged. "Look, Deke's a good guy. He and I go way back. We went to school together, hunted, fished, chased girls, and played basketball until we graduated in '06. Then he left his home here in Kentucky to see the world through the Marine Corps and saw action in Afghanistan."

Tim stood and walked to the window while Rita's eyes followed him. "Deke never returned home here permanently to Crittenden County ... only to visit his family. He took a job as a penitentiary guard at Joliet, Illinois, for a short time until he was accepted by the Chicago Police Department." He turned from the window. "In fact, he is the one who talked me into a law enforcement career when he came to visit. I was voted in as sheriff when my predecessor passed unexpectedly."

Rita shrugged. "I'm not sure what that has to do with this case. But since you started it, if he liked policing so much, why did he leave Chicago?

Tim stared at the slowly rotating ceiling fan and became aware of the clicking noise. He kept forgetting to lubricate that thing.

"Now, Ms. Courtney, I believe that's not my story to tell. Just know under that cavalier persona is a good man, and a good deputy, with a good heart. Suffice it to say, he wanted to return to his boyhood roots and find a better quality of life."

She exhaled softly, and a smile lifted the corners of her mouth. "I see, I think. Okay, Sheriff. I will take that into consideration. First, however, I must do what I believe is best for my client." She rose to her feet, extending her hand.

Tim returned the gesture.

"Ms. Courtney ..."

"Please, 'Rita' will suffice, unless we are in the courtroom."

"Gotcha. And Tim will suffice for me. Unless you are upset with my people or me."

They both chuckled, and Tim opened the office door for her. He stepped around the counter and gave a nod. "Have a nice day."

"Same to you." Rita left through the main door, her heels clicking down the marble hall.

He turned to see Amanda staring at him with a questioning look, which he ignored. Instead, he returned to the counter, picking up a delinquent tax warrants folder.

"Well?" Amanda's impatience took control.

"Well, what?"

"You know!"

Tim leaned over the counter and spoke in a mock-conspiratorial tone. "You know I could tell you, but I would have to kill you."

"Oh, you goober."

Tim chuckled. "Do you know where my prodigal deputy is?"

"In his inner sanctum, most likely."

"I will be visiting him. Don't call me. I'll call you," he admonished.

"Yes, Igor."

CHAPTER 2

The sheriff bounded down the marble stairs to the basement and strode to a closed heavy wooden door that still bore the stained outline of missing letters spelling the word, 'CUSTODIAN.' He paused to read the posted sign tacked below the former term.

THE HONORABLE DEPUTY DEKE CAMPBELL
IF YOU ARE NOT EVIDENCE, YOU ARE NOT WELCOME!

Tim snorted and reached for the knob, grateful Deke had trained as an evidence technician his final year in Chicago and that he'd wanted to come back to his roots. The change had been a win-win for them both.

"Who dares to disturb the work of a genius?"

"The one who signs your overtime card."

The door creaked open. Deke wore goggles and a surgical mask with pointed teeth drawn in black marker. "Okay. I'll grant you entrance, but don't try to snack on anything here."

Tim entered and waited while Deke switched off the ultraviolet ray light over a set of latent prints on glass shards. Then, finally, he switched on the overhead light and removed his protective gear, including the apron protecting his uniform.

"Sit! And I will reward you with a mint." Deke gestured to a metal folding chair as he sank into a rickety office chair.

"Very funny."

The deputy picked up a Tic Tac box, flipping it open with one hand, and offered the contents to him.

The sheriff sat in the metal chair, declining the mint with an upraised hand. "Still battling the nicotine gang, I see."

"So far, it's a standoff. However, another session with Lady Justice could cause me to wave the white flag."

Tim laughed. "I cannot believe Mr. Model for sports would let himself get hooked on the burley leaf. Did that happen in the corps?"

"Nah. I had to maintain my lungs for yelling at my recruits as a drill instructor. Actually, it happened when I spent some time undercover in Chicago. Lollipops don't exactly promote an image of toughness when you're working a drug deal."

"So, you escaped the grass, coke, and horse, only to be captured by a legal drug."

"Never heard it put that way, but ... sure, I guess so." Deke popped another Tic Tac and squinted at his friend. "You never make a social call to my lab. What's up?"

The sheriff leaned forward. "True. It smells like dirty socks and bleach in here."

Deke feigned a hurt expression. "I am trying to do my laundry more than quarterly. So, you have to have patience."

"Look, in all seriousness, Rita—Counselor Courtney—is a smart, good lawyer and has a great personality."

Deke leaned back with his mouth open. "I am shocked! Shocked, I say. Does Bev know about this?"

"Cut it out. My wife and I know her family well. They lived in Union County. Her mother, sweet lady, still lives in Union. John, her father, was a farmer and auctioneer. Unfortunately, he passed away a couple of years ago. I miss him. He had a great sense of humor. In his younger days, he had some issues with Kentucky bourbon. Got mean sometimes. But, he cleaned up, and a nicer guy you couldn't find. Then he was funnier."

"Evidently, Pop's sense of humor was not passed down in the genes."

Both men chuckled. After a few seconds, Tim broke the silence. "All I'm saying is this is not Chicago where there's a sea of people. Here you'll run into everyone again and again. You need all the friends you can get, especially a lady like her."

Deke tilted his head and smirked. "Trying to get reelected, Sheriff?"

"You're pathetic. I don't know why I just had to have you as a deputy."

Deke rose and smirked again. "Because you could not live without me. But don't worry, I'll never tell Bev." Deke gave a short laugh and dodged his friend's playful swing.

As they walked toward the door, Deke's demeanor became serious. "Oh, I had a weird experience this afternoon as I ended my tour."

"Oh?"

"I was driving on Crooked Creek Road near the bridge when a man appeared out of the woods on the shoulder. I didn't see him until I was right on him. He gave me quite a jolt."

Tim remained quiet, waiting for more to the story.

"When I stopped and got a good look at this guy, it was like Halloween in the spring. He seemed old, wore bibs and a straw Panama hat, but his facial features looked like he'd been rescued halfway through an attempted cremation. His face looked melted. Scary."

Tim nodded. "Waxman."

"What? Waxman? Sounds like a walking action figure."

"Do you remember the burned-out house on Crooked Creek? The old Burgess house? The chimney and the charred remains are still there."

"Yeah, I remember my parents talking about the house fire when I was a kid. Happened back in '85 or '86. Killed all the family, right?"

"Fire was in 1988 and took the life of Francine Burgess. Her husband, Dennis, had been killed in an industrial accident in Paducah about three months earlier. He fell about eighty feet while working on the power plant, leaving her pregnant and alone. Her baby chose to enter this world on the night of the housefire."

He had Deke's attention. Tim leaned on the still-closed door as Deke settled onto the workbench.

"Your aunt May was her midwife." He stopped, and a furrow creased his brow. "By the way, how is Mrs. Duston? I haven't seen her since she went to the nursing home."

"She is doing fine at seventy-nine, despite a broken hip. But unfortunately, her mind wanders a bit. I plan to see her tomorrow night." Deke frowned. "Go on, go on. Speaking of wandering minds."

"Well, a lightning storm knocked out the transformer. Knowing Mrs. Burgess would be without electricity and unable to call, Miss May drove down to check on her. When she pulled up, the back of the house was in flames. They think a kerosene lantern started it. Anyway, the story is Mrs. Burgess had already delivered the baby alone, and when your aunt raced through the front door, she found the woman unconscious on the living room floor. I think, if I got it straight, she heard a baby screaming in the bedroom, where the fire was, and rescued him."

Tim gazed at the evidence-packed shelves without seeing them. "The mother didn't make it. Burns and smoke inhalation. The baby survived, but he had bad burns all over his body."

He turned his eyes on Deke. "You just met that baby all grown up. Cecil Burgess, also known as the Waxman to the locals. You can see where he got the moniker."

Deke nodded, then frowned. "Wait a minute. Even with the distorted burn features, the dude I saw had to be at least sixty, maybe seventy, not in his thirties."

"Yeah, that's another part of the story. Besides Cecil's burns, he has a rare disease that causes a person to age faster than his years. It's called progeny, or progeria. I forget the word."

"Wow. I read something like that in Ripley's Believe It or Not. So, where does he live? How does he live?"

"He built a little place in the woods on the bluff above Crooked Creek near the charred house. The farm was in a trust left for him." Tim looked at the ceiling. "He makes a living selling herbs and lotions—concocts cures for everything from migraines to diarrhea. People are never charged, but they leave donations. They say he is pretty good. But no one wants to let out that they're getting help from him. Too spooky for their taste."

Tim pulled the door open and paused. "He even helped me once. I had a toe fungus I couldn't get rid of with over-the-counter stuff. So, he made me a salve, and in three weeks, it was gone."

Deke hopped off the workbench. "Maybe he could make a potent potion to cure himself of old guy's disease and slather on some good looks."

"That is cold, man." Tim's face hardened.

"Yeah, yeah. I know. I didn't mean it that way. If he is so good at healing, why doesn't he find a cure for himself?"

"I guess that's why he studies natural healing. He hasn't found a cure, so he helps others with what he knows will work for their ailments."

Deke shook his head. "Sorry for that crack. I just found him kind of unsettling, and I don't have much confidence in medicine men. Not that AMA doctors are all that great in my book either."

Tim recognized the buried anger in Deke's eyes. "I am sure the doctors did their best to save him."

Deke turned away. "Well, I was just speaking generally. Not my experience."

Tim patted his friend on the shoulder. "See you Sunday. One p.m. sharp. Don't be late. Bev will dump the mashed potatoes on my head for not getting you there on time and hot gravy on yours when you do arrive."

"I would think she would do both to you. Potatoes and gravy go together."

"Be there." The sheriff opened the door and departed.

After Tim left, Deke exhaled loudly and switched off the lights as he entered the empty hall, turning to lock the door. A freshness filled the air outside the courthouse, despite the cool spring temperatures partnering with creeping darkness. Deke headed for the Corner Cafe across from the courthouse.

The neon "open" sign blinked a tired welcome. Deke paused at the door to check the front window display. The building had been built in the early 1920s. It was once a two-story dry goods store. In the sixties, the first floor became a restaurant, and the upstairs was now an apartment. The plate-glass window display paid homage to a bygone era. A mannequin seemed frozen in time in herringbone wool, surrounded by antique tins and obsolete household items.

His gaze swept over kerosene lamps, baseball cards, rag dolls, a butter churn, a poster for Ringling Brothers and Barnum & Bailey Circus, sheep shears, and other eclectic displays. Mounted on a high shelf sat another mannequin—this one a bearded hillbilly in a rocking chair, his moonshine jug within easy reach.

Nope. Nothing had changed since Deke left the county.

The heavy wood and glass door groaned against his efforts, eventually relenting as he stepped inside, greeted by the fragrance of frying hamburgers. His eyes combed the sparsely populated booths and tables. Hank, the owner, leaned on a table, chatting with a couple of local farmers.

"Well, surprise, surprise!" Hank straightened. "What you see when you don't have a varmint gun."

Deke smiled and ignored his greeting. "I have been coming in here since I was a kid. You still haven't fixed that door. It takes fourteen men and a boy to get it open."

Hank raised his beefy arms. "Hey, it helped you become a man. That was the only exercise you got growing up."

The two farmers at the table joined Hank in laughter. Deke clapped Hank on the back on his way to the rear of the cafe.

"You guys won't think it's so funny when you leave here and find tickets on your tractors for being double-parked. And you, manager, you violate Health Department rules by storing the customers' food in the dumpster out back."

All three laughed harder. Deke shot a grin over his shoulder as he stopped near the kitchen and hung his hat on a rack attached to the end of a bench seat. He'd already turned to slide into the side facing the door when he made a discovery.

Rita Courtney already occupied the booth.

"Oh. I'm sorry, I didn't see anyone sitting here."

"And here I thought police officers had fine skills of observation."

Deke stood and regained his composure. "Well, Ms. Courtney, I did not anticipate this booth to be occupied by someone the size of a derby jockey at this time of the evening."

She squinted at him and smiled. "Call me Rita. You know, I could file a civil action suit against you for slander."

He took her hand and winked. "Doubt it would go anywhere around here, especially once the jurors saw you using a step ladder to take the stand."

Rita sighed. "Apology accepted. No suit."

Deke cocked his head. "What part of what I said was an apology?"

"Do you want to join me or not, Deputy Campbell?" Rita pointed at the bench opposite her.

"Well, thank you. If you don't think I will damage your reputation."

"My, my. You think you have that much power, do you?" She clasped her hands over her plate, elbows on either side of the half-eaten grilled chicken salad.

"You win." Deke dropped into the seat and extended a hand across the table. "Can we start again? And call me Deke. I think we got off to a bad beginning in the sheriff's office."

Rita formed her hands into a teepee over her salad, supporting her chin.

Deke kept his hand extended. She had eyes a guy could swim in.

18

Finally, she raised her hand to take his.

"Agreed. And your impersonation of Mel Gibson was spot on."

Deke, again, felt the color rising to his face. But then, he was jolted back to his surroundings by Hank and the farmers clapping. He jerked his head in their direction and saw their grinning faces. They had been listening.

"Ah, Hank, if it is not too much trouble, could I have a little service here? Otherwise, I will forget to include your premises on my patrol."

"Only time you patrol my premises is when you're hungry!"

The group guffawed, and Deke shook his head.

Nancy, a plump waitress in her sixties, approached the booth.

"Whacha want, cowboy?" She paused and tapped her pencil on her order book. "Oh, I know. Cheeseburger with bacon, burn the bacon, toasted bun, and brown mustard."

Deke put his hand to his mouth and widened his eyes. "How did you know?"

Nancy grinned and tapped her imitation diamond-studded glasses. "Because I am psychiatric!"

"I think you mean psychic."

The waitress scratched out his order. "Whatever. I am gifted at reading minds, not gifted in English."

Deke chuckled. "Thanks, Nancy. And black coffee."

Without looking up from her order book, the waitress said, "No, too late for coffee. Keeps you up."

"All right, then lemonade."

"No, it makes you pee the bed."

"Give me what you think I should have."

Nancy peered at him over her glasses. "Water. It's good for you, but tip me like you ordered a drink."

Not waiting for a response, Nancy retraced her steps to the kitchen.

Deke leaned back in the booth and smiled at Rita. "I get no respect."

"Seems like everyone knows you around here."

"Please, don't judge me on their conversations."

"Oh, certainly not. Folks do seem to like you. I am a lawyer, and I know things," she drawled in a down-home voice.

Deke nodded. "Why did you become a lawyer? Didn't your guidance counselor like you?"

"My counselor liked me very much. The legal field had always interested me, especially the idea of helping those who cannot defend themselves."

Nancy slammed a large water glass onto the table, splashing water on Deke's hand. "Hmph!" She did not slow up as she headed to another table.

Deke picked up a napkin and wiped his hand. "Well, my philosophy comes from a '70s song intro for the detective series, *Baretta*. 'Don't do the crime if you can't do the time.'"

At Rita's furrowed brow, Deke explained. "See, if you had a kid, and he steals a pencil from another kid in school, I would hope you wouldn't defend his crime and berate the teacher for disciplining him."

"I would make sure he was not innocent and examine whether his punishment would fit the crime," Rita answered.

"Hmm. So, you would take the little thief's word over the teacher's, then tell the teacher how to do her job. Have I got this right?"

"No! I just want justice to be served."

Deke had struck a chord. He grinned.

Deke's burger arrived. "Okay. That debate is for another time. Let's not ruin my appetite."

Before he could attack the burger, Rita laid her fork down.

Deke sent her a puzzled look. "What?"

"Sorry. I was giving you a chance for grace." Rita murmured. Her entrancing eyes were like inviting blue pools.

"That's Nancy, not Grace." Deke mouthed an 'O'. "Oh, right. Appreciate that. Eating in restaurants in Chicago in uniform could make you a target—eyes closed, bowed head, and all, ya know."

Rita reddened. "I didn't mean to be preachy. I am used to dining in the Bible belt. Sorry."

"No problem. I was raised in church. Guess I kinda got away from traditions."

They lapsed into small talk, trading inquiries into who they knew and how they were related to other people.

She seemed so proper, yet there was a fire in her. Deke tried to attend to what she was saying, but he found himself drinking in her natural beauty.

When Hank switched off the 'Open' sign and flickered the overhead lights, Deke looked up in surprise. He hadn't noticed the farmers leave or any other customers. The owner walked into the kitchen, saluting Deke as he disappeared.

Rita glanced at the tiny rectangular gold Bulova on her slender wrist. "Oh, my! I didn't realize how late it was getting."

"Time is a treasure when you're having fun," he said.

"Oh, are you having fun?" Rita gave a wry smile.

Deke leaned back, looked at the ceiling, and stroked his chin. "Yes. As a matter of fact, I am. But don't spread it around. I have a reputation to maintain."

A giggle escaped her lips. "Me too. But you can spread it around. I am a lawyer, so I could use a reputation as fun-loving."

The couple rose and walked to the register. Deke reached to pull Rita's ticket out of her hand.

"No, I'll take care of my own."

"Just trying to prove I'm a gentleman at heart."

Nancy, waiting at the register, faked a yawn. "Honey, I used to be a feminist but learned that if I continued down that trail, I couldn't afford my cigarettes."

Deke kept his eyes on Rita.

"Okay."

He handed Nancy his tab with some bills.

Nancy's eyebrows rose. "Did you say keep the change? I can't afford a new battery for my hearing aids."

"No, I did not, and I am reconsidering the twenty percent I had intended to give since I was baptized with my water glass."

Nancy took her pen and scribbled on Deke's check. "Oh, forgot. One dollar for Deputy Dawg's bath."

At their laughter, Nancy broke character and had to chuckle herself.

Outside, the night was cool and crisp. Deke walked Rita to her late-model red Mitsubishi Spyder convertible parked in front of the cafe.

He let out a whistle. "Nice. The county is probably paying you too much."

Rita ignored his comment. "Where are you parked?"

"Thar she is!" Deke gestured to a beat-up, muddy 2006 Chevy Silverado four-wheel-drive across the street.

Rita stared at the work truck. "And the county is probably not paying you enough."

"A legacy from my dad. Of course, he wouldn't have approved of my additions to his wheels. Like the tuned exhaust system and jacked suspension." Deke smiled and touched the brim of his hat. "Good night. See you in court."

Deke crossed the street and stepped onto the sidewalk. He turned his head enough to catch her watching him as he walked. She jerked her attention back to her car, opened the door to the sporty convertible, and disappeared inside.

Deke shook his head, grinning. He tugged at the unlocked door of his well-used work truck, which protested loudly. Jumping in, he turned the key in the ignition. At the rumbling greeting of the big engine and throaty pipes, he patted the dashboard.

Yeah, Dad. Your old friend has still got it. Now, she has become my friend.

The red convertible glided down the side street of the courthouse and turned onto Maple Street. He watched until the taillights disappeared.

Dunderhead! All that talking and he hadn't even found out where she lived!

Deke pulled out of the parking place and headed home. He turned on the radio and punched a button to a country and western station. Alan Jackson was singing "Gone Country."

Deke had not felt like singing for a long time. Now, he did. What would Alan think about him joining in a duet?

CHAPTER 3

Deke rose before sunrise and slid out of bed. He padded to the bathroom wearing only pajama bottoms and switched on the light, blinking in the sudden illumination. He splashed water on his face and paused to examine his upper body reflected by the mirror over the sink.

Dripping water coursed off his face and over the deep scar across his left breast—compliments of a psychotic rapist he had interrupted assaulting a young woman in a stairwell. It could have ended badly for him and the girl, but fortune had favored him.

Hard workouts had kept him trim. He took a deep breath and mentally marked the days of tobacco abstinence. He couldn't claim victory, but four days was a good start.

Dressed in his jogging sweats, Deke entered the kitchen, jabbing the Mr. Coffee start button before sitting at the table. He pulled on white cotton socks and Nike running shoes and gazed out the window at the reddening horizon.

The coffee maker had produced enough to fill his large cup, decorated with a U.S. Marine Corps emblem. Deke walked outside, still squinting at the dawn. He raised the overhead garage door where his truck waited on one side—

on the other side were mismatched dumbbells, a couple of bars, and a variety of steel plates. A worn weightlifting bench jutted out from the wall. In the corner hung a heavy canvas sparring bag with splits covered in duct tape.

After a couple of swigs of hot coffee, Deke began his intensive ritual with varied sets of lifts. This was his designated light day, for which he was grateful. Finishing his workout in under thirty minutes, he walked outside for a jog through the deserted streets of Marion.

By the time Deke finished his run, it was almost seven. He entered his little rented house to a ringing cell phone, which he grabbed on the fifth ring.

"Hello!"

There was a pause at the other end, then a crackling voice yelled out, "Who is this?"

The voice did not wait for an answer. "Is this you, Deacon? You should be up by now. Your daddy would have thrown a pan of water on you if you were still in bed!" The cackle of laughter was familiar.

Deke smiled. "Mr. Thomas, good morning, and I have been up an hour and a half. My daddy would have been proud of me."

Mr. Thomas again cackled a high-pitched laugh, then cleared his throat. "Deke, I gotta give you some bad news." There was a noticeable change to a serious tone.

"Horses all right?"

"Oh, yeah, yeah. Your animals are fine, but something else has come up."

Deke was listening intently now. "Go ahead, Mr. Thomas."

"You know, I've been pasturing and taking care of your horses for about ten years. Ever since your Daddy started having heart problems and you were off playing a cop in *Sheecahgo*."

Deke permitted himself a snort at the man's pronunciation of Chicago. "I know, and my dad and I have appreciated the way you care for Zorro and Mandy. Did you get the check I left for you the other day?"

"Oh, oh, yes indeed. That's not why I'm calling. I have to tell you that I am selling my farm and moving in with my daughter, Ruthie. You remember Ruthie, don't you?"

"I do. She still living in Evansville?"

"Yeah. She thinks I am getting too old to live by myself. After I fell out of the hayloft and cracked a rib, Ruthie said no more."

"I can understand her concern. Have you sold the place yet?"

"Yeah. I did. Didn't get what I wanted, but Lamb told me my taxes were going to go up, and you know that rooster has the power to see it happen."

Deke stiffened. "You mean Bryce Lamb?"

"That's the one and only. Bryce Lamb. That that son of a gun is buying up everything in the county. I use that name in consideration of your genteel ears, Deacon. But you can substitute another."

Deke pictured Lamb, five years his senior. Lamb had nicknamed him 'Bones,' alluding to his thin frame. They'd once come to blows in a basketball scrimmage. Deke had gotten the worst of it.

"You still there?"

Deke shook off the memories. "Yes, yes. I wish you had talked to me before you made a deal with him. I might have been able to purchase your place."

His response was harsh. "Hah! Deke, maybe you don't know, but he controls all the lending around here, too. You would have never gotten a loan."

"Didn't know he had that much power."

The tone from Mr. Thomas was gentler. "I know, son—just a word of advice. You are a public servant, and Lamb holds a lot of power. Lots of power. Don't cross him."

"Thanks for the words of wisdom. I had my fill of Bull Lamb in high school. I thought by this time, he'd have changed or got what he deserved."

"Naw. The devil takes care of his own."

"How long do I have to find a new home for my horses?"

"Thirty days, when the deal closes."

Deke nodded, deep in thought.

"Deacon, you hear me? You got thirty days. As mean as Lamb is, if Zorro and Mandy are not gone, he'll either sell them, claim them, or send them to the glue factory."

"I hear you. I'll be in touch. And thanks again for all you've done. You have been a good friend to my father and me."

When Mr. Thomas spoke again, emotion showed in his voice. "Son, it's been a pleasure, and I'll feed and take care of the horses for the next week. I will tell them you are looking for a new home. God bless ya."

The phone went dead. Mr. Thomas had always been abrupt.

Deke switched off his phone and placed it back on the counter. He stood for a few seconds, deep in thought, then exhaled loudly, reaching for the refrigerator handle. The top shelf was home to a smoothie he had made before going to bed.

The deputy finished his drink, showered, and dressed. He strapped on his leather gear and inspected the weapon. Checking the tools of one's trade every time you picked them up could be the difference between surviving and becoming a victim. Now, he was ready to face the day.

SUMMER OF THE WAXMAN

In his small room at the courthouse, Deke worked undisturbed, marking evidence from a petty theft case over on Main Street. After a few hours, he cleared up his work area and went outside to his Jeep to assist other patrol units.

A note was stuck behind the windshield wiper. "Deke— Clausen's bull is missing. He thinks somebody stole him. We need some hoof prints at his place. Mitch." This was followed by a smiley face.

Before Deke settled behind the wheel, he checked the back to make certain he had his evidence case and camera.

Deke headed for the Clausen farm just outside town. As he drove, he assessed the pastures and barns on parade on either side of the narrow blacktop.

He had to find a new home for his horses. He should have paid attention to the local farm talk on pastureland for lease. He had not seen this coming.

The deputy turned down Crooked Creek Road, a shortcut to the Clausen farm. Might as well do his community relations gig and see if ol' Virgil had found his meandering bull.

Besides, maybe he'll have some room for the ponies.

As he topped a rise, a late-model Ford pickup truck came into view, parked near a bridge on the shoulder. No driver, but Deke could see a head with a ball cap on the passenger side.

Deke slowed his Jeep and detected a male figure wearing jeans and a camo shirt and cap and standing near the bridge. The young man rocked back and hurled an object at an unseen target. Probably killing snakes in the creek.

As Deke's wheels crunched to a stop in the gravel beside the road, the thrower turned. He looked to be late teens or early twenties.

The youth threw down what Deke now determined was a rock and sprang to the parked truck. He leapt inside and

29

rabbited away, spewing gravel and dirt from the shoulder. The tires connected with the asphalt and screamed their indignation.

The passenger stuck his head out the window, and Deke slapped his fist against the steering wheel.

"Bobby Page, as I live and breathe! There is a story here." Deke focused on the license plate and vocalized the alphanumeric registration.

"Victor Juliet, eight seven three zero."

As he repeated the identifying license, he rubbed the side of his nose vigorously with his index finger, using the oil to hastily record the identifying plate on his rearview mirror.

He was almost to the bridge when the truck disappeared over the hill. A flash of color under the steel bridge support caught his attention. Deke slammed the brakes, turned his lights on, and leaped from the vehicle. He slid and hopped down the steep embankment sideways, trying to see what was under the concealment of the bridge.

The Waxman! What did Tim say his name was? Bruger? Burgess? Yes, Burgess. Cecil Burgess.

The frail man's hat hung down as he squatted, leaning his back against a bridge pillar. Despite the blue bandana he held against his head, a line of blood trickled down the side of his face. At Deke's hurried approach, Burgess started, and looked toward him with an open mouth and anxious eyes. However, when he saw the uniform, he relaxed. The injured man picked up a walking staff from the ground and, with its assistance, rose unsteadily to his feet. He continued dabbing and pressing the cloth to his head.

"Mr. Burgess, you okay? Was that boy throwing rocks at you?"

The dark eyes focused on the deputy's face. "Well, I don't think he meant to hit me, just scare me."

"You know him?"

Cecil nodded. "Know his father better. He had a good teacher." The thin-lipped mouth expanded into a troubled smile.

"Okay, first things first. We need to get you to the emergency room. It looks like you are going to need stitches. Then, I'll deal with your assailant."

Cecil did not answer. He seemed to be engrossed in the concrete nooks over his head. He leaned his staff on the support and reached up to gently retrieve a clump of spider webs with the freed hand. He made a final pat with the bandana, then delicately applied the gob of silky material on the wound, patting it lightly.

"There! That will suffice. I have some ointment to apply at home."

Deke gazed at the man. "You sure you don't want to get checked out?"

"I am sure."

"Well, at least let me give you a ride home. You own the Burgess place, right?"

"I take care of it temporarily. Yes, I am residing there."

Deke furled his brow. "Maybe I got the wrong information. I thought you owned that farm?"

Cecil shrugged his shoulders and drew a deep labored breath. "No one owns any land. The Lord God does. He has just allowed me to take care of it. I am a steward."

Hmm. Tim hadn't mentioned Burgess was a religious freak too. Perhaps, as ugly as Burgess was, God was the only friend he had.

"You probably think I have gone off the deep end."

"Oh, oh no, I was just thinking maybe you were referring to the bank owning your farm, and I understood you had inherited it from your folks."

Jeez, that was weird. Could the strange man read minds? Deke hoped he hadn't caught his 'ugly' thought.

Cecil nodded and started scaling the bank to the road. He paused and turned back to Deke, who was watching him climb the steep incline, slapping at his empty cigarette pocket.

"I guess I would appreciate a lift to my place. I am more unsteady than I thought."

"Good enough." Deke caught right up and opened his passenger door.

Deke stuck out his hand.

"Name's Deke Campbell." The frail man shook his hand. His grip was surprisingly firm.

"Cecil Burgess, aka the Waxman, but you already knew that, Deputy Campbell." He widened his smile.

"Uh, yes. I mean, I asked around about your identity after we first met. Um, after I tried to run you down." Deke reddened and grinned. "And you can call me Deke. As long as you don't have any outstanding warrants."

Cecil tilted his head to the side. "Well, I considered a career as an armed robber at one time, but I realized it would be short-lived. I am easily identifiable, you know."

"Yeah. You like to put people on the spot, don't you, Mr. Burgess?"

"Big believer in having fun. But call me Cecil. Or, if you have a mind to, you can call me Brad Pitt."

Cecil seemed not to be able to contain himself and broke into a high-pitched laugh.

Deke echoed his laughter. "Cecil it is. Brad is a good name too, but I have to focus on facts as a law enforcement officer. And Cecil is what is on your birth certificate. Right?"

Deke placed the man's staff on the rear seat.

"Still, you don't trust me. Getting all weapons out of reach."

Deke chuckled. "Department policy. Don't want to give the sheriff reason to write me up."

As he closed the door of the Jeep patrol unit, an older model Chevy Impala approached behind them. The driver pulled in behind the Jeep and stopped. A middle-aged man wearing a white shirt and tie stepped from the vehicle.

"Morning, Deputy!" It was a pleasant greeting, accompanied by a smile and nod.

"Morning—can I help you?"

"Oh, I don't mean to be intrusive, I am the pastor of Flat Rock Baptist Church about a half mile from here—Brother Mike. Uh, I thought I saw Cecil Burgess getting into your patrol car. He is a friend and neighbor, and I just thought I would stop and see if I could help."

"Well, Pastor, if you are thinking I am arresting him, I am not. He just took a rock to the head from some of the local rowdies, and I am giving him a ride home."

Deke recognized the man as one he'd seen in the cafe having Sunday lunches with churchgoers.

"Oh, brother! Who did it? Was it Calvin Lamb?"

Deke felt his neck hairs raise at the name. "Calvin Lamb? I don't know, he wouldn't say. I hoped to get it out of Mr. Burgess on the ride to his home."

Pastor Mike shook his head. "Well, innocent until proven guilty, right? However, I have seen that boy, along with Bobby Page, harass Cecil in the past. Calvin's Daddy's land borders on Cecil's, and Mr. Lamb thinks he should own it."

That name again. Now, it was all making sense.

"So, you are talking about Bryce Lamb. Is it his son you suspect?"

"Well, not to jump the gun, but yes, I know that history repeats itself. Look, is Cecil going to be all right?"

"I am sure he will. Thought he needed stitches in his forehead—it seems like the cobwebs he plastered on his gourd took care of the bleeding."

Mike nodded and smiled. "Yeah, Cecil is an expert at natural remedies. He knows natural herbs and oils, and he concocts treatments for the locals. He never charges. If he did, he could upset the medical doctors. But even they grudgingly give him credit on his fixes. He does not like getting out in daylight. As you can see, he can catch a lot of stares. So, I deliver his cures to folks in the county."

"Is he a witch doctor?"

"I don't think he would like that title, but you would never know it, 'cause he will never get upset at anyone."

Mike stared at the little hat-covered head in the Jeep's passenger seat as the he continued. "He's a brilliant, kind man who hides from the public because of his deformities. He used to come to my church and sit outside the open windows to listen to the service. When we got central air and heat, we closed the windows. I ran a speaker outside to the woodshed. Now, he slips into that and listens. He even leaves money on a log for an offering."

The pastor focused on the Jeep and seemed to drift off. "He has suffered his entire life, but that life will be short." He abruptly looked at Deke. "He won't tell you who did it, and even if you do know from other sources, he will refuse to testify against them. Sadly, the Lambs know it."

"I see. Well, nice meeting you, and I appreciate the info. I'll get him home safely and make sure he is all right."

No sense in spilling his guts to this holy man. He would deal with this in his own way.

Deke stepped back from the Impala and checked for traffic, and then directed the pastor on his way. The pastor waved to the figure in the Jeep as he drove past.

Deke started the drive to Cecil's farm.

First, he had to build trust if he hoped to make a case.

"I understand you are an herbalist or a natural healer?"

Cecil scrutinized Deke with his piercing brown eyes before answering. "I have studied natural remedies since I was a boy and have developed a knowledge of plants, herbs, and oils. God has given me the wisdom in their use."

Another holy man. What was this, a tag-team match?

"Hmm. Did you study someplace, I mean a college or institute?"

"Not really. I did take several correspondence courses, but mostly learned on my own and used a trial-and-error approach."

"You mean if the patient lived, then you bottled more— if they croaked, you poured it out?" Deke gave the little man a crooked grin.

"No, I would never subject a person to an experimental process that would be harmful. I only try possible cures that wouldn't endanger their lives or be harmful to them."

Deke cringed. Great, he'd hurt the little man's feelings with his warped sense of humor.

"I did not mean that seriously. I was only joking. Sorry."

"Oh. I guess I haven't socialized enough with law enforcement officers to be familiar with their sense of humor. Or, for that matter, most people in general. I only participate in Halloween parties." Cecil widened his tiny lips into a grin.

"Ahh! Ya got me. Now, I feel awkward." Deke gave him a sly smile. "Tell you what, Mr. Burgess, I mean Brad, no I mean Cecil, I'll teach you cop humor, and you teach me about witches' brews."

Both men laughed.

"Here is where I get off." He pointed a long, pale finger to an overgrown, rocky road that curved up an embankment into the cedar and oak-controlled woods.

"Okay." Deke wheeled off the blacktop and onto the creek-rocked roadway. He bounced up the rutted trail, ignoring the swish of weeds on the undercarriage.

"I can walk the rest of the way."

"No can do. I have to see you to your domicile. Policy, you know."

He halted the Jeep near a rusty cable with a padlock that showed no signs of being opened in years. Old telephone poles suspended the thick wire with two more posts on each side. Deep ditches on either side of the road prevented vehicular traffic around the barricade.

Both men stepped from the vehicle, and Cecil retrieved his staff. He looked up at the deputy.

"If you insist. Follow me." He turned onto a well-worn path that threaded its way between the two poles to the right of the cabled road.

Deke followed Cecil up the steep trail into the coolness of the woods. Ten feet from the cabled roadway, he noted a battered mailbox.

"I am guessing that you don't receive a lot of mail here, given the location of the box. You have another purpose for it?"

"Indeed, no deliveries by the US Postal System. People leave requests for my witch's cures. The victims, I mean the patients, pick them up here when they're ready."

"So, do you include your bill with the cures? How do you keep the payment from being stolen?

"I don't charge. Sometimes people donate. They might leave money or a box of cookies."

"I see. That's how you dodge being brought up on charges of practicing medicine without a license."

Cecil halted and turned to Deke. "Are you always so suspicious of people? Do you always look at them through a lens of criminality? That is sad."

"Cecil, I am a necessary evil. If I were not suspicious of people, you would get worse treatment than you got." Deke nodded toward his head wound.

"Point taken, but you must consider everyone is redeemable."

"Point taken, also. But in my line of work, I don't see many redeemable people."

Cecil smiled and brushed beads of sweat from his head. "You need to expose those people to redemption. Justice can still be served."

"You are not only a shaman, but you are also a prophet." Deke hurried on. "That was a joke."

Cecil shrugged and turned to continue the hike. "I am learning, oh great teacher."

A few minutes later, they arrived at a clearing with a small cottage made of logs. Solar panels lined the south-facing roof. Something moved on the porch, detaching itself from the shadows and bounding down the steps, emitting a series of joyous yips.

The dog raced toward them, tail wagging, and jumped up and down before his slightly built master. Cecil bent over and rubbed his head affectionately. "This is Plato. He wandered here all mangy and skinny. He is my buddy and listens closely to any thoughts I share with him."

"Is he a Blue Heeler?" Deke recognized the famed Australian herding dog characteristics.

"Mostly. Plato has got something additional in his background, but he won't share it with me."

The dog peered at Deke suspiciously from between Cecil's legs, but Cecil laughed. "Don't let that worry you.

The day he arrived, he was suspicious of me. I believe someone had mistreated him. I didn't look for his owner. He was probably about six months old when he ran away from home. Now he is about four and earns his keep here."

Deke did not inquire how so, but he grunted understanding.

Cecil straightened and climbed the wooden stairs to the roofed porch and leaned his staff against a wooden bench by the entry. He opened a dark outside screen door, then shoved the heavy wooden inner door with his shoulder until it creaked open.

"Gotta plane that down. Wet springs always make the door swell."

He waved Deke to follow him and entered the cabin. "Plato, you stay here." The dog had followed him up the steps and halted. Obediently, Plato resumed his resting place.

The dim interior was cool, and various fragrances assailed Deke's senses. It was dark but not foreboding.

"Just a minute. I will have light in a jiffy."

Cecil maneuvered around a large table holding neatly stacked jars and small plastic containers. He opened a closet door with shelves from top to bottom. Each shelf held three to four car batteries. He pulled a flashlight from one of the shelves and flicked it on. After a few seconds of crackle and sparks, he connected a cable to a battery post. The room lit up with dim incandescent bulbs in lamps on the table and a nightstand beside a beat-up recliner in the corner.

"Sorry about the inconvenience. I usually have most of the batteries fully charged."

Deke scanned the room of mismatched furniture. There was a wall with floor-to-ceiling shelves jammed with books.

He noted they covered a wide range of subjects. Classics, famous novels, philosophy, books of natural healing, and theology.

A framed photograph of a young couple sat on one shelf. Deke stepped closer to examine the man and woman.

Cecil called over his shoulder. "Would you care for some tea? It is herbal."

"No, thanks."

Cecil entered the kitchen area and grabbed the handle of a hand pump. He vigorously pumped the handle until it caught its prime and coughed up intermittent gushes of water, which filled a pan in the sink.

"You will have to excuse me. I need to wash this wound right away. I am prone to infections."

Deke continued to stare at the photo of the couple. "Uh, yeah, go ahead."

Cecil washed the spider webs from his cut and rinsed the soap from his face. He seized a towel and dried his face vigorously.

Deke turned to Cecil. "Are these your parents?"

Cecil walked back into the room while drying his face and hands. He paused to open a cabinet above a counter near the stove, selected a small bottle, and removed the cap. He drew a cotton swab from a pack near the bottles and carefully dipped it into the bottle.

He walked toward Deke, dabbing his cut and looking at the framed photo on the shelf—the only photo in the room. He had to look at it to decide who they were?

"Yes, it is. Don't I look like them?"

Deke ignored his dry humor. "Your mother was a pretty woman. And your father was handsome."

"That was taken about a year before I was born. It was mother and father's anniversary. Six months later, my father died from a fall at a construction site in Paducah. He was an insulator working on a power plant.

"That's tragic. I am sorry."

"Mom was six months pregnant with me. Then she joined my dad in eternity the night I was born." He glanced upward, as if saluting some cosmic joke. "I should have gone with her that night, but I guess it wasn't in God's plans."

Deke snorted. Why did these religious types think if everything went well, it was God's plan, and if it didn't go well, it was God's plan? It was like a weatherman—fifty percent chance of showers.

Cecil finished dressing his wound and cast the swab in a nearby waste can.

"Listen, you need to come down and press charges against young Calvin Lamb. He could have put your eye out or worse."

"How do you know it was Calvin Lamb? I never told you."

"Well, I got his license plate when I drove up."

No sense in ratting on the man's pastor friend. In truth, he did get the license plate. He just hadn't had a chance to run it.

"He just needs to be in church," Cecil said.

"He needs a butt-beating."

Cecil smiled. "Deputy Deke, you and I have a different way of looking at the world."

"For sure. Mine is the rational way."

"Please, I thank you for your assistance, and I do want us to part on good terms, but I cannot press charges."

Cecil extended his frail hand.

"All right. Have it your way. I will get the kid when he messes up again. I know the type, and he will mess up."

Deke gently shook the man's hand and walked out the door with Cecil following him.

"Oh, almost forgot." Cecil vanished into his cottage again.

Deke heard him pulling a drawer open. When he returned, he clutched a small glass bottle with a dropper and handed it to him.

"Here! Take one dropper full, four times a day."

"What's this for? And what is it?"

"It will help you quit smoking and lessen your withdrawal symptoms. As to what is in it—oat berry extract, Saint John's wort leaves, skullcap, valerian, and a touch of toad slobber." Cecil's eyes danced.

"How do you know I have an issue with smoking?" Deke ignored the man's joke.

Cecil answered with another question. "How many days have you gone without a cigarette?"

"Four days." Deke glanced at his watch. "And nine hours."

"If you had not been struggling with the addiction, you would not have been so quick and accurate with that answer. Every day, the tobacco demon rears its ugly head, and you have to fight it. Makes keeping count important." Cecil shrugged. "Besides, when we first met—when you tried to run me down—I saw you trying to fish a cigarette out of an empty shirt pocket. You did it again by the bridge a little while ago."

Deke looked at the bottle and back at Cecil. "If you ever need a job, see me about a role as a detective."

Cecil chuckled. "My social life is limited, so when I see other humans, I am observant."

"Is your social life limited because of your own making?"

"It doesn't matter. It is what it is."

"How much do I owe you for the bottle?"

"Aha! That is entrapment, Deputy. I am not asking for money, so you don't have a case."

Both men laughed.

"You sure about not preferring charges on the Lamb kid?" Deke coaxed.

"I am sure. Have a nice day." With that, the little man turned, climbed the steps, and softly closed the door to his cabin behind him.

Deke shrugged and trotted down to his waiting Jeep.

What a weird character. Interesting. The deputy kind of liked him.

But Deke wasn't finished with this. There was a crime, and there was a victim.

CHAPTER 4

The radio crackled in the Jeep as the dispatcher acknowledged Deke's communication. "Vehicle is a 2019 Blue Ford four-by-four half-ton pick-up registered to Bryce Lamb on Turkey Run. No warrants or hits on it."

"Ten-four. I will be making a follow-up on that vehicle at that address." Deke cradled the microphone in the clip on the dash and headed to the address supplied by the dispatcher.

The dispatcher's voice offered an additional comment. "By the way, cancel the APB on Virgil's bull. He's returned from a night of wandering."

Deke leaned forward and keyed the mic button. "That's a copy. Did Virgil say where he had been?"

"Negatory. Just a night on the country back roads."

"Ten-four." Deke could not help but chuckle. He patted his pocket for the nonexistent pack and felt nothing but the small bottle given to him by the Waxman. No time like the present.

Flipping up the pocket flap, he extracted the dropper-sealed bottle and unscrewed the dropper while steering with his elbow. Lighting cigarettes while driving had at least given him a transferable talent.

He filled the dropper, set the bottle in front of his instrument panel, and proceeded to squirt three drops under his tongue.

"Aaag! He wasn't lying. There was toad slobber in there!" Deke grimaced, seized a half-empty cold MacDonald's coffee container from the cup holder, and gulped it down to cover the taste. "That's nasty." Deke flopped his tongue between his lips.

The turnoff on Turkey Run was surprisingly near Cecil's farm, and the target address was only about a quarter-mile down the road. A large stone-encased mailbox announced Lamb's name and address in steel lettering. As if that weren't enough, wrought-iron arches over the drive from stone pillars spelled "Lamb Farm" in black steel lettering, shouting to anyone who neglected to read it on the mailbox. White horse fences stretching out from the asphalt drive on either side established the farm's boundaries.

Deke turned into the drive and followed the winding blacktop flanked on each side with evenly spaced, flowering white pear trees. The long drive ended at a large, two-story white mansion with a circle drive. The jacked-up blue truck sat in front of the stately house in front of the pillared veranda.

After stopping behind the truck to verify the plates, Deke strode around to the truck's front and stepped onto the stairs. A movement caught his eye. A blonde-haired little girl, no more than six or seven, sat humming on a short stool. Her attention was on a small cradle, which she rocked in rhythm with her song. The cradle contained a small doll wrapped in a blue blanket.

Not wanting to frighten the child, the deputy weighed options to approach her in a calming way. She stopped humming and spoke in low tones to the doll. Finally, she spotted Deke when the sound of a hummingbird zooming in for a drink of sugar water from a feeder diverted her attention from the cradle.

The girl's hair had been hiding her face as she leaned over the cradle. Now it was in full view. Deke could see she wore heavy black glasses with thick lenses. The glasses did not detract from her cuteness. She seemed to be looking at Deke without seeing him. Bright blues were searching for another presence besides the hummingbird.

The girl rose and stepped forward. Deke cleared his throat and spoke. "Hi, I am Deputy Deke."

For a couple of seconds, the girl said nothing. Then a broad smile replaced uncertainty on her face. "Hello, my name is Violet, but my friends call me 'Vi.'"

Violet took a few steps closer to Deke and adjusted her glasses on a tiny, upturned nose. She looked him over. "You are a real police officer, aren't you? I've met Sheriff Tim. My daddy knows him, too, but he doesn't like him too much. Don't know why."

She shrugged her shoulders, then turned her attention to the bird feeder and the persistent bird that kept jamming its elongated bill into the opening, trying to touch the sweet liquid.

Violet pointed at the hovering bird. "You know, hummingbirds are the only birds that can fly backward, and they can fly up to thirty miles per hour!"

"That so? Did not know that."

"I did not either, until Mr. Cecil told me."

"You mean Mr. Burgess? How do you know him?"

Violet nodded, then glanced around and lowered her voice. "Shhh. My Daddy does not like him. Our farm is next to his. He is a very nice man and teaches me a lot about plants and birds and animals. Then Daddy found out we talked and he, he ..." She turned suddenly and strode back to the cradle.

"Tinker is hungry, and I need to feed her." She thrust her hands in the cradle and lifted the doll. As the blanket dropped, Deke noted the child's toy was missing an arm.

"Is your dolly all right?" Deke inquired.

Vi quickly retrieved the blanket and covered the missing appendage. "Yes, yes. Are you here to see Daddy?"

"Is your daddy Bryce Lamb?"

"Uh-huh. He is out back by the pool. I can take you to him."

"Well, I am looking for your brother and Bobby Page."

"Why do you want to see Cal and Bobby? Have they done anything wrong?"

The child was mature beyond her years. She spoke like an adult.

Deke smiled. "I just want to talk to them."

Violet cocked her head to one side and then turned. "Okay. Follow me. They are out riding four-wheelers. I heard them talking about going honking tonight."

Deke furrowed his eyebrows as he followed Vi. "Excuse me? Honking?"

Vi stopped and turned to Deke, a puzzled look on her face. "Yeah, it didn't make any sense to me either. I guess they want to talk to geese."

The little girl shrugged. "They said they had to go over to Tennessee 'cause it's wet down there. I don't know. It's wet here too."

Deke put the girl's puzzling words together. "Did they maybe use the words honky-tonk?"

"Yes, that was it. Honking and tonking. That doesn't sound like much fun." She shook her head.

"No, it doesn't." He laughed.

Vi led Deke through a breezeway connecting the house and a garage. She stopped at a gate, which she unlatched and held open for the deputy.

"Thank you." Deke entered a patio area surrounding a large rectangular pool. He paused and looked at the large man reclining in a chaise lounge on the other side of the pool. The man wore Bermuda shorts and a Hawaiian shirt. A baseball cap and sandals completed his ensemble.

The man had heard the loud click of the latch gate over the strains of Glen Campbell singing "Wichita Lineman" from twin speakers. The sunbather sat up and shielded his eyes against the descending sun.

Deke hadn't had any contact with Bull Lamb since right after high school, but a familiar feeling welled within him. No, not the same. It used to be fear mostly, tinged with anger. Now only pure anger remained.

Get ahold of yourself, Campbell. You're an adult now. That period of your life is over.

Recognition flooded the barrel-chested man's face, and the corners of his mouth curled upward, not a smile as much as a sneer. "Well, well, Deputy Deke Campbell—or is it Deputy *Bones*?"

He kept his face devoid of emotion. "No, Deputy Campbell will do. I have filled out in the right places." He paused and nodded toward Bull's slight potbelly. "I see you've filled out too." He stared into the man's eyes, allowing a wry grin.

The sneer melted. Lamb broke into a loud laugh. "Well, ya got me there. Didn't need to maintain my football form over the years." He tapped his temple with his index finger and leaned his head forward. "My business brain has replaced it, and now I give orders to others to be physical." That familiar laugh came again. "Sit, sit!" Lamb swept his hand to chairs surrounding a glass-topped round patio table with an umbrella standing sentry in the center. He swung his eyes to the little girl standing behind Deke. "Moon Pie, get us a couple of beers from the kitchen."

Deke raised his hand. "Not for me. I am here on business, not to reminisce about old times." Deke remained standing with an unsmiling expression.

Lamb raised bushy eyebrows. "Hmm. Well, maybe another time. So, what's this all about?"

"I need to talk to your son, Calvin."

"Again, what about Cal?"

"I am assuming he is eighteen or over, and in the law's eyes, that makes him an adult. Therefore, it would be unethical for me to discuss my investigation with you, as he is not a juvenile." In check, thought Deke.

Lamb frowned and matched the deputy's stare. "Well, if you cannot tell his daddy, I cannot tell you where he is."

The sound of four-wheelers penetrated the silence between the two men. "I do believe I hear your son approaching now. So, when he arrives, we can talk here, privately, or take a ride to the department headquarters. Your call."

Checkmate.

Lamb's face reddened, and his lips tightened, and then the visuals quickly disappeared. "Okay, okay." He waved his hand in dismissal and reseated himself.

"Campbell, you're tougher than you were in your younger days. Maybe it's the gun?" Lamb leaned back, clasped his hands behind his head, and smirked.

"Don't need a gun. Did when I was thirteen, weighed a hundred fifteen pounds, and was being bullied by an adult gorilla almost twice my weight." Deke tapped his index finger on the side of his head and rolled his eyes skyward. "Let's see. What do they call it? Oh, I believe *karma*." It was his turn to smirk.

The noise of the four-wheelers grew louder on the other side of the barn fifty yards from the pool.

"It's Cal and Bobby," Violet spoke in a quiet tone.

Both men turned their eyes toward the girl as they became aware of her presence. She looked back and forth at both parties and nervously licked her lips.

Lamb's face squinted. "Violet, get your keister in the house and help your mother with the meal!"

"But Momma is not fixing a meal." The blinking eyes behind her thick glasses signaled puzzlement.

"Go! Get outta here!"

The little girl spun and ran to the patio doors, where she leaned her small frame sideways to pull the heavy glass open and disappeared inside.

Deke rolled his eyes and sighed. "Hmm. Big girls or little girls, I see ya haven't lost your cordial style."

Lamb jerked his head toward the deputy but refrained from rebuttal. The rumble from the motors behind the barn ceased—laughter and indistinct profanity-laced shouting filled the air.

Two figures came around the barn toward them, snickering and exchanging shoulder punches.

Cal and Bobby drew nearer the pool fence, oblivious to the two men's presence as they continued their mock combat. Then Bobby struck a glancing blow off Cal's shoulder that nicked his lip.

All play ceased.

The color drained from Bobby's face, and his mouth gaped open. Wide-eyed, Cal raised a hand with exaggerated caution toward his lip and then examined his blood-tipped fingers.

"You, you, son of a ...!"

"I ... I ... didn't mean it! It was accidental!" Bobby's voice trailed off in an anguished wail.

Cal balled his fist up and stepped closer to Bobby, making his friend flinch.

"Knock it off. You both get over here!" Lamb's anger startled Deke, and he found himself turning and lifting his right arm in a defensive posture but caught himself and transitioned into a reach for his cigarette pocket. He concluded his movement by buttoning the pocket. Fortunately, Lamb had not noticed.

Get over the old days. You are a grown man now.

The boys, eyes fixed on Lamb, cautiously approached him. They seemed not to see Deke standing by Bull when Cal opened the gate to access the pool. He entered and slowly approached his father with Bobby trailing him.

Deke studied Lamb's son. It was like seeing Bull again from his high school years. He was about an inch taller than his father, bulky in the upper body but lacking his dad's paunch.

Cal became aware of Deke's presence and halted as he entered the gate. His companion collided against him. Bobby tried to conceal himself behind Cal's broad shoulders.

"What's up?" The question was to his father, but his eyes went to Deke.

"You met Deputy Campbell before?"

"No. I Don't know him. Never met him."

"Think again. We might not have officially met, but we have met." Deke spoke with a measured tone. "Crooked Creek Road this morning."

Cal shrugged. "No, it was not me. I wasn't on Crooked Creek this morning."

"So, then you must have had your truck stolen. The same truck that is parked in front of this house. That's why I am here, and license plates don't lie. And Bobby Page must have been an accomplice to the theft, because I saw him clearly on the passenger side."

Bobby peeked around his friend's shoulder. "Hi, Deputy Campbell. I ... I ... ain't no accomplish! Didn't steal my buddy's truck. You remember, doncha Cal? We did drive down Crooked Creek. You just forget."

"Oh, hi, Bobby. Nice to see you again." Deke nodded. "You want to tell me what adventures you had when you were at Crooked Creek? Particularly at the bridge."

Cal flashed a stern look at his pal. Bobby stepped back, pressing his lips tight as he glanced alternately between Deke and his friend.

Lamb crossed his arms across his chest. "Look, Campbell, just give us the lowdown. Is my son being charged with anything?"

"I told you, your son is not a juvenile, so if you are not his attorney, go help your wife and Violet fix the meal. Then your son and I can have a meaningful conversation." Deke paused. "I have changed my mind. You can stay. Maybe when you hear about your offspring's adventures this morning, you will be willing to offer some fatherly advice."

Deke had no case without Cecil's testimony. However, Lamb did not know that.

51

"Okay, spill it, Cal. But if I say stop talking, you stop."
Lamb turned to Deke and continued. "Understand, you
have not given my boy his rights. So, nothing is admissible
in court. Right?"

It was more of a command than a question. Deke did not
like it but hid any sign of irritation.

"Didn't know you had a law degree, Bull. However, I
am just trying to intercede in a case of bullying. You are
familiar with laws against assault, aren't you?"

Before Lamb had a chance to respond, Deke addressed
Cal. "This morning, I witnessed a battery on Cecil Burgess
at the Crooked Creek Bridge. By you. A rock is considered a
deadly weapon. It is an aggravated battery."

"I was throwing rocks at snakes."

"You gotta problem if you cannot distinguish between
snakes and a man. I would hate to see what your dates look
like."

Bobby tittered. "That's funny!"

Both father and son gave Bobby withering looks. The
chuckles stopped.

"Cecil Burgess! That ugly piece of ...!" Lamb halted.
"Look, Campbell. I gotta accept some blame for that."

Deke did not expect the response. "How so?"

"Well, that creepy critter's land adjoins my farm, and
he refuses to join me in contracting with the gas company's
offer to explore our land. For the company to agree to
lease to me, his land had to be available too. His refusal is
causing me to lose out on a nice five-year contract." Lamb
was breathing hard. "Besides that, he makes eyes at my
Violet whenever she strays over close to his property and
picks flowers. I think he is a molester type."

"Has he ever done anything inappropriate?"

"No, not yet. But I know sickos. And it can happen."

"Well, my information is he has not bothered anyone. He stays to himself and has only been guilty of helping people with natural remedies. Besides, why would you say you're to blame for your son's actions?"

Lamb gestured to his son. "Don't you see? My son respects me and sees my feelings about the Waxman. He is only acting to protect this family. And now that I think of it, he did give my daughter some poison potion one time. I told him not to do it again or he would pay for it!" Lamb sighed and softened his tone. "I guess my son heard that, and maybe he was alarmed and wanted to protect his sister. But you know how kids overreact sometimes."

Deke turned to Cal. "Is that true? I need some truth here."

The young man looked at his father, who nodded.

"Well, I didn't mean to hit him. I was only trying to scare him. I was afraid of what he might do to my family and me."

Oh, you're good. Like father like son. Deke, you have the edge now, don't blow it.

"Okay. I can see where a frail old man terrifies you. I'm gonna cut you some slack and take you at your word. However, it better not happen again. I will build a case and see you prosecuted, and you can take that to the bank. Leave the man alone."

Deke kept his focus on the boy, but out of his peripheral vision, he could see anger on his father's glaring face.

"Yeah. Uh, yes, Deputy."

Deke restrained himself from the impulse to heap useless words on the situation and gave the boys a tight smile. "Okay, and you, Bobby, if you are with your buddy, you are a party to the crime. You can't afford any bad press, given your status. Know what I mean?"

Up until this time, Bobby seemed to have been enjoying the exchange. Now he shook his head and waved his hand as if swatting a fly. "Hey man, I done nothing, so you can't tag anything to my future trial. My defense attorney is going to get me off."

His jaw slacked, and Deke grinned at the boy's realization.

"Is that right? Well, dreamers dream. Just be careful not to add to your report card because I have a habit of showing up when you least expect me." Deke touched the brim of his hat. "Have a nice day, boys. Oh, and when you return from honky-tonking in Tennessee, make sure you have a designated driver."

The deputy ignored the surprise on the two youths' faces and turned to Lamb senior with a wry smile. He nodded farewell. "Been a long time, Bull. Can't say I missed you."

Deke didn't wait for a comment. Instead, he headed for the pool gate and let himself out. As he turned the corner to the circle driveway, he heard the sound of the front door opening.

Willa Lamb had been preparing sandwiches for lunch. Her son expected her to include Bobby Page. Bobby always brought trouble for her son. Why couldn't Cal find decent friends?

At the sound of the sliding glass door opening, she looked up. Violet entered, her lower lip thrust forward.

"What's a matter, Honey Chile?"

"Daddy says I have to come in here and help you." She continued scowling.

Willa peeked through the window and saw a man engaged in conversation with her husband. He wore a uniform, a sheriff's department uniform. Her knife hand froze mid-slice over the sandwich.

She heard four-wheelers announcing the boys' arrival. The man with her husband stepped closer to the poolside gate. She could now see his face. Vaguely familiar.

"That's Deputy Deke." Violet wrinkled her nose, pushing her thick glasses upward. "I think Cal may be in trouble again. But Daddy made me go in before I could hear what happened. Can we have chips?"

"*May* we have chips," Willa answered automatically, maintaining focus on the two men poolside.

"Sure, we can." Violet mischievously grinned as she maneuvered around the kitchen island to a cupboard that housed the chips.

"Deputy Deke, you said?" From the windowsill over the sink, Willa picked up some small binoculars she used for birdwatching.

"Yeah, Momma. He's a nice man. He talked to me a bit on the front porch. I like him."

Willa directed the binoculars toward the deputy and Bryce as she rolled the focus wheel. "Yes, yes. It is Deke Campbell. I haven't seen him since graduation."

Violet had returned to the island, her arms embracing two other packages of chips. "Graduation from kindergarten?"

Willa lowered the glasses. "Uh, no. High school." He looked good. Filled out that once-wiry frame. Much taller.

"Set the table, Vi."

Willa's son and Bobby approached the pool gate. She moved to the sliding glass door and eased it open.

She had to know what this was about.

She caught bits of the conversation from her vantage point, but not enough to determine the topic. When their meeting ended, the deputy turned and departed. She slid the door closed and began walking from the kitchen area toward the front of the house.

"Vi, finish setting the table. I will be back."

The little girl gave a questioning look. "Where are you going?"

"Never mind, just do as I said."

Willa rushed toward the front door and pulled it open as Deke rounded the house and came into sight. He halted and looked toward the shady porch.

"Hello, Deke." She smiled to cover the nervous tone.

She saw his eyes widen in recognition. He returned the smile. "Well, hello yourself, Willa."

He recognized me!

She brushed back some strands of wayward blonde hair, glad that she'd recently been to the salon for a style and that her nails sported new acrylics. She spoke again, this time with confidence.

"It has been a long time. I guess just after you graduated, and then you were gone to the Marines. Heard you became one of Tim's deputies. Chicago too busy?" She giggled at her joke.

"Naw. Just missed my horses and the fishing on the lake."

"I am sorry we didn't make your father's funeral to pay our respects. But Bryce was tied up with getting some gas leases." She thought it a weak excuse and bit her lip.

"Same Willa. The peacemaker. You know, and I know, attending my father's funeral never entered Bryce's mind. He had no use for me and certainly wasn't grieving for the man who procreated me."

"Same Deke, the sarcasm king." Willa looked at the ground. "I would have come, but yeah, Bryce wasn't interested. So, I just didn't want to make waves."

56

Deke shook his head. "Sorry about that sarcastic crack. Seriously, how are things with you?"

"Oh, got everything I want. Or everything I need. You know."

"You deserve it. I mean having what you need. You certainly saved me from a lot of harassment from your husband. Especially during basketball."

Willa sighed. "I don't know why he was so mean to you in high school. Oh, he was mean to others, but he took special pains with you. I guess the others cowered. You didn't."

Deke gave a wry chuckle. "I guess I should have cringed. I would have saved myself a lot of cuts and bruises. But that was then, and this is now."

"Yes, yes. And you are looking good. Marines and police work molded you into a fine specimen." The nervousness returned as she reddened and giggled."

"Well, thank you, Willa. And if I had been in your senior class, maybe I would have given Bryce competition."

"I remember when I was a senior and Bryce had graduated. He was picking me up from school. You were a sophomore, and we were in front of the school talking. He thought you were competition."

Deke chuckled. "I guess so. He jumped out of the truck. I never saw anybody as red-faced as he was. That's when I realized why he had the nickname 'Bull.'"

"But you stood your ground. Why?"

Deke shrugged. "We were just talking, nothing wrong. Besides, I figured he was over eighteen, and I was just turning sixteen. So, if I whipped him, they would say that kid did a job on Bull. But, on the other hand, if he whipped me, he could not brag about kicking a kid's butt." He paused, then grinned. "I guess I counted on the latter."

Willa nodded. "So, I take it you never married?

"Nah. No woman wanted to share me with the department. But I am settling down a bit, and who knows, I might start shopping."

They both laughed, then Willa spoke. "I will certainly keep my eyes open for an appropriate candidate." Her face grew serious. "Uh, what were you discussing with my son and his father?'

"I'll let them tell you about it."

"I need to know." She caught herself and softened the tone but repeated the assertion.

"It seems your son wanted to practice his rock-throwing skills down by the Crooked Creek bridge. His target was Cecil Burgess."

"Oh, dear! I hope the little man wasn't hurt. Are you sure my Calvin did it?"

Deke nodded.

"I don't know what gets into that boy sometimes. Is he in serious trouble? I mean, you didn't arrest him?"

"No, I didn't. I mean, I would have, but Burgess does not want to sign a complaint." Deke looked into her eyes and softly said, "Second chances don't come around too often. You might want to make your boy understand that."

"I will try. I guess Cal sees his father's anger at the Waxman, I mean Mr. Burgess. It seems Bryce wants to acquire his farm and mineral rights. That way, he will have rounded out his land investments, but Mr. Burgess won't sell." She stared again at the ground. "I will talk to Calvin. But it is a difficult situation."

"Do that. It can become more difficult if this gets out of hand." Deke touched the brim of his hat. "Well, honestly, it has been good seeing you again. Take care of yourself."

Willa nodded. A smile appeared on Deke's face as he looked around her to something else. She turned and saw

Violet standing behind her and peering out at the deputy. Her nose wrinkled as she tried to move the glasses up on her face.

"And goodbye to you, Miss Vi. I am sure Tinker needs care now." Deke nodded his head toward the cradle on the porch.

"Goodbye, Deputy Deke. Stop by and visit us again." Vi smiled broadly.

Deke nodded toward the child and then turned toward Willa, touching the brim of his hat. "Ma'am."

The deputy strode to his Jeep and fired up the engine. Willa watched him drive off.

Why am I the wife of a rich bully instead of a thoughtful cop?

CHAPTER 5

Sunday morning found Deke lounging in bed later than usual. He opened his eyes, only to be stabbed by brilliant rays of sunshine that peeked through slits in the closed blinds. He grimaced and sat up, swinging his legs over the side of the bed. Then, leaning forward, he brushed the venetian blinds downward to terminate the offending sunbeams.

He picked up his wristwatch. Just seven. Time for catching up. He yawned and swiveled back into bed. He soon found fitful sleep.

A car's taillights danced in front of him. Then it seemed to rise in flight, disappearing over dark buildings. Finally, the vision of the vehicle appeared to transition to an unkempt head wearing a stocking cap. A bearded face reflected a mix of terror and surprise as it hurtled toward Deke.

Deke's brain transported him back to that night in the squad car, wrenching the steering wheel to avoid the face. He relived the horrible thud as the body slammed into the car's grill and catapulted over the hood into the windshield. For a split second, the face expressed a voiceless scream, then exploded into a mass of blood.

His partner, Dwayne Goodlet, wailed, "Oh, Jesus!"

Deke bolted upright in his bed, sweating and panting as he returned to the present. His wristwatch still lay on the nightstand, but the time glowed 11:15 a.m. It was a nightmare after a six-month lapse. He'd thought they had stopped.

He lurched forward out of bed and rushed toward the TV on the chest of drawers. He needed to flood his senses with something else. As he turned the old set on, he noticed that his hand trembled. His T-shirt was soaked.

"Come on, man! It's over, and you can't change it."

He busied himself with trying to find the local news. As he flashed through the stations, he became aware of the programming. One after another displayed a preacher behind a pulpit. Some were calmly speaking or reading Scriptures, and others were sweating and yelling as they ran around the platform.

"That's what I need." Deke frowned, then paused.

I'm forgetting something.

He ran through his mental Rolodex—events from yesterday. He had exhausted a list of farmers he had called in search of a new home for his horses. No luck.

The background of preaching on TV supplied him with the forgotten item. "Oh, crapola! This is Sunday. Lunch date with Tim and Bev. What time was that?" Deke tapped his forehead.

"One p.m.," he muttered.

By noon, Deke had dressed, downed a coffee, and made a few more calls to farmers he knew in the county to check for available land for lease. No one answered his calls. At first, he surmised the recipients were looking at their caller IDs and deliberately not answering. "Hmm. They see a Chicago area code and figure it must be a telemarketer."

Then he realized again that it was Sunday, a day when most respectable farmers were in church. Deke shook his head and wandered to the refrigerator. He plucked his multivitamin bottle and the Waxman's smokers' concoction off the top. He had delayed long enough.

"Saved the best for last." Deke grimaced as he studied the bottle and its contents. He squirted the vile-tasting liquid into his mouth, then turned up the water bottle and drank more than he wanted.

Stuff seems to be working. But unfortunately, the cure is worse than the addiction.

Wait a minute. A thought flashed through his brain. *Cecil has acreage not being farmed!* He smiled. Perhaps he'd found a solution to his horse dilemma. "It's worth a shot."

The sheriff liked it when Bev cooked for guests. She'd always been a good cook, but her meals were extra-special when guests came over.

Tim had removed his tie and sport coat and was preparing to plunge into his leather recliner to catch the Cardinals' pregame speculations when Bev's voice interrupted his plans. He continued to drop into the chair but stopped short of picking up the remote.

"Tim, Tim! Where are you?" The mixer whipping up the potatoes was not loud enough to drown out her voice, so he could not feign deafness.

"Ohh, all right," he mumbled, bobbing his head from side to side. The downside of having company meant his lovely bride would become edgy, and he served as her stress-relief valve.

"In the living room," he answered.

"What are you doing?"

Tim glanced around. "Living."

"Honey, can you help me? They will be here in an hour."

Tim raised his hands in surrender and walked into the adjoining kitchen. Bev, banging the beaters on the stainless-steel mixing bowl, took immediate charge.

"Can you check the green bean casserole?"

"Where's it at?"

She rolled her eyes. "It's in the freezer. Where do you think it is? Check the oven."

"Remember it's Sunday, and we just came from church. I am sure there is a Scripture verse about sarcasm." Tim grinned as he opened the oven.

"Well?" Bev tried to peer over his shoulder as she transferred the mashed potatoes into a dish and covered it.

"Well, it's green. That be the right color."

"Oh, you. Is it bubbling?"

"It seems happy."

When his wife rounded the island and headed his way, Tim hurried on. "Yes, yes, it is bubbling."

She arrived at the stove and glanced at the beans. Then she turned to the deep fryer and checked the temperature.

"By the way, Bev, I thought only Deke was coming for dinner. Why the extra plates?"

"I told you yesterday, but you were not listening. I ran into Pastor Mike and Lois at Food Giant, and I invited them. They first said they had invited a single lady who was new to the area to their house for dinner and had to decline." Bev paused and looked at her husband. "I thought it would be a good opportunity for Deke to meet a single girl."

"Girl? Who is she? Do you know anything about her? And for Pete's sake, she might be older than dirt and uglier than homemade soap!"

Bev shook her head. "I didn't catch her name, but I assume she is young because she just graduated a couple of years ago from college or something. And Lois said she had a nice personality."

"You should have picked up on that clue. A 'nice personality' is something people say when the girl can scare the label off a perfume bottle." Tim sighed and crossed his arms on his chest, leaning back against the counter.

"Oh, stop it. That is unkind, even for a sheriff." Bev slapped Tim's bottom as she hurried toward the refrigerator. "Now, get out of my kitchen with that attitude. Why don't you check on Douglas in the backyard?"

"Suit yourself. Don't say I didn't try to fulfill your every wish." Tim hurried to the back door before she changed her mind.

He opened the door to see his seven-year-old son sprawled inside a tire swing attached to a large oak tree, swinging like a pendulum over the grassy ground. The boy did not notice his father's entry into his imaginary world.

Doug was staring grimly at something in the distance. One tiny fist extended in front of him, the other arm straightened alongside his hip. His red cape fluttered as he swung.

Superman. Doug's favorite fantasy hero.

"Hey, Sport! What are you doing?"

Doug jerked his head upward. "Saving the world." The boy's fleeting grin turned dark as he refocused his glare at some unseen enemy.

Tim chuckled. "Okay, but you need to start locally by saving the county. Better yet, by saving me."

He approached the swinging youth and seized the chain.

"Hey! I was traveling at supersonic speed!"

"It's time you travel at supersonic speed to the bathroom and get washed up. And stop by a phone booth to lose the cape."

"What's a phone booth?" Doug slid to the ground with a puzzled expression.

"Never mind. I have orders from the president of the house to make sure you get cleaned up and ready for our guests and dinner."

Tim could see the reference to food instilled urgency in the boy. "Okay. Beat you to the back door!"

Doug sprinted to the house with Tim in pursuit.

"You cannot escape me! I have a pocketful of kryptonite."

The boy squealed and entered the house, letting the storm door slam behind him.

As Tim entered the kitchen, Bev was repeating the orders he had already issued.

The doorbell chimed. Bev clamped one hand to her mouth. "Oh dear, they are early."

"Take it easy. It might be Deke."

"No, no. Have you ever known Deke to be on time for anything?"

Tim strode leisurely toward the front door. "Yes. When there is food involved."

"Please get the door, honey."

"I'm on my way." Tim opened the door and greeted his guests. Lois Paterson stood in front of him, smiling broadly and carrying what appeared to be an apple pie.

"Tim, I know this is a favorite of yours. But your pastor forgot to pick up the ice cream to go with it." She paused to glare at her husband. "I hope Beverly has some in stock."

Pastor Mike gave a guilty shrug. "What can I say? I was working on a prize-winning sermon yesterday, and it slipped my mind."

Tim joined the pastor in chuckling and stepped aside to allow entry. "Come on in. I just finished with the dinner preparations while Bev was taking a nap."

"I heard that." A voice from the kitchen elicited laughter from the three of them.

It was then Tim became aware of the third party quietly entering. His mouth gaped open.

Lois spun quickly to the young woman. "Oh, I'm sorry. May I present Rita Courtney. She is an attorney who recently moved here from Union County. She lives in Marion but drives to her mom's home to attend church with them."

Lois leaned toward Tim in a conspiratorial manner, "She plans to find a church closer to where she is living now. So, she will be visiting us!"

"Ah, Sheriff, or does 'Tim' still hold since we are not in court?" Rita smiled while extending her hand.

Tim's response was slow to come, producing an awkward moment of silence. *Didn't expect this. He'd have to give Deke a heads-up.*

"I'm sorry, I was expecting a guest, but my wife didn't reveal who it was." His hand shot out. "I am pleasantly surprised."

Bev entered the room, drying her hands on a towel. "Well, good afternoon, all. I have already greeted you two in church." Her eyes were on Rita as she walked up beside her husband.

"Hi, I am this rude man's wife, Bev. Evidently, you and Tim know each other?"

"Yes. Only in official capacities of sheriff and defense attorney. You might say we are friendly competitors. I am delighted to meet you and thank you for extending an invitation to dinner. I've heard all about your cooking from Lois."

Tim felt the warmth of introductions between the two women. *Oh my. Deke is oil and she is water.* He cringed and envisioned a replay of their meeting in his office. It was then he noticed a bouquet in Rita's left hand.

"Oh, these are for you. I didn't know what to add to your menu," Rita gushed.

"They are beautiful!" Bev accepted the flowers and buried her nose into their midst, inhaling deeply.

From outside, they heard a crunch of gravel and a throaty rumble of pipes. Deke had arrived.

Tim hurried toward the door, but Bev stepped in his way. "Hon, go ahead and seat the guests and introduce Doug to Rita. Also, put these in water."

"Well, er, I need to talk to my deputy so that I can bring him ..."

"I will take care of our Johnny-come-lately." Bev stepped out the door, leaving Tim to seat his guests.

Can't do anything about this situation. Must play it by ear.

"Please, come this way." Tim led the three into the dining room, where they met Doug as he emerged from the hallway.

By the time the guests had engaged with Tim's son, and all were seated, Bev reappeared with Deke on her arm. Tim thought Deke hid his surprise well. Deke surveyed the room, exchanged playful punches with Doug, and then looked into his boss's eyes. Tim responded with a palms-up, wide-eyed shrug.

Tim noted that Deke seemed not the least bit tense as Bev made the introductions. "Deke, this is our pastor and friend, Brother Mike Patterson, and his wife, Lois, from Flat Rock Baptist Church."

"Hello, Pastor," Deke leaned forward to shake Mike's hand as he rose from his chair. "We meet again."

"Oh, you two know each other?" Bev inquired as Deke acknowledged the pastor.

"We do indeed. It's a long, unexciting story. The pastor gave me some background information I needed for a case I was working."

Rita was staring at Deke with a half-smile. Tim sighed deeply.

The last thing Campbell wants is to have someone he is at odds with smiling at him.

He thought quickly. "All right, Pastor, I am sure everyone is hungry, so could you give thanks, and we can get started."

His abruptness surprised everyone. Bev looked at her husband with disbelief etched on her face. "Timmy, Rita has not been introduced to Deke."

"I think she has already," Tim mumbled.

"Yes, we know each other. How are you doing, Counselor?" Deke smiled and sank to his chair across from Rita.

Rita nodded. "Doing fine. It is good to see you again, Deputy. Um, Deke."

"That's wonderful!" Bev clapped her hands. "Everyone seems to be acquainted here. So then, we can skip the awkward small talk and have serious conversations—as an extended family should."

Extended family? Tim couldn't imagine anything further from that scenario. "Uh, can we pray now, Brother Mike? Unless yer all prayed out, then I can sub?"

Mike laughed, "No, I think I can handle it. Instead of singing for my supper, I am praying." With that, he lowered his head, closed his eyes, and began to say grace.

The others lowered their heads, all but Tim. He remained vigilant, trying to sort out what was happening.

Throughout dinner, Rita noted that Deke exuded a fondness for the sheriff and his family. She was becoming curious about this enigmatic man. Somehow, she found him fascinating as he and the sheriff shared stories from their youth. Tim extolled Deke's awards in sports, rodeo roping, and his commendations as a Marine and later as a Chicago cop. The deputy appeared to be embarrassed by the sheriff's profuse praise.

Quite different from his demeanor when they first met, she thought.

Rita found the pastor and his wife enjoyable, too. Although Mike took his pastoral calling seriously, he had room for fun and seemed to have a photographic memory for jokes and funny stories, as well as Scripture verses.

She studied Deke as Tim recalled humorous stories about Deke's edgy youth. Deke's chiseled features were inconsistent with his attire—a tweed jacket with leather patches on the elbows encased an open-collared white dress shirt. Professional cleaners had starched the collar. He wore Levi jeans with a western-style belt and an oval buckle with a turquoise stone in the center. Nice leather cowboy boots completed his wardrobe.

Hmm, half cop, half cowboy. No wonder I can't classify him coherently.

Bev broke into Rita's analysis. "Okay, everybody had enough? Don't want to cut anyone off, but if everyone wants to stretch and make room for dessert, feel free to do so."

Lois stood and started clearing the table. Rita took her cue and did likewise.

"Oh no. First-time guests are not allowed to labor. But, Rita, I can tell you love flowers by the floral selection you brought. So, I want Deke to take you on a tour of my mediocre flower garden."

Deke's raised eyebrows betrayed his surprise. "Bev, I don't know a flower from a weed. Just ask my lawn mower."

"Nonsense. I am sure Rita can teach you something about flowers. Go on, you two. Deputy, you are escaping KP. You should be rejoicing."

"Okay. You got me there." He turned to Rita. "Shall we?"

Rita met his eyes as he searched for approval.

"We shall." Her lips pursed, then the corners elevated into a smile.

They stepped through the sliding glass doors, Rita in the lead. The moment Deke closed the door, Rita spun around. She caught him appraising her from behind. He refocused on her eyes, but his reddened face gave him away.

"You think Bev has a hidden agenda?" *May as well offer him an escape path.*

"Uh, what do you mean?"

"We ladies know a matchmaking strategy when we see one."

"Oh. Maybe so. Bev wouldn't have done this if she had seen our first meeting in the sheriff's office." Deke chuckled and stepped alongside Rita, gesturing with his hand the way to the garden.

Rita let Deke off the hook.

He is playing dumb, and he is not dumb. Any cop worth his salt looks for a motive, friend, or foe.

She had learned that from her time grilling police on the stand.

"Let's humor her." Rita turned her face upward in the spring sunlight to look into this man's dark eyes. She brushed stray hair from her face and squinted.

Deke stopped walking and grinned at her. "Yeah, yeah. Let's do that. Humor her, I mean. By the way, did you see Tim's expression? He didn't have a clue that we smoked the peace pipe after our session in his office."

Rita snickered, touching her fingers to her mouth. "Now that you mention it, he did seem a bit uncomfortable."

The couple enjoyed a bonding laugh and resumed their walk through the garden, where Rita pointed out azaleas and various plants with insect repellent qualities. His eyes seemed to be attentive to her descriptive soliloquy on identifying the types and characteristics of the plants. However, she frequently caught him looking at her when she glanced up from the flower lecture. She hoped the breeze had not mussed her hair.

Rita forgot about time as the one-sided conversation flowed. Was she boring him? He seemed genuinely interested. Of course, his attention did sometimes wane when she caught him examining her. But that was all right.

An intruder's voice sounded from the patio. "Hey, Buddy! Time to get your nose out of the flowers and into a cup of coffee!" The sheriff beckoned to the couple and pivoted to reenter the house.

On their way back, Deke touched Rita's arm. "Say, do you ride? I mean, you like horses?"

Rita tilted her head. "Well, I have had limited riding experience, mostly on docile horses following trails at camps. I haven't ridden in years. But I do like horses and all animals for sure. Why do you ask?"

"How would you like to meet mine?"

The light in his eyes told her he wasn't joking.

"You have horses? The man from the city?"

He laughed. "Don't forget I grew up here. I've been a cowboy all my life at heart. I did some rodeo roping during my wild teen days. My buddies were all into drag racing, but I couldn't get into it."

Deke looked down at the ground, absently brushing a honeybee on a clover bloom with his boot. Rita wondered if he was mitigating the risk of being stung for them—he did not kill the insect.

"Tell me about them," she said.

"Well, I have two mature horses, Zorro and Mandy, who have been in the family for years, and they are itching to be ridden more. First, however, I have to find them a new home. The home they had has been purchased."

Rita waited expectantly.

Tugging at his earlobe, he continued, "I need to feed my ponies this afternoon, then check on a leasing prospect. And ... and if you are not busy the rest of this afternoon, you could go with me. I mean, I would *like* you to go with me."

Rita half-smiled as Deke extended the invitation. This confident, self-assured man behaved like a high school boy asking a girl on a first date. "No, I don't have any plans. I would like to meet your friends, the horses."

The smile widened, and Rita continued, "We'll humor Bev's agenda!"

"We will indeed. It'll make her day. Come on, we'll have coffee and dessert and then say our farewells."

CHAPTER 6

That afternoon, Rita found herself bouncing beside Deke in his old pickup over the rough pasture. They had passed the time reliving their departure from the sheriff's home.

"I wish I had a photo of the expressions on their faces when we told them we would be leaving together to visit your horses," Rita said, shaking her head.

Deke grinned. "The five-second silence was deafening, followed by the recovery with all of them talking at once, encouraging us to exit."

"Tim's open mouth was a portrait winner." She couldn't help but giggle. "What confounds me is that getting us together was their objective, at least for Bev and Lois, and then they were surprised when we did get together. That's rich."

Rita grabbed for the roof hand hold after a particularly jarring bump and nodded toward a point on the horizon. "Is that barn the destination? You think your truck is going to make it?"

"Oh, ye of little faith. This humble machine has made the trip many times. Lucy always complains, but she's steadfast."

"Why do men give feminine names to their vehicles? It seems to me they do it because then they feel justified in giving them derogatory characteristics." Rita hiccupped her question as a sudden jerk launched her upward, and the seatbelt tightened in restraint.

Deke grinned and plucked a toothpick from a row of five stuck into the plastic padded dashboard. "Well, I guess a masculine name would set up a combat situation that the driver would have to deal with—male pride. However, feminine names allow guys to overlook irritating behaviors. Being gentlemen, you know."

He turned toward Rita, the toothpick clenched between his grinning teeth.

"Hmm. That doesn't make a bit of sense." Rita pointed to the beaten grassy roadway as he deviated from it. "Watch the road!"

As they neared the fenced-in barn on Mr. Thomas's farm, she saw two horses grazing. They raised their heads, ears flicking in recognition, and started walking toward the old truck.

"My friends are thinking I'm running late."

Deke pulled up by the fence and stopped the truck. He sat for a moment, gazing into the horses' huge brown eyes. The ticking of the heated engine punctuated the quiet. Rita watched in silence. He seemed to be in a world of his own. The he pulled the pick from his mouth and returned it to the hole in the dashboard.

"Uhh, are you planning to reuse that toothpick?"

Deke seemed not to notice her look of dismay. "Oh. Well, yes. It still has a usable point. Besides, if I do that often enough, I save a tree."

He threw his shoulder into the door, simultaneously pulling the handle toward him. Lucy squealed her displeasure. He jumped to the ground and walked to a sagging wooden gate, stopped abruptly, and then retraced his steps to the truck, walking around the front to open the door for Rita.

"Sorry. I'm used to being alone when I mingle with Zorro and Mandy."

"Oh, don't mind me. I am not a complainer like Lucy here." Rita allowed Deke to assist her to the ground. He held her hand for a few seconds as they exchanged smiles. Despite his strong, calloused hands, his grip was light and gentle.

What a paradoxical man.

He released her hand and said, "Come on. I want you to meet my family."

Zorro and Mandy stood quietly with their heads thrust over the gate. Rita followed Deke as he approached them, and they vied for his attention.

What beautiful animals.

Zorro was a muscular black gelding with a white star on his forehead. Mandy, a sleek chestnut mare with bright brown eyes, was a little taller and had a mischievous light in her eyes.

Deke alternately rubbed their muzzles and murmured to them in a calm voice. Rita could not make out the words, but all three seemed pleased with their meeting. Then each horse started nosing Deke's chest and snorting.

"What do you want? Are ya glad to see me or want something ya think I brought?" Deke laughed and reached inside his shirt pocket and brought out two lumps of sugar. "Is this what you want?"

The horses greedily consumed his offering as Deke pushed the gate open, and they backed up.

"Come on in."

"Will they bite?" Her heart thudded as she stared at their large heads.

"Not unless you are an apple or a carrot." Deke stroked Mandy's neck. "Come on. The way to introduce yourself is to rub her like this. Not like you're afraid, or she might be leery. Act like you want to make friends."

Rita took a few tentative steps toward the man and his beast. Then, she raised her hand, gulped down her fear, and imitated Deke's firm strokes on Mandy's neck.

"She's so large up close—majestic, even." Mandy's mane felt coarser than she'd expected, but her sleek hide was soft, and Rita could feel the horse's powerful muscles ripple at her touch. Mandy pressed toward her, filling Rita's heart with warmth as she took in the heady, earthy smell of barn and pasture.

"I think she likes me," she whispered.

"Not surprised. You're quite likeable." Startled, Rita looked up to see Deke gazing at her. His face reddened, and he quickly changed the topic. "Ahem, Mandy was my first horse. Well, after Trigger, a Shetland pony that my mom and dad gave me for my ninth birthday. But unfortunately, I only had him for a few years when he died from Equine Infectious Anemia.

"Then came Mandy. I was about thirteen. She is a Tennessee Walker. That means a gaited horse that has a distinct running walk. The Walkers were bred in the eighteenth century and used by a lot of generals during the Civil War because they were comfortable for riding long distances. For example, Robert E. Lee had a part-Walker. His name was Traveler.

"Let me introduce you to Zorro." Deke moved around Mandy and scratched the second horse under his neck. Rita gasped as she took in the horse's mass.

"He's amazing." She still could only whisper. "I love those soulful eyes. How did you get him?"

"I loved riding, but I wanted more exciting stuff, so I got interested in rodeoing. That's where I met a couple of old-time bronco riding and roping cowboys. Brothers who lived south of town. I used to watch them work cattle and do some roping. Fascinating stuff. I helped take care of their horses, and they taught me the ins and outs of roping and riding cutting horses."

Zorro dipped his enormous sleek head and nuzzled against Deke's shoulder. Deke rubbed the horse's neck as he continued.

"Long story short, the older man, Abe, passed away. His brother Zeke was never the same, and then his wife died of cancer. Sold his farm and moved back to West Texas, where he was from originally. He gave me Zorro."

"Wow, he could have probably sold him for a good price, right?"

"Yeah, but he knew I loved that horse. So, I became Zorro's family. He is a quarter horse and has seen his share of calf roping championships. He's never let me down." Deke paused and sighed. "But they're not in their prime anymore. Mandy is twenty-two, and Zorro is pushing twenty. They were true to me, and I will give the same treatment for the days they have left. And they know that."

After a long silence, Rita asked, "How long do horses live?"

Deke shrugged. "Most domestic horses' life spans are twenty-five to thirty years. Some live to thirty-five or more if they are taken care of——and loved."

Rita noted his emphasis on "loved" and quietly added, "Just like human beings."

Deke looked from Zorro to Rita. "Yes, I guess so. Never really thought of that."

Rita watched Deke feed the horses, spray them down for pesky flies, and check the water in the trough. Then, when he seemed satisfied with their well-being, he escorted Rita to the gate, securing it behind them. Mandy lifted her head from the feed trough and whinnied goodbye. Zorro, focused on his feed, jerked his head up to meet Deke's gaze, then resumed his meal.

Deke fired up the truck and circled back to the bumpy pasture road, retracing his route. "I dream of the day when I can purchase a place of my own and have some acreage. Then I could have my horses right there by my back door."

"Are you shooting for this dream?"

"Matter of fact, I am. I have a little inheritance from my parents. I could finance a little place, but then the payments would only permit me to eat every other day." Deke chuckled as he retrieved the used toothpick from the dash.

"That's disgusting." Rita wrinkled her nose.

"What? To have a little farm of your own?"

"No! Reusing that toothpick. It's unsanitary!"

"Now, think about it. You order a meal in a restaurant, and the food is on a plate. Everyone from cooks to customers passes by and breathes on it. Then you eat it. Germs! Billions of germs! I stick this in my dash so it can be protected from germs. The sunlight and heat disinfect the pick and everything around it. Just like a surgical operating room."

Rita stared at him. "Are you for real?"

"Hmm, I have heard that before."

They broke out in simultaneous laughter.

When they were back on the road again, Deke gave her an apologetic glance. "Listen, I know you're probably getting bored and wanting to go home. However, if you can spare me another hour, I need to run and check on some land to rent where I can move my horses. It's a short distance from here. The guy that owns it is a bit eccentric, hermit-like, but a wealth of knowledge, and a nice person. They call him Waxman."

"Waxman? Why?"

"You will see if I can locate him. Then, I will take you home, but not before I buy you something from the Dippity Do."

"That sounds like a bribe. Okay, but it has to be a double-caramel fudge frosty."

Deke eyed Rita, making no effort to disguise his assessment. "Then it's done, but how do you maintain that figure the way you're eating today? Apple pie and ice cream, and then a double-caramel fudge frosty to weigh it down?"

Rita squinted at him. "Considering I have to run around the rest of the week burning up physical and emotional calories dealing with cops like you pushing the limits of jurisprudence, I need all the calories I can get."

Deke rolled his eyes. "I knew I was good for something."

Rita stared ahead, suppressing a smile as they made their way to Crooked Creek Road at a speed that defied the posted limit.

CHAPTER 7

Deke pulled into the drive leading to Cecil's home and parked the truck.

Rita did not wait for him to open the door. Instead, she pulled the latch and threw her petite shoulder against the door as she'd watched him do earlier. It yielded with a high-pitched squeal. She slid from the seat and dropped lightly to the ground.

Dismissing any thought of protecting their Sunday dress, the couple approached Cecil's cabin like a hiking competition. Deke forged ahead, taking long, purposeful strides, and Rita kept pace by nearly doubling her steps and picking up speed.

Plato, who had been asleep on the porch, sprang to his sentry posture—stiff-legged, tail pointed straight, and nostrils sniffing. He watched the intruders, then let out a low growl. Deke slowed his approach. Behind him, Rita slowed as well.

"Easy, boy. Remember me?" Deke extended his hand, palm up, and cautiously moved closer while she watched the scene play out.

Plato sniffed, then tilted his head. He barked three times, then paused and studied him. Deke slowly approached the porch, his scent wafting toward the animal on a slight breeze. Instantly, Plato's demeanor changed. His tail wagged, and he bounced down the steps to greet Deke like a long-lost buddy.

"Yeah, you remember me. I am friends with your master."

Rita remained still, watching the encounter.

"I am sure he understands your language, although your slight Chicago accent may have thrown him," Rita teased.

"Don't tell him you are an attorney. His friends have probably told him horror stories about lawyers suing for dog bite victims and canines having to face execution."

"Very funny. Come on, Plato, I won't bite." Rita bent and slapped the front of her leg.

Plato regained his friendly tail wag and trotted to Rita, allowing her to pet him.

"Ah, she charms both juries and dogs too!"

"I'll have you know all beasts like me." She straightened, one hand still caressing Plato's ears. "It worked on you."

Deke tilted his head. "Hmm, a beast, huh? I guess I've been called worse."

They both laughed, but Rita stopped abruptly. Her eyes widened at something over Deke's shoulder, and she gasped.

Deke swung around. "Oh, Cecil, didn't hear you come up. I was introducing Plato to my friend."

The Waxman stood near the corner of the house, dressed in his bibs and Panama hat. He held a small baby food jar in one hand and some green plants in the other. Plato left Rita and bounded over to his master, who wore a half-smile but remained silent.

"This is Rita Courtney. She is a friend and a local attorney."

Cecil nodded. "Pleasure to meet you, ma'am. Sorry to startle you. I have that effect on people. The deputy should have warned you." His small mouth widened into a smile.

Rita reddened. "Oh no, I, I thought your dog was home alone." She dipped her head.

Deke nodded toward the plants. "Cecil, looks like we're interrupting you."

"Oh, this stuff." Cecil glanced down at his hands. "Yes, it's an emergency. I don't normally work on the Lord's Day. But, Deke, could I impose on you to give me a hand?"

Deke welcomed the request. A good deed might bring him closer to a potential lease for his horses. "Sure, whatcha need?"

Cecil was already climbing the stairs to his cottage, talking at the same time. "Come on in. Violet, the little Lamb girl, found a deer entangled in barbed wire, and she wants me to help her free him. The little creature has himself in a mess, and she is standing by keeping him company. I came back to get some wire cutters and some medicines to treat his wounds."

"Sure, I can help. But, Rita, are you game, or are you worried the chiggers and ticks will eat you up?"

Rita answered Deke's tease. "I am familiar with insects, and it is an emergency. So, I feel compelled."

"Okay. But seriously, you can wait here." Deke shrugged. "Suit yourself."

Cecil opened the door and turned to the couple following him. "Miss, you're welcome to stay here, but there is a well-worn path I use to collect plants and herbs, so it is free from vegetation. And I have some natural insect repellent you can apply."

"Naturally." Deke smiled at the little man.

At Rita's raised eyebrows, Cecil added, "It's not dangerous. It is composed of vegetable oil and healing oils of pennyroyal, citronella, eucalyptus, and cedar."

She flashed Deke a defiant glare. "Okay, I'm always looking for new fragrances."

Cecil approached the shelves on the living room wall. His eyes swept the display of bottles and tins marked with masking tape labels. Long, thin, pale fingers waved in parallel with his sweeping eyes until he found what he needed.

"Aha! I will give you some cotton balls to rub the repellent on your legs and arms." He selected a bottle, removed the cork, and handed Rita some cotton from a tin box.

"Here! Have a seat there and just rub it on your skin. Pay particular attention to your ankles."

Cecil moved briskly to retrieve a small olive-green bag from a peg on the wall. Deke had seen that bag hanging from his shoulder on their first surprise meeting.

Deke watched with interest as the frail man moved deliberately and confidently back and forth from his scarred worktable to shelves in the windows with an assortment of glass jars. He selected several vials and some gauze and quickly thrust them in the bag.

Deke turned to Rita as she diligently applied the repellent to a shapely calf.

"Need some help?" Deke gave her a mischievous grin.

Rita paused in her application. "Thanks, but no thanks! I am quite capable of applying my own."

Deke shrugged. "Suit yourself. Just trying to be helpful."

Cecil said, "You should be doing the same thing to yourself, or are you immune to chiggers and ticks?"

"Naw. Bugs don't find me tasty. Besides, I keep my boots rubbed down with cattle insect repellent."

"Delightful." Rita intoned.

When Cecil had gathered his supplies, he slung the bag over his shoulder, then stepped to a drawer and pulled out a heavy-duty wire cutter and placed it into a side pocket in his overalls. He looked at both of them. "Ready?"

"Ready!" Rita stood and walked toward the door, passing Deke.

"You smell good." He said in an almost surprised tone.

"You mean, I did not smell good before?"

"The repellant does have a pleasing fragrance," Cecil commented as he followed the couple out of the cabin. "Most people are not averse to using it."

As they neared the woods, Cecil turned to the excited dog bounding by his side. "No, Plato. You need to stay here. That deer has had enough trauma and seeing you would not be good."

Plato's tail stopped wagging, and his head dipped low. He sat dejectedly on his haunches.

"I think he understands," Deke said, impressed with the dog's obedience.

"Oh, yes. We have some great conversations, Plato and I."

As they walked along the path that divided woodlands and pasture, Deke thought it was the right time to pose his question.

"Um, Cecil, are you farming your land out?"

Without looking back, Cecil responded, "No. Some acreage is under a conservation program—the soil bank. I have Bert Langley bushhog it twice a year. Mr. Langley owns the cattle farm near Ford's Ferry Crossing."

Deke processed this information, and they walked in silence for about a minute. "Cecil, I have two old riding horses that have been with me since my teen years. I was pasturing them west of Marion. Then the property was sold. Now I have to move them to another place. Do you have some land available for lease, and would you allow me to graze my ponies and ride them over your property?"

Cecil stopped abruptly and turned toward Deke. His deep-set brown eyes, one eye partially hidden by scarred flesh, seemed to pierce Deke's skull. Cecil's mouth pursed, but he remained silent.

Deke continued. "Look, I would be responsible for all fencing and repair of existing fencing. Also, I plan to buy a small tractor and bushhog, and I could mow your fields for you. Free!"

Does he not like me? Maybe he is happy with no people on his property.

Cecil squinted at the open fields from the sheltering woods. "I think maybe we can work something out. I like that offer to mow the fields a couple of times a summer. But, as far as rent on the land, I couldn't ask you to pay me anything."

"I don't expect you to let me do this for nothing."

"I have everything I need. If I had more money, I would probably be tempted to blow it all on wine, women, and song."

His words caught Deke off guard. Had he looked at himself lately? Then he heard a high-pitched chuckle.

"Uh-oh." Deke grinned. "I thought I was the only one who would inject a Don Rickles joke into a serious conversation."

Cecil cocked his head. "Who's Don Rickles?"

"A comedian famed for his one-liners and insults. He appeared on the Johnny Carson show in the late seventies and—oh, never mind. You don't have a TV."

"Don't have a use for it. It would cut into my reading time."

Deke changed the subject. "When could I move in? I mean, bring my horses here?"

"Anytime." Cecil resumed walking, then swung back. "By the way, I also have a usable barn. Beside it is a well with a hand pump. Water is good." He pointed a long finger to a distant structure. "You're welcome to it."

"That's great. I will make any needed improvements. Thanks a bunch!"

Cecil nodded and picked up his pace.

Rita had been silent during this exchange, but she now smiled and nodded at Deke, who checked that Cecil's back was to them, then clasped his hands in victory and grinned.

The couple quickly caught up to their guide.

After a few more minutes, they heard a child's voice talking in slow, soothing tones. They entered an open field and saw Violet kneeling and stroking the back of a brown form near a barbed-wire fence.

"It's gonna be all right. Mr. Cecil is getting some tools to cut this nasty fence off your legs."

As the three of them approached, she turned and rose.

Violet squinted through her thick glasses and then smiled broadly. "Mr. Cecil, I thought you would never get back. And you brought friends!"

"I told you I would be back as soon as possible. How's our patient?"

"He is scared, but he just wants to be free." Violet's face brightened. "Deputy Deke! Mr. Cecil got you to come to help! I thought you only arrested bad guys, but you are a deer rescuer too."

"Good to see you, Violet. So, what are you doing out here by yourself?"

"Oh, I like to walk and pick flowers and visit Mr. Cecil." She waved her hand toward a small plastic sand bucket. "But today, I was hunting mushrooms."

Deke looked at the bucket filled with morel mushrooms. "Wow, quite a haul. But you know you have to be careful. Some mushrooms are poisonous."

"Oh, I know. Mr. Cecil taught me which ones are good to eat and which ones are bad."

She turned to Cecil, who was kneeling beside the deer, examining the back legs tangled in barbed wire. "Mr. Cecil, I found them at the edge of the woods. Mayapple plants surrounded them like you said they would."

He glanced at the girl but then returned his attention to the struggling deer. "That's great, Violet. But remember, always check with me before you take any plants home to eat."

"I will. I was on my way to your house when I found Bambi."

Deke approached the deer quietly. Its movements became more frantic. "Let me do this and get him to calm down." Deke removed his sport coat and gently laid it over the deer's head. "You want me to cut the wire off his legs?"

Cecil nodded. "I think you have a stronger grip to manipulate the side cutters."

The two men swapped places, and Cecil surrendered the tool to Deke.

It wasn't long before Deke cut the rusty barbed wire and freed the deer. He quickly grabbed the thrashing deer's legs. Its hooves were sharp and could be lethal weapons. Deke had seen deer kill snakes by dancing on them.

"If you can hold him steady, I'll apply some ointment."
"Go ahead."

Cecil reached into his bag and produced a tin of salve that he delicately applied to the deer's cuts. Next, he reached back into his bag and retrieved the small baby food jar with the slurry he had made in the blender. He applied the thick paste on the wounds and followed up with wrapping gauze around the legs and taping it to hold it into place.

"You think this guy is going to be a good patient and leave that gauze on?"

"Oh, certainly not. However, it will stay on long enough to do its work."

"Okay, Violet. Say goodbye to your friend, and we will let him go to join his family." Cecil regained his feet and prepared to lift Deke's coat from the now-docile deer.

"You ready?" Cecil looked straight at Deke, who nodded.

Deke released the legs as Cecil removed the coat. The deer struggled to his feet and momentarily stared at the humans around him.

Violet lifted her hand. With sadness in her voice, she sniffed, "Bye-bye, Bambi."

The young deer bolted toward the woods. At the edge of the trees, he stopped and turned as if to thank his rescuers. Then, he resumed his flight, and soon, the last tip of his white tail disappeared.

As Rita watched quietly, Violet became aware of her presence. She stepped closer to her. "Who are you? Are you Deputy Deke's wife? Girlfriend?"

Rita touched her finger to her lips and blushed. "Oh, no. Neither!"

Deke grinned. "What? I thought we were friends!"

Rita scowled at him. "Violet, we are just friends. But it is very nice to meet you. You must be proud that you saved one of God's creatures from certain death."

Cecil twisted his face as he handed Deke his coat. "I wouldn't advise you to wear that again until it's cleaned thoroughly. Deer ticks."

Deke muttered, "Yeah, I figured. I feel them on my arms."

Deke looked for the tiny red dots as he turned his arms over for inspection.

"Here." Cecil fished out a small bottle of spray from his pack and sprayed the fragrant liquid on them as Deke extended his arms. It smelled like Rita's new scent.

"Violet probably needs this too."

Deke handed the spray back to Cecil, and he turned to Violet and sprayed her arms and hands. "Violet, wipe it on your face and be careful not to get it into your eyes."

From a distance, there came a high-pitched motor. A motorcycle from the road? Deke shrugged and walked toward Rita, holding the jacket at arm's length. "Well, I guess I needed a new sport coat anyway."

"You're not so tough. To sacrifice your wardrobe for a deer was very sensitive."

"It was the least I could do. I probably shot his daddy last fall."

"Oh, stop it! You are incorrigible."

The noise from the motor grew louder. Deke could now make out the source—a Kawasaki, side-by-side utility vehicle approaching the fence on Bull Lamb's side. Lamb was driving, and his son, Cal, sat in the passenger's seat. The vehicle turned sharply to avoid a pile of rocks and old boards. A rusty bucket with a chain perched on a locust post stood sentry over the material as a warning. Perhaps a vacated well.

The vehicle slid to a halt beside the fence. Lamb cut the ignition and leapt to the ground. Cecil looked up at the red-faced man storming toward them.

He cursed as he pushed down the old, barbed wire and crossed over into Cecil's property. "Get away from my daughter, you ugly piece of—" The barbed wire caught the beefy man's pants, and he almost fell but caught himself.

Cecil finished applying repellent to the child's neck and stood as the angry man closed the distance between them.

"Whoa! Lamb. You need to settle down." Deke was already moving to intercept the charging figure.

"You stay out of my way, Campbell. I'm going to teach Halloween here a lesson."

Deke dug his heels in front of Lamb's intended target, assuming a ready-for-combat pose.

"Lamb, you will not touch this man. I would like nothing better than to haul your big butt off to jail for assault."

Lamb stopped short. Deke had his full attention now, but his fists remained clenched.

"Think before you do something you'll regret." Deke spoke in a low voice and kept his face devoid of expression. "Now, what is the problem? Your daughter found a deer tangled up in the fence, and she saw Mr. Burgess and asked for help to free him. I was available and came with him to help."

Deke wondered if the de-escalation would work. Lamb's veins strained in his neck, and he was breathing hard. The last thing Deke wanted to do was to take the man out in front of his daughter, but he would not allow him to hurt Cecil—or himself for that matter.

Lamb turned his attention back to Cecil. "I warned you to stay away from my daughter, perv."

"That was uncalled for. This man treats everyone kindly, including punks who throw rocks at him." Deke raised his voice and looked at Lamb's smirking son sitting in the side-by-side.

"Daddy, he was just trying to help me with the deer. But, please, let's go." Violet stepped closer to her father.

Violet timidly put her hand on the clenched fist that was now by his side. The inflamed man seized her upper arm and jerked her around. "Yeah, we are going, and I will deal with you at home."

Deke closed the gap between himself and Lamb. His words now had volume. "Still the ultimate bully. But now you are reduced to jerking little girls around."

"I got a right to discipline my kid!"

"That's not discipline. That's child abuse. They got laws against that, and I would love to shut a cell door on you."

"Campbell, I own this county, and you will find out what happens to people who cross me."

"Your time is over. Don't push me. You cool down and leave this man's property."

Rita's voice rang out.

"Mr. Lamb, please just leave quietly. Deputy Campbell is right about the treatment of children. The State protects them. So, everyone should consider this a misunderstanding, and let's not allow this to get out of hand."

All three men stared at her. She spoke in calm, measured words as if addressing a jury. Deke half waited for her to say, "I rest my case." But her clear articulation was just enough to defuse the situation. He noted the redness had left Lamb's face.

"Okay, I will let this slide." Lamb pointed at Cecil. "This time. But remember what I said. Keep away from my family."

"Mr. Lamb, I have no intention of bothering your family. I have always tried to get along with everyone. I am sorry if you find me offensive."

"Let's go home." Lamb whirled around and started walking toward the fence, but Deke noted that he had loosened his grip on Violet's hand.

"My mushrooms." Violet pulled her hand out from her father's hand and stooped to pick up the pail.

"Leave them," snarled Lamb. His foot beat her hand to the pail, spilling the contents on the ground.

Deke walked rapidly to the retreating father and daughter, pausing only to bend and sweep up the now-empty pail. He reached the fence row as Bull Lamb roughly picked up Violet, lifted her over to the other side, and then crossed the fence and stalked to his side-by-side.

The little girl was on the verge of tears, whether from embarrassment or loss of her treasured mushrooms, Deke couldn't tell. Maybe a combination.

"Here, Violet." Deke rescued some of the spilt mushrooms and thrust the pail across the fence, setting them down by the fence post. He smiled encouragement and whispered, "You can come back later."

"Thank you." She returned his smile through tear-blurred eyes and quickly ran to the utility vehicle, jumping into the short bed behind her brother.

Lamb looked back to see if Violet was aboard, then scowled at the deputy, doing nothing to hide his contempt. Both men exchanged challenging looks, but then Deke spoke over the sound of the motor.

"Lamb, you were a piece of work as a teen, and now I see you are still a piece of work. And that's complimentary." There was an edge to his address.

Lamb opened his mouth to respond but seemed to think better of it. He gave Deke a sarcastic salute. "See ya around. Make sure 'creepy' knows my family is off-limits." With that farewell, he engaged the transmission and stomped the accelerator.

Deke stared at the disappearing side-by-side. His heart ached, watching the fading face of the little girl with the thick glasses. He remained facing the departing trio, allowing himself to regain some semblance of composure. Then he turned to Rita and Cecil.

Cecil seemed undisturbed at the encounter. The name-calling and threats had not affected his placid expression. Rita, on the other hand, shook visibly, crossing her arms in a self-hug.

Deke tried to minimize the event. "Takes all kinds to make this world. But unfortunately, this kind doesn't do anything to improve the world."

Rita shook her head and turned to Cecil and said in a gentle voice, "Mr. Burgess, what he said was most unkind and mean. I guess he has underlying issues."

Cecil gave her a thin smile. "Oh, Mr. Lamb was uncharacteristically gentle. Maybe the presence of a lady softened him. And it's Cecil. All my friends call me Cecil. What friends I do have." He chuckled at his joke.

"I have known Lamb all my life, and he has always been a jerk." Deke approached the duo.

Cecil's manner took a serious tone. "He needs Jesus."

Deke glared. "He needs his butt beat."

Cecil shook his head in quiet reprimand.

Deke sighed. "Okay, first a butt-beating, then he may be more accepting of Jesus."

Rita put her hand on Cecil's arm. "Ignore Deke's strategy. You are right, Cecil. The man needs the Lord."

Deke shrugged. "I feel outnumbered."

Cecil smiled. "Let's go back to my place and celebrate our new stabling arrangement with some tea, Deke."

Deke was glad to escape the Bible talk. He had heard enough of it in his youth. "Sounds good. And do you have any more of that nasty concoction you gave me? I confess, it seems to be working."

CHAPTER 8

Cecil awoke with the sun, as usual. However, his mind was cloudy with the cobwebs of sleep. Joint pain reminded him he faced another day of life. He rose from his homemade wooden bed. The soft feather mattress did little to alleviate his aches.

The deformed man inhaled shallow breaths that filled his lungs with magnolia-scented air wafting through the open bedside window. The cooing of a dove drew his attention. His sparse, wispy hair fluttered as he turned to search for the source of the call.

He spotted the soloist on a tree branch nearby. "Good morning, Mr. Dove. I hope your morning is pain-free."

Today he would alter his daily schedule. Pastor Mike had left him a note in the woodshed in the back of the church, asking if he could take him to visit Miss May in the mornings this week to free the pastor for evening revival preaching in Princeton.

He moved to the railroad depot clock near his front door, ticking off the slow march of time. Cecil gently pulled the glass face to wind the ancient timepiece with its brass key.

He smiled slightly, grateful for what few items he had of his parents'. According to Miss May, the clock with the discolored brass pendulum had survived the house fire because it had been in a small workshop in the barn. Cecil's father had brought it there to repair, but he never had the chance before his death. Cecil had lovingly restored the clock and repainted the Roman numerals and the manufacturer's name, 'Ball Watch Co.' inscribed on the face.

Cecil finished winding the clock and stepped back to listen to the musical tick-tock. His eyes slid to the bookshelf, stopping at the black-and-white photo of the parents he had never known. A lump formed in his throat. If only he had known his family. Any of his family. His only aunt, Clara, had died when he was ten. She was his mother's sister and had visited him in the Methodist Home when he was six. He could still remember the horror on her face when she saw her nephew for the first time.

Aunt Clara had been gracious enough to visit him occasionally, but those times were rare, made difficult by the long trek from her home in Charlotte, North Carolina. He'd been nine when she gave him this photo of his parents, along with a small cedar jewelry chest made by his grandfather. She told him her father—his mother's father—had been a gifted carpenter. He had made a chest for each of them. Of course, his mother's chest perished in the fire, so she was giving him hers, saying she wanted him to have something that he could connect to the family.

He recalled his aunt's last visit to him—how strangely different it had been from the first. She did not shrink from his hideous features any longer. She even kissed him on the forehead as she said goodbye.

On her way out, she stopped in the doorway of the children's home lounge and gave him a long, sorrowful look.

"Sweetheart, I have cancer. Doctors do not give me long to live." Tears formed in her eyes. "Your mother would have loved you. I should have taken you in after her death. I am sorry I did not. Please forgive me."

After her confession, she walked out, leaving Cecil conflicted by hurt, sympathy, and anger. Anger had never been a common emotion for him as a child, nor even as an adult. However, now Cecil relived those feelings, turning his head toward the jewelry box she had left with him.

Cecil kept all he deemed most valuable in this box—coins he had found in the burned remnants of his birthplace and a silver, heart-shaped pendant he'd pulled from the ashes. The silver chain had melted, but the pendant itself was relatively unmarked by the fire.

The pendant. The jewelry box. The clock. The framed photo. Not much, but they were his. All that remained of his parents.

Cecil sighed and glanced at the ticking clock, which had once graced the railway waiting room. Six-fifteen. He had time to check on his ginseng crop before Pastor Mike arrived. Already dressed in clean overalls and a blue dress shirt, he put on the brown felt fedora he wore during his rare daylight forays into public areas. The crisp newness of the hat attested to its limited socialization.

He stepped outside and was greeted by Plato, who jumped up, tail wagging vigorously.

"Plato, you just saw me last night. Did you miss me, or are you getting a touch of dementia?" Cecil laughed as he playfully rubbed the dog's head.

A heavy dew covered the grass. Cecil tried to protect his shined work shoes by taking slow, measured steps. He should have put on his everyday shoes for this.

Plato forged ahead, sniffing trees and bushes, pausing now and then to leave a liquid message for animals who had passed this way through the night.

After a few hundred yards, the dog paused in front of a mulberry bush and expectantly looked back at Cecil.

"Yes, we are going to check it out."

Satisfied, the dog resumed his trot, forcing the bush aside. Cecil smiled and followed him, turning sideways to forge through the bushes. Once clear of brambles, he stopped and surveyed an enclosed area. The cleared area was enclosed by a six-foot chicken wire fence. It also had barbed wire woven through chicken wire with two feet of separation. In addition, climbing vines grasses clung to the fencing making it almost invisible.

Cecil stepped closer to the gated entry, and one plant caught his attention. The earth on one side had been disturbed. He entered the plot and knelt to examine it more closely. A deer or squirrel? No, the fence was high enough to keep deer out. Maybe, squirrels or a coon? Strange. It didn't look like an animal dig. It was too straight and clean.

Worry for his precious crop surged through him. When it matured, this small medicinal plant garden could be worth three to five thousand dollars. He counted on this market to supplement his social security and donations for natural healing products.

Should he put chicken wire around his plants in addition to the fence?

He had to determine the trespasser's identity before making a plan to stop it. Hopefully, the invader wouldn't inflict too much damage before then.

Cecil looked at Plato, who sat quietly studying his master's face. "Well, old friend, we do what we can, but our lives are in the Lord's hands, right?"

Plato rose and walked over to Cecil and licked his hand in agreement—then, both dog and master retraced the path to the cabin.

Cecil poured dry dog food into Plato's bowl on the porch. He refreshed his drinking bowl and found a rag under the sink to clean his dew-kissed shoes.

As he closed the door, he spoke to Plato, who had turned from his breakfast to accompany Cecil.

"No, buddy! You can't go with me. I will be back by noon." The man bent and rubbed the dog's ears, then trudged down the path to await his ride.

CHAPTER 9

Cecil disliked daylight trips to town, mainly because of the stares. He nervously patted the breast pocket on his bib overalls to reassure himself he had the tin of homeopathic salve for Miss May.

Thinking of Miss May always made him smile. She was the only regular visitor he'd had during his childhood years in the Methodist home.

He had looked forward to those visits. Miss May had been comfortable around him, and he, in turn, felt comfortable around her. She always brought a surprise—candy, cookies, books, or a toy. Staff had told him how she rescued him from the fire when he was born. Now, it was his turn to visit her in a time of need. He knew she had a nephew in Chicago who occasionally visited when he came to see his family. Strangely, she never mentioned those visits.

At precisely seven a.m., Brother Mike's car rounded the curve and pulled into the weedy drive leading to Cecil's home. Cecil opened the door, bent low, and smiled at the pastor.

"Good morning!" Cecil said.

"Morning! Get in and make yourself comfortable."

After Cecil had seated himself and closed the door, Mike checked for traffic and then backed out onto the blacktop. "I appreciate you being flexible and changing your schedule for me. I know you prefer evenings to visit Miss May."

"Oh no, I'm the appreciative one. You have been providing a taxi service for me for years. So, a little adjustment on my part is only to be expected. It's not like I am punching a time clock." Cecil grinned at the driver.

Mike chuckled. "If you were punching a time clock, I bet you'd find the hours you have put in growing plants, hunting cures, and concocting medicinal treatments for people really paid off. You probably have made about four cents an hour."

Cecil shrugged. "Well, I enjoy my homeopathic hobby, and I enjoy helping people if I can."

Mike nodded. "You do indeed." The pastor changed the subject. "Cecil, I wish you would come inside the church and listen to my sermons instead of hiding out in the woodshed. It gets hot out there in summer, and cold in the winter."

"You know I'd be a distraction. You have a fine congregation, and you don't need another pretty face to preach to."

Mike frowned and shook his head. "You know you would be welcome."

Cecil looked out the window. "Maybe for some, but for others, it would be uncomfortable."

Mike changed the subject again and proceeded to give him the community news. Cecil liked to keep up with events in the county and looked forward to the times spent with the pastor to keep him updated.

"Last Sunday, Lois and I had dinner with the sheriff and his wife." Mike paused and then continued after his famous chuckles. "It turned out to be a special event for a couple of people. His single deputy was there for dinner, and Lois had invited a local attorney, who was also single, to come with us. You know Lois is always playing cupid.

"Long story short. The deputy and Rita hit it off and left the dinner party to visit the deputy's horses. I think they are now seeing each other regularly."

Cecil turned his head and looked at Mike. "Rita. What was the deputy's name?"

Mike gave Cecil a puzzled look. "Why, his name is Deke. I believe it is short for Deacon, although he is not a regular church attender despite the moniker. Wait a minute! That was the same deputy who rescued you from that rock-throwing brat!"

Cecil bobbed his head up and down. "Yes, yes, and I met Miss Rita last week. Deke is using my pasture for his horses."

"Well, I'll be! Did you know that May Duston is Deke's aunt? His mother's sister."

"She once told me that she had a nephew in Chicago but never said he moved here." Cecil pondered this development. "Maybe he never visits her?"

"No, I know for a fact he visits her. I have even seen him on my rounds once or twice. But, of course, he wasn't wearing a uniform then, so our first official meeting was when Cal was rocking you under the bridge."

Cecil looked at Mike, squinting his eyes. *But Aunt May always told me everything. Why did she not mention his visits?*

Mike glanced at Cecil, deep in thought. "Maybe, she didn't want you to know because she thought you would curtail some of your visits. I mean, she is a lonely woman and is delighted when any guests show up."

Cecil shrugged. "Maybe so."

They pulled into the nursing home parking lot, and Cecil sighed heavily. Even at twenty minutes after seven, the place teemed with people entering and leaving. Some must be workers, likely changing shift for the day. Others were visitors going in to see their loved ones before work.

"Well, we are here. I will make some quick rounds while you visit Miss Duston. I'll come to her room last."

"Uh, could I ask you to please go to her room first and get her to meet me outside in the garden?"

Mike gave Cecil a questioning look. "Well, sure. But wouldn't it be better inside her room? You know, cooler?"

"There are already patients fully awake in the halls or room doors open to see me waltzing down to her room. Half of them have dementia, and the other half have lost touch with reality. Do you really want to see folks having seizures or heart attacks when they see this creature invading their safe place?'

Mike frowned. "Cecil, you are too hard on yourself."

"Please, Brother Mike. I always come at night when the folks are in bed, so I don't cause a disturbance. I am just trying to avoid making a name for myself here."

"Okay, okay. I'll take her to the garden. Give me about ten minutes to sign in and get her ready."

"Thank you. I will walk around back to the garden."

Mike patted Cecil's leg and smiled at him.

Cecil appreciated the man's concern. "It's fine. I get along well with people, as long as I stay under the radar."

CHAPTER 10

May had just finished her breakfast and was being wheeled back to her room by an aide. She had missed some of the local news, and she did not like that.

"Patty, can you step it up? You were already running late when you came to my table to take me back," May did not disguise her irritation.

"Miss May, I told you I had to take care of Mr. Meese. The poor man, his stroke left him with one good hand, and he dumped his tray on the floor."

May saw the evidence on Patty's uniform tunic, stained with jelly and oatmeal. Remorse coursed through her as the nurse wheeled her into the hall.

"That's right. I'm sorry for jumping on you."

Patty touched her shoulder and said, "That's all right. You're forgiven." They both laughed.

As they neared her room, May could make out a lone figure standing in the doorway. Her eyes were not the best. Macular degeneration had taken its toll. Nevertheless, she could vaguely make out the stranger.

"Pastor Mike! What brings you out this early?" Patty questioned.

May turned her piercing blue eyes his way, hoping they still danced behind her glasses. She wanted no one to know that those eyes had lost some of their acuteness.

"Yes, indeed. To what do we owe this honor?" May lifted her hand, and Mike brought it to his lips.

"Well, I just wanted to see if you were as beautiful in the early morning as you are in the evening."

"Oh, go on!" All three laughed.

"I will leave you in the capable hands of this man of the cloth while I go and take some temperatures. Pastor, would you kindly get her settled in her room, and I will be back."

"Certainly. Oh, but is it all right to take her to the garden first? She has a visitor waiting there for her."

In response to Patty's puzzled look, he whispered, "It is Cecil."

"I heard that. My eyes may have some issues, but my ears don't."

"I am sorry. It was to be a surprise."

"Cecil, huh. He usually comes at night," Patty said.

"Yes, well, my schedule changed, and so we arranged to have a morning visit."

Patty shrugged. "Okay, make sure you get her back to her room in about twenty minutes. Remember you're a preacher—I don't want you running off with my prize girl here." She laughed and waved as she turned to make her way down the hall to other responsibilities.

"Okay, May. Are you game to go to the garden? Or do you want to go into your room to attend to anything?"

"You are getting pretty personal, Pastor."

"Just trying to be considerate."

May waved her hand. "Let's roll!"

Mike wheeled May outside. The warm air infused with the fragrance of flowers from the well-kept beds greeted them.

Mike halted and looked around for Cecil. "Where is he?"

May sighed. "You got the only good eyes here," she confessed.

They found Cecil on a bench on the backside of a giant shady maple. The tree blocked him until he rose and stepped from the shadows.

"I don't know why he insists on hiding," May murmured.

Mike rolled the wheelchair closer to the lone figure.

"Hi, Miss May. I hope you are well." Cecil approached her and grasped her hands in both of his. "I'm sorry to force you out into the heat."

"Oh, not a problem." May winked. "This is a refreshing change from smelling pee-pee in the hall."

The pastor shook his head. "I will leave you two alone and make my rounds. Cecil, I will be back in about twenty."

"Thanks, Pastor! I will be ready."

Mike turned and reentered the nursing home, leaving the two friends to their visit.

"It's good to see you in the daylight, May."

"That goes both ways. Sit, sit!! I can wheel myself closer to the bench. I only pretend to be helpless. They give you more attention then."

May demonstrated her ability to roll her chair nearer to the bench. It was not easy, and she was conscious of her weak, translucent hands as they rotated the chromed circular hand mount on the wheels. Nevertheless, she succeeded in hiding her intense effort.

Cecil leaned forward as though he was going to help her. Cecil's burnt skin reminded her of the painful skin grafts he had endured at the burn medical center at Vanderbilt in Nashville. She later placed him in the Methodist Home for orphans and oversaw his care. She also ensured that his parents' land would be preserved for him if he made it to adulthood. A local farmer cropped it, and the profits paid the taxes with a bit of leftover for Cecil's savings account.

Cecil knelt and removed her house shoes, setting them aside. She watched the quiet man, so focused on gently rubbing the ointment into her ailing feet. At first, it burned and hurt, but then gradually, she felt the soothing balm.

They talked about the news, the weather, Cecil's latest medicinal project, and other mundane topics until they ran out of words. Then they just sat and enjoyed the birds singing and a distant dog barking. She knew Cecil well enough to sense there was something on his mind.

He continued to rub his hands with a blue bandana that usually protected his head. He stared at the ground and his hands alternately.

May broke the silence. "I am sure there could not be any salve left on your hands. Out with it."

Cecil looked up and took a deep breath. "You didn't tell me that your nephew was back here in the county. It seems that he has been visiting you for some time. Didn't you want me to meet him?"

May's lips opened and closed, but nothing came out. "Why, Cecil, I just forgot. Certainly, I have nothing against you meeting him. He is a deputy sheriff now. Used to be a Chicago policeman."

"I know. We've met. Deputy Deke will be pasturing his horses on my land. I was curious why you would not tell me that he was back. I mean, we always tell each other everything, I thought."

"You know my mind isn't what it used to be. You need to understand that."

Cecil nodded his head and stared at the ground.

A few moments passed before May broke the silence. "Deke is a good man. But he had some problems in Chicago and wanted to get back to his horses and the county. So, his old buddy Sheriff Tim got him on the payroll."

"What kind of problems?"

May wondered if she should share any more. Cecil had so few friends, and he seemed to trust the deputy.

"He accidentally killed a homeless man while chasing some armed robbers with his patrol car. He doesn't like to talk about it. He was a very intense man as a police officer, and he takes the job seriously. I wish he would find a woman who would put up with him. And marry her."

Cecil's face lightened, and he smiled. "I think he's found someone. Her name is Rita. She is an attorney. Very pretty and sharp. Just a thought."

"So, you ah, are getting to know him pretty well?"

"Well, as I said, he keeps his horses in the old barn by Mom and Dad's old place. He comes to feed them. I'm helping him stop smoking. He says the cure is worse than the addiction."

Both of them laughed. May leaned forward and touched his leg. "That's good."

Pastor Mike appeared beside them. "So, did you get the world's problems settled?"

May tried to focus on Mike's face. "Well, at least in the county. The world is going to need more of our sessions."

"All right, you two. Time for farewells. I have to get Miss May back to her room before Patty has me tarred and feathered."

Mike rolled May back to the door, then turned her around to tip the chair backward and cross the threshold. She could see Cecil's fading face watching her from the tree line. She wondered what he thought as he disappeared from view.

CHAPTER 11

Deke entered the courtroom and sat behind the rail in the second row on the defense side of the aisle. It was his regular court date, and he was wearing a tie with a white-collared shirt. It fit a little tighter than he preferred. However, he'd bought it on sale, so he decided he could live with it for a short time.

The county prosecutor, Frank Croft, was already seated behind a stack of folders that were scheduled for a hearing. A potbellied bailiff leaned over the table on his knuckles, talking with Frank about the day's cases.

Frank rotated in his chair and spotted Deke. He smiled and gave a subdued wave. Deke responded with a nod, then looked around for the person he most wanted to see.

Where was she? What could she possibly use to defend Page's theft of the meds? Would she try to obscure Bobby's guilt by trying to get the judge to buy into Deke's unorthodox apprehension using his Jeep's door? Maybe he shouldn't have been so flippant when explaining his actions in the sheriff's office.

Naw, she's interested in justice. Then again, she is a lawyer representing a petty thief. We are on different sides.

Deke turned and scanned the courtroom full of people. A mixed bag. Some career criminals, but some just caught up in petty violations or lapses of conscience. All ages, but mostly under forty. Some sat with parents or significant others. You could tell the career criminals by their expressions of boredom. Two were dozing.

Hmm? No Bobby. Surely, he didn't jump bail.

Deke returned his gaze to the front and focused on the nameplate on the judge's bench. "Honorable Constance Graham," it declared in burnished brass lettering.

Not exactly a "hang 'em high" judge, but decently fair.

A self-conscious-looking legal intern hurried down the aisle with an armload of files. She paused to knee open the gate and then dumped the cases on the table adjacent to the prosecution's table. The young lady turned and plopped into a seat in front of the railing that divided the spectators and accused from the inner sanctum of the judicial machinery.

She seemed aware of the eyes burning into her back. She fumbled in a large briefcase slung over her shoulder and retrieved a yellow legal pad and pen. Deke theorized that was all she had in the bag, given its faux leather slimness.

Deke shifted in the seat discreetly moving his elbow to adjust the butt of his nine-millimeter off-duty automatic under his sport coat. Where was Rita? Moreover, where was Bad Boy Bobby?

The courtroom door swung open. At the sound of heels tapping, Deke turned to see Rita striding down the aisle to the front. She looked neither left nor right. Her shapely figure was clad in a conservative blue skirt and jacket. She wore a crisp white blouse with a blue and white scarf tied loosely around her neck. Her left hand clutched a fully packed leather briefcase. She was a model for a professional woman who tempered her beauty to project her business acumen.

She nodded at her opposing counsel and smiled a greeting, then turned to her intern.

They whispered back and forth. The intern shook her head, and Rita tightened her lips and looked out into the congregants filling the small courtroom.

Probably looking for her client. Had to be Bobby.

She has to see me, but she doesn't act like it. Deke suppressed a chuckle. He could envision himself waving to her, wearing a cheesy grin, but thought better of it.

"All rise!" The bailiff's deep voice even disturbed the two sleepers. A robed woman entered the courtroom from a rear door and strode to her judicial bench. The bailiff continued, "For the honorable Constance Graham presiding over the Crittenden County Court."

In a mass cacophony, everyone in the courtroom rose but not in unison. Judge Graham showed no expression as she ascended the platform and sat on the high-backed leather and oak chair. The small woman with graying hair pulled back into a bun settled in her chair, adjusted her robe, and pulled her billowing sleeves up, exposing tiny hands. She picked up a wooden gavel, then paused to look over her reading glasses at the assortment of people.

The judge banged the gavel on her desk. "Court is now in session. You may be seated." Again, the room echoed with noise as people settled.

The bailiff approached the bench and conferred with the justice in subdued tones. Deke watched Rita turn and look at the door, shaking her head and checking her watch. She looked at her intern, who stiffly shrugged.

The sound of the heavy courtroom door being shoved open caused heads to swivel. A thin man stumbled inside. Deke saw deputy Chuck Delaney pulling the door open. Deke grinned as he analyzed what had happened. The man was trying to open the heavy door and the deputy must have tried to assist him in his efforts, causing him to stumble from the hall into the room.

The man righted himself and turned, red-faced, to the gawkers inside the courtroom. He stood stiffly for a few seconds trying to orient himself.

You did make it, Bobby. What a grand entrance.

Bobby, dressed and clean-shaven, wore a purplish shirt with a yellow tie adorned with various birds. The blue checkered sport coat he wore was about two sizes too small and exposed about three inches of purple shirt sleeves. The pants, on the other hand, were about four sizes too big, the excess cloth cinched into a bunch by a worn belt.

Bobby looked around like an owl adjusting to bright sunlight and met Rita's glare. He flashed her a sheepish grin and awkwardly started down the aisle to the front of the courtroom. He looked back and forth as he made his way down the aisle to the front. Bobby spotted Deke and slowed. Deke fixed his gaze on the front of Bobby's baggy trousers and affected an expression of horror.

He halted, looked down, and frantically fumbled with his zipper. He found the zipper and a look of relief flooded his face. When he looked up, a chorus of titters rose from the spectators.

Bobby gave Deke a questioning look. Deke shrugged and silently mouthed the word, "Mistake."

Deke grinned as he turned to the front of the courtroom, right into Rita's penetrating glare. She stared at Deke while addressing the plaintiff in a low whisper, "Bobby, come on down here."

The embarrassed man hurried forward, and Rita opened the gate to admit him. Only then did her stern countenance leave Deke, who assumed a look of misunderstood innocence.

She wasn't buying it.

The bailiff's announcement diverted Rita's attention not a moment too soon. "The court calls the case of the people versus Robert Louis Page, charged with misdemeanor theft."

The judge's finger slid rapidly along the lines of Bobby's case docket as she speed-read the details underlying the charge. In seconds, the judge removed her glasses and gazed toward the table of the defense attorney. "Who is representing Mr. Page?"

Rita rose and stated the obvious. "Your Honor, I am."

"Let the record show that Mr. Page is being represented by Counselor Courtney."

After the court stenographer had duly noted her command, Judge Graham again looked at the standing attorney. "Counselor, how does your client plead?"

"Mr. Page will enter a plea of guilty and request the court's leniency."

The expression on the judge's face was one of puzzlement. She frowned, replaced her readers, and reread the elements of crime in the docket. She looked up and again removed her glasses to stare at the nervous plaintiff whose right leg bounced spasmodically under the table.

"Mr. Page, are you pleading guilty to this crime with which you are charged?"

Rita grabbed the elbow of the seated client and jerked upward. Bobby quickly found his feet.

"Yes, ma'am—Your Honor. I done it. Guilty as he ..." He chose not to finish.

Deke watched the prosecutor, who was twiddling with his pen. His absent expression suggested he was in another place.

What gives?

Deke knitted his brows. *Surely Rita knows that this will probably mean jail time.*

Deke had an 'aha' thought. He looked at Frank, who wore a wry smile.

You cunning little devil.

They had not mentioned the charge of fleeing the arrest, only theft. Rita must have convinced Frank to drop all charges except theft and be agreeable to court supervision. She would not pursue Deke's unorthodox methods of the arrest.

Interesting, and maybe good to have this end here.

"Mr. Page, you realize with your record—this is not the first time you have been before me—you could be facing jail time?"

Bobby's head bobbed up and down. Rita touched Bobby's arm and whispered to him.

"Your Honor, we recognize that Mr. Page has had his share of misfortune, but he has never been guilty of violence, and all his record is for petty offenses. He is trying to make a new start for himself and is actively seeking employment."

The judge sat for a few seconds looking back and forth from defense to prosecution. Then she cleared her throat. "Will the prosecution and defense please approach the bench."

Both attorneys complied and engaged in a vigorous discussion. Deke could not hear the conversation but could tell it wasn't hostile. Bobby looked confused and at one point started to sit down, but he decided against it.

The jurisprudence group ended their secret discussion and went back to their respective seats. Following their lead, Bobby sat.

"It is the decision of the court—please rise, Mr. Page— that because of your admission of guilt, your counselor's assurance that you are trying to make amends in your social behavior, and the agreement of the county prosecution—that leniency of this court will follow, and you will be placed on probation. Certain stipulations accompany this probation. First, it will extend twelve months from this date, and you will be supervised by the court. Second, you will abstain from all illicit drugs. Third, you will seek legal employment and report back to the probation team assigned to your case at dates established by them."

The judge leaned forward and spoke slowly. "Mr. Page, do you understand this, and the conditions of your probation?"

Bobby glanced at Rita. "Uh, yeah." At her quick jab to his ribs, he added, "I mean, yes, I think so—Your Honor."

"I will leave the details of the probation between Ms. Courtney and Mr. Croft."

Both attorneys responded in unison. "Yes, Your Honor."

The judge looked at Rita. "Make sure your client understands what a break he is getting and the stipulations of his probation."

Rita assured the judge she would carry out the instructions. The justice banged the gavel, making an ear-piercing sound. Deke wondered how a woman with such tiny hands and wrists could make such powerful noise. She must've practiced in her off time.

The bailiff approached the judge and whispered, then she said aloud, "We will have a short recess of ten minutes and then resume." The gavel banged again, and the robed justice rose and left through the chamber door.

Deke thought it best to slip out, too. Didn't want to be seen fraternizing with Rita. Besides, she did not seem to find humor in his practical joke on Bobby. He rose and Deputy Delaney opened the door for him.

"Hey, funny prank," Delaney said. "But I didn't see his lawyer laughing. Maybe she thought that was cruel and unusual punishment."

They laughed, and Delaney swatted Deke on the shoulder, then abruptly grew serious. "Say, are you going to join us in Leather and Ladders this year?"

"Wow, I nearly forgot about that," Deke recalled the fellow deputy's skills as the center for their high school basketball team. His six-six frame had served them well in conference competitions, and he still looked as if he had a few layups in him. "I don't know. It's been a while, and I'm not sure I want to make my return debut at a public charity event."

"Come on, we need you," implored the center. "The game is still five weeks away. We've got Sheriff Tim, so it's the three us from the original team and four new guys from Marion PD."

Deke pondered the prospect. "Yeah, maybe it's enough time to get the feel of the ball again. I haven't touched a B-ball in three years."

"You are just trying to make an excuse in case you aren't the usual high-point man." Delany jabbed an index finger at Deke's chest, then leaned toward him to whisper, "And as a bonus, you get another shot at Bull Lamb. Ya know, he is going to be playing for the Ladders."

Other than a twitch at the corner of his mouth Deke let no emotion show. "Well, that's frosting on the cake."

"Thought you would like that. He always gave you a hard time. Don't know why. Maybe because Willa had eyes for you? Too humiliating for him to have his girlfriend licking her chops at the sight of a peewee player." Delaney snorted.

"What are you talking about? We were just friends."

"Girls talk. And my girlfriend, Gina, said she talked about you being more than just a friend."

"Dee, you're crazy! That was a long time ago, and the only thing that set Bull off against me is that I wouldn't kowtow to him. Nothing more, nothing less."

"Uh-huh. Hey! Gotta get back in there and earn my keep. Practice Thursday, at five. Veterans Park, outside court. Be there." Delaney was already backing toward the courtroom door. He spun around, almost colliding with Bobby Page.

"Sorry, sorry," Bobby muttered.

Delaney said, "That's okay. Lucky for you I am in a good mood, so I won't shoot you this time."

Bobby stared open mouthed at the deputy. Then Delaney exploded in laughter. "Just funning you, silly rabbit."

A light went on for Bobby. "Oh, I get it."

He turned toward Deke. "I guess you wanted me to get the chair."

Deke shook his head and held up his hands. "Bobby, I just wanted to protect widows from you stealing their meds. Understand, she could have died."

Bobby stared at him, and Deke continued. "Look, you would not get into half the trouble on your own if you just stayed away from Lamb. He does not care about you. He will throw you overboard anytime he can. Trust me. I have seen guys like that before."

Bobby looked down, stood on one leg, and rubbed his cracked leather shoe on the cuff of his pants. When he looked up, he had a quizzical look on his face. "Calvin is my only friend."

"He's using you. Okay, now to another subject. Do you have any leads on a job?"

"No ... I'm famous in these parts. No one wants to hire me."

The sadness of his statement touched Deke. He took out a notebook and pen from his shirt pocket and paged through the notebook until he found what he wanted.

"You know Dwight Kensington?"

"Yeah, he lives in the bottoms by Piney Creek."

"Right. I was driving by his farm the other day, and I stopped to chat. He's in a pickle. His hay harvest is coming in a week or so. He just had a square baler and said he could not find young guys who were willing to work hard bucking the bales. He asked me if I knew anyone. I wrote down his number and said I would check around. So, here's his number, and I am recommending you for the job."

"Wow, thanks, Deputy Campbell."

"Just work hard and make me look good. And, Bobby, break ties with Lamb. Go to church and find new friends." That last sentence even surprised him.

"I will work hard. Thanks again." He grinned wide and took the piece of paper, and almost ran out of the courthouse.

Maybe he will seriously try.

Deke felt eyes on him. He looked to the courtroom door and saw Rita striding toward him with tight lips. He gave what he thought was his most disarming smile. She ignored it.

"What were you doing? Giving Bobby an address of your tailor who specializes in uncooperative zippers?"

Deke chuckled. "That's a good one." He cleared his throat, "Look, I am sorry. I thought I could just relax the kid."

"Relax the kid?" Rita responded. "You made a mockery of the justice system. What you need is training in impulse control."

"Impulse control training? If I had that, I would have never asked you out the first time." Deke tilted his head to the side and assumed a forlorn expression.

The corners of her mouth danced, threatening to smile.

"If you ever pull that again on me, I will brain you with this briefcase in open court."

Both began walking toward the stairwell.

"By the way, what was that note you gave to Bobby?"

"It was your number and home address. I said you needed a butler and chauffeur."

Rita swung her briefcase into the back of Deke's leg.

"Ouch! Now, who needs impulse control training?"

CHAPTER 12

Deke's shirt was sweat soaked by the time he had unloaded Zorro and Mandy from the trailer and led them into the corral around the old barn.

"Here is your new home, my friends. Hopefully, it will be your last."

Deke removed their halters and allowed them to explore. They took a few tentative steps into the corral, sniffing the air in puzzlement. Mandy swung around and stepped closer to Deke, nuzzling him for reassurance. Zorro tossed his head and began a slow trot around the fenced-in area.

"I expected you to be the first to show that you're not the least bit scared."

He rubbed Mandy's ears and patted her neck. "Go on. Join your buddy."

Mandy swung toward Zorro with slow steps, gradually breaking into a trot. She followed him around the corral until they both discovered the horse trough and drank greedily.

Deke entered the barn to ensure the two stalls he had prepared for the horses were ready, and he had not forgotten anything. He hung the halters in an empty stall, along with the riding tack he'd already stored on pegs. When he was satisfied the stall gates were open, and the floor was well strawed, he returned to the sunlight and watched the two animals settle into a grazing routine.

He sensed he was not alone and looked around. A high-pitched laugh at the corner outside the barn, causing him to jerk.

A shadowy figure stood with his chin resting on the top rail of the corral. Cecil.

"Sorry, I did it again. Didn't intend to make you jump," said the frail man under the straw hat.

Deke grinned and shook his head as he walked toward him. "No need for apologies. Jumpiness comes with the territory of being a cop. Although ... could I ask you to consider wearing a cowbell around your neck?"

"If I started doing that, folks around here would link it with me, and every time an ice cream truck or bicyclist sounded a bell, they would run screaming." He chuckled at his joke.

"You're too hard on yourself." Deke approached the man and turned serious. "Cecil. I know you grew up in a children's home. Did kids give you a hard time?"

The man did not answer for a few seconds. He seemed to examine the horses, then sighed and looked into Deke's eyes with equally penetrating dark eyes.

"Oh, sometimes. But those who I grew up with did not notice my beauty until they reached their teen years. Then like teens everywhere, I guess, they sometimes made fun of me." He paused as Plato came around the front of the barn, panting from exertion. He bent to pet the dog, and Plato responded with a vigorous wagging tail. Plato noticed Deke and stuck his head inside the corral—to identify the visitors to his farm. His tail stilled as he sniffed the air.

Deke squatted on his heels and rubbed the suspicious dog's head. Then, he looked up and saw Cecil watching him.

"He likes you. He does not like many people. But he does like Pastor Mike. It seems he senses when people are comfortable around me. He is my administrative assistant." Cecil pointed his long index finger, "and he screens folks he senses will not like me or be disgusted with me."

Deke rose and smiled at the dog, who was now distracted by the horses. He'd crawled under the bottom rail and was approaching them slowly. Plato showed more curiosity than caution. Zorro and Mandy paused their meal to study the dog.

"Cecil, I don't want to be nosy, but no—I do want to be nosy. I know you have a rare type of affliction, and it is serious. It must be a double whammy with your burns."

The man rubbed his one eye and turned to watch Plato make friends with the horses. Seconds passed, filled with quiet.

Oh man, I stepped out of bounds. How do I clean this up?

Cecil tilted his head upward and smiled. "You're not being nosy. That, too, comes with being a cop, along with jumpiness."

He scraped the earth below the fence with his worn work shoe before he continued. "I have what they call Werner Syndrome, aka adult progeria."

Deke nodded. "Go on."

Cecil inhaled before speaking. "It causes premature aging. I was diagnosed with it in my late teens. I stopped growing at about fifteen, started graying around seventeen, wrinkling— of course, you don't discern much of the wrinkles because my burns hide them. So, my disease was not diagnosed until I was about twenty. I am thirty-four now."

Cecil once again leaned on the top rail of the corral.

"It produces lesions, abnormal fat depositions. That's why I have abnormally thin arms and legs. A Charles Atlas course couldn't even save me. My beautiful singing voice is a by-product of this affliction. But I do have the honor to have this very rare condition. Fewer than one in one hundred thousand people in the world are affected. And there are internal issues. Most of us develop cardiovascular disease or cancer. Oh, and diabetes. But I can say that diabetes is not an issue for me. The other two, well, I have been diagnosed with them. Heart disease and non-Hodgkin's Lymphoma. Thanks to my herb supplements and modern medicine, they seem to be stabilized."

His narrative seemed to have worn him out, and he was breathing a little more rapidly.

"I am sorry. Is there a cure?" he asked softly.

Cecil pursed his lips and shook his head. "Death, which for me will come sooner than later. I have periodic visits to Dr. Barnett in town. He mainly monitors my heart. He is kind enough to see me in the evenings, after dark, at his home. Pastor Mike usually takes me. Or his wife, if he is busy."

Deke searched for words. He recalled his callous comments to Tim when he first encountered Cecil. Cecil's age admission stunned him. *He's my age.*

"Why do you insist on hiding from people, like the folks at Mike's church? I know there are people in the congregation who have deep-seated issues of their own making. Yours are not. Furthermore, if you give people a chance to get to know you—such as the people who stop by your mailbox to pick up your cures—they surely are indebted to you and would welcome a relationship."

Cecil formed a crooked smile and responded. "You better get your money back from the police academy, Deke.

Folks don't want to have anything to do with a mishappen ugly old man. It will ruin their image. Didn't they teach you anything about human behavior when you were going through training? And if I were a gambling man, which I am not, I would bet you shared some descriptive language about me to your fellow officers when we first met."

Deke hoped that his face would not show any red. "That's, that's not true!"

Crapola. Why did I lie? He knows I am lying.

Deke rephrased his answer. "Cecil, there is some truth in it. I have a sick sense of humor—compliments of ten years in law enforcement. But I still contend you have to allow people in your life to develop friendships—like Mike and yours. And of course, me."

"You're a friend now?"

Why does this guy insist on putting me on the spot?

"Look, you are a nice guy and likable. You are a well of wisdom. Also, I see your kindness."

The two men stood looking at each other before Cecil broke the silence. "You are a kind man too. However, you do your best to hide it. Miss Rita sees that characteristic too."

Deke wanted to change the subject. "I appreciate you allow me to lodge my horses here. I am looking at a used tractor and bushhog. As soon as I make a deal, I will get your farm cut. It needs it now. Hopefully, I can get it done soon."

He surveyed the field. "I will treat your property like it is mine."

"I know you will." Cecil smiled and glanced at the sun. "Well, Plato, we need to go."

Deke glanced at his watch. "Yeah, I need to go too. I have an appointment tonight."

"Appointment or date? Appointment with Miss Rita, perchance?"

How does he know these things?

Deke laughed heartily. "You got me. I do have an appointment with her. I will give you and Plato a ride back to your place."

"You should do that more often." Cecil cocked his head sideways.

"Do what?"

"Laugh. Laugh hard. It wears well on you."

He's right. I have not laughed in some time. But I came close with Rita.

"Make you a deal. I will laugh more if you agree to meet more people."

"It is easier for you to laugh. That's something you can control. I'm not in control of how people react to me." He turned to walk off and slapped his leg to summon Plato. "No need for a ride. Need our exercise."

"Where are you headed? Your cabin's the other way."

Cecil halted and looked back at Deke. "I like to study the habits of wildlife as they go about their daily schedules. Toward evening, it is a whole different world. Similar to a city of people. During the day, professional people are in their offices. Blue-collar folks are repairing streets, fixing power lines, and so forth. I have my binoculars to help my ancient eyes."

Deke nodded. "Sounds fascinating." Then he had an idea. "Hey, just a minute. I have got something you might enjoy. Follow me to my truck."

Deke placed a hand on the top rail of the fence and launched himself over.

Cecil grinned. "You must teach me how to do that."

Both men laughed as Cecil and Plato followed Deke to the truck. He approached the Chevy and pushed the side button on a toolbox secured to the truck bed under his rear window.

"Let me see." Deke scavenged among tools and various containers until he located what he wanted.

"Aha."

He pulled out a camouflaged trail camera with a strap. Then he redirected his attention inside the box and pulled out the companion charger.

"This is what you need. You can strap it to a tree where you want to observe your wildlife and leave it to take photos. It has a rechargeable battery, but you have experience with recharging in your home. This bad boy takes some sharp photos even under low light."

Deke handed Cecil the camera. He turned it over and over in his hands and examined the item closely.

"So, where do the photos pop out?"

Deke chuckled. "Nowhere. You have a small card. See? The picture is on the card anytime it detects movement. Then you remove the card and stick it into your computer, and you can see all the photos."

Cecil smiled and handed the camera back to him. "That's nice, but unfortunately, I am fresh out of computers."

Deke handed the camera back to him and placed one hand on his shoulder. He could feel the bones, with very little muscle to hide them.

"Don't worry about that. I have one and am in the process of replacing it with a more up-to-date one. So, I will bring it by tomorrow and show you how it works."

"That's very kind of you. So, you don't think I'm too old to learn about this stuff?"

"Hey, you are a walking encyclopedia, and you might as well add this to your repertoire."

"I do appreciate this. But I need to pay for these things."

"Tell you what. Give me another bottle of that tobacco demolition stuff, and we'll call it even."

"I think I'm getting the better part of the deal."

"Hey. What can I say? I have always been a sucker who makes bad deals."

The two men shook hands as Deke concentrated on keeping his grip soft. He knew he had a viselike grip. In the past, he had caused men to wince.

Deke watched as the spindly man made his way across the field. What a cruel world he had been born into—through no fault of his own.

Yet, he exudes a better attitude than me.

Deke jumped into his truck and fired it up. He smiled as he thought about the upcoming evening with Rita.

CHAPTER 13

He looped the string over the open ashtray and closed it with a solid push. As he backed out of the vehicle, his eyes were drawn to the half-dozen toothpicks protruding from the dashboard foam upholstery.

What was it she had said? Oh yeah, disgusting and unsanitary.

"The things I do to please a woman," Deke muttered as he pulled the toothpicks out of the dash and placed them in his pocket with the deposed cigarette butt.

He hurried into his house to clean up before his date. The answering machine winked red from the darkened kitchen. He stabbed the play button, and Rita's lilting voice floated in the empty room.

"Hi, Deke. I am sorry to get this message to you this late. I tried to call your cell but no answer. I left a message but ... Anyway, I am stuck at work in my office. I will certainly be finished by six, and I am already dressed for dinner. So, could you give me until ten minutes after six and pick me up here?"

The time of her call flashed a few minutes after four. Deke consulted his watch.

Five o'clock! Good thing she changed the pickup. He would have been running late to her house. Now, he didn't have to rush.

Deke entered the bedroom and selected a light brown dress shirt with a classic green and brown tie. His hand hesitated over the string cowboy tie with turquoise slide. No, too flashy. He would stick with the sophisticated look of the classic tie. A new pair of Levis with a silver-buckled belt and soft leather Tecova boots rounded out his wardrobe.

Deke snapped his fingers, stuck his head in the closet, and grabbed a tan sport coat. He looked it over to make sure it was presentable but noted a tiny drop of barbeque sauce on the front. Souvenir of the church lunch he had gone to after the funeral of an old family friend. He went into the bathroom and moistened a towel to remove all vestiges of a previous meal.

After showering and dressing, he still had time to spare. He drove to the Main Street car wash, and quickly inspecting the truck bed, he determined nothing there would be damaged by the hard spray. He parked his truck next to the firehouse and glanced up at the second floor of the nearby building housing Rita's office. He thought he caught a movement.

Rita shoved file folders into the cabinet on the second floor of her office. The clock on the wall hummed as though urging her to speed up—half-past five.

Rats! I don't know if I can wrap up here in time.

She passed by a window and caught a movement on the sidewalk below. She leaned her head back to identify the solitary figure. It had to be Deke. Although he was not wearing his uniform, the erect no-nonsense walk and broad shoulders gave him away. She shook her long brown hair.

He certainly was on his way up to her office. She tidied her desk, picked up her purse, and walked to the closet. She opened it to reveal file cabinets, boxes of old court documents, and legal books, as well as a full-length mirror inside the door. She pulled a brush from her purse, ran it through her hair, and then touched up her lipstick.

Not bad for a first date. She blushed briefly. Was she really doing this? From what she'd seen so far, she and Deke had almost nothing in common. He was impudent, headstrong, and self-assured. Or was that arrogance? She couldn't be sure. Still, she'd glimpsed the man beneath that bold facade and liked what she saw.

Tilting her chin for a final inspection, she nodded and snapped her purse closed. At any rate, it was just one date. If it wasn't going to work out, better to learn now.

She closed the closet door and returned to the window. Leaning close, she could see Deke talking and laughing with a couple of firefighters who were cleaning their equipment.

He wasn't exactly anxious to see her.

Rita pursed her lips in a tight pout. Something she did as a child to show displeasure to her parents.

Okay. If that's the way he wants to play it.

Rita stepped from her office, locked her door, and clicked down the hallway to the stairs. When she reached the street, she walked with the deliberate steps toward the firehouse and corner traffic light. She regretted not having picked up a folder for her ruse.

Deke's back was toward her as she approached the station's front, but the two men paused in their conversation with Deke and looked toward her. Deke swiveled his head to follow their gaze. When he saw Rita, he grinned.

"Hey, I was just on my way up to see you!"

"Oh, hello, Deke." Rita feigned surprise, then smiled back. "I was just headed over to the courthouse to, to ... check the roster on a pending case."

Deke's dark eyes swept to her hands, clutching only her purse.

Shoot! He knew she wasn't going to the courthouse.

Deke spoke quietly as he openly admired her. "You look elegant. I am afraid I don't clean up like you do." Deke nodded and smiled, showing cute crinkles around his eyes. "Care to bypass the courthouse and head straight out?"

He looked so innocent. To talk like this in front of his buddies, it must be sincere.

A gravelly voice interrupted the couple's preoccupation. "Well, well—two love birds."

Deke stiffened, and the smile disappeared—replaced with a stony military countenance. He slowly turned toward the voice. The countenance of the two firefighters had changed too.

"We'll talk at you later, Deke," one man said, and the other grunted and nodded. Then, they both moved toward the gleaming pumper truck and proceeded to rub its already shiny brass and chrome with chamois cloths.

When they stepped aside, Rita saw a hulking figure in a fireman's attire, the same as the other two but wearing a white shirt of a supervisor. The graying close-cropped hair had been hidden by a John Deere cap when she had first met this man. The voice was the giveaway. Bryce Lamb. What an odd last name for a man that contentious.

Lamb watched the men depart before turning his attention back to the couple. He pointed a meaty index finger alternately from Rita to Deke.

"I am wondering if the county would consider this relationship a conflict of interest. You know, public defender and law enforcement. Like, let's make a deal."

"Bull, the only conflict of interest around here is you. First, having a position of captain on the fire department, then violating burn laws on your acreage. Now that's a conflict of interest."

Lamb's eyebrows raised. "Whattaya mean?"

"I didn't stutter when I said it. Everyone knows that you use your position to push the envelope. And everyone is too nervous about reporting you. But I would be delighted to catch you." Deke rocked back on his heels and smiled.

Lamb's face was devoid of expression. Then he exploded in a laugh. "Campbell, you could not handle me as a kid. Don't try it as a grown-up." The laughter faded. "You need to be careful."

Rita glanced from man to man. Finally, Deke spread his hands with palms up in a mock questioning attitude.

"Careful? Why? I am careful around skunks and rabid dogs. Oh, I gotcha. I will add you to that list." Deke maintained his smile.

Rita watched the two firemen polishing the truck. They were staring, inattentive to their task as their polishing cloths made slow automatic circles on the metal.

"Ahem, Deke, we need to get going. We don't want to be late for our reservations." Rita spoke quietly.

Lamb took a deep breath and chuckled. "Okay, okay, Campbell, let's declare a truce. We'll settle this on the court just like old times."

Deke cocked his head to one side, "You talking county, state, or federal court? Oh, oh. I see. You meant the basketball court. Okay by me."

Lamb shook his head and smirked at Deke. "You know, Bones, you were always clever talking. But the walking—well, that's another story."

Rita felt Deke stiffen again, but he showed no sign of offense.

"Bull, you were sure proud of the creative name you gave me. But did you ever think why the kids called you 'Bull'? Not because of your 'Hulk Hogan' body. News flash—when you were not around, they added another word after Bull and enjoyed a good laugh."

Deke waved and turned away from Lamb. "See ya. Looking forward to the game."

Bull looked confused. The two firemen had stopped their cleaning and looked at each other. They snickered, which provoked the angry fire captain to turn his attention to them.

Lamb had pivoted to his underlings. "Get back to work!"

They turned toward back to their polishing. Although the men faced the truck, one man's shoulders were shaking from subdued laughter.

CHAPTER 14

Rita sighed at Deke's jacked-up four-wheel-drive truck sitting beside her sporty car. "Hmmmm, let's take my car," she hurried on, "You can drive."

"What? I just washed and cleaned my machine for you. I usually do that only once a year."

"I appreciate that. However, mine gets better mileage, and besides I'm not sure these heels would make that Everest climb into the cab." Rita fished through her purse and dangled the keys. "We can put the top down. It's going to be a nice evening."

Deke sighed and accepted the extended keys. "Okay." He gave her a mischievous smile. "Just know that I was looking forward to lifting you into my truck. That tight skirt wasn't going to make the leap."

"You're incorrigible." She answered his smile with one of her own.

The top-down drive to Evansville's Cork 'n' Cleaver was pleasant, weatherwise. Deke's fresh short haircut barely moved in the slipstream while her long brown tresses waved wildly in the flow. She reluctantly removed a scarf from the glovebox and captured her rebel locks. Deke was unusually quiet.

She couldn't imagine what he was thinking. Most likely mulling over events at the firehouse. Perhaps his run-in with Lamb at Cecil's farm had been more serious than he was letting on.

She searched for a way into his thoughts. "This evening is made for a convertible ride. Not cool, but not warm. Right?"

Deke gave no evidence of having heard her. She leaned forward, entering his peripheral vision, but his face remained fixed on the road ahead—his eyes hidden behind the defensive sunglasses. She remained leaning forward as his right hand came off the wheel and patted his sport jacket at the inside breast pocket.

"Right?" Rita inquired.

Deke seemed suddenly aware that he had a passenger, "Huh? Sorry, I missed that. Wind, you know."

"Oh, never mind," she shouted over the noise of the rushing air. She turned on a country-western station and cranked it up.

They arrived at the restaurant ahead of their scheduled reservation, but a smiling, dark-haired young woman still led them to their table. She made small talk, and Rita politely responded while Deke's busy eyes scanned their surroundings.

"Enjoy your dinner." The hostess smiled as she handed them menus and left them alone.

"I have never been here before. What would you recommend?" Rita asked.

Deke clutched his menu as he eyed the approaching waiter. Rita continued to study him but did not repeat the question.

The waiter, Phillip, about thirty with gleaming white teeth, welcomed them and asked for drink orders.

Deke finally looked across the table to his date. "Do you want a wine list?"

"No, thank you." Rita looked up at the waiter with a frozen smile. "I would like an unsweetened iced tea, please."

"And for the gentleman?"

Deke looked at Rita. "Mind if I have a beer?"

Rita shrugged. Why would he ask her permission?

"Your choice. You're driving." Rita saw a slight reddening in his face and wished she hadn't said that.

Deke twisted in his seat, exhaled sharply, and spoke low and slow. "I know I'm driving. I intended to have one beer, not a twelve pack."

The waiter tittered nervously, looking back and forth between his diners. Rita held her hands in mock surrender and smiled. "Just didn't want to carry you to the car."

Deke bowed his head, then raised it with a slight smile on his face. "I will have whatever's on draft." The waiter waved his pen and started to speak. "A large one. As long as the glass does not have the capacity of a twelve pack."

Phillip snickered again as he marked his pad—smiling even more broadly, if it were possible. Rita drew a deep breath, nodding at Deke's humor—hoping it was humor.

When the waiter departed, they sat quietly for a few seconds, looking at each other. Deke broke the silence.

"I am sorry. I was looking forward to this time with you. But I guess I am not great company tonight." He shrugged with open hands. "I am not this moody. Usually."

Rita had learned to choose her words carefully dealing with male clients or witnesses. It could drive them into a defensive posture if she framed a question like "do you want to talk about it?" For strong men like Deke, that would sound patronizing.

Instead, Rita faked cluelessness. "What do you mean? I never saw a moody side to you."

Deke leaned back in his chair and smiled at her. A genuine smile, she thought.

"I appreciate you giving me some space while I was self-indulging. But I didn't mean to be inconsiderate. I guess I'm ruining our dinner."

Now was the time for a peek at this man's wounds. "We haven't even started. There's plenty of time to ruin it, but I think we're good so far. Look, I don't want to pry, and I know you are not the kind of person who gets hostile for no reason. But, this man, uhh, Bryce Lamb, seems to get under your skin. I saw that the first time when he showed up while we were helping little Violet with the deer. I have not seen you act that way with any other person.

"Yes, yes, I confess, I did my homework on you. And if you are the man I think you are, you also did your homework on me." Rita extended her hand across the table and whispered, "You don't have to tell me anything—I just care."

Deke looked down at her hand and slid his hand over, gently covering hers.

"Thank you. I've seen that you care for people, even me. I owe it to you to explain my behavior tonight. I think, well, I know I have a good reason in my mind. You might not think so, but what's the word they use in church? Justified?"

Rita giggled loudly, raising her free hand to her mouth. "I'm sorry. You make me laugh, whether it's intentional or not." She quickly covered his hand and squeezed. "I am not laughing at you."

Deke affected a hurt look. "Well, you're certainly not laughing with me."

They both laughed in unison. The waiter returned to their table with their drinks. Rita reluctantly pulled her hands back. Was that a twinge of disappointment in his eyes?

"Seriously, when you are ready to share, I can be a good sounding board." Rita touched his hand again and smiled.

Phillip lit a candle on the table. As he waved the match to extinguish its flame, the scent of sulfur momentarily stung Rita's nostrils. The candlelight bounced off his expectant smile. "Ready to order?"

Deke looked at Rita. "I can recommend either the filet or the New York strip."

"Well, I will accept your recommendation. The filet, medium."

Deke nodded. "The strip for me. Make it blood-transfusion rare."

"Yessir. It will still be mooing." Again, the flash of teeth.

When the waiter left for the kitchen, Deke turned to Rita and whispered, "I gotta find out what brand of toothpaste Phillip uses. He probably has a dental hygienist in his family."

Her laugh started as a snort. She reddened and quickly used her napkin to dab her lips. "Oh, you embarrass me."

"I like it when you get embarrassed. It gives color to your face. Say, you could save a fortune in cosmetics if you just maintained a steady case of embarrassment."

"You're a creep."

Deke and Rita ate their meal and enjoyed the lively conversation. Deke made no effort to circle back to the story of his hostility toward Lamb. She left it alone.

CHAPTER 15

The coolness of the evening prompted them to put the top back up before they started the drive home. Deke and Rita left the city lights behind them and were bathed in a full moon so large they could see the shadowy features of the terrain.

Rita leaned forward to get a clear view of the nocturnal delight. "Beautiful."

Deke turned his head toward her as the sports car slid through the night. "Oh, I thought you were talking about me." He grinned in the glowing dash light, then quietly agreed, "Yes, it is. I missed those full Kentucky moons when I lived in Chicago. As a kid, I used to saddle up my horse and go night riding when the moon was like this."

Both were quiet for a time, letting the moon do the talking. Then Deke spoke softly. "That was when I used to dream of what the future would look like and felt like I could do anything. Those were happier times."

Rita nodded. "I guess when you're a teen, you always think things will turn out the way you dream or plan. Then you become an adult, and reality slaps you and wakes you up."

Deke raised his eyebrows. "I guess I did not expect you to have experienced similar things. I was under the impression you were a practical, by-the-book kid and that your dreams, if you had any, were grounded in reality. I mean, you don't seem like a risk-taker, so I figured everything was planned and assessed."

It was her turn to look surprised. "So, you don't think I had dreams, disappointments, and mistakes? Am I that robotic?"

"Oh, I didn't mean that as a negative. On the contrary, I envy you in your pragmatic planning. I admit I failed at that." Deke slowed after a curve to allow the car following them to pass on the short straight section of the road. He cleared his throat. "Look, I did not answer you about why Lamb and I harbor animosity. I didn't think you would understand. Or worse, you would understand and think less of me."

He seemed to be trying to summon the courage to continue. She sat quietly, observing his expressions, but without staring.

Deke gritted his teeth. "Lamb was the reason I became a cop. He motivated me. He was my first genuine bully." After a few seconds of silence, Deke drew a breath and continued, "He was a senior, and I was a freshman. He was a fully-grown man, muscular, athletic, and tipped the scales at two-twenty. He claimed he and Willa, who's his wife today, were high-school sweethearts."

He shook his head. "I was the exact opposite of Bull. I was skinny and did not have a hostile bone in my body."

Rita looked straight at him—no pretenses. She let him talk. His focus on the road probably made it easier to keep going.

"I don't know why he made me his special bully project. He used to beat me over the head with a textbook on the bus ride. Once he smeared lipstick on my face while his senior buddies watched and laughed." The muscles in Deke's neck tightened. He gave Rita a terse smile. "One morning when I got up and looked at a bruise on the side of my head, compliments of Bull the day before—I said, '*no más*.'"

Deke's voice dropped to a whisper. "I started to fight back. I couldn't beat him, but he learned not to touch me unless he was willing to accept the consequences of a few lucky punches. So, he stopped the physical assaults, but the insults persisted until he graduated."

"Willa was a year behind him and two years ahead of me. She always had a smile for me, and when he was not around, she laughed and joked with me. I think she had a thing for me. Or maybe she just felt sorry for me." Deke seemed lost in his memories. "Well, it all came to a head after Bull graduated. On that day, he came to the school driving his Chevy to pick up Willa. He caught us talking in front of the school. He parked his car in the no-parking zone and came across the lawn toward us. Bull grabbed Willa by her sweatshirt and started smacking her in the face."

Deke drove on, staring at the moon. It seemed to Rita even the heavenly sphere was hanging on his narrative.

Rita touched his arm. "What happened then?"

Deke pulled the sports car to a stop before a bridge at a boat launch. He shut off the engine and looked at her. The moonlight bathed his face.

"It is such a beautiful night, and we are close to Marion. I know it may be a little chilly, but would you mind if I lowered the top to appreciate the night? I'll give you my jacket to wear, and we can turn on the heater." Deke said it like a schoolboy on his first date.

Rita shivered, but not from the cold. In some ways, it did feel like a first date. She nodded. "I think that would be nice."

He opened the door, unlatched the locks on the convertible roof, and lowered it to the well by the trunk. He took off his coat and walked around the car, setting it carefully across Rita's shoulders. Its subtle smells of Old Spice and leather reminded her of her father—not the father of her youth, but the one who finally triumphed over his many demons.

Back in his seat, Deke started to turn the key, then halted, tipping his head up at the stars, and picked up his story where he'd left it.

"What happened then? I think about it off and on through the years. My fear went by the wayside. I yelled at him, and he turned to me, shoving Willa to the ground. I didn't give him a chance to prepare. I delivered a right hook that sent him to his knees. I think it surprised both of us. I was ready to fight to the finish. I am a firm believer a man never touches a woman like that."

He chuckled. "Then reality set in, and I thought, 'Uh-oh, what have I done.' Story of my life—act, then figure out what's going to happen. I stunned Bull, and his eye was already starting to puff up, but he staggered to his feet and came at me. By that time, Willa had semi-recovered. She jumped between us and would not let him get past her."

Deke laughed. "It was a strange sight, me dancing around in imitation of Muhamad Ali, and tiny pixie-like Willa pushing Bull back with all her strength, while he's shouting that he's going to kill me."

Deke spread his hands and pressed his lips tightly. "Luckily for one of us—and my money would've been on Bull—the track and basketball coaches saw what was happening and came running up. Even Bull did not want to mess with them, and he departed in a huff without Willa. But not before he threatened to finish the job on me."

"Did he?"

"Naw, he went back to college, and I was a big man on campus for a while. Everyone knew Bull, and even those who made like they were buddies with him were secretly happy I popped him. They were too scared of him, and it didn't matter I was too stupid not to do it." Deke grinned.

He then leaned closer to Rita, and his face sobered. "I never forgot what Bull put me through. I didn't tell you half of it. I'm serious in that I became determined to do my part to stop bullies in their tracks. I trained in karate, did some amateur boxing, worked hard on building up, and the Marines did wonders for me. I also schooled myself in talking to bullies. It came with my cop job. Most bullies are just selling wolf tickets—trying to scare you, but they cannot deliver on their threats. The bullies I dealt with found out I was not buying their tickets."

The moon had slipped below a tree branch, but still cast a soft beam on his wide, somber eyes. "So, then I get away from Chicago and other issues—which is another story—and find myself having to deal with my old nemesis again. But this time, I am ready."

Rita nodded. "I think I understand a little more. I mean, I am sorry that you went through this. I hope you will consider it history. In a way, you might want to thank Bull, er, Mr. Lamb."

"What?" Deke retorted. "Thank him for what?"

"Well, he made you into a fighter for a just cause. What doesn't kill you makes you stronger. Isn't that what they say?"

Deke burst out laughing. "Rita, you are *so* baffling. So smart in the courtroom, so by the book, but so unpredictable."

"I am not sure if I should be offended by that." Her lips formed a pout.

Deke gently cupped her chin with his hand, and she saw the moonlight reflecting gentleness in his eyes. He leaned closer—and their lips touched briefly, then reengaged as he wrapped his arms around her for a long, lingering kiss.

She had wanted to kiss him. He must have wanted to kiss her too. He leaned back and looked at the floorboards, but then flashed her a smile.

"Conflict of interest, huh? Bull was wrong—no conflict, but a lot of interest on my part."

Rita giggled and coyly tilted her head. "It's getting late. Take me home, Deputy."

"If it wasn't up to your standards, all I need is more practice," Deke said in mock seriousness.

Rita shook her head and giggled again. "It's my standards I am watching." The two settled into a comfortable silence as he fired up the engine. She leaned toward him and laid her hand on his arm as he reached for the gear shift.

"And for the record, you do *not* need more practice."

CHAPTER 16

The gravel crunched as Rita pulled up in front of Mike and Lois's modest home. She stepped from the sporty convertible and then reached back inside to pluck a casserole dish from the passenger seat. No need to ring the bell—Lois was already opening the door.

"Well, come in, come in!"

"Oh, I don't want to interrupt anything. I just wanted to return your dish, of course sans the delicious chicken casserole."

"You didn't have to make a special trip to do that. I have plenty of dishes. You could have waited until Sunday to return it." Lois raised an eyebrow and asked, "Did you really like it?"

"Oh, indeed! I just worried that Pastor would be upset with both of us 'cause you let the leftovers from the potluck go home with me."

Lois laughed. "I keep him well fed—no need to worry about that. Besides, I figured as busy as you are defending the defenseless, you needed it more to sustain you."

With a chuckle, Rita handed the empty dish to Lois, shifted her weight from one leg to another, and looked down at a stone duck holding a welcome sign in his beak beside the door.

Lois spoke quietly, "Is there something else, Hon?"

Rita lifted her eyes and spoke tentatively, "Uh, is Pastor Mike busy? I mean, I'm sure he is working hard on his next Sunday's sermon, so I don't want to distract him ..." Her voice trailed off.

Lois now wore a concerned look. "Well, certainly. He always has time for his backup piano player."

"Oh, I just know a few hymns to fill in if Mrs. Debosse is ever under the weather."

"Come on in." Lois widened the door and allowed Rita entry.

"Mike! Mike, where you at?" Lois called out in the direction of the pastor's study.

"You rang?" A deep voice spoke softly behind the two.

Mike stood with a half-smile in the kitchen hallway, holding a steaming cup of coffee.

Lois spun and jabbed an index finger toward the docile pastor. "Stop that!"

Mike assumed an innocent look. "Stop what? This is only my second cup of coffee."

"You know what I mean. You're always padding around and showing up unexpectedly."

Mike held out his free hand, palm-up. "I live here. For now, at least." He looked at Rita, his face breaking into a smile. "Good morning, Miss Rita. I thought I heard your voice out there. How ya doing?"

"Good, Pastor. I'm sorry to intrude, but I was wondering if you have a minute to talk?"

"Of course. You can see my wife does not allow me too many breaks anyway. So, let's go into my study. Would you like coffee?"

"Oh no. I've had all I can handle this morning." Rita turned to Lois. "I don't mean to exclude you from our conversation—"

Lois smiled. "Think nothing of it. This is a common occurrence, and that is what he gets paid for. Just let me know if you get your money's worth."

Mike rolled his eyes, and Lois laughed as she took Rita's elbow and guided her to Mike's study.

Mike motioned to a worn, padded chair occupying a space near his desk. "Please."

As Lois backed out of the office, Rita decided Lois made an excellent pastor's wife—efficient, unobtrusive, and focused on the visitor's comfort.

Rita swung her attention to Mike, who ignored his desk chair and pulled a straight-back chair from the corner to the edge of the desk, where he placed his cup.

The office smelled of old books—and no wonder. Rita's eyes swept the wall that held the tools of his trade from floor to ceiling. Bibles, commentaries, counseling guides, Greek guides, and curiously—fiction books that were not limited to the Christian genre. The shelves also held Hemingway, Steinbeck, and several detective novels.

Mike saw her eyes scan his collection and linger on his fiction section. "I find reading fiction expands my insight into behaviors and perspectives. Fiction writers are experts in stripping away the mystery of humans." He chuckled and sipped his coffee.

Rita nodded. "Makes sense."

"But you're not here to discuss my literary collection." Mike tilted his head. It was not a question.

Rita drew a deep breath. "I'll get right to the point. You know I have been dating Deke since we met at the sheriff's home. Nothing serious, but we have a good time, and I find him interesting."

"For sure. Deke is a good man. Sharp and dedicated to his job. And you have been able to get him to church a few times. That's more than I could do."

Rita stared at the ticking mantel clock that served as a bookend on the shelf. A few seconds passed. He was waiting for her to talk.

Mike took another sip, set the cup down on his desk, crossed his legs, and folded his hands in his lap.

Rita fired her thoughts like a cannon. "Look, deep down inside, Deke is an angry man. You wouldn't know it, but I have gotten to know him, and I know that he has that anger bubbling deep inside. And ... and I want to help him."

Mike showed no emotion at Rita's outburst. His slow nod seemed less like agreement and more like affirming he had heard her.

Why had she come here?

Mike drew a breath and calmly said, "It was difficult for you to share this with me, I can tell. I believe you are sincerely concerned."

"I am." She fought it, but her eyes welled up, and one rebel tear ran down her face trying to distance itself from its origin.

Oh God, he must think me pathetic.

The pastor, as if on cue, leaned toward his desk and handed her a Kleenex box. She gladly took a couple of tissues and dabbed at her eyes and cheek.

"I may have damaged my reputation as an unflappable attorney." She sniffed.

Mike smiled. "Your reputation is safe with me—as is Deke's."

Rita lowered the tissues to her lap. "I think I am falling in love with him."

"There are worse things you could do."

Rita appreciated this pastor's permission to vent. "I didn't mean to lose control. But I had to talk to someone, and I couldn't think of anyone in this county who could keep their mouth shut."

"Thank you. I think. I have interned for thirty years in my marriage, so I have it down quite well."

Rita could not help it. She burst out laughing. "You have an odd approach to counseling, just letting the person ramble, but it's effective."

"Well, my style wasn't in the books at the seminary, and I failed my practicum, but I know of no other way." His face turned serious. "You say he is angry. At what, or who?"

"It is a 'who' I'm worried about. Bryce Lamb. He told me that Lamb bullied him in high school. Now that he's back here, he still holds a grudge. But it's different this time. Lamb is still a bully, but Deke is no longer bully bait. Lamb still pushes his buttons, and he controls it, but I am afraid he will settle the score one of these days. And I think the results could be disastrous." Rita leaned forward, and her voice trembled. "Deke is a good man. Inside he's a peaceful man. He cares for people. But he carries so much baggage."

"But ...?" Mike raised an eyebrow.

"Pastor, tonight they'll be facing off at the Leathers and Ladders game. If Lamb provokes him, I'm afraid Deke will rise to the bait."

Mike nodded. "Sometimes a man is repeatedly tested. It may be the Lord is trying to get his attention. Remember, Joseph was sold into slavery by his brothers. When he rose in the ranks under the Egyptian Pharoah and had the power to get revenge on his brothers, he didn't."

"That doesn't sound like a textbook analogy." Rita frowned.

"I told you—I flunked my practicum." Mike held up his hands in mock surrender. "Seriously, I think the Lord is working with Deke. Give him time. As far as Deke doing something tragic, I don't think you have to worry. Maybe he has a hot temper, but he didn't spend all those years being a Marine and a cop and not learn coping defenses. Else they would have drummed him out of the force a long time ago."

"You're probably right. I know he is a man of many talents."

"Lois and I will be there for the game. The police have lost the game the past five years, but they didn't have the high school champs like Sheriff Tim, Delaney—and of course your Deke."

Rita smiled sheepishly and blushed.

Mike chuckled. "Look, Deke and Lamb are adults. Not teens. Things change."

"You didn't see Lamb trying to incite Deke at the firehouse the other day. He hasn't buried the hatchet. I don't think Deke will start it, but he will certainly not take anything."

"Have you talked to him about your fear?"

"Well, no. But men are thick sometimes and take de-escalation efforts as a challenge to their masculinity. No disrespect intended."

"None taken." Mike leaned forward in his chair and spoke softly. "Talk to him. Don't give him your attorney ultimatums, but sincere concerns. Unless you're afraid you'll reveal your true feelings."

"I want to remind you, as I have client-attorney privilege, you have counselee-clergy privilege." Rita squinted at him.

"I remember, I remember. I will take your secret to my grave. And we'll be praying for cool heads to prevail tonight."

Rita shook her head and chuckled. "Thank you, Brother Mike."

"You are very welcome, and anytime you need to talk—I am here." Mike stood and extended his hand. Rita rose and grasped it.

Rita nodded. "That means a lot. And do not tell anyone about my tears. Everyone thinks I've never cried—even as a baby. I was never here, and I never cried."

"Your secret is safe. But consider leveling with Deke about your concerns."

Deke allowed himself a trip down memory lane as he drove to Rita's house to pick her up for the game. It would be good to play with Tim and Delaney in a competitive game again. Their practices had gone well, and the city cops and deputies were a real addition to the team. Those guys were younger, mid-twenties, and were closer to their high school playing days than his crew. However, Tim, Delaney, and he had contributed some strategic magic to their practices.

He knew all the other players in their professional roles before they connected on the court. All were good cops, and he had cemented working relationships with them long before this game.

Deke glided into a parking place in front of Rita's small brick rental house. He resisted the urge to announce his presence by tapping his accelerator and allowing the pipes to sing their throaty solo.

He grabbed his gym bag and stepped from the vehicle, catching a glance of himself in the side-view mirror.

Looking good. Like in my school days. Well, not quite.

He bounded up the steps, noting the well-tended flowerbed in front.

When does she find time to do all that?

When he heard footsteps from inside, Deke grinned, leaned closer to the door, and knocked rapidly.

"All right, all right. I've got neighbors, you know." She giggled and leaned out the doorway looking left and right.

"That's all right. I know a good attorney."

"Even she can't help you."

"Who said it was a she?" Deke laughed.

"You are entertaining. I can say that. Let me grab a sweater."

They filled the drive to the high school with small talk. The parking lot was already half-full. Folks looked forward to the annual competition between firefighters and police.

"Wow, I did not expect this," Deke said.

Rita scanned the parked cars and smiled. "It has a good turnout every year. Lots of money is raised for children. Tonight's game is for cancer research."

Deke found a parking place and shut off the engine. Rita sat staring out the side window.

"You ready to go in? How about a kiss for good luck?"

Rita turned her head but did not look at Deke. She stared straight forward.

"Whassa matter?"

After a few seconds, Rita replied, "Deke, there is something. I don't know how to say it or if it is any of my business at all."

"Go on."

She turned to look at Deke. "I know you have issues with Lamb. And I have seen the hostility from your two past interactions. I mean, could you promise me you will not allow this hostility to escalate during the game? It will be easy for things to get out of hand in this physical competition."

Deke studied her face before he answered. Truth be told, even he didn't know what he might do tonight, given the right incentive. "I am looking forward to a friendly competition. I don't give a flip about what Lamb feels. I believe our team can regain the title. I do look forward to humiliating him with superior athleticism—but not my firefighter friends."

"Okay, I just want to know you are in control."

"Babe, my middle name is control." Deke chided.

Rita smiled slightly, "Oh, what's the use. Go on and get inside with your team. I will find a seat."

Deke leaned toward her.

She was already opening the door. "Not, now. There are people."

Deke affected a confused look. "Oh, that's what they are. I thought they were beings from another planet. I can always count on your perceptive attorney skills to see through any pretense."

CHAPTER 17

The memories flooded back as Deke entered the gym. Just like the old days. The same shiny hardwood court, the retractable bleachers now in full extension with fans already stair-stepping to find their favored seating. There were even the same indistinguishable crowd murmurs and the smell of popcorn. His heart beat a little faster. Someone called his name, and he looked toward the stands. Café owner Hank and a couple of familiar patrons were grinning at him and giving a thumbs up. He returned the smiles and waved.

As he headed to the locker room, he bumped into a woman carrying a soda and bag of popcorn. "Oh, sorry." He automatically reached out to steady her. Then, he recognized her.

Willa coyly allowed his hands to steady her. "We have to stop meeting like this."

"Sorry. Pregame jitters," he said, ignoring Willa's flirting.

She leaned closer. "I don't believe that for a moment. You were never nervous, even as a boy. You've got enough confidence for five men."

Where was this conversation going?

Deke released his light grip as she brushed his bicep with the back of her polished pink nails—still clutching the bag of popcorn.

"It's all right, silly, and you should know I can withstand roughness. I am married to Bull."

Deke glanced at the gathering crowd and spotted Rita intently watching him. She sat with Pastor Mike and Lois along with the sheriff's wife. The hooting and shouts from Deke's fans had alerted them to his arrival. But, judging by their expressions, they had also witnessed the encounter with Willa. Bad timing.

"I gotta get ready. I won't ask you to wish me luck. I know that is reserved for Bull." He chuckled.

"I can root for both sides. I got friends on both teams."

Deke stepped again toward the locker room, choosing his parting words carefully. "You have a good time."

Deputy Delaney stood by the entrance to the locker room and let out a shrill whistle. "Deke, come on! You're holding up the team meeting."

Thanks, Delaney. As if he hadn't attracted enough attention.

Deke waved and jogged across the end of the court under the basket, where he risked a glance at Rita. Expressionless, she followed his progress with her eyes.

What was she thinking?

You dummy. You know what she's thinking.

He looked around to see who else might have observed the encounter with Willa. It was then he saw Lamb standing statue-still by the water fountain glaring at him. No escape—he had to pass by his archenemy. Deke slowed and met Lamb's scowl with a carefree smile.

"Good luck. See you on the hardwoods."

Lamb said nothing. Deke stole a glance backward as he entered the boy's locker room. Only then did Lamb head toward the girl's locker room, which had been reserved for his team.

The rest of the team members greeted Deke in the locker room, which reeked of stale sweat and camphor.

"Well, well. Better late than never." Tim scolded.

"Man, enough. I am striking out with friend and foe alike."

Tim shook his head. "Don't know what that means, but we got to huddle up for the game."

The team had unanimously chosen Tim as the captain. Deke could tell he was pleased but tried to play it down.

"Where's Rex?" Deke asked. "We need our coach."

Tim shook his head as the rest of the team murmured and shrugged. "We don't know. So, we need to proceed without him.

"Okay, this is what we prepared for. I think we got a chance. It is the first time we—Deke, Delaney, and me—are getting to play with you young bucks in this game." Tim nodded toward Roger, the Marion cop, Gillian, the twenty-five-year-old constable, and three other deputies. "We've learned you youngsters play a fine game, and we senior citizens will be passing the baton in the near future." The team chuckled.

His face turned serious. "Even though you have maybe more experience than you guys, we recognize our limitations. We are not as agile as we once were, we get winded easier, and we are poster boys for injury. Not saying we are delicate, but we are injury prone. Comes with age. So, we only got three subs that we can put in for exhaustion and injuries. Keep that in mind."

Delaney looked around the group and pointed a warning finger. "First guy who wimps out and asks for a sub buys the beer for the team."

Good ol' Delaney, ever the stress reliever. Even in high school, his deadpan humor had dulled their nervousness.

Tim wrapped up his counsel as coach and captain. The men placed their hands over each other's hands in a circle and shouted in unison. "Let's go, Leathers!"

Deke shed the jogging suit that covered his shorts and jersey. As the team made their way to the gymnasium, they were met by their tardy coach, Rex. Although Rex had mediocre athletic skills, he was a fantastic equipment manager and shrewd strategist.

"Sorry, guys, I had a flat," Rex panted like a freight train.

"No sweat. We're all ready to play, and you can take your place on the bench with us," Tim said.

Multiple balls thumped on the court. The Ladders were warming up. Deke broke into a trot. "Let's go, team." He patted Rex on the shoulder.

When the Leathers entered the gym, almost three-quarters of the crowd came to their feet cheering. *Amazing! The crowd has grown. Standing room only.*

They began their half-court warmups. Players from both teams took covert glances at the others to size up their opponents.

Deke felt good as they formed for layups. He even surprised himself at the altitude he was able to get for a right-handed dunk. His one-handed shots from the baseline were laser swishers. *Now, if I could only do this in the game.*

The rude bellow of a horn marked the end of warmups, and both teams entered their respective huddles on each side of the officials' table.

Rex was all business. "Sheriff, confer with the refs, and both you and Campbell play forwards. Rogers and Dusty at guard, and Delaney center."

Dusty, the shortest man at five-eight—but fast and a superb ball-handler—wailed, "But I wanna play center."

"Oh, hush up," the towering Delaney said, adding a playful shove.

Rex ignored the bantering. "We will start man-to-man defense and go to zone when you start getting tired. Don't kill yourselves. If you need a break, we got three good men to spell you."

Tim trotted out to meet the captain of the Ladders. Deke watched as the referees waited on Lamb to jog to center court. "Surprise, surprise. Bull is not only the fire captain—he is the team captain."

Rogers snickered. "Betcha he claimed that title, and no one argued."

"That be true, I'm sure."

Tim returned to his team, the horn burped the start of the first quarter, and the teams took their positions for the tip-off. Deke crouched, confident that Delaney would control the tip-off against the Ladders' shorter center. He saw Lamb move toward him, anticipating the tip-off would go to him.

The fire captain smirked and said in a gravelly voice, "Campbell, prepare to get humiliated."

The ball floated up from the referee's hand, and Delaney timed his jump. His reach was not even threatened. Instead, the ball was swatted cleanly into Deke's hands, and he dribbled toward his goal, evading both the guard and Lamb's efforts to double-team him.

Dusty's short legs could move at surprising speed. Deke saw him out in the open as he raced toward the basket and shot him a pass with just the right lead and height. Dusty could jump, too, and he was already airborne when the pass reached his extended hands—the layup patted the backboard and sank into the net. The crowd roared.

First points on the scoreboard. Must be an omen.

Deke slowed to a jog as he circled to get back on defense. "Way to go, young'un!"

Dusty grinned. "Nice feed."

Suddenly Deke felt his foot being swept from behind. He stumbled but quickly recovered his balance.

Lamb shrugged as he matched pace with Deke. "Sorry."

Deke flicked him a tight-lipped smile. "Still as graceful as always, I see."

Lamb's jaws tightened. Few of the spectators caught the exchange, and even if they did, the words were inaudible. Then, as Deke set up a defense on Lamb, the firehouse guards brought the ball down the court, signaling with two fingers to set up a play.

The guards exchanged passes and sought an opening to their center, but Delaney denied the pass by batting it away. Lamb raced to rescue the ball with Deke glued to him. Lamb spun and dribbled to the side. Deke knew his plan. He'd played against that strategy of his in high school. Deke outpaced Lamb and planted one foot firmly outside the court baseline marker. Lamb would have to go out of bounds to get past him or go around him on the court. Deke was ready for him.

Bull is a ball hog. He won't pass. I'll get a chance to steal.

Lamb lowered a thick shoulder like a football player and jammed it into Deke's solar plexus and lower ribs, knocking the wind out of him. A shrill whistle stopped the action as a ref called the obvious charging foul on Lamb. Scattered boos rose among the crowd.

Deke straightened, hiding the pain of the blow. He forced his face to remain expressionless. "Tickles."

The older ref, vice president of the Farmers Bank, approached to take the ball from the fouler. But instead, he glanced at Deke's face. "You good, Deke?"

"Yeah. You need to be more concerned about fat boy's shoulder."

Lamb gritted his teeth and drew closer to Deke, but the ref had stepped between them. He took the ball from Lamb's hands and walked to the foul line. Deke walked to the foul line, giving no evidence of his pain.

Deke positioned himself at the free-throw line as the ref announced the call.

"Charging! Number thirty-eight, red." The ref handed the ball to Deke and backed out of the key outlined under the basket.

The sheriff crossed the court and took a spot to ready himself for a rebound. As he passed by his teammate, he swatted Deke's backside. "Let's go. This is just beginning."

Deke's two foul shots swished into the net, and the spectators applauded. Deke and his team raced down the court to set up the defense. The Ladders' guard quickly took the ball out of bounds and passed to his fellow guard. The team's demeanor had become intense.

Deke glanced toward the bleachers and saw Rita was sitting rigidly.

Bull is just getting warmed up. Keep your cool, Deke. The night is young.

CHAPTER 18

At the blast from the horn, signifying halftime, Deke glanced at the scoreboard after his successful rebound and tip-in.

They were tied up—forty to forty. These firemen had proven to be great competitors.

Deke trotted to the bench, retrieved his towel, and wiped the sweat from his face, grateful for his daily cardio workouts. He glanced at Rita, who smiled and gave a discreet wave.

He turned to see the other team on their way to the locker room for halftime pep talks. They seemed to be in good spirits and exuded confidence.

A lone Ladders member remained seated on the bench, elbows on his knees, clutching a towel. Lamb was red-faced and breathing hard. His once muscular body bulged out above his shorts. He glared hard at Deke as he sucked in air.

Deke had to fight to keep from smirking.

He may have outscored, out-maneuvered, out-rebounded, and stolen the ball from Lamb several times, but Deke couldn't get overconfident. Bull was tired, but he would come out of halftime with a vengeance. He was still formidable.

"Locker room. Let's go. Time for my amazing coaching," said Rex.

He paused to swat Deke and Delaney on the backside. "Playing good ball, guys."

"Hey, I wanna get spanked too," Dusty whined.

"Oh, shut up," The whole team laughed as they made their way to the locker room.

Great camaraderie. Deke smiled, hooking his towel around his neck. Still smiling, he looked toward the opponent's bench where Lamb remained seated, his eyes following Deke's departure.

He couldn't resist. Deke snapped out a salute to Lamb. The captain gritted his teeth and stood, towel clenched in his two hands.

Some in the crowd were descending the bleachers to visit the refreshment stands in the hallway. He saw Willa moving with the group, but she had stopped, looking toward her husband, then toward Deke. Deke recognized that terse grimace and twist of her head. It was something she did in high school when she was nervous about what Bull was about to do or say. Old habits die hard.

In the locker room, Rex called for quiet among his exuberant team. "All right, all right! You haven't won yet. So, take a seat and give me your ears."

Dusty grabbed both ears and contorted his face as he demonstrated the effort to detach them from his head. His antics elicited hooting and chuckles.

Deke held up his hands. "Guys, settle down and listen to Rex. That's what we hired him for."

Rex frowned at Deke. "Thanks, 'D.' I think. By the way, I want a raise. Okay, I see you guys are holding up pretty well. So, let's stick to the man-to-man defense. By fourth quarter, you will probably need to switch to zone."

The team turned off their comic acts and became serious. Deke sighed, relieved. This was the one game he wanted—needed—to win.

Rex reaffirmed their playing and described a couple of plays they might try. Deke looked around at his teammates. It seemed like they were back in high school. Those were exciting and simpler days. They were teens again.

As Rex's talk ended, the players stacked hands. "Let's go!"

A refreshed team trotted out the door and down the hallway to the court. Deke paused to take a long draft of water from the water fountain.

Rex stopped by the fountain as the rest of the team left the hallway.

"Don't drink too much. It'll give you side stitches."

Deke raised his head from the fountain wiping his mouth with the back of his hand. "Old wives' tale from our school years, Rex. No medical evidence."

Deke grinned. The banker looked down the hall to ensure the team had disappeared.

"What's a matter, Rex?"

Rex stared intently into Deke's eyes. Seconds elapsed before he spoke. "Deke, you have to be careful. I am not worried about the Ladders' team. They are good guys, and they will enjoy the game, win or lose." Rex broke off his stare. He sighed. "You know Bull's temper from high school. It hasn't dissipated. If anything, it has grown more violent. I have seen him jerk one of my tellers across the counter because he thought the guy was disrespecting him. It scared the bejeebers out of the young man. Of course, he wasn't insulting him, but it didn't matter. I had to move him to another branch."

"What are you telling me?" Deke asked.

"Be careful. I see you are trying to get on Bull's nerves, and it won't take much. He will get you. Maybe not physically. You are a match for him now. But politically, socially, job-wise—he will get you."

Deke took in the coach's sincere demeanor. "Rex, thank you for your advice. I know you know him and his capabilities to throw down—be it hand-to-hand or using other agents." Deke laid his hand on Rex's shoulder. "However, I took his abuse all through high school, and I won't, I repeat, I won't, allow him to do it to me again."

Rex shrugged. "It's your ball game."

Deke leaned forward and smiled. "So, let's play ball."

Rita held her breath as the second half began, with both teams exuding a fervor not seen in previous years. Rita had attended the last year's competition, and it was not like this one. She recalled the good-natured bantering between the uniformed departments. The police had been defeated in a close game, and both teams left as comrades. But this year was different. Spectators and players alike seemed on edge about the duel between Deke and Lamb.

Lamb attempted a jump shot at the foul line. Rita was surprised by the altitude he attained, despite carrying so much weight. The captain's determined eyes were focused on the basket. Then a figure raced across the court and leaped upward. Deke nimbly jumped in front of Lamb and batted the ball a split second after it had left Lamb's hands. Only the guard, Roger, had anticipated Deke's move and was racing with expectant hands ready to receive the struck ball.

On its first bounce, Roger received the batted ball and dribbled down the court while one of the Ladders guards raced to cut him off. Deke did not hesitate after the steal and shot toward their basket to intercede in case the pressure of the defensive guard forced Roger to pass.

Rita almost couldn't watch as the defensive guard cut Roger off, but he seemed to have anticipated that interruption and shot a high pass toward Deke. It was high enough that Deke became airborne to catch the ball a foot away from the rim and stuff it into the waiting net. The rim and backboard shook from the assault.

Rita jumped to her feet along with the fervent crowd as they exploded over the well-executed steal and bucket. She was dimly aware of Pastor Mike's enthusiastic leap and yell. "Attaway, Deke, you got the moves!"

She gave a surprised look at her pastor, but with a small smile in accompaniment.

Mike reddened. "Well, even preachers sometimes succumb to worldly events."

Rita chuckled at his shrug and grin. When she turned her attention back to the court, the Ladders guard was racing to their basket, apparently conscious of the winking scoreboard clock ticking off the time.

She watched Deke retrieve the ball after scoring as the crowd continued their raucous applause. He seemed oblivious to the fans and the ref behind him but walked toward Lamb, whose scowl and clenched teeth spoke volumes. Deke kept walking, spinning the recovered ball on his index finger, then let it drop to the floor in front of Lamb as he passed him with a tight smile.

To everyone's surprise, Lamb turned and smashed the ball into Deke's retreating back with such force he lurched forward in pain. "Umph!" Deke gritted his teeth as he spun to face his assailant.

Rita's hands flew to her mouth—but she was not praying. Her heart pounded. "Oh, no!"

She heard Mike whisper, "Lord, Lord. Don't do it, Deke."

About three-quarters of the crowd vocalized their anger at the cheap shot. The remaining people stared, open-mouthed.

Deke's coach leaped to his feet, thrusting his hands skyward and shouting something, but his words were drowned out. The referees' shrill whistles were the only sound that penetrated the crowd's continued roar.

As the referees raced to intercede in the coming battle, Tim also ran toward his friend. He knew better than to grab Deke's arms, but he jumped between the two potential combatants with his back toward his deputy.

Rita watched the verbal exchange between the two men on the court, but their demeanors were quite the opposite. White-hot rage accompanied Lamb's menacing body language. She could barely make out what Lamb was saying because of the crowd's shouts. She did hear the words 'high school' and 'punk' shouted at Deke. Deke's demeanor, however, was peaceful. He seemed calm and controlled, not in the least disturbed by Lamb's apparent antagonistic behavior.

The refs were talking rapidly to Lamb. They guided him to the team bench. His teammates seemed bewildered. There was no clearing of the benches to show support.

Lamb walked toward his bench accompanied by scattered boos—which he answered with a quick display of his middle finger, missed by most fans. A young man standing near the players, mouth agape, offered him a towel. Lamb jerked the towel out of his hands, yanking the kid forward.

SUMMER OF THE WAXMAN

The head referee gave some final words to Lamb, but Lamb seemed to ignore what he said. Lamb wiped the sweat from his face and glared at Deke, who moved toward the Leathers' bench and accepted a bottle of water from Rex.

The referee said something to the other ref, who responded with a nod. Then, he turned to face the crowd and the officials' bench and took a deep breath.

He lifted his head and, in a booming voice, shouted, "Intentional foul on number thirty-eight, red! Two shots!"

Rita watched Deke, who was now sipping his water on the sidelines and seemed to be sizing up Lamb's state. Across the court on the bench, Lamb looked sullen, elbows on his knees. One of his teammates seemed agitated and was standing over him saying something. Rita could not make out what he said, but she had no trouble lip-reading Lamb's response—"Shut up."

The referee held the game ball in one hand and nodded to Deke to approach the foul line. Deke handed the water bottle off to a teammate and walked to the offered ball to the background of applause. He bounced the ball three times. The crowd grew silent. His two shots sank in the hoop only rippling the net. Rita's eyes shifted from Lamb to the crowd behind Lamb's crew. She spotted Willa, sitting rigidly with a half-smile on her face. Her eyes were not on her husband, as Rita anticipated, but on Deke. She moistened her lips, but it didn't seem out of nervousness at the antics of her husband. What was this all about?

CHAPTER 19

The Leathers were leading in the closing minutes to a hard-fought game. Rita found herself wishing the game over, no matter who won.

Beside her, Mike tilted his head, and with a tight smile said, "It's getting a little tense."

Rita nodded, noting although Lois, seated beside Mike, was intent on the game, her hands were tightly clasped in her lap.

Deke seemed to be in his element, playing team ball, but also taking his shots when the opportunity prevailed. He scored a high percentage of his attempts.

Then it happened.

Lamb took a throw-in from the sideline and dribbled to half court. Deke saw he was focused on his teammate's drive to the basket and trying to time his pass. Deke drove in and made a slap at the ball. A surprised Lamb looked down in disbelief—Deke had made a clean steal and was racing toward the basket unchallenged.

Rita watched as Lamb recovered and pursued the stolen ball. He hurtled toward the basket, his speed belying his girth. The crowd roared as Deke went airborne and dunked the ball through the net. Lamb never slowed as he drove into Deke's still-airborne legs. The force flipped Deke over his shoulders in a complete turn. Deke lessened the impact on the hardwood with his arms. His palms slapped the floor. "Oof!"

Rita gasped. "Oh, Lord!"

Now everyone was on their feet. Both teams raced toward the two men, whether anticipating a fight or out of concern, Rita couldn't tell.

Lamb swung around as Deke leaped to his feet. The furious fire captain swung his right fist in a hook.

Deke deflected his strike with a twisting motion of his arm, connecting with Lamb's thick forearm. Deke seized the back of Lamb's fist, twisting his arm and simultaneously slamming an open palm to his elbow. Deke stepped backward, keeping pressure on the arm lock, and swept Lamb in a circular motion. Lamb had no choice but to follow the controlled swing.

A stunned photographer from the press who had situated himself under the basket to snap some close-ups as he captured some dramatic aerials found himself scrambling to get out of the way when Lamb's body came hurtling in his direction. Deke released his grip on Lamb, allowing him to sprawl onto the floor as his nose collided with the heel of the retreating journalist's boot.

Rita could not follow all Deke's maneuvers, but she knew the actions of a trained martial artist—one who had used his skills in real-life situations. It was over in seconds. Deke's expression was devoid of emotion.

A few firemen went to Lamb's aid as the ref's whistles shrieked. The photographer had regained his feet, but he seemed at a loss what to do next. Rita caught Deke's attention as he looked toward the bleachers. His mouth formed the word 'sorry' as he gave her a helpless shrug.

The remaining firemen showed no malice toward Deke. One even patted his shoulder in passing and gave him a slight grin.

The top ref called a time-out, and all the players and coaches took their respective benches. Spectators sat down slowly, but some remained standing. A murmur swept through the crowd. Deke sat on the bench beside Tim as he talked to him, punctuating his conversation with light pats on his leg. Deke's eyes were on her.

The chief referee walked over to the officials' table, spoke to them, and returned to center court. The crowd became quiet, awaiting his announcement.

"Technical on both teams!"

He then called out numbers on both Lamb and Deke. "Out of the game. No shots for either team."

That caused an uproar among the spectators. One middle-aged man shouted, "What kind of call is that? You can't blame a man for protecting himself!"

A couple of voices from the spectators started a chant, with others joining in. "Only one, only one! Bull goes, Bull goes."

Deke turned his head toward the opponents' bench. Lamb was nursing a bloody nose but glaring at Deke. The coach was patting the injured player's shoulder and nodding.

The clock registered three minutes left in the game. Before it resumed, Rita saw Deke rise and make his way to the locker room. There was scattered applause, and someone yelled, "Yaaa, Deke. Good game!"

Rita searched for Willa in the crowd, wondering how she was processing the event. When she found her, Rita could only stare. The woman was smiling at the back of her husband.

What kind of reaction is that?

In the men's locker room, Deke let the steamy shower pummel his body as he leaned on his hands against the tiles. The hot needles felt good. He opened his eyes and tucked his head into his chest to examine some painful souvenirs of the game. Three angry bruises decorated his rib cage and chest. He thought he could see them changing color from blue to deep purple as he watched. He had a memory of the two on his lower ribs as he recalled Lamb's slashing elbow. Then he lifted his arm to examine a painful bruise on his left forearm.

Hmm. My gymnastic backflip.

He turned off the showerhead, grabbed his towel from a hook, and gingerly made his way back to the lockers. Deke paused before a mirror and touched a minor laceration above his left eye.

I don't know how I got this.

Deke dressed and went down the hall. He peered into the gym, trying not to be seen. Then he realized he didn't need to worry as the crowd was fixated on the game before them.

Mike and Lois remained in their seats. But he could not find Rita. As the final buzzer sounded, he looked at the scoreboard. The glowing lights pronounced that the Leathers had defeated the Ladders ninety-two to sixty-eight.

Deke gave a terse smile. Finally. The cops had regained their trophy.

The crowd was up and moving. Deke thought maybe Rita would be waiting at his truck and turned to move to a hallway fire exit. He did not want to meet anyone and discuss the game.

As he walked to his truck, his eyes roved over the parking lot. There. She looked so small, leaning against his massive truck.

Deke smiled. "There ya are."

She did not return the smile. "You just had to do it."

"Do what?"

"Start a war with Lamb."

Even with the parking lot's subdued lighting, he could read the anger and disgust on her face. His smile switched off.

"Look, you saw the game. I wasn't the one who declared war. I tried to avoid it."

"Making faces and smirking is not what I call de-escalation."

"Rita, I did not throw any punches or elbows to injure any player, let alone Bull. But I cannot allow him to injure me without protecting myself. Part of protection is intimidating bullies. You need to communicate you don't fear them and you are able and willing to defend yourself."

They stared at each other in silence. Deke thought he had struck a chord with his response. Then she drew up to face him.

"You came to this game intent on getting revenge. You knew you could provoke him. You brought your Chicago cop tactics to the basketball court."

"Wait a minute! That's cheap. You're the one doing the bleeding-heart defense attorney tactics." Deke changed his voice into a whiney, high-pitched declaration. "I don't care if he is guilty or that you stopped his evil attentions. He's just a lonely victim of society."

As soon as he said it, regret settled over him like a lead blanket.

Rita turned and started across the parking lot. "I'm through here. G'night!"

"For gosh sakes, Rita. Let me take you home."

He watched her stride toward Mike and Lois, who had apparently been waiting by their car a short distance away. As she approached, Mike opened the door to the back seat. Rita never slowed her pace and jumped in without a backward glance.

Mike gave Deke a shrug and raised his hands in mock surrender. Deke returned the sign of submission and walked around his vehicle, opened the squeaky door, and cast his gym bag to the passenger side.

The fans were now filling the parking lot. He'd have to move quickly to avoid conversation. Deke climbed behind the wheel and brought the engine to life, then paused to watch the disappearing taillights of Mike's car. He took a deep breath and let his head drop.

So, that's it. End of story.

CHAPTER 20

"Well, at least my horses want to see me." As Deke rumbled his way toward the corral in his truck, he could see his horses trotting toward the barn, their heads and tails raised in greeting.

He pulled out his cell phone to see if he'd had any calls since he had left the courthouse. None recorded. He tilted the screen up and waved it slowly around.

Rats. No bars. If Rita tried to call, she might think he didn't want to answer.

Well, serves her right.

He switched the phone off, jammed it back into his denim shirt pocket, and closed the button. He brought the truck to a halt by the barn as the horses jostled each other in their excitement. His hand slid across his chest to his other pocket. Empty. He found what he wanted in the ashtray: Cecil's snake oil. Only a few drops remained in the bottle, but one squirt was enough.

Good thing Cecil didn't prescribe a shot glass full of that panther pee.

Deke stepped from the truck and spat on the ground to purge the bitter taste of the elixir. Then, he strode to his horses and rubbed their noses. "You miss me, guys?"

They vied for attention, pushing their heads against each other and snorting.

"Okay, okay. Let me get you fed."

Deke entered the barn, retrieved some feed from one stall, and poured the grain into the two troughs attached to the horses' stall walls.

Tending the horses and listening to their gentle whinnies reminded him of the times growing up when things didn't seem like they would ever come together. Like after altercations with Bull and his minions.

Once upon a time, he wished he were a cowboy and spent all his free time caring for them. Sometimes, on his worst days, he'd race to the barn as soon as he got home from school. As he ran, it seemed each stride would strip off a little hurt, anger, fear, and humiliation. When he arrived at the barn, the combination of pungent odor of horse and the sweet smell of hay calmed him almost immediately. As he fed and brushed his friends, he'd find himself envying their simple lifestyle. Get fed, run around, and occasionally allow a human to think they are in control as you trot around with them on your back.

Funny. Now that he was back, he still felt that way sometimes.

Deke shook his head to end his reverie and re-entered the barn. Despite ducking, he still managed to jar his worn Stetson on the low opening. A lasso hung on a peg in the open tack stall as though it was waiting for him. He retrieved the rope and walked past Zorro and Mandy, busily devouring feed from their troughs.

"You two should have been pigs instead of horses."

Mandy paused briefly and tilted her head at Deke. Zorro continued unabated. "Oh, Mandy, I guess you are a lady, but your friend there is no gentleman."

Chuckling as he entered the corral, Deke walked to an old barrel topped with a home-made wooden cow head. The barrel had four cedar posts on two bowed planks. Deke had created the imitation cow in high school to practice his roping skills.

"Well, Clarabelle. Ready for another round?"

The black painted eyes and nostrils were sorely in need of a touch-up.

Deke dragged the wooden calf to the center of the corral and stepped off twenty paces from it. Both horses had stopped their feeding and watched.

"No, no. Y'all go ahead and eat. I am not looking for a partner to ride this time. I'm a little rusty, and I'll practice my ground game."

Zorro did not need much encouragement and bowed his head. Mandy kept her eyes on Deke as she nibbled.

Deke loosened the rope and twirled it. He gracefully cast the loop toward his wooden target. It settled over the head on the barrel but hung up on one wooden ear. He frowned and flipped the lasso off on the ground.

He drew the rope back to him, recoiling it for another try. His frown gave way to a mischievous grin. "Your touch with roping is the same as your touch with women—both need practice."

The second attempt was a clean throw. It settled down around the neck, and Deke tightened the loop.

"That's better." Deke strode to the wooden calf and freed his lasso. As he walked back, he mused over the many hours he'd spent engaged in this exercise as a kid, and the peace he'd always found there.

His thoughts were interrupted by a tinkling sound. He swung around looking for the source, his hand automatically going to the Berretta .380 he carried in the waistband of his jeans.

He recognized the Panama hat first, then Cecil's dark eyes peering over the top rail of the fence. The tinkling sound came from a jar Cecil dangled in his boney fingers as he tapped it with a rock hammer.

Cecil grinned, revealing two rows of small straight teeth. "Sorry, I didn't wear a bell. I thought this was the next best thing." He nodded to Deke's hand posed over his waistband and chuckled. "I hope you won't shoot a man for making noises." He chuckled.

Deke strode over to the fence and noticed Plato coming around the other side of the barn. When the dog spotted Deke, he bounded toward him, tail wagging.

"No, I don't shoot people for minor noises." He smiled at the old man.

Deke squatted to pet the dog through the fence. "Hey, Plato. I know I haven't seen you in a week. I'm sorry I got nothing for you."

Then he squinted upward. "How you been, Cecil?"

"Fine as frog's hair."

Deke stood up, grimacing and touching his ribs.

"Get that during the game?"

"How do you know about the game? I didn't see you in the bleachers. And you sure weren't one of the cheerleaders."

"Naw. I never could do the splits. I don't have to be there. I can boil a caldron, toss in some snake skins and buzzard eggs, a little sulfur, and my special blends, then the entire game comes to life in that pot."

Deke tilted his head.

Cecil perched his head on his arms on the top rail and shrugged. "When that doesn't work. I pull my old radio out and tune in to the local station."

"Ah. I forgot the game was on the Marion station."

"That and I got an instant replay from Pastor Mike when I went to see your aunt."

"I see. I thought a man of the cloth was supposed to be sworn to secrecy."

"Obviously, when the whole town witnessed the game, there is no secrecy to be had."

"You got me there." Neither man spoke for some time.

Finally, Deke lifted his eyes from the lasso he was fidgeting with and spoke. "I suppose he told you about Rita's reaction?"

"Well, he indicated she was none too happy about you and Mr. Lamb exchanging love pats."

"He patted me first." Ouch, that sounded juvenile.

Cecil pursed his tiny lips. "And you always pay your debts, right?"

"Come on! You sound like Rita."

"I thought you liked the way she sounded."

Deke approached the fence and leaned beside Cecil. "Seriously, you don't know what it was like under the hammer fist of Lamb in high school. The humiliation and torture. I swore one day I would not take it anymore."

Cecil responded in a quiet voice. "And you are not taking it anymore. You have arrived. So, you returned the favor by torturing and humiliating him. That feels good, right?"

Deke shrugged. "Well, when you put it like that ..."

"And by the way, mister, you-don't-know." He formed air quotes. "I have a little inkling of what it means to be tortured and humiliated. Look at this face. Do you think I didn't have hard times growing up? At least your bullying stopped. Mine is ongoing."

Deke shook his head. "I am sorry, Cecil. I was unbelievably crass to say that. That's my self-centered personality. Forgive me."

Cecil touched his arm lightly. "No, no. You were just expressing your feelings. I am honored you trust me to do that. Some hurts never go away without you packing them up and sending them away."

"How do you not stay angry with those who abuse you?"

"I would like to say it is simple, but it is not. You have to have help."

Deke knitted his brows. "What kind of help?"

"The kind only God is capable of giving us. And I have found that offering kindness to those who are against you often changes them. So many people who mistreated me in the past are now kind to me because I helped them and did not return their unkindness."

Deke spoke slowly. "Well, how many people who you killed with kindness invite you over for dinner? I mean, if they intend to be kind in return, why don't they openly claim friendship with you?"

Cecil shrugged. "Perhaps they are ashamed of themselves because they're afraid of what others might think or because they are just unhappy souls. In the end, God is who they answer to. I can only deal with my own sins."

With a sigh, Cecil laid a hand on Deke's shoulder. "I know you have had some bad times, my friend. But you need to let them go and focus on the good times. If you don't, you will never find peace. Just like the potion I gave you to let go of smoking. It will have no effect if you don't want to quit. In this case, your Creator holds the potion. You need to want to forgive, then ask him for help."

Deke scuffed the ground with his boot then looked up. "I appreciate your advice—in fact, I need another batch of your nonsmoking potion. As far as the Creator's help, maybe he has given up on me."

"I don't think even you believe that."

"I can't get past the picture of God forgiving people. I mean, how can he forgive real sinners, like murderers, rapists, those who are just evil?"

Cecil studied Deke's face. "Nor can I. That's not our place—to understand God. Our place as men is to believe he can and does forgive because of the extension of grace. And it's a good thing because everyone sins. Sin is sin."

"Even sins that cannot be corrected. I mean, that are a done deal?" Deke persisted.

Cecil nodded. "Yes, because the Lord has a done deal too. It is called his death on the cross. We humans cannot fathom God's mercy."

"Someone is coming," Cecil lifted his head and stepped away from the fence.

"What?" Deke inquired.

"I don't hear anybody." Deke could not help staring at Cecil's deformed ears.

Deke looked around and scanned the horizon toward the road. He removed his hat from his head and placed it behind his ear to capture any sounds. "Don't hear anyone. Don't see anyone."

Deke grinned and turned around to face the fence where Cecil and Plato had been standing. "You think this is odd. I picked this trick up from my father ..."

Cecil and Plato were gone. Not a rustle from the nearby woods. Vanished. Then he heard the sound of a motor. A familiar bright red convertible had turned off the main road and bounced toward him over the rutted field. Deke left the corral and closed the gate behind him. He stood wiping invisible sweat from inside of his hat with a bandana.

What would he say? What would she say?

Rita halted her sports car twenty feet from him and switched off the engine. The ticking hot motor spoiled the distant call of a whippoorwill.

The wind had beautifully disarrayed her hair, which contrasted with her professional attire. She opened the

BRENT I. BRANTLEY

door and slid out. Deke walked toward her, and she closed the distance but halted about six feet from him. He did the same.

Deke spoke. "Glad to see you again. Didn't think you wanted to see me."

"I had to talk to you." Her voice was musical.

"Go ahead."

Rita glanced around and stared at something behind him. Deke looked around and saw Zorro and Mandy's heads over the rail curiously regarding this meeting.

Deke shrugged and grinned. "I have no secrets from them. They're family."

Rita relaxed and smiled, nodding her head. "Well, I guess I'll embarrass myself in front of three creatures instead of one."

"Uh, a man and two creatures, if you please."

"The jury is still out on that." Rita raised a stern eyebrow.

They laughed awkwardly. At least she was laughing.

Rita grew serious. "I'm sorry for unloading on you like I did Saturday."

Deke was silent, and she went on. "I hate fighting. And people being treated unfairly. It's one of the reasons I became a defense attorney."

What should he say? He so wanted this to end. "If you are implying I like fighting, that's not true. I fight when I believe there is no other option."

Rita had been staring at the ground but lifted her eyes. "My father was abusive. He was a drinker ... an angry drinker. Many nights I would tremble under the covers as my mom endured his tirades. I know he experienced abuse at the mines where he worked. He was a foreman and came under fire from his supervisors because he advocated for his men. They told him it was an exercise in futility. So, the heads would give him hell—his words, not mine."

The setting sun cast an orange glint against Rita's tear-filled eyes. She took a deep breath and continued. "He often came home drunk—Mom would express her disappointment. Then—then, there would be loud arguments.

"Dad was a powerful man. One night he shoved her, and she fell, gashing her head on the sink. She recovered, but still takes meds to prevent seizures. I almost hated my dad."

Deke turned his hands over and shook his head. "I am sorry you went through that."

Rita smiled through her tears. "Their story did have a happy ending. My father felt so guilty about that shove, he finally realized he couldn't fix himself and turned to the Lord, with help from my mom and me. He quit drinking, resigned as foreman, and got an agricultural job."

"Did it help?"

"Absolutely. Dad changed. He became a caring, loving man. Their marriage became a model of God's plan for relationships. Three years ago, we lost him." Rita took a step toward him, her eyes drilling into his soul. "When I saw your intensity on the court, it took me back."

Deke hated being at a loss for words. He tried to look away, but her gaze held him.

"I see the good qualities in you, Deke, but you seem ready to explode because of your past experiences. I don't want to see my angry father in you."

Anger surged within him. Who did she think he was? First, he wasn't a drunk who shoved people. Second, he wasn't a coward.

Deke turned to gather his wits and cool his anger. He focused on a flock of doves seeking their perches for the approaching night. Doves. Peace. Was that irony? He sighed heavily, then turned back to Rita. Her face showed concern and innocence. How could he be angry with her? She was the first good thing that had happened to him in a long time.

Deke sighed. "I've learned everyone has a story. It might not be understandable to others, but it controls that person's life. What happened to you molded you, and I can see why I may remind you of your father. And, yes, I have issues to deal with, but I am *not* your father. Is that your fear? If it is, get to know me. Give me a chance."

Rita's hand flew to her mouth, and she nodded rapidly. "I know. It sounds silly now, and that's why I am here. I have thought about this for the past few days. I think maybe I was unfair. As an attorney, I try to read between the lines. I didn't do that Saturday."

She closed the remaining distance between them. "Forgive me?"

"I don't know why, but I would've preferred if you had demanded an apology from me." Deke looked down, then back into her misty blue eyes. "Because I'm sorry as well, and I ask you the same question."

Rita stepped forward and stood on her tiptoes—reaching both hands around his neck, she pulled his head downward and lightly kissed him on his lips.

Deke drew a breath through parted lips, then took her in his arms and returned the kiss—but this one lingered. Her warmth brought peace and was a healing balm on his battered soul.

CHAPTER 21

Cecil moved silently through the woods. He paused every few yards and listened for unnatural sounds. A faint bark came from the direction of his cabin.

Poor Plato.

Cecil hated tying his pet on the front porch. Plato was used to going with him wherever he went on the property. Today though, secrecy was of the utmost importance. He had to protect his treasure. Plato didn't understand that Cecil counted on him to sound an alarm at the house if someone stopped by. The thin man paused to analyze the dog's message. A single bark meant pleading with his master to come back.

Cecil smiled and proceeded on his walk. Plato would forgive him.

The thick hardwoods captured the heat, and sweat ran into his eyes. He should have waited until the cool of the evening, but he wanted to claim the treasure while nothing else stirred. He leaned on his staff, breathing hard. His heart pounded in his ears. It seemed the months were aging him, instead of years.

Cecil continued to strain his ears toward the world around him but heard only the buzzing gnats in his ears and the hammering of a woodpecker.

He gripped his staff tighter and moved on, occasionally sweeping the ground and bushes in front of him to scare any copperheads or rattlers that might be on his path. He arrived at his destination sooner than expected.

The well-hidden area seemed undisturbed.

Cecil carefully surveyed the location. Massive white and black oaks shaded an area about a hundred square feet. The close-woven chicken wire fencing that enclosed the area was inter-twined with leaves and vines, making the site practically invisible to all but the most discerning eye. He'd done such a good job hiding it, even he had trouble finding it.

Cecil paused and said a quick prayer of praise and gratitude. He could not help a small chuckle. Cecil leaned his staff against the fencing and unwound the wire that held the gate closed. His heart soared as he looked over the clearing with rows of plants, some with red berries and four to five leaves neatly radiating out from the main stem.

If the leaves were any indication of the roots, he had a great crop of ginseng.

Cecil stiffly knelt by one particularly huge plant and pulled his rock hammer from the side loop on his bib overalls leg. He carefully removed the soil six inches around the plant using the chisel blade on one side of the hammer. He worked the plant back and forth with one hand and used the other to pry with the pointed side of the hammer.

The plant broke free from the earth, and Cecil rocked backward, holding his prize before his face. The man-shaped root dripped dirt.

"Eureka! My treasure."

He scanned the area, praying his outburst hadn't been heard.

He had nursed this crop too long to tip-off any 'seng thieves in the area now. It had taken almost six years for them to bear mature fruit. Cecil knew from the approximate weight of the root he'd pulled it would command a good price on the market, even taking into consideration it would be dried. In the current market, it could fetch from five hundred to eight hundred dollars a pound.

This crop could feed him for a year. It would buy supplies and equipment. And if he didn't find a cure for his disease, it would buy a funeral plot by the church.

He halted his reverie and reconsidered that last possibility. That was something Deputy Deke would say. He chuckled aloud.

Cecil dropped the plant and swung the rock hammer into the ground. Next, he pulled a burlap bag from his bib overall strap. He rose and searched the garden perimeter until he found what he was looking for: several pieces of bark that all but concealed a plastic bucket that had once held dill pickles (compliments of McDonald's).

He strode over to the bucket, silently giving thanks to God again for a successful crop.

He lifted the bark concealing the upturned bucket.

He would have to make a lot of trips from here to the creek for water. But it was better to wash them here.

Cecil dragged the bucket out of the growth that had formed around it.

"Uhhh!" He felt several jolts of pain—two on his hand, and then a third hit his chin.

Bees!

Cecil dropped the bucket and jumped backward. He had surprised a nest of them, and they were angry. No doubt that was the first attack. The sentry bee would be joined by more of his comrades. He covered his head with his arms and ran to the exit.

The pain in his hand crept up his arm, and his face was beginning to swell. Time was of the essence. He had to get home to get his epinephrine.

He hurried down the overgrown path, oblivious to thorns grasping his clothing by multiflora rose bushes. His pounding heart and panting breath cautioned him to slow. He couldn't afford to. He wouldn't make it back to the cabin in time. Cecil found himself wondering if Deke would find him before the buzzards or other predators did.

"I see it! Lord, give me strength." A sudden calm and peace came over him as he staggered into the cabin clearing. Plato strained at the rope attached to a front porch post. Cecil's airway was becoming more restricted. He fought for air like a drowning man. Whining concern, the dog tried to get to his master.

Where are the stairs? Panic started to return, but a silent prayer held it at bay.

Cecil's shin connected with the bottom step, and he pitched forward, smacking his forehead on another step even though he attempted to catch his fall with his hand. His world went dark.

He dreamed he was lying on his back in a clearing surrounded by woods. The smell of damp wood was strong. Someone knelt by his side, wiping his face with a warm wet towel. Shouldn't it be cool? He felt his face being soothed.

He fought to open his eyes but couldn't see clearly. The kneeling form was wearing a white robe. He could see an indistinct face.

Was it Jesus?

He struggled to rise as the figure moved away from him without any apparent locomotion of his legs. The face smiled. A thought entered Cecil's mind.

"Not yet."

Not yet?

The retreating figure smiled again and raised a hand in farewell.

Not yet. Darkness again threatened to overcome him.

Cecil again tried to open his eyes and felt pain again. He was lying on his back on the steps. The damp cedar wood assailed his nostrils. Something warm and wet was again bathing his cheeks and forehead. This time it was Plato's tongue vigorously caressing his face.

He tried to sit up. "Stop Plato. Stop, boy." The voice did not seem to belong to him. It was weak and crackling. He peered through swollen eyelids at Plato, who sat gazing at his master's face with a look of concern.

Cecil reached out a shaky hand and petted the canine on the head. He used the other to steady himself on the stairstep. The memory of what he had to do rushed his brain.

"I'm okay. Just help me up." Plato seemed to understand as he moved a couple of steps down and allowed the injured man to place his hand on his shoulders. Cecil pressed himself up to stand erect. The dog quivered from the weight but stood firm.

Cecil paused as he struggled to inhale. His head spun. His eyes were slits. He fought to keep himself from toppling backward and pitched himself forward. He managed to plant his foot on another step on his climb. Another step and he was on the porch, reeling like a drunken man toward the wooden door. He slipped his hand around the rebar lever and thrust it downward. The bar on the inside lifted upward in response and allowed the door to swing open as Cecil fell against the wood. He continued his uncontrolled entry, tripping over a cane-bottom chair. Only the heavy oak table kept him from falling, but it did not prevent the variety of jars, Petri dishes, and the notebook of plants from being swept to the floor by his thrashing hands.

With one eye still not entirely closed, he searched the nearby counter. "Help me, Lord, help me!" He croaked.

His good eye passed over the books and items stored on the shelf until he saw it. He reached and clutched the epinephrine and syringe. Cecil sank to the floor with his back painfully sliding down the rough cabinet doors. It must be now!

Calvin Lamb pulled his truck crosswise to the driveway at the farm where Deke's horses were stabled. He pulled a pair of binoculars from the console and focused out the passenger window on an oak barn grayed by age. A foggy blur obscured his vision.

He lowered the field glasses to address Bobby Page's gaping face. "Outta the way, stupid."

"Oof!" Bobby grunted as Lamb elbowed his friend's chest to clear him from the field of vision and resumed his watch.

"Whataya looking for? Why are we here?" Bobby looked from the driver to the farm scene and back. "Man, I don't like this. Suppose Campbell shows up."

"Relax—your buddy Deputy Dog is in court. I drove by there and saw his jeep and truck parked in the lot behind there before I picked you up." Calvin moved the field glasses to scan the property. "The Waxman is in his cabin or gone. His mutt goes everywhere with him, so I'm just lookin' to see if the dog is there." He frowned. "I can't see his cabin from here. You need to get closer and check it out." He stuck the binoculars back into the console. He leaned sidewise against the door and grinned. "We're going to make some money."

Bobby's knee bounced up and down. "I don't follow you?"

Calvin balled up his fist and struck the thigh of his passenger's leg. "Stop that jerking."

"Ow," howled Bobby, rubbing the wounded area.

"Then knock it off."

"I can't help it. You make me nervous. I am still on parole. Besides, Campbell got me a job, and he gave me a break."

Lamb wagged a finger six inches from Bobby's nose, and he leaned back in his seat.

"A cop is a cop. He gets paid for busting people. Don't you think he is setting you up for a bigger fall? Cops aren't that smart. They gotta go by the book and anything that's not in it, well, they get confused."

"Cal, *I'm* confused."

Lamb sighed and pulled his finger away and rubbed his chin. "Look. Sure, you're confused. But that's why I am here. You need money, and I like a little extra. Right? I like a little weed or coke. So, I have a plan to satisfy both our needs. Comprendo?"

Bobby gave him a blank stare. "I don't talk Mexican. So, I don't get it."

Calvin spoke slowly, emphasizing each word. "Idiot. It's Spanish. Secondly, I don't expect you to get it. That's why I do the planning, and you do what I say."

Calvin glanced down the road and watched an Amish buggy pulled by a trotting horse. Probably going home from town. An unexpected passer-by.

"You got to move quickly. Get out and hurry to the edge of the woods where the old ugly guy lives. If that mutt is still there, you'll know he's home. If he is tied up, better still. That means the Waxman is delivering his cures and doesn't want the dog to follow him. I will pick you up by the big sycamore tree near the bridge. Now hurry."

"But, but ..." Bobby began.

"No 'buts.' You get your butt outta here, now."

Cal leaned over and shoved open the passenger door. His passenger hesitated.

"Get out!" Cal yelled.

CHAPTER 22

Calvin's truck bounced over the fields behind the house where he lived.

"Hey! Take it easy, you're gonna break something," protested Bobby as he was tossed around in the passenger seat.

"Fasten your seatbelt, you dummy. We got to get to the back of his property before Ugly gets back. He's probably delivering secret potions or visiting the nursing home. I've been watching his movements for a couple of months. And you say his dog was there. Right?"

Bobby screwed up his brows. "Yeah, I got close enough to see him sleeping on the porch.

"Now we are going for the Waxman's buried treasure."

"What buried treasure?"

Calvin chanced a look at his inquiring passenger, "'Seng! An exotic root that sells at the markets in the orient. And it brings big bucks."

Finally, he saw the light go on in his partner's eyes. "Oh, oh. Ya mean we're going to steal the Waxman's ginseng?"

"Nooo! We're going to surprise him by doing the hard labor of harvesting his crop, so he doesn't have to work!"

Calvin glared at Bobby longer than he should have. He hit a bottomless pocket which sent the truck airborne. The truck slammed to the ground.

"Sheeee—! You dimwit. I gotta draw you a picture? Let me concentrate on the driving."

Bobby turned to Calvin with hands extended in supplication. "I dunno about this, Cal. I'm on patrol anyway. I can't mess up."

"Parole. It's parole, you dip."

Bobby ignored his correction and plunged on. "I got nothing against Mr. Cecil. He helped my granny with her arthritis before she died. No doctor was able to help her. She paid him with blackberry cobbler pies and cookies. He didn't want money."

"Look, pea brain. You need money, and I do too. My old man won't advance me anymore allowance. I can't even buy a nickel bag of weed with what I got. If he has a good crop, it could be worth thousands."

Bobby lowered his head to his chest and shook it. "I just don't know, Cal. I got a job because of Deputy Campbell. He was good to me even after he busted me. I deserved to go to jail. He got me that job. Even helped me out with a few bucks until I could draw pay."

Cal's hand shot out and slapped Bobby's bowed head. "I don't want to hear any more about that Deputy Dawg! My pop hates him, and I do too. You saw the shiner that cop laid on Dad?"

Bobby rubbed the back of his head and grimaced at the driver. "You had no call to do that. That hurt." He lowered his voice and looked straight out the windshield. "Besides, I heard from folks there that your old man started it. Deputy just finished it."

Calvin gritted his teeth and drew his hand back for another strike at his friend. "You son of—I'll educate you later."

He scanned the neighboring woods, separated from his father's land by four strands of rusty barbed wire and locust fence posts with intermittent steel fence posts. He slammed on the brakes. "Here 'tis. That big sycamore tree marks the spot." He licked his lips and leered.

"Get out and grab the feedbags and the shovel from the back." Lamb didn't wait for a response but bailed out of the truck and eased the door shut. He surveyed the woods behind the stately sycamore. No movement.

Bang! A door slammed.

Calvin ducked and spun around. Across the bed of the truck, Bobby stood with his hand on the doorhandle.

"You idiot, be quiet." Cal shook his head. "Man, you're as useless as a one-armed wallpaper hanger."

"My old man used to say that to me all the time." Bobby frowned, "Never made sense then, don't make no sense now."

"Just get the shovel and bags out of the truck and be quiet about it."

Bobby let out a deep sigh and plodded to the tailgate. He stood on the bumper to retrieve the items as ordered.

"Move quickly, but quietly."

Calvin headed toward the fence, but he paused until his friend caught up to him. In the meantime, he searched the undergrowth in the woods listening for any human sounds. Finally satisfied, he straddled the barbed wire and crossed the fence.

"Come on," he whispered.

Bobby quietly placed the items he carried on the other side of the fence and then joined him by crawling between the barbed wire strands. A single barb caught him by his T-shirt at the shoulder, gouging his skin and tearing fabric. "Ouch!" He pulled loose, leaving a scrap of his shirt. "Man, that was a Christmas shirt from my uncle Irwin."

"Crap. Your uncle Irwin has been dead a couple of years. You stole that out of his underwear drawer when they were having a yard sale."

"Oh, yeah, I forgot. But he would've wanted me to have it. Anywise, he's got nice white robes now, and he's playing a harp."

"Your uncle Irwin is probably dancing naked in flames while little demons jab him in the butt with pitchforks."

"He is not." Bobby stuck out his chest. "He wuz a good man. I got good T-shirts too. Fruit of the Loom."

Cal shook his head. "Keep moving."

Both men crept through the undergrowth. Overhead, towering oaks, hickories, and other varieties of trees formed a dense canopy that sunlight fought hard to struggle through. Despite this, the high humidity heat clung to their bodies. Perspiration on their exposed body parts lured sweat bees with the promise of sustenance.

The bees were soon joined by other insects-in-arms—gnats. Gnats that made them miserable by dashing in and out of their nostrils and ears. Calvin cursed himself for forgetting the bug spray.

As they neared their target area, thirsty mosquitoes from stagnant pools in the creek bed swarmed upward with the other pests in quest for human blood.

It was as if the ugly Waxman had trained these bugs to guard his treasure. The thought made Calvin a bit uneasy. *That's dumb. Almost there. A little to the left.*

SUMMER OF THE WAXMAN

Although he had visited the garden site only a few days ago when he trailed an out-of-season deer he had wounded, it wasn't easy to locate the spot. He hadn't wanted to place any markers to guide him. The old Waxman knew these woods and would spot any alterations.

He stopped abruptly, with Bobby almost colliding with him. Calvin searched the steep hill. He swept the surrounding area. A section of vines reaching skyward seemed to be too organized. He moved toward the growth, then spotted some chicken wire attached to a wooden frame.

Got it.

He stopped abruptly when he saw the gate wide open. Was the Waxman there?

Calvin signaled Bobby to stay put, then turned, bent low, and crept up to the open gate. He tried to subdue his exertion and tell-tale panting for a few seconds. Then, when he could reasonably quash his heavy breathing, the trespasser peeked around the entry corner.

No one there. Calvin surveyed the neatly rowed plants then looked for a clue on why the gate was left open. An overturned white bucket in the upper corner of the enclosed garden caught his eye—as did the bees circling their disturbed home. They were far enough away that he did not feel threatened. He then saw the empty burlap sack on the garden floor and the rock hammer embedded in the ground in a nearby row. The hammer lay within inches of a missing ginseng plant.

Cal tried to reconstruct what had happened for Waxman to leave the gate open. It had to be an urgent departure, and it would not have been their arrival that sent him packing. Calvin straightened.

"What d'ya see?" A voice right behind him made him jump.

"Jeez, Bobby, I told ya to stay back."

"No, you didn't. You didn't say a word."

An irritated Calvin spoke through clenched teeth. "I mean, I signaled you to stay put."

"Oh. I knew I didn't hear anything."

Calvin turned his attention to the ginseng once again. "I don't believe the Halloween man will bother us. He left a sack and his precious pickaxe. Look at the overturned bucket and that lonely plant. Right beside a bee's nest. Yep! He left in a hurry, and he's not gonna be returning anytime soon."

Calvin turned to his partner in crime and grinned. His grin slowly faded as he gazed upon Bobby's puzzled countenance. "Oh, for crying out loud, he got hit by bees, and he headed out for home. Betcha they got him good from the looks of it. He left everything. He's hurting."

"Should we go and see if he needs help?"

Calvin stared at his accomplice for a few seconds and then spoke slowly. "Yeah, we should do that. We should tell him we found his 'seng's hiding place, and we were going to steal his crop, but we figured bees got him, and we wanted to get our Boy Scout 'bee badge' by helping him."

Bobby furled his brows. "Didn't know the Scouts gave out bee badges. But I was kicked out when I was fourteen for sticking an M-80 firecracker into a watermelon while my troop was picnicking. It went off and spattered the pack leader when she walked up to the table. Bad timing."

"No, stupid. We are here to steal his plot and not to help that creep. Get to digging. Go!"

Calvin wheeled and approached the crop, stooping to free the rock hammer from the soil, then knelt beside a particularly lush-leafed plant. He vigorously dug at the base of a plant with the broad point of the ax. Then, seizing the plant with one hand, he wrestled the hidden man-shaped root into daylight. "Gol darn—this is huge. It must be at least ten or twelve ounces!"

He swung his head toward Bobby, grinning broadly, then his grin faded. "Why are you still standing there? Get to work. Make some money."

Bobby appeared transfixed, staring vacantly at his partner. His mouth opened and closed spasmodically. "I ... I ... I can't do it. The Waxman depends on this stuff to live. I know how hard it is when you have nothing. I been there."

Calvin's jaw dropped. He rose and shook his head, his face reddening. "Don't tell me you can't do it. After all I've done for you! You get your butt over here and start digging."

Bobby stood his ground. Through jagged breaths, he spoke in quiet measured words. "I ain't afraid of you anymore, Cal. I got a chance to fix my life. So that's what I'm going to do."

Bobby dropped the shovel and bags and walked away from the plot.

"Where are you going?"

Bobby stopped but didn't turn around. "I'm going to try to help the Waxman. He done good for a lot of people. Never hurt anyone. Maybe I can make God like me again like when I was a baby."

He glanced back briefly, and Calvin saw tears in his eyes. Bobby opened both arms and seemed to have run out of words. He turned around again and headed for the path toward Cecil's cabin.

Calvin's heart quickened. *He's going to do it. He's going to not only screw up this money maker, but he may get me jailed.*

"Bobby, stop! Get back here. You can't do this, you, you idiot!" Calvin's words came out in a harsh whisper. He clutched the rock hammer tighter and started after him. A walk became a jog.

"Stop, you son of—"

Enraged now, Calvin raced toward Bobby's retreating figure.

Fear welled inside him as he processed all that could go wrong if Bobby defected.

"I will kill you—you scum!"

He raised the rock hammer and threw it with all his weight. Time seemed to stand still as the weapon sailed through the air, rotating a full two turns before the pointed pick-like side of the hammer struck Bobby squarely between his shoulders. His body pitched forward, hands outstretched, and he sank to his knees. He remained on his knees with his hands raised as Calvin froze at the slow-motion scene. Then Bobby collapsed face-down, making no effort to break his plunge with his hands.

A wave of nausea washed over Calvin. He could not feel his legs as he knelt beside his friend. A red stain spread rapidly across his T-shirt from the point of the protruding rock hammer.

"Oh, Jesus! What have you done? You lunatic, you caused this."

Calvin pulled at Bobby's shoulder to turn him over. The rock hammer prevented him from rolling all the way. He seized the weapon and pulled it out, increasing the free flow of blood and eliciting a combined groan and gurgle from Bobby's lips.

Bobby's eyes were wide, his nose was bloody and covered with dirt from his fall, and his breathing was labored.

"Oh man, I didn't mean to hurt you. I wanted to hit you with the top of the ax—not the pointy tip. I just had to stop you before you ruined it for the both of us."

Bobby's eyes widened more, and he strained to talk but only coughed.

"Hang on, buddy. I will get help."

Calvin fought to work his arm under Bobby's knees and the other arm behind his back. He then gathered his legs under him and attempted to stand with his burden.

Bobby groaned, coughed, and stiffened momentarily. His wide eyes shifted, then went dim, as he gazed skyward.

Calvin sank to his knees and rolled the lifeless body back onto the path. He buried his eyes in his hands and sobbed.

CHAPTER 23

Gotta think. I have to protect myself. Need an alibi.

Calvin swatted mindlessly at the gnats and mosquitoes harassing his exposed skin. He stood, alternately looking at the body of his friend and the surrounding area. Suddenly he bolted into action, grabbing Bobby's body under the arms and dragging him past the ginseng plot toward Lamb's property. The exertion left him winded, but he had to relocate the body and hope the law would ascribe a motive to the Waxman.

He hurried back to the spot where the body had lain. Streaks of blood decorated the scene. He found a clump of three-foot Johnson grass and cut it close to the roots with his Buck knife. He followed up by mopping up the still-moist blood on the trail. Finally, he eliminated the blood spore from the scene. Satisfied, he tossed the grass into the underbrush.

Calvin picked up the bags for ginseng storage near the garden gate and retraced his steps to where Bobby had fallen. He picked up the blood-stained rock hammer and used the feed bag to wipe the handle. He placed the rock hammer and some fallen limbs inside one bag to give it ballast. Clutching the bag ends, he dragged the weighted ends down the path where the two would-be thieves had walked. Slowly, he pulled the bags backward up the trail to the garden, including where he had dug the ginseng plant.

He surveyed his work. No traces. Good. Now, from the garden to the body.

Calvin scanned the ground, erasing any footprints between the plot and the site of Bobby's still body. Flies had already started to collect on the corpse. He had to hurry. He moved quickly to the overgrown creek bank with the bag of evidence and swung it open in an effort to empty the contents. The limbs dropped from the sack, but the hammer caught on the fabric. A second attempt was successful. The tool somersaulted down the bank and hid under buck brushes. Peering down the bank, he could see the hammer caught in the bushes. It was more hidden than he wanted, but he knew the cops would comb the area and find the murder weapon.

Satisfied, Calvin turned and jogged down the trail he and Bobby had taken to the crime scene. Arriving at the barbed wire fence, he once again became cautious. His eyes took in the expanse of his father's property. No humans in sight. This would be a critical part of his plan.

A small herd of Angus cattle had found shelter from the summer sun in a grove of trees. He had to smile. Great. As if they'd volunteered to help him.

Stepping on a lower wire and clutching the steel fence post, he swung his other leg over the top wire, crossed into the open field, and briskly walked to his truck. Punching the lock button on the side of the bed toolbox, he lifted the lid to expose an eclectic collection of goods— tools, beer cans, oil cans, sprays, feed sacks, and a smoky bong. He removed a pair of fencing pliers and a half-filled bag of cattle feed.

Calvin returned to the fence, dropped the feed bag, and, using the pliers, he cut the top two wires near the fence post he had crossed. The rusty wires retracted in a coil to the opposite post. He stuck the pliers in his hip pocket and placed his booted foot midway on the steel post where he had cut the wires free. Repeated shoves accompanied by grunts caused the fence support to lean at an angle in the soft earth. He grasped the top of the post and let his body weight finish his goal—leaning the post over to within eight inches of the ground.

He picked the feed bag off the ground and sprinkled some of it four to five feet on each side of the broken-down fence. He had covered everything to his satisfaction.

Now to get the cows to help finish the story.

Calvin jumped back into his truck and threw his bag of feed, with a quarter of grain left, on the passenger side floor. He started the vehicle up and bounced across the field to the lazing cattle. The dull-witted bovines watched his arrival. He was counting on their curious nature. His truck often had feed or hay on board. Finally, he arrived and swung the rear end around to face the waiting herd. He grabbed the feed bag and leaped out of the truck, leaving the vehicle running.

The herd showed no fear as he approached. He came within fifteen feet of the interested group when he stopped, spread a line of grain back toward his truck, and tossed the empty bag into the bed.

"C'mon, cow!" Calvin started backing to the side of the truck.

For a few seconds, they seemed to debate whether they should leave the cool comfort of the trees. One cow swung her head back and forth, then started forward. She lowered her head, grazed the grass and the feed indiscriminately. The others slowly followed.

Calvin glanced at his watch. "C'mon, you stupid cows."

Several others joined the lead cow in foraging a brunch. He had them. Calvin walked backward and stood by the vehicle's open door until he was satisfied that they would follow the source of their goodies. He carefully seated himself in the truck and closed the door as quietly as possible. Slipping it into gear, he let out the clutch hoping that the deep-throated boom of his pipes would not intimidate his entourage. It didn't.

Calvin drove slowly and allowed the beasts to leisurely follow him even after they exhausted the feed trail. He swung his truck to one side as he approached the downed fence. The cattle hesitated, but the same lead cow crossed the downed fence and discovered the dropped delicacies. Calvin jumped from the vehicle and quietly slunk to the rear of the herd, giving them a wide berth.

"Hey, Hey!" The herder encouraged the rest of the cattle to move closer to the downed wire, then over the fence. Calvin did not need to urge them much. The feed and natural curiosity about the newly discovered location motivated them to explore.

Okay, okay. Now I gotta get to the house and call the cops.

Sheriff Tim Holloman was grateful for a slow Wednesday. However, he wouldn't be lulled into a state of relaxation. The weekend was coming, and with it would come an influx of tourists checking out the Amish community and those escaping their city jobs to dream about idyllic small farms they could buy cheaply in a search for solace from their hectic lives. And of course, the peak of summer meant multiple revelers seeking out-of-the-way places to party.

Only a few deputies were working today—Delaney, Dusty, and Deke. He would need a full contingent this weekend. He signed the last of his paperwork at his desk, rose, removed his hat from the rack, and left the office.

Amanda hummed quietly as she sorted through files and did not look up. As Tim entered the filing room.

"Anything going on? Who's dispatching?"

Amanda straightened, looked at the ceiling as she processed his questions. "Nothing to speak of, and Theo is the radio jockey. Oh, Deke is handling a car and buggy collision out on Black Ford Road."

Tim raised his eyebrows but said nothing. Amanda read his mind.

"No one hurt. A Chevy Impala with a herd of one hundred twenty-five horses crested a hill and surprised a one-horse buggy. The Chevy clipped the back end. As I understand, Deke let dispatch know that no humans or animals were injured. He said the horse might need trauma counseling, though."

Tim shook his head and grinned. "Bet Deke never had to investigate accidents in Chicago like he does here."

"That's true." Amanda turned her attention back to her filing.

He grabbed a report of a downed stop sign and nodded. "I'll take this. I'll also be checking on traffic and watching for possible flooding on Cave Springs Road. The weekend is coming, and I want to make sure we don't need to put barricades up to prevent any hotshot drivers from seeing how their vehicles will perform fording flooded creek crossings."

The assistant nodded and started humming again.

Tim donned his hat at a tilt, left the courthouse and bounced down the few steps to his waiting vehicle. The blue sign on the street in front of the diagonal parking place sternly reserved this spot for the sheriff.

Tim chuckled aloud as he thought about the games that Deputy Deke would sometimes play with him. No one dared to park in his place—except Deke.

As Tim drove down the state highway toward the Repton crossroad, he cut the AC and enjoyed the warm air licking his short hair through the open window. Repton consisted of few buildings that once housed a restaurant, a store, auto repair, and a church. Today the only activity centered around the community church. The office had received a report of a stop sign down at the intersection. Some folks around the area had viewed the sign as a suggestion, not a command.

Tim was always prepared for these events with a spare sign and wire in his Jeep.

The sheriff was a couple of miles away from the location when the radio crackled as the deep-voiced dispatcher queried, "Unit six, you clear from that buggy accident, Deke?"

Deke's voice broke the airway. "Ten-four, just finishing up. Whatcha got, Syd?"

"Complainant, Calvin Lamb, reports an assault by a neighbor, Burgess, upon him and Bobby Page where the two farms join. He escaped. His friend, not so lucky." There was a brief silence. "Got Lamb on the phone. He says he thinks his friend is deceased."

Tim slammed on his brakes and made a bootlegger's U-turn on the highway to head back in the opposite direction. He reached for his mic as Deke's terse voice broke the airway again.

"Ten-four. I'm in route."

Tim flipped his lights on and kept his mic close to his lips. But he was unable to transmit because of Syd's message to Deke. "I am dispatching an ambulance to the farm."

The radio click afforded the sheriff to key his mic. "This is unit one. I will take this call. What's the ten-twenty of this assault, and is the vic still there?"

"That's affirmative. It happened on Cecil Burgess's property, between his cabin and Lamb's farm." The dispatcher still had his mic depressed, allowing those listening to hear a faint phone conversation.

"You say the Waxman did it?"

CHAPTER 24

Deke sped down the backroads to Lamb's farm. A familiar voice broke through, overpowering the sound of the winding motor of his Jeep. "Unit one to unit six."

Deke leaned to the inside of a curve while his vehicle threatened to lose traction. His firmly set mouth showed his intentions as he entered the turn. He tap-danced on the brake pedal to slow his entry. He knew these turns from boyhood. But now, they were not encountered as youthful fun and exhilaration.

"Unit six, come in." The sheriff's voice was demanding.

A few seconds rolled by, and Deke took a deep breath, pulled the mic from its holder, and spoke with forced calmness. "Unit six, responding. I am about three minutes from Lamb's farm." He lied to his friend and had a twinge of guilt.

Immediately the sheriff clicked on. "Negative, six. I say again, negative, Deputy. I will interview the complainant. Six, check the woods behind the Burgess cabin. Cover the alleged scene."

Deke slowed the Jeep slightly and nodded his head as though Tim could see him.

Tim is not only concerned with the case but also worried I would forget my professionalism.

Deke's jaws tightened. "Shoot! Who does he think I am? I've handled more serious cases than he has ever dreamed of."

That's not fair. He was right. Deke, control yourself.

Deke's finger closed on the mic button. "Ten-four, understood. I will try to enter the scene where the remains of the Burgess homeplace were. Can you get a little more specific on the location in the woods of the assault?"

"Syd, I'm almost at Lamb's place. Can you get more specific info for Deke from Calvin?"

Deke sighed. He and Tim had a resolution. The kind that only longtime friends understood.

The dispatcher relayed information from the landline to Deke. Deke was satisfied he could find Bobby—or his body—if a crime had taken place. He turned onto Cecil's farm and bounced toward the old barn. Mandy was the first to recognize the Jeep patrol vehicle and danced near the fence in excitement. Zorro stared suspiciously at the approaching car, but recognition was soon evident. They both raced back and forth, delighted to see their friend and master.

Just before he reached the corral, Deke stopped and engaged the four-wheel-drive option. He then turned to the wooded area and bounced over the pasture. He looked in the mirror and half-smiled at the bewildered horses who had stopped dancing and stared after the retreating Jeep.

Deke's eyes and mind returned to the situation at hand as he tried to translate the description of the location where the assault happened. Ominous thoughts now crowded into his mind. Was Cecil all right? Could he have attacked Bobby and Calvin as the conversation indicated?

Impossible!

Deke shook the intrusive thoughts off. *Concentrate, Deke. Show your skills, not your bias.*

He braked when he saw the towering gum tree beside the creek. The rusty three-string barbed wire fence abruptly ended there with the years of the tree's growth capturing each wire and embedding them about two inches. Where the wires ended, an old oak plank gate began. The ancient gate no longer served its purpose as it leaned toward the creek, almost touching the ground.

Deke paused to turn his radio on clipped to his belt and exited the vehicle. He wrestled the gate further down until it lay flush with the ground. He then walked down to the shallow creek. The high banks of the creek and thorn bushes on the other side made his progress difficult. He retreated from the impenetrable multiflora rose bushes lining the creek bank and walked on the wet creek bed looking for an opening in the thicket towering on the steep bank.

Mosquitoes and gnats challenged his presence. He moved faster, seeking an exit from the creek. "Aha." Deke found the opening. It was where deer crossed the creek to enter the fields to graze. The vegetation on the bank was completely obliterated by heavy deer traffic. As he struggled up the slick bank, he lost his balance and pitched forward, reflexively grasping at a buck brush. It saved him from planting his face in the bank.

Deke grunted, then stopped his attempt to upright himself. "What is that?"

He leaned in closer, trying to discern the object that seemed incongruous with the vegetation. He reached out one hand while maintaining his balance on the steep bank by tightly grasping a sapling tree with the other. "Ow!" A thorn punctured his thumb as he reached in to investigate the curious item.

He realigned his feet and grip on the sapling and cautiously extended his thumb and forefinger, disengaging the partially protruding item from its leafy hiding place. Deke strained to reach the oddity, then pulled it halfway free. It was a rock hammer.

Like, like—Cecil carries.

When he realized what the object was, Deke stopped trying to extricate it from the brush. He cursed his carelessness and replaced the hammer gingerly. Then, working himself upward to the crest of the bank, he turned around and knelt. The hammer was evident from this angle. He leaned forward, squinting at the tool. The pointed side of the hammer was dark. Blood. Very possibly blood.

He then remembered to advise Tim that he had arrived at the scene and to report to central dispatch his status via the walkie-talkie to begin radio documentation. It was significant evidence—if needed. And it was starting to look like it would be required.

Deke saw the fenced-in garden before he saw Bobby's body. He only took a few steps toward the garden before he spotted a leg extending into the path. He halted abruptly and surveyed the scene before trotting forward to the still leg of the victim.

The entire lifeless body came into view. The eyes were half open and gazing skyward, the mouth gaped open, and insects explored the nostrils. Bobby was beyond help, but Deke still checked for a pulse and breathing. The ground was moist under his back with blood. He gingerly lifted one shoulder and saw the wound near his spine. He lowered his shoulder gently.

Deke slowly stood erect. He pulled his radio from his belt. "Unit six to dispatch."

"This is central dispatch. Come in, Deke."

"Notify paramedics to come to the scene. They should enter by way of the Lamb farm so they can drive over more solid ground. At the fence of the Burgess farm, they can cross on foot. Tell them to bring a gurney. Notify the coroner and see if Dan Trimble from the state lab is around. Tell him I need his expertise and evidence collection."

Although it was clear Bobby was deceased, since Deke was not a licensed medical professional, his determination would be considered inadequate. That was the first thing a defense attorney would rip into a cop for—assuming the victim was dead. An old-timer had once told him, "I don't care if their arms and legs are missing, throat's slit, and blowflies are having a party on the corpse. Yer not a doc or a coroner. Call it in and grab your medical kit like yer going to save their life. Better to squirm at the scene than in court."

Deke stood listening for a response from the dispatcher. He almost thought the transmission had not gone through because of the lengthy time-lapse.

"Ten-four, will advise." Syd's voice finally responded.

Deke returned his radio to his belt. He looked down at the lifeless body. Sadness gripped his heart. "Oh, Bobby, Bobby. I don't know what happened here, but I am sure you didn't deserve this."

Deke looked down the path to Cecil's invisible cabin. Could he have...? No, Cecil was not a killer.

Deke hurried back to his Jeep, taking the path and avoiding the creek obstacle course. It was a longer route but generally clear of vegetation. Arriving at the vehicle, he grabbed his forensic bag and camera from the back. He hurried back to the murder scene. Lots to do before a whole lot of people started trampling the site. He started with photos of the body and surrounding area. Then Deke donned plastic gloves and knelt to examine the body. He turned Bobby's hands over and noted that rigor mortis was starting, sped up by the heat, no doubt. The small muscles in the hands were usually the first to be affected. He had probably been dead about two hours. How did that square with Lamb's call?

Hmm? No indication of defensive wounds on his hands. Deke rose and rummaged around in his case until he found what he wanted. String and u-shaped staples—chalk to outline the body didn't work well on a forest floor. Deke used bright yellow cord to outline the body. When he finished, he further isolated the crime scene with yellow police tape.

Deke fought to focus on his role of evidence tech. But, despite his efforts, his mind turned to Cecil. Where was he? Could he possibly be tied into this? The man didn't have a mean bone in his body.

The deputy shook off the worrisome thoughts and concentrated on his job. He placed a V-shaped plastic numbered marker at the bush holding the ax, then measured from that point to the body.

He paused to catch his breath in the oppressive humidity. His eyes combed the surroundings and then sucked in a deep breath and plunged down the bank. Slipping and sliding until he reached the place where the rock hammer hung, he picked up the Nikon suspended around his neck. He clicked eight frames with differing perspectives. He then pulled off the dirty plastic gloves and pulled a fresh pair from his hip pocket.

Deke pulled out an evidence bag he had inserted into his shirt between buttons before descending the bank. Slowly and carefully, he grasped the tip of the handle of the rock hammer and deposited it into the open bag. He sealed the container and wrote his name and pertinent information on the bag over the seal.

Deke cocked his head at the approaching sound of a motor. "The calvary is here." He climbed up the bank and started examining the foliage protecting the garden. Then he spotted the open gate and walked to it. Deke straightened. "Well, I'll be."

The cultivated ginseng plants stood in orderly rows. His head spun as he processed the events leading up to Bobby's demise. He prided himself on following the facts, examining the evidence, and not allowing any distractions. He had to hear from Calvin Lamb. There were several thousand dollars in this ground. Bobby could not talk, but Calvin could.

CHAPTER 25

Deke stood at the downed fence watching the rescue ambulance lurch over the pasture. He had snapped a few photos and was examining the fence posts and wire. Hoofprints told him cattle had been in the woods, but the nearby presence of a small herd in Lamb's pasture indicated they had not found worthy grazing on Cecil's farm.

Deke squatted down and picked up a strand of barbed wire. Holding it close, he turned it at different angles. Next, he fished through his bag and drew out a magnifying glass. He moved the glass back and forth until he could focus the end of the strand.

"Hello," Deke said. The wire showed signs of a clean fresh cut. No cows he knew carried tools.

Deke rose and photographed the cut wire. Then he saw something caught on one of the barbs. It was a piece of cloth with just a streak of red. It could be from a shirt. He snapped another picture and then placed a marker at the scene and again photographed the cloth. Carefully he disengaged the impaled fabric with tweezers, dropped it into a plastic container, and set it into his bag after marking it with relevant information.

No one had lain down on this wire. The fence had to be standing to grab clothing.

The rescue squad arrived, and Deke stepped over the fencing to meet them, then paused. He again squatted and picked up a few grains. The grain was placed in evidence and disappeared into his bag.

Two uniformed men approached Deke. One carried a folded gurney, the other an emergency medical kit.

Deke rose. "Hey, Red. Anson, how ya doing?"

Both men smiled at Deke and returned his greeting. Then, Red said, "what you got, Deke?"

A door slammed on the passenger side of their vehicle. It was Farley, the coroner. He rounded the front end and gingerly walked toward the gathered men. His focus was on the ground, as if watching for anything that would cause him to stumble and send his ample body face-down on the ground.

Red followed Deke's gaze and grinned. "Dr. Farley didn't want his caddy to take a beating over these fields, so he hooked a ride with us. He wanted us to drive closer, but I told him we didn't want to pollute the scene—not knowing where it was exactly."

Anson snickered. "The doctor is a sharp coroner, but he thinks God gave him legs to operate an automobile, not to walk."

"Hey, Doc. Come and get in the shade."

"Shade. It'll still be hotter'n blazes under the trees."

Deke and both men chuckled. "Well, you got me there. Where's your medical bag?"

Farley drew near the group, breathing hard and mopping his forehead with a handkerchief. He gestured to Red's medical kit, exposing a sweat-soaked white shirt underarm.

"He'll have everything I need."

"Okay, gentlemen, follow me." Deke swiveled and retraced his steps to the body. He paid close attention to the area in case he had missed something.

The radio crackled again. "Unit one, the Madisonville Tech is here. I will send him back. You are familiar with Agent Trimble, correct?"

Deke was relieved to hear the agent assigned was a friend, and he had the utmost respect for his expertise. "That's a big ten-four. Tell Dan to look for the rescue wagon and follow the path. And oh, he needs to bring his gallon jug of tea—not just his mug. He will understand."

Deke finished his communication and was grinning. He caught Red looking at him.

The paramedic crinkled his bushy red eyebrows. "Let me guess. Is it Dan? Didn't hear it all, but I know that Dan doesn't stray far from his iced tea."

They arrived at the scene of the crime, and the men became all business. Solemn countenances replaced nonchalant ones. Dan Trimble arrived fifteen minutes later. After the coroner declared Bobby dead and with no urgency to transport his body for medical treatment, they initiated an in-depth investigation.

Another hour and a half passed before the professionals felt they had covered all details. Then Red and Anson loaded up the body and transported him from the scene to the morgue. Dr. Farley looked more than happy to seek the cool shelter of the rescue unit. Only Deke and Dan remained in deep conversation.

"So, you got a person of interest?" Dan said.

Deke frowned and drew a deep breath before he answered. "Well, a so-called witness said he saw the owner of this property exhibit his displeasure about trespassing on his land with the rock ax." He nodded to the plastic bag he had given to the agent for a lab screening.

"And you're not buying it?"

Dan looked over to the concealed garden of ginseng. "Seems like as good a motive as any to be upset with someone trying to nick your high money crop."

"The witness is a lying mutt!"

Dan opened his arms wide with one hand grasping the inevitable mug handle. "Whoa. Don't bite my butt, Doggy Deke. Just saying it looks like a case of property protection."

Deke shook his head and sighed. "Sorry, my friend, but I know the man he is accusing of murder. And I know the so-called witness. It's a frame job."

"You know I cover the western counties and have done a lot of crime scenes. One thing that sets me apart in law enforcement from the rest of my colleagues is that I don't know the vics or the perps the way the cops know them. Everyone involved is a stranger. So, I can remain objective."

Deke looked straight into the pale blue eyes of his friend. "You think I'm not? You got a point there. But I also have the advantage of being familiar with people on my beat, the good, bad, and ugly. I have the advantage of insight into what a person is capable of, or not capable of."

Both weighed each other's position. Dan broke the silence. "You got a point there, too. Just be careful. You can remain like 'Lady Justice,' blindfolded."

Deke nodded.

"Unit one to central." Tim's voice broke the airways.

"Central, go ahead, Sheriff."

"I am clearing from the Lamb farm. I have a statement from Calvin. I am in route to Mr. Burgess's farm. Advise unit three to meet me there. Expedite."

"Ten-four. Dispatching three to the Burgess home—"

Deke mashed his mic. "This is unit six. I'm in the area, and I will take that call for backup for unit one."

"Negative, unit six. Unit three will assist. You copy?" Tim's voice was firm.

Anger surged through Deke from top to bottom. He keyed, then unkeyed the mic, mouth at the ready, but with no words. Dan watched in silence. Deke read his thoughts.

He keyed the mic and spoke in measured words. "Uh, unit one, Sheriff, requesting permission to be on site for any evidence gathering need."

The radio was dead for what seemed like minutes. Then, finally, Tim spoke softly, "Ten-four. Deke, it may be necessary, so rendezvous with us. Wait for my arrival at the gate."

"That's a copy, sheriff."

Dan extended his hand and smiled. "I will make like a sled and slide on out of here."

Deke grinned. "Catch you around. I owe you a tea."

"You owe me lunch."

"Oh, by the way, you might find my print on the ax. Unfortunately, before I realized what it was, I took hold of it. My mistake." Deke grinned sheepishly.

"Right. I have your prints and your ugly DNA on file, so you got an alibi. But I could set you up if you refuse to buy me lunch." Dan chuckled. "I'll process this evidence tonight. I'm going fishing with my kid tomorrow, so I want to get it done. I know you do, too."

Deke barely heard his last words. He now focused on getting to his Jeep and getting to Cecil's house.

CHAPTER 26

The sheriff had already arrived. Deke swung into Cecil's drive and slid to a halt beside Tim's Jeep, just inches from the cable stretched across the road. He leapt from his vehicle and strode around the cable and up the path.

Tim turned as Deke approached him. His face was blank, and his usual smile absent.

Deke nodded, but the sheriff spoke first. "Where's your lid?"

"In the unit." Deke frowned. "Didn't think I was going to be in a parade."

The sheriff's long, piercing gaze jolted Deke's confidence. He spoke slowly—almost in a whisper. "This isn't a case of graffiti on a county road. We are investigating a murder. You need to look professional and behave professionally. Get your hat."

Deke gritted his teeth. "You don't have to instruct me on professionalism. I have investigated more murders than you have."

He regretted the words instantly. "Sorry, that was uncalled for." Deke lowered his head and lifted his hands.

Tim cleared his throat. "You can't be objective here. Cecil's your friend, and your investigation will be tainted by that."

Deke started to speak, but Tim raised a hand. "Even if you do everything by the book, an attorney will filet you on the stand. You're pasturing your horses on Cecil's property, giving him rides to the nursing home—in short, you're buddies. Not to mention your animosity toward Lamb and his kid."

Tim put his hand on Deke's shoulder and squeezed lightly. "If you believe your friend is innocent, don't set him up for a mistrial. Stay out of this. I need you to gather evidence. But understand, this may clear him or convict him. If you cannot do this, sit this one out."

His hand remained on Deke's shoulder. "And for the record, you may have investigated more murders, but I've solved more graffiti crimes than you."

Deke relaxed at the familiar smile crease in Tim's face. "Point taken. Tim, I don't care what the wolf in 'Lamb's' clothing told you. Cecil doesn't have a wicked bone in his body. I do know him well."

Tim nodded and removed his hand from Deke's shoulder. "I understand, and I trust your instincts. You've never let me down. I just want to get ahead of your emotions and prevent you from hurting yourself and Cecil. Copy?"

"Yeah."

"Okay, let's go, and let me do the talking. I will give Burgess his Miranda warnings, and you will be a witness. Then we will take him down to the interrogation room and ask questions. Finally, I will ask Detective Mueller from the State Police to come in and assist me."

Deke cocked his head, but Tim broke into his thoughts. "Think about it. Evan is a good guy, a good detective, and he is not intimidating. We need an objective investigator. And even I am at risk of being subjective. Whether Cecil is innocent or not, no judge, jury, or prosecutor can be given reason to say something smells about this case."

Deke rocked his head from side to side. "And I thought I was the only one who had the cunning to handle cases in western Kentucky. You are giving me competition."

Tim smiled and punched Deke on the shoulder. "Let's go."

They both moved down the path toward Cecil's cabin. As they neared the porch, Plato rose and went into a stiff-legged stance. A low growl emanated from his muzzle.

Tim slowed, allowing Deke to pass him. "I believe you when you say Cecil doesn't have a wicked bone in his body, but I am not so sure about his dog."

Deke chuckled. "Plato, is that any way to greet an old friend."

At the sound of Deke's voice, Plato wagged his tail excitedly. He ran down the steps to greet Deke.

Deke stepped onto the first step and petted Plato as the dog licked his other hand. "Where is Cecil? Oh, this is Sheriff Tim. He is a friend—you can trust him."

Tim stepped closer and offered a tentative hand. "How ya doing, boy?"

Plato looked at Tim suspiciously, but a few sniffs of his hand sponsored a tail wag. Acceptance.

"Cecil usually answers his door when Plato alerts him." Deke stepped up onto the porch and approached the door.

"Cecil. Cecil, you home?" Deke called out.

No answer. Deke reached for the door handle, then saw it was already open a few inches.

"Wait." Tim stepped up beside him, hugging the exterior wall with his back. He unstrapped his holstered weapon but did not draw it.

"That's not necessary," Deke whispered.

"Police protocol. You know that."

Deke nodded, and his hand hesitated on the door handle. Could Tim be right? Cecil's ginseng crop was a lot of money. Suppose he found Bobby and Calvin on his property? Suppose the little man just snapped?

"Cecil, this is Deke. Are you home? Please let me in. The sheriff is with me."

He tapped on the door and waited for a few seconds. Then again.

"Cecil, you alright? I am coming in."

Deke looked at the sheriff, and he nodded as he flattened himself against the wall and slowly eased the Glock out of its holster. He held it, pointing downward with his trigger finger extended along the barrel. Despite his friendship with Cecil, he respected Tim's caution. He had learned a long time ago to expect the unexpected.

Deke shoved the door open. As his eyes adjusted to the dim interior, he noticed a cup lying on its side on the table and a book and note pad on the floor. He stepped into the cabin then he saw a scrawny white leg protruding from a denim pant on the floor behind the table. Deke rushed around the table and found Cecil on his back, with a cloth over his face. A medical injector lay beside him.

"Oh, Cecil." Deke started to check for a pulse, but Cecil stirred slightly and moaned. He slowly reached up with skinny gnarled fingers and pulled the cloth from his face.

"Oh, jeez—what happened?"

A dark face, disfigured by swollen flesh, stared upward at Deke. Recognition slowly glinted in Cecil's eyes.

"Bees," his raspy voice intoned.

"We have to get you to the hospital, Cecil." Deke spoke in what he hoped were assuring tones.

"No, no. I'll be all right." His hand brushed the injector on the floor. "Got them meds in time. Just let me rest a minute. Deke, would you get me a drink?"

"I'll get it." Tim had returned his weapon to the holster. He walked to the kitchen area, his head swiveling, trying to take in all the eclectic array of bottles, plants, mushrooms, and stacks of books. He glanced at the photo of the hermit's parents on the wall.

Deke returned his attention to the injured man.

"Bees? You mean they got you, and you had a reaction?"

"Even though I live in nature, sometimes nature is unkind." Cecil grinned, showing his tiny but gleaming white teeth.

Tim returned with the cup and held it out to Deke.

"Let me sit up." Cecil was already struggling from the floor.

Deke assisted him and spoke softly. "Just sit here against the cabinet until you can regain your strength."

Cecil nodded and accepted the glass of warm water. He took a long drink, then breathed heavily.

Cecil nodded toward Tim.

"Who's your friend? I see he is wearing the same club uniform as you."

"Oh. I'm sorry, Cecil. Where are my manners? This is Sheriff Tim Holloman. And a high school buddy."

"Yes. Now I recognize you. My eyes were injected with the wrong vitamin to boost my sight. Vitamin 'Bee' instead of vitamin 'A.'" Cecil laughed at his joke.

Deke smiled but sobered immediately. "Cecil, I found your ginseng patch. Is that where you got stung?"

Tim stepped forward and leaned toward the seated man. "A pleasure to meet you, Cecil. Not under these conditions, of course. I would like to ask some questions, but first, we want to get you medical care. Is it all right if we give you a lift to the ER?"

Cecil seemed to be recovering as they studied him. "Oh no. I will be all right. This is not my first time being stung. Thank you, though." He hesitated. "What questions?"

Tim spoke gently, but with authority. "Well, I know you and Deke are good friends, but the questions I have for you are on a professional legal level. First, are you familiar with Miranda rights that police use to advise people before they talk to them?"

Cecil peered at the sheriff, as if sizing him up. "Yes, I am. I have never been the recipient of those advisements, though. Am I to assume that you consider me a *person of interest*?"

"Well, certain events have occurred that warrant my advising you of your rights. I just want to get this out of the way. Okay?"

Cecil nodded. "Go ahead."

Deke studied Cecil's face as Tim intoned the rights. "Okay, you have the right to remain silent ..."

Tim finished and asked Cecil if he wanted to speak to them.

Cecil said, "Sure. But what is the charge?"

Tim glanced at Deke, who stared at him blankly.

Tim cleared his throat. "Mr. Burgess, Calvin Lamb is accusing you of murdering Bobby Page."

Deke could practically sense the birds stop chirping, and the cacophony of insects lowering their volume. Seconds lapsed while Cecil looked from face to face.

"I did not murder Bobby. I wouldn't murder anybody." His soft voice was almost inaudible.

"We would like you to help us clear your name. If you come down to the office willingly, we won't have to place you under arrest. You can answer some questions, and maybe we will just detain you for a short time. That is if you want to talk to us. At this point, we must take you in, but we are still sifting through evidence." The sheriff waited.

Cecil fixed his swollen eyes on Deke. They held no fear—just sadness. "Okay. I am willing to go with you." His eyes never left Deke.

"I will have to search you. Police policy. And I will have to place handcuffs on you." Deke realized then his friend was taking precautions against arrest procedure violations.

Without waiting for an answer, the sheriff quickly patted him down, relieved him of the pocketknife he was carrying and handed it to Deke. While Tim reached for the cuffs on his belt, Cecil broke the awkward silence. "I'll be wanting that back. It would be all right if you sharpened it, too." A wry smile creased the man's face.

Deke nodded. "I'll take care of it." God. The man didn't realize the seriousness of this. Maybe he had snapped.

Tim lightly gripped his left arm and started to pull it behind his back. A groan escaped Cecil's mouth as he winced. The lawman paused.

"Is that necessary, Tim? He has severe joint pain."

Tim sighed. "Look, it is not by the book, but I will cuff you in front. I don't want you to suffer any discomfort."

Cecil said, "Well, I am already discomforted with a murder charge. Any side benefits I can get will be welcome."

While Tim underwent the process of cuffing him in front, Deke discreetly removed his notebook and pen from his pocket. He glanced at the two men, satisfied they were engrossed in the mechanics of cuffing.

Deke scribbled on the bottom of a blank page, creased the page above his writing, and used the crease to tear it cleanly from his book. In a matter of seconds, he had returned pen and notebook to his shirt pocket and folded the piece of paper in half.

Deke looked up to see the sheriff straighten and ask Cecil, "Too tight?"

Cecil shook his head, and Deke stepped closer to the pair. He grasped Cecil's arm while Tim still had a grip on the cuffs. The deputy spoke in a matter-of-fact tone. "I will steady him. You lead the way, Sheriff."

Tim gave his deputy a quizzical look. "Oh, okay."

The trio started down the trail with the sheriff in the lead. All three heard steps and heavy panting. Plato was following.

Deke squatted and petted the dog. "No, Plato, you have to stay here. Cecil will be all right. Honestly." Deke could see the questioning look in the dog's eyes.

Cecil turned his head. "Plato, I will be back." His eyes were on the dog, but he addressed Deke. "My friend, will you make sure he is all right?"

Deke's throat tightened. "You know I will."

The men again started down the path. They glanced back to see Plato sitting on the edge of the clearing, looking forlorn.

As Deke and Cecil followed Tim down to the parked vehicles, Deke placed the scribbled note he had in his free hand and tucked it into Cecil's bib overall chest pocket. Cecil glanced at Deke but said nothing.

When they arrived at the vehicles, Tim opened the door to his unit and assisted Cecil inside. When Cecil was belted in, he shut the door. Tim started the engine to keep the Jeep cool and stepped out.

He nodded toward the back of the Jeep. Deke followed his head motion to the back.

"Okay, Deke," the sheriff began, "I am giving you what we got, and I need what you have too. Young Calvin claims he and Bobby Page were looking for cows that had strayed onto Burgess property. He said the fence was down, and they rounded them up and drove them back onto Lamb's property. Well, it seems they had one lost calf not accounted for, and they pushed deeper into Cecil's property. They discovered a partially hidden garden. A ginseng garden. Calvin claims that while they were looking at the garden, they heard a war hoop behind them and turned to see the Waxman, Cecil, charging them with a pickax. From the description, I think it's a rock hammer. Cal said he was like a crazy man, and before they could explain their trespassing, they decided he wouldn't listen. So, they ran, trying to get back to a safe zone. He said he figured if he got on Lamb property, they would be safe."

Tim paused and looked in the rear window. Cecil's head barely rose higher than the seatback. Then, still studying the form, he asked, "Now, what did you find?"

Deke gave the sheriff a summary of what he had seen, and the evidence collected. He also reported finding the rock hammer.

Tim scuffed his boot in the gravel as he pondered the toe. Deke knew he was preparing how to say something to him he did not want to say. Finally, he looked up and fixed his sky-blue eyes on his friend.

"Deke, aside from the cut wire and oddly placed feed corn, this doesn't look good. I know you are fond of Mr. Burgess, and I don't want to see you go out on a limb that will break."

Deke let his breath out in a snort. "Cecil is not capable of hurting anyone—physically, mentally, emotionally, or ... spiritually." He hadn't meant to add the descriptive terms. His words even surprised himself.

As they traded looks, unit three pulled up and Tim turned his head to the young deputy driving. "Carl, we got it covered, you can resume patrol."

Carl saluted and backed onto the blacktop.

Tim laid a hand on Deke's muscular shoulder. "I know you believe that with your whole heart, but you have only known him for about three or four months. Do you know him? He is a hermit, and his garden keeps him fed. Even a normal person could snap given these conditions."

Deke forced a smile. "Tim, you know I am a walking polygraph machine. That's why you hired me. I know people. Lies make my synapses start firing."

"Okay, okay, but just don't burn out your synapses. I also hired you because you are a critical thinker. Use that gift. I am taking him to town, and I need someone to witness it if he decides to talk. Can you play cop for a possible interrogation?"

Deke scowled. "Play cop! I *are* one."

Tim shook his head, "All right, 'are one,' let's go."

CHAPTER 27

Deke followed Tim and his detainee to the courthouse. He fought the urge to call Rita and enlist her help. It would be unethical for him to execute his duties while simultaneously playing co-conspirator with the defense.

Lamb was lying, for sure. He wanted to turn off and race to the boy's home and jerk a confession out of him. But Cecil needed him, and such action wouldn't go over well with the sheriff or the courts. He hoped—no, he prayed—that Cecil would follow through and call Rita.

Please let Rita be available.

At the courthouse, Deke grabbed his evidence bag and camera while Tim assisted the cuffed prisoner out of the Jeep. After he closed the door, he nodded at Deke. "I will take Mr. Burgess to the interview room. Meet me there after you dispose of your gear. I'll see if Amanda is available to take notes."

If Cecil decided to talk, it would be recorded. Tim was arranging Amanda's potential presence as a witness to the interrogation. He gave Tim a blank stare. "Okay, give me ten."

Deke rushed ahead and went to his basement office. As he stowed his gear, he gazed at the black phone on the wall with the blinking lights designating internal lines. He paused and lifted his hand toward the phone, then stopped. "No."

He noted the laceration on his thumb and turned toward his desk, pulling open a drawer. He rummaged through the miscellaneous collection—paper clips, pens, pocketknives, chewing gum, antiacid tablets—until he found a box half-filled with bandages.

Deke grunted at his find and selected the appropriate size to cover his wounded thumb. He quickly unwrapped the adhesive pad and applied it to his injured area. Then he opened his office door. The phone still beckoned. He shook his head, stepped into the hallway, and locked his door. Finally, he bounded upstairs and strode down the hall to the sheriff's office.

Dusty stood behind the counter. "Hi, I'm Amanda." He giggled in a high voice while patting an invisible hairdo.

"Hmmph. Amanda, when you greet customers, you know the protocol. Yer supposed to be standing."

Dusty frowned. "I am standing ..." His voice trailed off.

Deke peered over the counter. "Oh, I see. You are."

"Okay, you're one up on me. I will get you back." Dusty's tone became serious. "They are in the interrogation room—with the Waxman."

Deke started around the counter to the closed door of the room. He glanced back to Dusty. "He has a name. Cecil Burgess."

Dusty reddened. "I'm sorry, buddy. I messed up."

Deke paused with his hand on the doorknob. "It's okay. I'm more politically correct about Cecil. Funny thing about it. I get more offended than he does." He pushed the door open and stepped inside. He heard Dusty's subdued "sorry" behind him.

The sheriff looked up as the grim-faced deputy entered the small room. Comfort-challenged chairs guarded the heavy oak table. The fluorescent lighting cast a surreal glow to the scene.

Tim nodded toward one of the chairs. "Deputy Campbell, have a seat." He had deliberately insinuated an atmosphere of formality. Deke met his eyes, nodded, and seated himself.

Deke looked at Cecil and smiled reassuringly. "You doing all right?"

Cecil returned a tight smile and nodded. "I don't know how to act like a criminal. This is all new to me."

The sheriff cleared his throat. "Mr. Burgess, you have been informed of your rights, and you elected to speak to counsel, not to us. So, we wait for Ms. Courtney's arrival."

Tim spoke to Cecil, but his eyes were on Deke. "It seems he had Ms. Courtney's phone number handy."

"Oh. Well, that doesn't surprise me. Cecil has met her several times."

"Uh-huh," Tim responded.

Deke gave Tim a wide-eyed look and shrugged. Amanda sat in the corner of the room with a legal pad on her lap. She nervously recrossed her legs, making a rustling sound. All three men looked at her.

"Oh, Amanda. Didn't see you. Are you taking orders for lunch?" Deke grinned.

She scowled. "Do I look like a short-order cook?"

It was a welcome relief from the tension. Deke and Tim chuckled. Cecil let a slight smile cross his face.

The chuckles were interrupted by a slight tapping on the translucent glass of the door. Then it opened slightly as Dusty's head and shoulders appeared. "Sheriff, Ms. Courtney is here to see her client."

"Okay, send her in."

Dusty opened the door wider while turning, but Rita was already through the gate and striding toward the interrogation room. The deputy quickly stepped aside to grant the defense attorney entrance.

Tim and Deke rose, the sheriff gesturing to a seat beside Cecil. "Please."

Rita searched both standing men's faces.

"I understand you are acquainted with Mr. Burgess?" Tim queried.

"Yes, I am. I have been selected to represent Mr. Burgess. I would like to know the charges." Rita sat and laid her small leather briefcase on the oak table. She did not wait for an answer but turned her head and focused on Cecil.

"You okay?" She placed her hand on the back of Cecil's scarred hand and looked at his head. He turned with a wistful smile to Rita. She recoiled from his swollen face.

Tim did not give her a chance to ask what he knew her question would be. "We found him like this. But the swelling has already gone down dramatically. He said he got into a nest of bees."

Rita's gaze remained fixated on Cecil. Finally, after a few seconds, she seemed to gather her wits and licked her lips. "Why didn't you take him to the emergency room? That looks serious."

Tim cleared his throat and spoke softly. "When we arrived, Mr. Burgess had treated himself and appeared to have recovered. He expressed a desire for no further treatment."

"Isn't department policy to let the medical professionals determine the status of injuries? Do any of you have your medical licenses?"

Quiet ruled the room, then Cecil spoke. "Oh no, Miss Rita. I was on the mend and did not want to go to the hospital. These officers treated me quite well."

"Did they ask you if you wanted to see a physician?"

"They did."

"Sheriff Holloman, on behalf of my client, I demand you provide him with professional medical care. Before you incarcerate him—if that is your intent."

Ohh, Rita. Was she stalling to keep her defendant out of the pokey? Deke really didn't want to see that happen either. But she was just postponing it.

"But it's my choice. I don't want to go to the hospital." The little man had panic in his eyes.

Deke moved toward his phone. "Listen, why can't we call Doc Sullivan? He's retired but still licensed. He's helped us in a pinch when we had combative suspects and didn't want them to have hospital staff at their mercy. I'm sure he'd be more than willing to check Cecil—I mean Mr. Burgess out. Ease the pressure a bit. The doc's a stress-free medicine man."

Tim grabbed the ball from Deke and ran with it. "Yes, we can do that. Would you be agreeable to that, Mr. Burgess?"

All eyes turned to Cecil, whose panic attack seemed to dissolve. He gave a wry smile. "Yes, yes. I would like that. Dr. Sullivan was a patient of mine."

"Okay, counselor, then it's settled." Tim nodded to Deke, who started punching in Sullivan's contact number into his cell phone. He stood to step out of the conference room. "We'll get Doc over here right away, and he can check Mr. Burgess out."

Rita assented and jotted some notes in her memo pad. "Okay. I need some private time with my client. Again, what's the charge?"

Deke paused, not wanting to hear, but unable to leave before the words were spoken.

"I am afraid right now it is suspicion of murder. However, no formal charges have been brought by the county prosecutor's office."

"So, you are not going to hold him?" Rita stopped writing and looked up.

"Ma'am, we will get the full reports over to the attorney's office, but I am afraid it will be tomorrow before he can come before the judge for arraignment."

"Then you will be holding him. Which makes it all the more important to have a doctor check him out before you incarcerate him overnight."

"Deke, go ahead." The sheriff nodded again at his deputy.

"Okay. While you're contacting the doctor, could you give me some time with my client? In private." Both men and Amanda exited the room.

CHAPTER 28

Deke completed his report. He pushed back from his desk and thumped his pen on the side of his jaw—opening and closing his mouth to emit variations in hollow tones.

Cecil could not commit murder. He didn't have it in him. That Lamb kid was tied into this in some way. Could Cecil have snapped? All those years of living alone? The illness? The threat to his livelihood? Could any of these have sent him into a fit of rage? No. It was not possible.

Deke stood and looked at his watch. Almost six o'clock. He hadn't heard from Rita, but she'd probably completed her interview with Cecil. He retrieved his hat from the deer antler rack in the corner and grabbed his completed report before leaving his basement office.

As soon as he pushed the glass doors open and walked onto the marble floor hallway, Deke saw Rita clutching her small leather case and coming out of the sheriff's office. Her erect posture and clicking heels reminded him of a model on a runway. She sure was pretty. No—beautiful. But unlike other women he had known, she did not seem to know it.

Deke grinned. "You know your walk makes these stern halls melt."

Rita drew closer, and he could see her blush. "Stop it. You will never change."

Her eyes radiated warmth. She gave a furtive glance around.

"Nobody but these walls can witness a kiss I plant on your lips." Deke smiled.

Rita smiled and shook her shoulder-length brown hair. They stopped a few feet from each other, and her face grew serious. "Deke, we need to put our relationship on hold until this is resolved."

"Okay. Let's go over to the cafe and strategize how we'll carry on a clandestine affair. I know you'll struggle, but absence makes the heart grow fonder."

"I am serious. We don't want to jeopardize Cecil's defense in any way. The optics of arresting officer and defense attorney being in some relationship is bad enough, but the actual case could be compromised."

"Oh, goody, goody. You said we had a relationship. True confessions." Deke clasped his hands under his chin and hunched his shoulders in a caricature of uncontrolled glee.

"Will you behave?" Rita giggled.

A serious Deke replied, "Okay. As much as I am going to hate that, I agree. Cecil's life is on the line."

Rita nodded, and Deke spoke again. "Look, I was going to get Cecil something to eat from the café. Would you take care of that for me? Then I don't have to enter the premises and cause you to swoon."

"I already had planned on that."

"And I'll talk to Tim and see about getting Cecil held in a solitary holding cell and not stuck in the county jail with the general population."

Rita said, "Done. Tim already told me he would place him where he would be safe from others, and the doctor could examine him privately."

Deke exhaled. Tim, for all his by-the-book adherence, had seen fit to give Cecil a special consideration. "Good ol' Tim."

Rita's brows raised. "Oh, almost forgot. He asked me if you would feed and water Plato." She lowered her voice. "Tell him what is going on. He said Plato would be worried. So, I told him if you couldn't do it, I would take care of it."

"Yeah, I guess when you are alone, you share your secrets with your pets. But, come to think about it, I got Zorro and Mandy. If they exposed our conversations to the outside world, I would be in a heap of trouble."

"And you got me to share with, too," Rita spoke in a hushed voice.

Deke did not have his usual comeback. "Do I? I like that." He wanted to kiss her, but he refrained.

A few seconds passed, and they just looked at each other. Then, finally, Deke cleared his throat and spoke. "Yeah, I will take care of Plato. You take care of Cecil."

Rita nodded and turned to leave the courthouse. "I'll see you in the morning, I guess. At the arraignment."

"You betcha." Deke's eyes followed Rita's petite frame as she descended the stairs to the main doors of the courthouse. As she stepped through the door, she glanced back, and they locked eyes one last time.

God ... I know I haven't talked to you in a while. But please let this be resolved quickly

The face of the homeless man crashed into the windshield of Deke's patrol car. Wide eyes on a bloody face slid down to the hood and slowly morphed into another face—Cecil's face. The panic-stricken eyes matched Cecil's look on hearing he was a suspect in a murder case. Deke shot up in bed. The sheets stuck to his sweating body.

Deke's waking brain fought for order and understanding. He wiped the perspiration from his face with both hands and placed them on his knees, which he'd drawn up, cross-legged. He looked around the room, attempting to get his bearings. The digital clock on the nightstand glowed in the predawn darkness. Gradually, Deke's breathing returned to normal.

No more sleeping now—his mind had already started working on what faced him this day. Cecil's arraignment. Yesterday's events streamed back into his consciousness as Deke sipped his coffee. Cecil would be arraigned by nine or ten today. Poor guy. Hopefully his night in jail hadn't been too taxing.

Some niggling thought probed his mind, but he could not pinpoint it. Something he was missing.

Memories of the interactions he had had with Cecil over the summer flooded his brain. The distorted man with a quiet demeanor and gentle helping spirit could not have committed murder. If he had committed the act while in a fit of rage, he would have confessed no matter the consequences. He was that kind of man.

What was he missing? He glanced at the clock on the kitchen wall. Now it was showing five twenty. Funny how clocks stood silent guard over you and reminded you of your obligations.

"Stand guard. Stand guard. That's it!" Deke slammed the cup down on the counter and grabbed his keys.

In a minute, he was out the door and coaxing his truck to life. The old truck seemed to sense his urgency. It dispensed of its usual coughing and demands for a warm-up and engaged the engine with the transmission.

SUMMER OF THE WAXMAN

The truck left the driveway and traveled down the quiet street toward the rising sun as one-by-one, the streetlights relieved themselves from duty.

CHAPTER 29

Deke halted his Jeep at Cecil's driveway a few feet from the padlocked steel cable. He hurried down the path to Cecil's cabin.

Plato leapt to his feet, hackles raised and started with a rumbling growl that rose to a series of deep-throated barks.

"It's only me, Plato."

Plato relaxed at the familiar voice. His demeanor abruptly changed as he bounded down the steps, tail wagging. Deke squatted and tussled his furry neck. Plato reciprocated by licking the deputy's hands.

Deke laughed. "Okay, okay. You're glad to see me." He glanced at the trail into the woods and stood with a sigh. Plato gave a plaintive whine.

"All right. I am in a hurry, but I'll take care of your breakfast first." He strode toward the door of the cabin, stooping to sweep up Plato's empty dish. Plato remained outside, staring toward the hidden county road.

Poor guy. He is expecting his master to show up. If my hunch is right, he will be showing up.

Deke filled Plato's dish and freshened his water bucket. Then he gave the dog a final pat as it started to nose the food and descended the steps, walking down the path toward the murder scene. The sound of running paws and panting breath caused him to turn. Plato stopped beside him and looked imploringly into his eyes.

"Okay, you can keep me company, but stay out of my way."

Deke entered the small clearing beside the concealed garden. The stillness was only broken by chattering squirrels chasing each other in the upper reaches of the black oak trees. He stood still, and his eyes swept the lower parts of the bushes and trees surrounding the ginseng garden. Dividing the area into quadrants, he surveyed the growth:

He studied the quadrants in a general overview.

He inspected the details of the quadrants. Minutes went by as he made his 360-degree reconnaissance.

Plato seemed to sense his friend was doing important work and sat quietly on his haunches.

Nothing. Deke stretched and rubbed his eyes before beginning his second survey of the higher quadrants. At the third quadrant, he stopped.

"Hello." Just maybe.

Deke moved around the garden's perimeter, forcing his way through growth until he stood in from of a medium-sized red cedar tree. He moved closer, and the tiny fragment of what he had seen became wholly visible.

"You little turkey. You knew what you were doing." Deke grinned.

The game camera that Deke had given Cecil was solidly strapped to a branch about twelve feet above the ground. It was mounted so that lens and motion sensor had an unobstructed view of the garden and down the trail to

Cecil's cabin. Choosing the evergreen of the cedar to provide year-round camouflage was the crowning touch.

Deke made his way to the base of the tree and looked upward. He wouldn't be able to get close enough to retrieve the camera by climbing the cedar tree's limbs.

"Cecil, you fox. You must have used a ladder to get up there."

Deke mused at the image of Cecil's frail body transporting a ladder to this spot and then his struggling climb to mount the camera. "Wait a minute. He must have the ladder near here to check the card."

Leaving the tree, he scouted outward in ever-widening circles. He found the aluminum ladder about thirty feet away. Cecil had covered it with a green plastic tarp. Ferns in woven baskets sat on the covering, making it almost invisible.

Deke brought the ladder back to the cedar, working it into the branches and propping it on the trunk near the camera. He climbed up until he could reach the instrument and opened the card storage. The card seemed to be in good shape. Placing it in his shirt pocket, he descended the ladder and left it as he hurried back to the cabin.

"C'mon, Plato. I've got what I need to hopefully get your master back home." Plato, as if he understood, ran beside Deke back to the cabin.

He bounded up the steps, threw the door open, and entered. Deke's eyes combed the dark interior for the familiar computer he had given Cecil to read the photo card. His eyes stopped and returned to the glass case over the workbench. There it was—the computer with its familiar Chicago Bears sticker adorning the top. In a matter of minutes, he had the computer up and running by hooking the battery to an AC converter. When the computer booted up, Deke inserted the card into the reader slot. He dropped into a wooden chair and placed the laptop on the battered table.

Be there—be there.

Images sprang to life on the screen. First, a close-up of a robin settling on the branch in front of the lens. Then two does made their way up the trail, stopping to graze. Finally, several frames recorded their dining experience.

Come on. Don't fill up with wildlife. God, please help him.

Had he inadvertently prayed?

The ensuing photos were short bursts of Cecil examining his crop. He watched as Cecil's crooked grin was recorded when he unearthed a sizeable ginseng root. Finally, a photo showed him standing. Beside him was the rock hammer embedded in the ground—the murder weapon.

The next photo froze him, as a bucket fell from his hands near the fencing of his garden. An agonizing look on his face as his hands waved in the air. Although Deke could not see the bees, he could see his friend's painful reaction. The next photo was of Cecil hunched over, running down the trail.

"Okay, God. I am praying that the camera batteries lasted, and the card is not filled up. Yes, Lord, it's me asking for help."

Two figures appeared walking on the trail from the opposite direction of Cecil's cabin. Deke leaned forward. He could only see the backs of two men. The following still photo was of Calvin Lamb entering the open gate to Cecil's ginseng garden, followed by Bobby Page. They were there—another image of the two men engaged in conversation.

Another click and Calvin was shown picking up the rock ax forgotten by Cecil in his panicked retreat to his cabin. Then the photos he'd been searching for appeared.

Bang, bang. I gotcha Lamb.

A sequence of photos activated by the motion sensor showed the murder in progress. Calvin throwing the ax—striking Bobby in the back with the pointed blade—penetrating the area near the spine.

Deke leaned back in the chair, watching as photo after photo showed Lamb's efforts to extinguish all evidence. He had done a good job of obliterating bloodstains and footprints on the trail—and the transfer of the body. He found himself breathing hard, then the rising of sadness for Bobby. Bobby never had a chance.

His introspective mood was interrupted by the old clock on the wall ticking. A quarter until nine. Cecil's arraignment. "I gotta move."

Deke's hands moved quickly as he shut down the computer, unplugged it, and ejected the small card from it. He noticed Plato lying in the open doorway. "Plato, I'm in a hurry. Cecil's coming home."

He shooed the dog outside and, clutching the computer, jogged to his truck. Gravel spewed from the tires as he backed onto the blacktop. He seized his cell and called the dispatcher. "Orville, get hold of the sheriff and tell him to stall the arraignment. I am on my way. I'll be there in five. Over and out."

So, I lied about the time. I know, Lord, you will forgive me, but Tim might not.

CHAPTER 30

Rita arrived early at the courtroom. Judge Whitmore, a crusty old-timer, sat on the bench. She liked him. Despite not having kept up with changing jurisprudence, he had a reputation for calling cases as he saw them, which to her recollection, had never been anything but honest. A glance at her watch informed her she had a twenty-minute countdown to Cecil's arraignment hearing.

An attorney from Princeton was trying to convince Judge Whitmore why his client should not face jail time for confiscating a city park bench while in an inebriated state. Courtroom spectators tittered, prompting the judge to strike his gavel on the wooden block.

"This is a courtroom, not the Jimmy Kimmel Show."

Oh boy, the judge was not a happy camper this morning.

Rita looked at the closed side door with expectant eyes. They should be bringing Cecil in at any moment. He must have been terrified at what was happening—especially being innocent. He said he was, and she believed him.

The judge's verdict brought Rita back to the present.

"Your guilty plea for theft of city property is stained by your admission of being publicly intoxicated and driving your vehicle home, for which no charges have been brought. My sentence in consideration for these factors will be fair. You are hereby ordered to three days in jail, granted one day off the sentence for time already served, and a two hundred dollar fine."

The gavel banged loudly, causing Rita to jump.

"Pay the clerk." The judge twisted around in his robes as he pulled a white handkerchief from his pocket and blew his nose loudly.

This brought another round of giggles from the crowd, to which he elevated his brushy gray eyebrows. Rita watched his hand tighten on the gavel, and he lifted a few inches but laid it back down. Then, while eyeing the spectators with a stern look, he snatched the gavel so fast and delivered another blow to the block on his bench that caused some in the court to jump again.

Judge Whitmore surveyed the group, now sitting upright and quiet. They relaxed again when he directed the clerk to action. "Next case."

The side door opened, and all heads swiveled to Deputy Delany and the small figure in bib overalls.

Rita appreciated that they had not placed Cecil in an orange jumpsuit. Anyone looks guilty in orange before they even are tried.

Delaney had turned to uncuff the prisoner and blocked the view of the courtroom. The sheriff followed the two but did not remain with them. Tim stepped away from his deputy. The bailiff returned from taking custody of the bench burglar and approached the bench, leaning over the clerk as they spoke in whispers.

Cecil was freed from his cuffs. Delaney turned and faced the court. A collective gasp filled the courtroom as the people took in the sight of the little hermit. Rita whirled around in her chair and scowled at the occupants. "Shush!"

She returned her attention to the front. The judge's stern countenance was focused on her alone.

"Counselor, I will do the 'shushing.'"

"I apologize to the court." She felt her face heating.

The judge turned to the courtroom. "Shush!" The gavel came down as an emphasis.

Rita lifted her eyes in surprise. The judge met her gaze. Was that a wink?

It was a fleeting expression, probably not caught by anyone. But she had embarrassed herself and needed to regain the high ground. She nodded a thank-you.

Delaney guided Cecil over to her table. "Have a seat, Mr. Burgess. If you need anything, I will be sitting right behind you."

"Thank you."

Cecil turned slowly toward his defense attorney. His sparse hair floated in a breeze generated by a ceiling fan. "Good morning, Miss Rita. Thanks for being here."

Rita smiled and touched his frail hand. "Wouldn't miss it. You're my friend, and I'm honored to help you."

The main doors creaked open and curious eyes were drawn to the latecomer who dared to interrupt Judge Whitmore's courtroom proceedings.

Rita, too, turned in her seat, wondering why the bailiff was not attempting to intercept the interloper. It was Deke. The burly deputy strode toward the prosecutor and the sheriff, seated at the table adjacent to Rita and her client. The judge frowned but remained silent. Deke didn't slow until he reached the wooden gate separating the spectators from the court floor. Then she noticed the laptop computer tucked under his arm.

"Your Honor, I ask the court to forgive my intrusion, but it is imperative that I speak to the prosecution on an urgent matter relevant to this case. The evidence may amend his filings."

The judge sighed, pursed his lips, then spoke. "This is highly irregular. Deputy Campbell, I have witnessed some of your irregularities in the past. Nevertheless, if memory serves me correctly, your actions have proven to be historically appropriate. Counselor, I will adjourn for fifteen minutes for you to consult with law enforcement."

His hand raised the trusty gavel, but it stayed its descent with the appeal from Deke. "If it pleases the court, I will need only three minutes or so. No need to adjourn."

Rita cringed. The judge was not one to take guidance from anyone. She was relieved when the judge returned the gavel to the block quietly, and his frown disappeared.

"Very well. I will give you four minutes."

Deke had already opened the computer and turned it on. "Thank you, Your Honor."

He placed the computer on the table in front of the State's Attorney, Jim Croft, and Tim, who was leaning forward beside him. As the computer booted up, Deke whispered to the prosecutor. She strained her ears to hear but could not make out his words. Deke inserted a photo card and, with an open hand, gestured to the screen. Spectators moved around in their seats, attempting to see what was being shown. Rita tried to read the faces of the three men.

The judge leaned back in his high back leather chair, absently tapping his cheek with a pen regarding the group huddled around the screen. The three men straightened their postures in unison. Tim and Deke's faces held blank expressions. Croft stared at the screen, then threw his hands up, mouth agape, and blurted out, "Holy cr ..."

He looked abruptly at the judge, whose eyebrows arched, and offered an apology. "Uh, pardon me, I ... If it pleases the court, may we approach the bench?"

Judge Whitmore lifted his hands in surrender and sighed. "Yes, you may. I seem to have lost all control of this operation anyway."

The prosecutor started toward the bench and then paused to wave Deke forward. Rita could see the judge stiffen. "It appears that by 'may we approach the bench,' you are including Deputy Campbell. Do you also want to include the custodian sweeping the hallway outside?"

"No, Your Honor. I don't think he could add depth to this case."

Rita tried to keep the smile that tugged at her mouth at bay as a few giggles rippled through the spectators. Deke carried the laptop as he approached the bench while the prosecutor spoke in low tones. The judge leaned forward with a puzzled look.

Deke placed the computer on the bench and rotated it to face the judge. He curled his head around to view the unfolding shots using his pen to point out essential details, then clicked the keys to advance to photos. His back was to Rita, and although she strained to hear what he was saying, she could only make out an occasional word.

The judge watched with rapt interest. Rita saw movement at the prosecution's table. Delaney had moved up to a chair beside the sheriff. Delaney stared at the table and nodded as Tim whispered to him. Tim stopped talking, and Delaney leaned back in his seat. A pat on his shoulder from the sheriff and the word 'go' formed on his lips. The deputy lurched out of the chair.

Rita jerked her head around to see the judge's response. He was oblivious to the creaking of the chair as Delaney stood. That was a first. Deke had shown what he wanted the judge to see and was quietly closing the screen on the machine. The county attorney said a few words, and the judge nodded, deep in thought. It was seconds, but it seemed like minutes before he spoke.

Whitmore cleared his throat. "The prosecution has gathered additional evidence in the case of the State versus Cecil Burgess. As a result, they have declined to prosecute and have requested all charges dropped. I concur with their decision."

The judge swiveled his high back chair to face Rita and her client. His eyes focused on Cecil, but his first words were directed at Rita. "Counselor, your client's charge of murder or manslaughter, to be determined by a grand jury, is now dismissed."

The judge turned to Cecil. "Mr. Burgess, on behalf of the Commonwealth of Kentucky and Crittenden County, we offer our apologies for any distress and inconvenience this has caused you by your arrest and subsequent legal actions. A sworn statement from an eyewitness has proven to be false. We will be proactive in clearing your name of any charges."

A smile creased the judge's face. "I hope you will accept our apologies. I, for one, am truly sorry. And I am grateful for the blessing of your homeopathic treatments with which you gifted my mother, Hazel. Momma's last few years were without arthritic pain."

Cecil studied the judge's face, and then a light came on. "Oh, Miss Hazel. I did not connect you with her." He grew solemn. "I am sorry about your loss. But you know she is with Jesus."

The judge's eyes became moist but not for long. He straightened in his chair. "Case dismissed; the court is adjourned." The gavel echoed again.

Deke approached, smiling at the hermit. "Justice has prevailed, my friend. I will take you to pick up your items and bring you home. Plato misses you."

Cecil grabbed Deke's hand with both his hands and swallowed hard. Then, finally, he choked out a "Thank you."

Deke covered both of Cecil's hands with his other hand and whispered, "That's what friends are for."

Rita watched the bonding in silence. Finally, Deke slowly released his grip on the gnarled hands and turned toward Rita. "Good job, counselor."

Rita bristled at his grinning face—then she realized what he was trying to do. He wanted to detach himself from the emotional conclusion.

"Well. We both know if you had done your job competently, this would have never gotten this far."

"Oh, methinks that is an insult. Score one for the clever lawyer." Deke looked over at Cecil.

"Methinks you both are good at your jobs. And I am glad I know you," Cecil said with moist eyes.

Rita impulsively hugged the little man and kissed his cheek.

"Hey, right in front of me. I thought I was the only one." Deke feigned offense.

Cecil shrugged. "Can't help that women are attracted to me. It's a curse." Cecil gave a full-throated laugh, and both Deke and Rita joined him.

Rita grew serious too. "But I don't understand. What happened to throw the case out?"

The group discussion was breaking up, and Tim headed toward them. "Mr. Burgess, I am sorry for having to put you through this," he said. "For what's it worth, I didn't believe you did it. And you had this big bear challenging my authority as sheriff." He nodded at Deke. "I am thinking about putting a written reprimand in his file for talking back to me. That is, if I can find the policy number addressing it."

Cecil extended his hand. "That's all right. Unlike your deputy, you follow the rules and the procedures. But please do give him grace."

"Miss Rita, may I borrow your undercover boyfriend?"

"Be my guest. I need a reprieve from his jokes."

Tim laughed and patted Rita's arm. "Good job!"

Rita said, "Everyone keeps telling me that, yet I did nothing. I'll need to disguise myself to pick up my paycheck."

CHAPTER 31

Tim opened the gate and escorted Deke toward the front courtroom doors. They halted by the closed doors. The prosecutor approached the two men.

"Deke, you will need to supply the evidence of the photo card and make an addendum report to my office. I assume that you are preparing to submit a request for a warrant for Calvin Lamb."

Both officers nodded.

Croft patted Deke's shoulder. "Nice piece of police work, Deke. I was hoping it wouldn't be Mr. Burgess. Now, the real test begins."

"What do you mean?" Deke asked.

"You know better than anyone that the Lamb kid has a powerhouse daddy. He will get the best attorneys to get Calvin off." The county prosecutor replied.

Deke stopped walking and turned to the prosecutor. "The ball's in your court now. You're the one who can make this case stick."

"Yes, yes, I know. But it's going to be a challenge." The lawyer shifted his briefcase from one hand to another and sighed.

He's prepared for failure.

Deke regarded the nervous attorney for a few seconds before he spoke. "A challenge, huh? Listen, I know Bull backed you in the last election. I don't know how much money was thrown in the kitty." Croft reddened and opened his mouth, but Deke raised his hand and continued. "This is a slam dunk. Don't blow it."

The prosecutor lowered his eyes and nodded. Deke reached out and laid a hand on his shoulder. "Look, Frank, I know the pressure you must be feeling. You are not afraid of losing this case. You are a first-rate prosecuting attorney. Don't even consider any outside interference. Stand firm. I believe in you."

"Thanks. I just had some concerns about what the family might pull. You're right. Not to worry." A faint smile touched his lips as he squared his shoulders.

Deke nodded, and he lowered his hand. Frank looked around and spoke in a conspiratorial tone.

"Okay. We don't want this to leak before we have the arrest warrant in hand. So, I am headed back to the office to draw up the documents for Judge Whitmore. He's already agreed to sign the warrant. News travels fast. I wouldn't put it past Calvin's old man to hustle the kid out of the country as soon as he hears. Sheriff, can you post—"

Tim raised his hand. "Already taken care of. Delaney is babysitting Cal until we get that warrant in our hot little hands."

Deke grinned and cocked his head. "Sheriff, that's why you make the big bucks. You're always thinking ahead."

Tim's swat to the gut came out of nowhere.

"Oof! Did you see that? I should have grounds for an HR complaint. Maybe a lawsuit for his next month's paycheck."

"I didn't see nothing." Croft grinned. "I gotta get back to the office. See you guys later." The attorney pushed the door open and walked rapidly to the stairs.

Deke glanced at Rita and Cecil, who were signing paperwork with the court clerk.

"Looks like they're about to finish. I have time before we get the arrest warrant. Think I'll take him upstairs to pick up his personal effects and maybe grab him a bite to eat before I take him home. Then I'll partner with Dusty to pick up our murder suspect."

Tim shook his head. "You got it right until the last sentence. I will partner with Dusty."

Deke started to open his mouth in protest but thought better of it. "I know. You don't want to taint this case with a vindictive deputy targeting his arch enemy's son."

Tim squinted his eyes at Deke. "You know it's more than that. You are the evidence tech who is key to the prosecution and an eyewitness. Think of how a crafty defense would decimate your testimony."

"Point taken. Can I at least be there as a backup if Bull gets rambunctious?"

"You can come and direct traffic as we transport Calvin to lockup."

"Very funny."

Rita and Cecil joined them. She still looked every bit as puzzled as when they'd called the case.

"So, Cecil is a free man and has a clean bill of health. Now, could I be privy to what Deke showed on his computer that turned things around?"

Deke looked at Tim. "I don't see any leakage here, but can you give me permission to go ahead and get Cecil's things, then I can fill them in over lunch?"

Tim nodded slowly. "I think we'll be in the safe zone by then. Okay, permission granted."

"Cecil, come with me, and we will get you fixed up. I know that jail grub is not the finest dining. Oh, and

Counselor, you're welcome to join us since this case has been adjudicated."

Rita brushed some hair from her face and wrinkled her nose in a way that stirred Deke every time he saw it. "I have a better idea. There may be reporters or curious folks at the cafe. So, what say I pick up the food, and you bring Cecil to the Lake George picnic area. This time of the week, we should have the place to ourselves."

"Sounds like a plan. What do you like, Cecil? I am going for their fried chicken plate special today."

"Oh, I need to get home and don't want to put a burden on you two."

Rita frowned. "As your attorney, I will require your presence for lunch."

Tim spoke up. "And as your arresting officer, I require you to go to lunch as thanks for your cooperation."

"Besides," added Deke, "Plato has waited this long—a couple of hours won't matter."

"Okay. You win. Thanks to you all." His mishappen face beamed.

"Tim, can you check the hallway for paparazzi?" Deke inquired.

Tim nodded and opened the door for a peek. "All clear."

Deke watched from the county sheriff's window as Tim and a new deputy named Coursin climbed into his vehicle to go to the Lamb place. Calvin Lamb's arrest warrant had been prepared faster than any Deke had ever seen. Possibly because the county prosecutor wanted to enact what he knew to be right before Bryce Lamb could get his political and legal machine in motion. Tim and his deputy pulled out of the parking place and were on their way. Delaney had radioed that Calvin, Willa, and Violet were home, but

Dad was not. Deke could visualize the encounter that was about to go down.

In one way, he wanted to be there and place cuffs on young Lamb. Specifically, he wanted to do it in front of Calvin's father, Bull. But a sudden sense of sadness squelched his fire as he considered the mess the Lamb family had generated for others over the years. Calvin had grown up with a sense of entitlement and the desire to bully others. The boy hadn't had a chance. Now, another boy lay in the morgue.

Deke was sure Bobby had headed down the path to Cecil's cabin because he didn't want any part of the theft. The photos clearly indicated his intentions.

Still, Deke felt sad for the entire Lamb family, especially for little Violet. And maybe her mom. Lamb had abused Willa even before their marriage. A small cough broke his dark musings. He turned to see Cecil holding a small paper bag.

"Well, I am ready to go. I miss my farm. And freedom."

Deke exhaled. "I'm sure you are ready and do miss both farm and freedom. However, Rita is going to meet us by the lake. It's a nice day, and it should be a quiet picnic. You do need to eat."

"Trying to spare me of being around gawkers?"

Deke pounded the counter, surprising him and causing Amanda to peek around the corner from the file room. "Cecil. We don't care about being seen with you. Don't ever convince yourself of that."

Cecil blinked rapidly. "I didn't mean that you are ashamed to be seen with me. You, Rita, and Pastor Mike are the only people who haven't been ashamed of me. It means a lot to me."

"Sorry, I didn't mean to respond like that. I guess I was thinking about how things turned out in the lives of people

I know. Both ones I like, and ones I dislike. But, if it's any consolation, you belong to the category I like."

"I know. I'm not used to being liked."

Deke chuckled. "Let's go meet Rita."

CHAPTER 32

As Deke and Cecil approached Deke's truck, the deputy heard a familiar voice. "Hey! You guys are hard to chase down."

Pastor Mike was striding toward them, out of breath. He looked from man to man with his bushy eyebrows knitted. "Cecil, are you alright? I was visiting the hospital this morning, and I heard you had been arrested. For murder?"

Cecil shook the pastor's hand. "A case of mistaken identity. But for me, it ended well."

Deke walked around to the front of the vehicle and shook Mike's hand. "Sorry. I thought Rita might have contacted you."

"No, my wife and I were in Evansville. I had to deliver a eulogy for a former member. Heard the news from the nurses on my morning rounds."

"Seems Calvin tried to frame Cecil for the murder of Bobby Page. His body was found on Cecil's property.

"I tried my best to reach Bobby for the Lord, but bad actors easily influenced him." Mike stared at the ground, shaking his head. When he looked back up, Deke saw a sorrowful pain in his friend's eyes. He averted his gaze and changed the subject.

"Cecil's all right. He's had a rough twenty-four hours. The whole case is going to come out in full soon. I just can't talk about it now. We are on the way to get some lunch, and then I will take him home."

"Okay. I will be waiting for the full scoop. Thank the Lord you are all right." The pastor turned to walk away but paused and snapped his fingers. "Oh, almost forgot. Miss May is asking for Cecil to come to see her."

Cecil nodded. "Does she need something?"

"Well, I'm not sure. She seemed a little confused. I think she is low on the foot ointment you gave her. It seems like she has good days and bad. Say, I can take you to her tomorrow night."

"That works for me," Cecil said.

"See you in church, Deke. I couldn't get you there when I first met you. It took a woman. Always takes a woman." Pastor chuckled as he walked away.

"Very funny." Deke looked at Cecil. "Don't say a word."

Cecil got into the truck. "You, attending church? Why, that's a modern-day miracle."

As Tim drove toward the Lamb farm, he weighed what might happen. Bull still hadn't appeared on the scene, and he wasn't on duty at the firehouse. Tim hated not knowing where he was. He did not like surprises.

The rookie interrupted his thoughts.

"Sheriff, you expect he will go peacefully?"

He'd almost forgotten Coursin was there. "Huh? Oh, we plan on bringing him in peacefully—three strategies we use for peaceful arrests. First, surprise—never give the perp a chance to prepare or think. Second, superior force—that means manpower, firepower, and competence. Third, nonconfrontational—you can provoke someone to resist, or you can give them a reason to cooperate."

Even as he spoke, Tim was aware of his own misgivings. He could not shake the dread of Bull returning to the farm during the arrest procedure. He glanced at his deputy and saw his right-hand white-knuckled on his knee as his tongue darted out to moisten his lips.

Oh boy. I could sure use Deke. But no—that's a surefire way to end up with an unpeaceful resolution.

As they neared the driveway entrance, Tim picked up the mic and keyed the button. "Delaney, what's your location and the suspect's location?"

The radio crackled at the release of the button. "I am on foot, north of the house. Viewing back. The suspect is in the pool area."

"Ten-four," Tim responded. He would rather approach Lamb with backup from Delaney than the untried deputy. Beside him, Coursin now had a white-knuckled hand on each knee.

"Delaney, start moving toward the suspect when you see us park. Any sign of anyone in the home?"

"Negative."

"Copy. We are on the drive."

Without looking at the deputy, Tim spoke tersely. "Okay, relax. You cover the front. Let me know if someone else comes down the drive. Got it?"

"Yessir."

The Jeep glided around the circle in front of the stately home and came to a halt. "Don't slam the door," ordered Tim as he opened his door.

Tim approached the side gate that led to the pool area at the rear of the home. He quietly lifted the latch and opened the gate. For a few seconds, he stood still, touching the folded warrant in his hip pocket. No movement or sounds coming from the house. Then, there was a familiar sound of escaping carbonation from opening a drink can. He peered into the pool area. Lamb sat in a lounge chair tilting a beer can into his mouth. He wore knee-length swim trunks and a UK blue T-shirt. Beside the chair sat a pair of blue flip flops.

Tim saw no weapons within reach, and Cal's dress could not conceal anything. He looked to the side of the pool patio and saw a tall frame moving stealthily. He stood behind Lamb's vision scope about twenty yards away, hoping their luck continued.

He strode into the open and walked toward the man as Delaney closed the distance behind him. Not until Calvin lowered the can from his lips did he see the approaching lawman.

Lamb's eyes widened as he stared slack-jawed at the sheriff.

"Morning, Cal. Need to talk to you," Tim walked around the pool toward the staring man.

"Sheriff. Yeah, yeah, good morning." Cal sat upright and swung his legs to the patio. "I thought I—I had given you all you needed to bust Burgess."

His face twisted into a scowl as he noticed Delaney at the back gate. "What's going on! Why do you need your deputies to talk to me?"

"Cal, I'm afraid this visit isn't just to talk to you." He slipped the warrant from his back pocket. "I have a warrant for your arrest, for the murder of Robert Page. Please stand. I am going to advise you of your rights."

Tim watched the man closely. If Cal wanted to rabbit or resist, it would happen now. Delaney had cuffs at the ready as Cal rose with clenched fists.

A gate clinked behind them, and a voice boomed. "What do ya think you're doing?"

Tim cursed under his breath as Bryce Lamb stormed toward them. Lamb was probably packing.

Deputy Coursin followed the enraged man. "Sheriff, he came in and jumped out of his truck. I didn't have a chance to call you."

"It's all right, Coursin," Tim spoke calmly, even though he didn't feel calm. "Mr. Lamb, you need to settle down. I wouldn't be here except for carrying out a court order."

"What court order?" Lamb bellowed.

Delaney had recovered from the intrusion and was reaching for one arm as he softly ordered Cal to put his hands behind his back.

Bull Lamb stood within striking distance. Tim could be a formidable opponent, but the angry father had about fifty pounds on him and a longer reach. In his recollection, Lamb had never lost a fight. The problem was, he would have to wait for him to make the first move.

"Your son is under arrest for the murder of Robert Page. I'm sorry, we need to serve the warrant and take him into custody. Bull, you know me. He will be treated fairly. Don't complicate the situation."

"Murder! You know that ugly, slimy Waxman done it." Spittle shot out of his mouth. "Leave my son alone and get off my property."

The sound of the gate again. "What's happening, Bryce? What are they doing to our son?"

Oh, Lord. Things could not get better. Tim shouted to his deputy, "Keep Mrs. Lamb outside the gate." A small figure followed in Willa's wake. Violet. The child was blinking in confusion behind thick glasses.

The sheriff was rapidly losing control of the situation. No longer did they have superior numbers and the element of surprise.

"Oomph!" Delaney gasped as Calvin drove a sharp elbow to his midriff. Only one wrist cuffed, and the painful strike caused Delaney to release the cuff and stagger backward.

Calvin swung the dangling cuff in a backhand motion reaching up to the deputy's face. The edge of the cuff just missed the police officer's eye but struck a vicious blow to his cheek. Blood spurted everywhere.

Tim spun toward the assailant as Cal leapt over the lounge chair barefooted. He ran around the pool to the fence enclosure and jumped over it, sprawling to the ground.

"Run, baby, run," Willa shouted as Violet broke out in a plaintive wail and tears.

Delaney had recovered his wind, and although blood flowed from his face onto his uniform, he jumped over the lounge chair, following the path of the escaping suspect with long strides.

An angry Tim pivoted toward Lamb with gritted teeth. "Don't. Don't even think about it." He reinforced his command with a stabbing index finger toward the father. He brushed Lamb with a tight shoulder and ran to the gate to head off their escapee. A confused Coursin looked back and forth at Lamb and his sheriff's back and fell into a run behind him.

Calvin had regained his feet and raced toward the side of the house. He was fast. Tim cursed himself for not having enough manpower for a contingency plan. Too late.

Calvin had just about disappeared around the corner of the house when he abruptly halted, as if driven back from an unseen force. "Oomph," Calvin gasped. He fell onto the ground and rolled into a fetal position, clutching his abdomen. Powerful arms reached out, and Calvin's body straightened as the arms drew him out of view around the corner of the house.

Delaney vaulted the fence, then stopped. His entire demeanor changed as he walked toward the corner of the house with a slight smile, pressing a bandana to his cheek.

"Ooh, uhh. Ow, ow. Let go ..." Calvin, wrists cuffed, wriggled like a cornered animal as Deke led him over to Tim.

"You have the right to remain silent. Please take advantage of it. You have the right to counsel ..." Deke intoned Miranda warnings as he walked the man toward the sheriff, who met him at the front of the house.

Deke looked over his shoulder as Delaney followed the pair. "Hmm. Cut yourself shaving?"

"Yeah, wise guy."

Delaney turned his attention to Calvin. "You're lucky, punk, that our department comedian caught you instead of me."

Sullen and red-faced, the cuffed man spat out grass and dirt. His T-shirt had rolled up, exposing a reddened abdomen with the faint outline of a shoe sole. "You'll pay for this, and I know my rights."

"I know you do. I just informed you of them. Did you forget?" Deke feigned concern.

Tim waited for the three men to approach. "I thought you were serving a summons."

Deke grinned. "I finished and thought I would check on my favorite sheriff and comrades. And aren't you glad I did?"

"Let's get him in my unit." Tim heard the footsteps and quickly rolled down Calvin's shirt. No sense in adding to Bull's anger.

Lamb rounded the corner and stopped short, eyes wide, neck veins throbbing. "I should've known Campbell was a part of this. You're not going to get by with this. I will sue you and the county for this. You piece of ..."

"Easy, easy." Tim held up the warrant. "You can do what you want, but we have a legal document to take Calvin into custody right now. So, cool down."

Tim seized Calvin's free arm and whispered, "Deke, it's better I take him in."

Deke nodded and released Calvin's other arm. He turned to Delaney. "Let me see."

Tim paused and looked back as Deke examined Delaney's cheek. "Buddy, I think you're going to need a few stitches ... seriously. You gonna need stitches." Deke squinted up at him as Delaney applied pressure to the bandana.

"You're the one who keeps me in stitches."

"Ha! I knew I had a purpose." Deke chuckled and then turned dark, peering more closely at his friend's cheek.

"I'm okay." Delaney gave a dismissive wave. "I'll get it checked out later. Annie will do it."

"For crying out loud. Your wife is a music teacher. She gonna sing to your cheek?"

Tim interrupted their debate. "Delaney, if you are good enough to drive, go to the emergency room. Coursin and I will take Calvin in. Deke, go make out your report."

Tim didn't waste any time marching the prisoner to his Jeep. But the sight of Willa standing near the corner with Violet clinging to her leg moved him.

"My patrol car is parked on the field road. I'm all right, I got it covered, Deke." Delaney turned and headed to the vehicle obscured by bushes and trees.

Bull growled, "Don't say anything, Cal. I'm getting my lawyers." Then, with a scorching look at Deke, he raced toward the front door of the home.

As Coursin frisked the prisoner and settled Calvin into the Jeep, Tim looked back to see Willa running after Deke with the child in tow. She caught up with his deputy, seized his arm, and faced him, grabbing his other arm tightly. He strained to hear what she was saying. Was she pleading with him? Then Willa abruptly embraced him, crying.

Deke disengaged himself and appeared to talk softly to her. Tim was more concerned that Bull would return and witness his wife's display. "Deke, let's go."

Then kneeling, his deputy pulled little Violet close and spoke to her. Violet wrapped her arms around his neck for a few seconds and sobbed.

Deke broke off from the girls and walked toward his unit, pausing at Tim's vehicle.

"Lamb doesn't deserve his family. He's destructive to all of them. What a piece of work." Deke continued to his Jeep.

Tim shook his head. This would not end well for anyone. Not young Calvin, his family, or the community as a whole.

CHAPTER 33

Rita smiled as she peeked through the blinds at Deke's battered truck gliding to a stop in front of her house. His efforts to tamp down the throaty exhaust on a Sunday morning were endearing. She thought of his rebuttal to her past inquiry about considering getting quieter pipes installed on the aging vehicle—He had looked at her askance and replied, "Are you for real? That'd be like asking a cowboy to trade his boots for sandals." She had tittered, then saw he was serious.

Rita watched Deke place his cowboy hat in the folding hat roof ring above the mirror and pause to check his close-cropped hair. She smiled again. What on earth could be out of place in his hairstyle? Secretly, she hoped he would one day allow his dark thick hair more length—perhaps even a part on the side.

Deke bounced up the walkway, his erect posture bordering on a military march. But, Lord, he was good-looking.

Rita glided into the entry hall, checking her brunette locks in the oval mirror over a tall table. She'd lined up some dolls on the table from different stages of her childhood, starting with a soft sewn infant doll to a Raggedy Ann, culminating with several pre-teen Barbie dolls.

The doorbell rang, but she delayed, examining her makeup in the mirror and sliding her hands over her hips to smooth out any wrinkles, then giving one last pat to the hair. The bell demanded her attention again. He needed to learn patience.

But then again, he's a man who believes in being on time. That's responsible.

She turned and placed her hand on the doorknob. Then came a rapid-fire knock on the door. She yanked it open as Deke was lowering his fist.

"What are you trying to do? Disturb the peace and tranquility of the neighborhood?"

Deke's brown eyes danced as he took in her form. "This neighborhood needs disturbing. You look good enough to be seen with me."

"At my worst, I look good enough to be seen with you. I'll get my purse." Rita turned and leaned over, sliding open a lower drawer in the hallway table.

Deke stepped into the hallway. Rita felt him studying her as she retrieved her purse from the drawer. She didn't mind.

She picked out a color-coordinated purse she had stocked with miscellaneous items. Closing the drawer, she stood and faced the deputy. "There. All ready to go."

Deke frowned. "I don't like your purse. Choose another one."

Perplexed, Rita said, "What are you saying ...?"

She then saw an impish grin tug at his lips. "Oh, you."

"You look great, all over. Front sight and hindsight."

Deke gently pulled her close and kissed her soft lips. She slid her hands to the back of his neck and held their lingering kiss.

When they broke their embrace, she tilted her head and wrinkled her nose. "Let's not forget the plans. Church. We are attending church this morning."

"Oh, yes. I knew I got dressed up for something."

Both laughed and walked out to Deke's waiting vehicle.

They made small talk as they drove to church. When the conversation lulled, Rita posed a question. "Deke, have you seen Bryce Lamb since the grand jury hearing on Calvin?"

Deke's eyes were on the road. He drew a deep breath. "Not since Lamb's lawyers entered the guilty plea last month. I was surprised at the quickness of the trial. I guess Daddy knew we had the goods on the boy, and his lawyers got him convinced he should make a plea deal. He was facing life imprisonment on the murder charge. Involuntary manslaughter was a stretch, but the legal eagles convinced the judge Calvin had only intended to scare Bobby by throwing the rock hammer at a tree near him."

A silence fell over the conversation. She wondered if he shared her foreboding picture of what the future might hold.

Rita turned her head toward Deke as he drove toward the little white frame church surrounded by idyllic woods. Searching for a parking spot close to the church, he guided the truck past the old cemetery. The freshly painted parking stripes beckoned vehicles to park in an orderly fashion. Rita's eyes remained on the man she had come to consider something more than a friend over this summer. *He was different from me, but I feel comfortable with him. Strange. Love?*

He turned off the Chevy's ignition and met her eyes with a half-smile. "Well, let's get churched. Then we will be good to go for the week. Right?"

She returned his smile, then adopted a serious look. "Deke, I worry about Lamb. He's a vindictive man, and for some illogical reason, he thinks you're the reason his boy's in prison."

Deke regarded her for a few seconds before he spoke. "That's because Lamb is insane. He has always had delusions of grandeur and had his way from his teen years to now. So, any failures are someone else's fault."

He reached for Rita's tightly clasped hands. "Don't worry 'bout me. Lamb is tricky, yes. But I may be the trickiest. Is that a word?"

"Maybe, but I want you to be serious with me. I mean it. Just be careful." Her voice was tight in her throat—she hated when her emotions took over.

Deke squeezed her hands lightly, then leaned forward and gently kissed her on the lips. "I will."

"Hey, don't smear my lipstick."

Deke jumped from the truck and jogged to the passenger side to open it. He helped her down from the heights. "You're not supposed to wear a dress in a luxury limo truck like mine. Jeans are more sophisticated."

Once on the ground, she straightened her clothing and was about to reply, but Deke snapped his fingers. "Oh. Almost forgot. After we have lunch, do you mind if I pick up Cecil, and we all three visit my aunt in the nursing home? She has more confusing moments, but it seems she has more on the ball in the daytime. You know. They call it 'sundowners' when dementia is at its full influence."

"Sure. Why don't we invite Cecil to lunch? Is he in the outbuilding in the back?" She craned her neck toward the building, but the church obstructed her view.

"Maybe. But he usually waits in the woods until everyone has arrived and is seated in the congregation. However, this whole murder scene has been hard on him. He seems warier than ever. I'm sure he will decline the invitation."

"I understand."

"Listen, go on in and grab a couple seats. I'll go check if he's in the back storage building. Stay away from the front few pews in case Pastor Mike gets on a roll and starts yelling and spitting."

"That's terrible. I am going to tell him you said that."

Deke grinned and started walking to the back of the church. He turned and said, "Aww, just tell him he's supposed to be a Baptist, dunking folks in water—not a Methodist sprinkling them."

Rita suppressed a laugh. "You heathen."

Deke ducked low as he walked, to avoid being spotted by congregants looking out the windows. At the back of the church, he made his way around the galvanized water trough—empty now—but filled with water when it was needed for a baptism.

Deke took a second look at the elongated tub. It made him uneasy. He had been baptized in a church as a preteen. However, it seemed to him now at his current age that his twelve-year-old self had wanted to go under more for fear of hell than the love of heaven. Pastor Mike had talked about his relationship with the Lord over the months when they were alone, and the preacher had been able to answer all the questions he had raised. Mike was not pushy and did not make him feel guilty about anything. However, he was firm about the need for a "personal relationship with Jesus."

Deke's attention was drawn by singing coming from the little workshop. Music was being piped into the shed. He stood by the door with his hand positioned to knock. "It's me, Deke." Then he tapped several times. No sounds but that of music from the inside.

He started to tap again, and then he saw a little hand push aside burlap curtains in a darkened side window. He jerked his head toward the movement and saw a jack-o-lantern face expose tiny teeth with spaces between them. The vision quickly vanished as the curtains closed and swung until they were still. The door creaked open.

"Come in, friend, come in. How are you on this Lord's Day?"

Deke entered as Cecil stepped aside. He peeked outside the door, turning his head like an owl, left to right. Then, with a satisfied nod, he closed the door softly and turned to Deke. "No girlfriend?"

"Rita is getting our seats in church."

Cecil shrugged. "So, you admit she's your girlfriend. You wouldn't have come to church if she weren't here."

Deke gave Cecil a playful swat on his shoulder. "Very funny. I didn't come to be roasted."

Cecil wore clean bibs and a white shirt, washed and pressed. His hatless head had sporadic long gray-brown hairs forced under control by some sort of oil. His black leather shoes were spit-shined, worthy of a Marine inspection.

"Say, I know we are on the schedule to visit May in the nursing home at two, but why don't you join Rita and me for a Sunday lunch? We can leave from here. Then we'll go on to the home."

Cecil walked across the room and plugged in an old fan mounted on the wall. It woke up and started to turn from side to side, drawing the air from a screened window below it. He watched until the clicking start-up noise subsided and turned to face Deke.

"Oh, I thank you for your invitation, but you need your quality time with Miss Rita."

"Cecil, you need to eat, and I see you are already dressed to go out. I mean, if I had kept my uniform pressed and boots shined like yours in the Marines, I wouldn't have been in so much trouble with my drill sergeant."

Cecil looked down at his attire and slid his fingers down his creased dress shirt. "Allean Shuecraft launders and irons my formal wear. She has done that for years. Twice a month, on a Tuesday, I leave my duds hanging in a plastic bag on a hook on the post of the pick-up box. She has them all spic and span on Thursday in the same place."

Cecil sat down on an old cane chair near a small homemade table attached to the wall. He picked up a worn Bible lying open on a shelf below the window beside the door. "Well, I was taught at the Methodist home to wear your best when you come into the Lord's house of worship." He waved a frail arm around the shed. "Even if it is a shed on the grounds."

"So, will you join us?"

"For a police officer, you're not good at picking up on the obvious, are you?"

Deke chuckled. "Maybe not, but maybe I'm just persistent. Come with us. It'll be fun."

He was silent, and Deke waited. Cecil seemed deep in thought. Finally, he looked up from the floor. "My friend, I am still recovering from the incident involving the boys. One killed, and the other serving time. It was bad enough to be gawked at in the daylight hours, and now I have an arrest record. I'd rather not be out in public."

"Cecil, you were not guilty, and the photos cleared you of all suspicion. You do not have a record. Calvin Lamb tried to frame you, and it turned around to bite him. He got what he deserved."

"Oh no. Calvin needed guidance. His life is ruined, and he has to live with killing his friend. Maybe if I hadn't been cleared of the crime, there would have been a chance to redeem young Calvin."

Deke couldn't believe what his ears were hearing. "That's ridiculous. Innocent people should not go to prison. Furthermore, I am not a social worker or a preacher. I am glad he went to jail. You should be relieved because you could have been the one. Don't feel sorry for mutts."

Cecil stared at his open Bible and pensively stroked the worn pages with his inked notes.

Deke stepped forward and put his arm around the boney shoulders. "My friend, let it be. Justice was served. Now, if you don't want to join us for dinner, okay. I don't want competition for my lady anyway."

The little man looked up and smiled, but the eyes were sad. "Tell Miss Rita thanks for the invitation. And yours too."

"Will do. But I will be back about one-thirty to pick you up to visit the nursing home." Deke jerked his head toward the black speaker on the wall. "Ooh, I got to get in there. The preacher is starting his gig. See you later."

Deke double-timed it back to the front of the church, staying low under the windows.

CHAPTER 34

Rita couldn't explain it, but she enjoyed sitting between Deke and Cecil. One man exuded physicality, security, and charm—the other was spiritually wise and charming in his own way. Their conversation on the drive to the nursing home drifted from local affairs to Cecil's homeopathic remedies to the morning sermon. A sense of peace washed over her. These men were genuine—they had that in common. The fact Deke had been drawn to Cecil and Cecil to him was proof opposites did attract. Both seemed to recognize they had something to learn from each other.

As they drove into the parking lot of the neat, single-story, red-brick building, Cecil's mouth opened, and his head swiveled back and forth. "Lots of visitors," he mumbled.

Rita heard his breath quicken. She laid her hand on his and squeezed gently. "Oh, it's all right. Folks will be busy in the rooms of their loved ones just visiting. They will not notice us."

Why had she said that?

Deke cleared his throat and spoke calmly. "I think we will park on the backside near a side door. Cecil, you can wait in the truck until I open the door and signal. Okay?"

Cecil sighed. "Thanks."

Deke had bailed her out.

"That's great. The walk will do me good after that fried chicken meal." Rita assured Cecil.

Deke found a non-official parking spot near the side door meant as a fire door and parked. He rolled the windows down and removed his ignition key. "I'll take my keys with me. I have seen how you eye my ride, Cecil."

"Well, it wouldn't be grand theft auto that I committed. That would be petty theft, given the condition of your vehicle." Cecil sat with a straight face. He remained expressionless as both Rita and Deke responded with spontaneous laughter.

Deke paused with Rita to sign the guest register in the lobby, listing all three of them. Rita had accompanied Deke on his visit to his Aunt May on several occasions. She had been impressed with the softer, caring side of Deke with his failing aunt.

"Okay." Deke laid the pen down on the stand that held the guest log. "Let's see what mood my aunt is in today. She will probably lambast me for not visiting sooner ... even though she forgets my visits."

They walked side by side, acknowledging greetings by some of the fellow visitors they recognized. The couple paused at the half-open door of May's room. Deke lightly tapped and received no answer. He tapped again. "Aunt May, it's Deke. Are you ready to receive guests?" Still no answer.

"Maybe she is sleeping." A puzzled look creased his face. "Not like her to be sleeping at this time of the day. When she does nap, it is later and only for ten minutes, give or take."

He pushed the door open slowly and revealed two beds. The bed closest to the door was occupied by a frail, wrinkled woman. Her hair fanned out on the pillow. She was softly snoring with her mouth open. The other bed, usually occupied by May, was empty and made up with fresh linens. The nightstand, usually cluttered with his aunt's miscellaneous items, was starkly clean with only the corded call button and tv control residing on it.

"What's going on?" Deke leaned backward and checked the name holder beside the door. There was no card with May Duston's name. Only Wilma Crockett.

"That's May's roommate. But where is my aunt?"

A heavyset nurse with a stethoscope draped around her neck softly padded down the hallway toward them.

"Naomi. Good to see you."

The nurse's smile affirmed Rita's assumption that they knew each other. "Well, Deputy Deke. I have missed seeing you since I got on the day shift. How are you doing?"

Deke ignored her question. "Naomi, this is my friend Rita. I need some help. Where is my aunt? It looks like they moved her out."

"They did." Naomi frowned. "Didn't anybody notify you? That was done several days ago. I believe on Thursday last week."

"No, nobody let me know. I'm the only one listed as a contact, so I should've been notified."

"Deke, it seems like your aunt took a downturn in her memory department. She would be very articulate and normal for one hour, then go off babbling and going back to when she was fifty or sixty years younger. It came on all of a sudden. The problem was, I guess she was disturbing her roommate, so they moved her to a single."

"Where?"

"I'll take you to her." Naomi started walking down the hallway with Rita and Deke in tow. She turned down a side hallway and walked two doors down. The door was wide open, and May appeared to be sleeping.

Deke touched Naomi's elbow. "Thanks. Could I ask you another favor?"

"Shoot. Oh, sorry. I forgot I was talking to a lawman."

Deke smiled at her joke. "Listen, I have Cecil outside. In fact, he is waiting near this side door. Would you be so kind as to use your security card to let him into the building? I don't want to start a panic among the staff thinking the alarm is sounding for an escapee patient."

"Gotcha covered." Naomi walked to the door with red letters printed on it announcing that an alarm would sound if opened. She slipped her card through the electronic device on the door and pushed the crash bar to open the door. Deke pushed the door open and stepped outside.

"Thanks. Naomi." He leaned closer. "This will be our secret policy breakage."

She giggled and looked back at Rita. "You got a wild one here."

"Don't I know it."

Naomi retraced her steps down the hall. She passed by Rita. "Have a happy Sunday."

"Thanks. You, too."

Cecil hurried to the door, slipping past Deke while glancing around for witnesses.

The two men joined Rita and returned to May's room.

"Well, as I live and breathe. Welcome to my world, Ms. Attorney."

Rita had entered the room first to see May operating the control button to elevate herself in the bed to a semi-reclining position. She was clear-eyed and smiling.

"Miss Duston, I hope we are not disturbing you?"

"Not at all. Come in." She leaned forward in her bed. "And bring those two in with you. I declare. You need to be more selective about the company you keep."

Rita laughed. "Yes, I do. But they are the only ones who will associate with me."

Deke entered and took his aunt's proffered hand and brushed it with his lips. "You moved and did not give a forwarding address."

"Did I? Oh, my roommate was disturbing my sleep. So, I got this nice place all to myself. Costs a little more, but I have saved my pennies for such a time as this."

"Nephew, get out of the way. I want to see my special doctor." She weaved around, trying to see Cecil.

"Miss May, how are you feeling?" Cecil stepped up to the bed beside Deke. May grasped Cecil's hand with both of hers. Rita could not help observing that the hands were remarkably similar. A woman in her eighties with ancient hands identical to Cecil's hands, although he was in his mid-thirties.

"Oh, here's the ointment for your feet." Cecil fumbled in his pocket until he found what he wanted: a white jar that had originally held cold cream but now held his concoction.

He set it on her nightstand. "Make sure to apply it in the morning and before you sleep at night."

"I was waiting for you to deliver. Now, put that in my top drawer. The nursing home police will not allow me to use anything that doesn't have a prescription.

"Sit, sit everybody. Darling, you take my rocking chair I brought from home. I don't want that big cowboy breaking it. He can sit on the hospital-reinforced one designed for baby elephants."

"You cut me to the quick, Aunt May," said Deke with feigned hurt. He sat with exaggerated care.

"Cecil, you can have a seat on my bed."

The three visitors and the patient engaged in a lively conversation. Rita saw no signs of the diminishing mental capacity that had concerned Deke. However, about fifteen minutes later, she noticed a change coming over May.

After a lull in the conversation, May looked out the window. When she turned back, she gave a little jump as her eyes focused on Cecil's face. Her mouth spasmodically opened and closed. Then she looked about the room, eyeing Deke and Rita with puzzlement.

Deke spoke with a quiet, reassuring manner. "Aunt May, what are you thinking?'

No answer. May lifted a boney finger toward a corner where the ceiling met the walls. "There she is again." A smile tugged at her wrinkled cheeks.

Three heads followed the finger and tried to discern what she was looking at in the corner.

"Uh, who do you see?" Deke inquired.

She gave Deke a bewildering look. "Why, my angel baby doll. She has come alive. You know I took extra special care of her when I was a little girl. Now she has returned to take care of me."

May stared at the corner, smiling and nodding her head.

"Maybe we should go, Aunt May. You need your rest." Deke rose and approached her bedside.

"Deke, Cecil. Boys, I need to talk to you."

Rita saw a glimmer of recognition come into her eyes. *Poor woman. She is struggling.*

Tears flowed down May's cheeks as she looked back and forth at the two men. Her head suddenly dropped. "So, so tired."

"It's all right. It would be best if you had your nap time. We're interrupting." Deke looked at Cecil and Rita and jerked his head toward the door.

Cecil rose from the bed and uncovered the woman's bare feet. He grimaced at the sight of the deep fissures in the heels. May had returned to staring at the corner and seemed oblivious to her visitors.

Cecil went to the nightstand and drew the drawer open. "I'm going to at least apply the ointment before I leave. So, you two go ahead, and I'll meet you at the truck."

Deke nodded and started toward the door, then turned. "You know you can't leave the building by the way you came in unless you want alarms going off and the staff converging on you. Why don't you go out by the back garden door? The alarm's not set this time of day. I will drive around and meet you there."

Cecil nodded, "Sounds good." He was already gently applying ointment to her feet. Rita heard May faintly singing a nursery rhyme, but she could not remember which one.

The couple exited the room and walked the hallways, now clearing of visitors.

Naptime, Rita thought.

Deke and Rita entered his truck and pulled around to the rear of the hospital. Only one older man in a wheelchair was there in the shade of a pin oak tree with a nurse's aide. His head drooped to the side, and the aide gently moved it from the uncomfortable position. They waited.

Rita broke the silence. "I watched my grandmother go down this road. I know it's difficult to see someone you love to go through this."

"You know, my aunt has always been a high-energy, wise lady. So, to see her change is depressing. But it also underscores that I could be there someday." Deke chewed his words out rather than his usual rapid-fire speech. He covered his face with one hand and his shoulders shook. "She is the last living relative I have, and I may lose her soon. Worse yet, she may end up living for a long time, but not know me."

Rita had never seen this side of this man before. She wanted to hold him but did not want to break his mood. So instead, she slid her palm over his free hand, which rested on the steering wheel, and waited while he grieved.

He finally broke the silence with a huge sigh.

Rita moved her hand up his forearm in a gentle caress. "I am falling in love with you."

Deke jerked his head upward and appeared confused, but the look soon melted and was replaced by a warmth in his eyes she had rarely seen. He leaned forward and cupped her chin. They both closed the distance, and their lips met for a long kiss.

They separated slowly, and Rita opened her eyes to meet his.

"Likewise," he whispered. "The only difference is that you're falling—I already fell."

They embraced again. Rita wondered if someone could be watching, perhaps from the windows. But she didn't care.

They released each other and traded smiles. Deke seemed suddenly aware of their surroundings and started surveying the back of the building and the garden. She joined in the watch. A good length of time had passed, and Cecil had not appeared.

"Deke, do you think we had better check on him?"

"Don't know. May has only two feet. She's not a centipede."

Rita giggled. "You missed your calling. You should have been a stand-up comic."

Deke adopted a humorous contortion of his face. "You think I could make a living?"

Rita placed her index finger on his lips. "No. Don't quit your day job."

Deke snickered, then looked around Rita. "Oh, here he comes."

Cecil hurried to the truck and strained as he pulled the reluctant door open. Grabbing the door's armrest, he hoisted himself into the vehicle. He had to slam the door three times before he could get it securely closed. Cecil sat staring straight ahead and breathing hard from the exertion.

Deke started the engine but did not engage the transmission. He and Rita stared at the hermit, who seemed to be deep in thought.

Rita cautiously intruded on his thoughts, "Cecil, are you okay?"

The little man didn't seem to hear the question.

"Cecil, is something wrong?" At Deke's rumbling voice, Cecil jerked back into consciousness.

"Oh, I'm sorry. I just was thinking about Miss May. She saved my life at birth and made sure I was taken care of until I was grown. I am deeply grateful ...

"She was the only person who visited me regularly at the Methodist home. She never forgot my birthday or Christmas. Hard to believe we are losing her." He turned to Deke. "And I know you were close to your aunt too."

Deke nodded and sighed again, seemingly not wanting to repeat his earlier demonstration of humanness. "I guess that's life. It ends in the end."

"No. Life on earth ends, but eternal life is waiting for us— if you trust the Lord." Cecil fixed his dark eyes on Deke.

They both said nothing but stared at each other. Deke sighed and engaged the truck's transmission. "So I've heard."

No one spoke on the ride home.

CHAPTER 35

Deke had looked forward to this September Saturday as the summer was cooling. The calendar and the temperature heralded deer hunting season. On top of the joy of hunting, things seemed to be getting back to normal. Calvin Lamb, who was out on bond, would get some time. Not the time he deserved, probably, but some time. Bull's legal team was working overtime as they sought a deal. It had been a month since Calvin had been arrested and Cecil freed.

All's well that ends well.

Deke smiled as he pumped gas into his truck at the convenience store in Marion. He seized the squeegee from the container of water between the pumps, set the lock for automatic on the nozzle, and bent low and duck-walked around to the passenger side of the windshield. He leaped up and slapped the squeegee on the windshield as Rita squealed in surprise.

Deke widened his eyes and scrubbed the windshield vigorously. Leaning over to the open side window he spoke with an exaggerated accent from an old vampire movie. "I am the vindow viper, I come to vipe your vindow."

Rita was still breathing hard when she attempted a slap at his shoulder. "You ... you. You could have given me a heart attack. Next time we go out, I think I will carry a can of mace." She tried to hold back a smile, with little success.

Deke laughed loudly and returned to the pump nozzle. He surveyed the bed that held the portable deer stands, seed corn bags, two feeders, two compound bows, and all the paraphernalia an avid deer hunter could wish to have. Only disappointment was he would not see Pastor Mike.

Pastor Mike had arranged to meet him at the barn that day for a short practice with the bow Deke had lent him. After a month of learning archery, Mike had proved to be a quick study. However, Mike had just called to cancel. He needed to make an emergency hospital visit.

As the pump slowed, signaling his tank was full, he stepped closer to his open driver-side window and peered inside. "Want some coffee, Babe?"

Rita smiled and declined with a raised hand. "Two cups in the morning are my limit. Otherwise, you would think I talked too much."

Deke placed his fingertips along his cheek and declared his disbelief. "Well, shut my mouth and call me crazy—I would never dream that, let alone believe that."

Rita leaned toward the window and removed her Stetson, swinging the hat toward Deke through the open window. He jumped back and laughed.

"Be right back. I need a caffeine booster shot."

He entered the adjacent convenience store and strode toward the back, tipping his own hat toward the thin blonde behind the cash register as he passed. "Morning, Bonnie."

"Morning, Wyatt," she responded with a mischievous grin.

He filled a foam cup with strong black pecan roast coffee and spoke over his shoulder with his back turned. "You know I don't look anything like Wyatt Earp."

He turned with a full cup and walked toward her.

"You ever met him?" Bonnie inquired.

"No. Have you?" Deke retorted grinning.

"I have a fertile imagination—don't be trying to take over my fantasy."

Deke chuckled and slid a five-dollar bill across the counter.

"You know the rules. Cops don't pay for coffee." Bonnie glowered at him.

"I'm off duty. I will pay."

"Okay. I don't want to cause a scene while your girlfriend might be watching."

"That's better." Deke recognized he had not corrected Bonnie's reference to his and Rita's relationship. Girlfriend. It sounded good.

Bonnie handed the change back to him. "How is Miss Rita doing?"

Deke was surprised at what sounded like a genuine question. "Oh, she's doing good. We're doing some riding today."

"Good for y'all. She is a keeper. You agree?"

"Well, Bonnie, I think you are right. She *is* a keeper."

Deke left the store deep in thought, swapping the hot coffee cup back and forth in his hands to avoid being burned.

The sound of squealing tires jolted his attention back to the present. A white Cadillac jumped the street curb and lurched straight toward Deke before braking hard. He had already started evasive action, but it was not necessary. The car stopped crossways of the pumps behind his pickup. The door flew open, and long slender legs appeared first, then the woman who owned them. Willa. What was going on?

Willa was crying as she walked toward him. She seized his forearms, sloshing some of the hot coffee onto his hand.

"Please, Deke, help my son. Look, I know he does some wrong things but consider who raised him. I can't stand the thought of him going to Eddyville Pen. He won't survive. You can get him off. I know you can."

The hysterical woman plunged her head on his chest, wrapped her arms around his body, and sobbed.

Deke stood with his arms outstretched, not sure what to do. Finally, he sat the coffee cup on top of a newspaper vending machine and grasped Willa's shoulders, disengaging her gently.

"Willa, I am sorry this has happened to Cal, but you have to recognize he brought it on himself. He's fortunate they reduced the charge from murder to manslaughter, so he is not going to a maximum-security place like Eddyville."

She tilted her mascara-streaked face upward toward him. "Deke, you can say you made a mistake on the evidence or, or, there is some technicality that can save him. We have known each other for a long time. Bull has often said that you had a thing for me. If you do this for me, I will be good to you."

"Whoa, whoa. You are upset and desperate. But I cannot do anything. And if I could, I wouldn't." Deke let his words sink in. "Yes, our friendship goes way back. But you belong to Bull. I respect you, and you need to respect me as an officer and a man. I wouldn't think about taking advantage of you—in any way."

He wished he could tell her to flee, but he knew she didn't have the means. Where would she go? But if she thought for one minute he was still interested ...

"Willa, go home and rest. If Cal can use this bad experience, he could come out a new man. Understand?" He released her shoulders and took a step backward.

Willa nodded as her sobs diminished.

"Are you all right to drive?"

She nodded, sniffing into a silk scarf that hung around her neck. "Don't tell Bull I tried to get you to help Cal. When I said I wanted to talk to you, that maybe you could help, he got angry, very angry."

"Then you better go home. This never happened. I know you are feeling pain. See someone that you can trust. A counselor or a pastor. Someone competent to guide you through your emotions."

She looked exhausted. Her life could have been so different if she had chosen another man. She had chosen wrong.

He became aware of other eyes on them. He looked up to see an expressionless Rita staring. Then, twisting his head, he saw Bonnie gawking out the window. She hurriedly started arranging some displays as though she had seen nothing.

"Yes, you're right. I'm driving myself crazy trying to help my son." She looked at the ground then back to Deke.

"I'm sorry that put you on the spot. C'mon. Let's get you to your car and get you home."

Willa nodded as Deke took her elbow and guided her to the car. He opened the door, and she slid in slowly, her short skirt displaying her long, tanned legs.

Deke hurried to close the door, hoping no one had seen that seductive maneuver. Get her out of here. No, get *me* out of here.

Willa's window glided down. A slight smile pulled at the corners of her mouth. Her decorative fingers cleared a lingering tear at the corner of her eye.

"Goodbye. I hope to see you again—under better circumstances," she said in a hushed tone.

"Drive safe." Deke touched the brim of his cowboy hat, pivoted, and walked to his truck after retrieving his now-cooled coffee.

He entered the vehicle and glanced at Rita, who had her arm resting on the open window frame. Her head was resting in her hand as she studied him.

Through the mirror, Deke watched the Caddy pull onto the street at a decidedly slower rate than it had entered the gas station.

He started the truck and looked at Rita. She hadn't changed her position.

With a shake of his head, he left the gas pumps behind. "Well, that was a surprise."

As he drove, he risked another look at Rita. Still, no movement even though the wind was whipping through the cab of the truck. She seemed oblivious to the rearrangement of her hair.

"Maybe more awkward for you than a surprise."

"Oh, come on. You're acting like I provoked that attack. She is still in shock over her son. And give me a break."

"I could not hear most of the conversation, but I was able to fill in what I felt were the appropriate words."

"Listen, I was trying to calm her down. I didn't do anything wrong," Deke retorted. "You're making me feel uncomfortable. You're a defense attorney. You can recognize innocent and guilty people. Right?"

Rita sat upright and closed the window, making conversation easier. Then she leaned forward and, in a conspiratorial voice, said, "Does she have nicer legs than mine?"

"What?" Deke reddened. "What kind of question is that? I never noticed. I mean, yes, I saw her legs, but I didn't pay any attention."

"Now, Deputy, you're beginning to perjure yourself."

Deke was trying to watch the road, but he slammed on the brakes and jerked to the curb. He turned to Rita.

Rita's scowl disappeared and became a grin. "Deke, Deke, honey. I know you did nothing wrong." She touched his arm.

"Incredible! *You* were playing *me*? And I fell for it."

"Accountability, precious. Just keeping you honest." The giggles came again.

"Okay, you can score a point for your prank. I thought I could read people. You're going to have to carry two cards. One reads 'serious,' and one reads 'prank.'"

"Small correction of your statement. You can read men, but you're not so good at reading women." Rita leaned toward Deke, emphasizing her last word. She turned and faced forward, rocking her head side to side. "I know that for a fact—because I am one."

"Well, then you can teach me."

"Sadly, I don't know if old deputy dogs can learn new tricks. But on a serious note, pretend you see the serious card I am holding up."

"I'm listening."

Rita chewed her lip. "I am not sure, but while you were romancing Willa, I thought I saw Mr. Lamb's truck drive through the intersection at the corner of the station. Very slowly. I couldn't see the driver because of the tinted windows, but there are not too many of those high-dollar four-by-fours around the county."

Deke leaned back in his seat, absently drawing a toothpick stuck in a hole in his vinyl dashboard. He chewed on it as he contemplated what she had said.

"Hmm? I never saw him."

"That's because you were too involved in admiring your old girlfriend's legs."

"Would you quit?"

Rita let loose with a peal of laughter. "I'm sorry I forgot to display my prank card."

Before Deke could answer, the police radio that he had installed in his private vehicle crackled to life. As an evidence technician, he was always on call, so he found it to come in handy. Sometimes too handy.

"Central to Deke."

"Now what?" Deke removed the microphone from its clip on the dash and keyed it.

"This is Deke. Whatcha got, Patty?"

"Deke, you've got someone at the office who wants to see you?"

"A name?"

"Dan Trimble, from the state lab."

Deke dropped his head on his chest and blurted out to no one in particular. "Oh man, I forgot to follow up." He turned to Rita. "I have got to see this man. I failed to contact him after the disposition of Lamb's case. It shouldn't take long. I'm sorry. This day just gets better by the moment."

"Tell you what, on your way to the courthouse, drop me off at my house, and I will get my car. Then I'll meet you at the farm." She jerked her head toward the bed of the truck. "After we go riding, you can go ahead and do your 'deer' thing, and I can take my car and go home. I assume you can get your deer stands up by yourself?"

"Yeah, sounds like a plan. Oh, be careful driving out to the barn on the field road. The heavy rains we've had the last three days have made the ground pretty soggy. If you find it questionable, just leave your car at the gate."

CHAPTER 36

Willa pulled up in front of Gretchen Mobley's small, well-kept white frame house with its picket fence. The heavyset matronly woman wearing a tight bun had not seen her yet. Instead, she was talking with Violet and pushing her in a swing.

Willa pulled down the visor and flipped open the lighted mirror. Oh, Lord. Her face was a mess. She looked ready to play a witch with the streaked mascara. Seizing a tissue, she tried her best to erase the dark streaks. She jumped when she heard a rap on the passenger window. The smiling face of Violet appeared. Willa pushed a button and slid the window open.

"Hi, darling." She looked and saw the babysitter standing with her hands on the picket fence. Willa didn't think she ever frowned. "Hi, Mrs. Mobley. Sorry, I am running a little late."

Mrs. Mobley's smile widened. "Perfectly all right. Vi and I were enjoying ourselves. It seems I learn something new every time I'm with her."

"Thank you for taking care of her. You are excellent. If you don't mind, I will call you the first of next week to drop her off while I meet with my ladies' group. Then we will settle up."

"I should be paying you for the pleasure of seeing Vi."

Willa unlocked the door, allowing Violet entry. "Thanks again." She needed to get home.

Violet jumped into the car, and using both hands, tugged the door closed. She turned to her mother. "Where you been?"

Willa closed the window and looked away from her, pretending to check traffic, but in reality to hide her of a tear-streaked face from the girl.

"You knew I was at the salon, getting my hair fixed."

Violet sat quietly, observing her mother. "You should go back there and get your money back. They robbed you."

Willa shook her head but focused on looking ahead. "Hush, child. I had other business to take care of, too."

"What kind of business?"

Willa snapped her head around to look at her daughter. "That's enough. It's adult business."

Violet started to say something else but seemed to think the better of it. She sank back in her seat and started humming quietly. Both mother and daughter rode in silence until they reached home, when Willa drove slowly past the house.

Violet raised her head. "You missed the drive."

Willa continued to a small wide place on the shoulder where she could turn the car around. "So, I did."

She let out a sigh of relief when she saw no sign of her husband's truck. He was supposed to meet with his fire department leaders this morning, then play a round of golf in the evening at the country club. Yes, yes. She could relax now. She was safe.

Willa punched the electric door opener and drove carefully into the garage. They left the vehicle and entered the kitchen.

"Vi, go to your room and take a shower and clean up. I will start dinner after I get changed. You're a big girl. Let's see if you can wash up well. Including your hair."

"Okay, Momma. What's for dinner?"

"It's a surprise. You will like it." Violet smiled and bounded upstairs to her bedroom.

Willa sat down on a high counter stool and held her face in her hands. She sat rubbing her face and trying to process what had happened today with Deke.

She suddenly sat up straight. What if that lawyer girlfriend was in the truck when I made my grand entrance? *No, no, I didn't see her. Maybe the windows were too dark? Crazy. No, she couldn't have been in the truck or else she would have flown out and read me the riot act.*

She looked out the window to the pool area. "Better check." She rose quietly and pulled the curtains back. The pool was still.

Willa passed into the dining room and the adjoining living room. All quiet.

She passed by the empty glassed-in music room. Then, moving down the hallway, she stopped at Bull's office door. Her heart thumped faster. The ornate, heavy wooden door was closed, but he always kept it closed. She tried the handle, and it rotated downward smoothly. She felt a little dizzy but finally shoved the door open. Her last thought before the door opened was that she would break into a smile and ask Bull how he liked her hair.

Panic seized her as reason edged out her plans. Vi had said that she didn't see the results of the salon. And the way the girl squinted behind thick glasses told her that her face was still a mess. Oh, jeez, too late.

The door swung open wide into the office, and she stumbled in as her mind screamed. Only the empty high-backed leather chair behind the ornate wooden desk greeted her. Her breath came in short gasps as she leaned on the oaken bookcase by the door. The only sound was the ticking of the clock. She vented her relief in sobs.

Pull yourself together. You're your own worst enemy. He's not here. Why should he be?

Willa straightened and stepped out of his office, making sure to close the door, then walked down the hallway to their master bedroom. She crossed over to the window and pulled the drapes back to allow a little more natural light. The king-sized bed occupied the center of the wall. She had picked the furniture and decorated the sleeping quarters. She was proud of her flair for decorating. She had been careful not to go overboard on the feminine touch—she knew her husband would not stand for it. She knew just how to avoid pushing his buttons. But she knew just how to push them, too.

Willa needed to straighten her face and change clothes. Then, when Bull came home, she'd be ready for him. She made her way to her walk-in closet, opened wide the partially open door, and switched on the lights in the twelve-by-twelve room.

Willa screamed and fell into the door frame. Bull was sitting in her chair, one ankle crossed over his knee, left hand resting on his ankle. The right hand clutched a glass of bourbon whiskey, neat. Probably Old Grand Dad.

"What are you doing? You scared the ..." Willa's face darkened. "What are you doing in my dressing room!"

Bull took a sip of the amber liquid then spoke slowly. "Dressing room. It's just an oversized closet fully stocked

314

with every piece of clothing a woman could want. Where ya been?"

"Why do you want to know? And where's your truck?" The best defense would be an offense.

The man downed the rest of the whiskey and turned to her cabinet with cubby holes holding her shoe collection. He pulled the Old Grand Dad bottle from the space and poured another generous pour.

He's not sure I did anything. Willa felt emboldened.

"And how many glasses have you had? It looks like you killed half a bottle."

She stayed leaning against the door frame, folding her arms over her chest.

I got him confused.

He set the bottle back into the shoe compartment then leaped out of the chair, sending it falling on its side, and lunged toward her. His speed caught her completely off guard. One hand grabbed her arm. The other hand, holding the bourbon, allowed just a few drops to slosh out. He shoved her into the bedroom.

"No more," he said through gritted teeth. "I ask the questions."

He slung her onto the bed, her ribs and head striking the tall post at the foot.

"Ooh!" Willa cried. She sat up quickly, rubbing her ribs in pain. She trembled as he carefully placed the glass on her dressing table.

"Okay, I'm a considerate husband, so I will answer your two questions. My truck is parked behind the barn." He gestured toward the window. "Out of sight."

He turned and gestured toward the glass on the dresser. "How much? Enough."

He moved menacingly toward her, where she was still seated on the bed. "Now, answer *my* questions. Where ya been?"

Willa trembled. "To my salon. To get my hair and nails done."

He grabbed her hair. "No work done there." Then he released her hair and grabbed one hand. "Don't see work done there. You still got those old false nails."

He released her hand and stepped back. "I'll give you one more chance. Where were you?"

"I am leaving!" Willa stood, and he blocked the doorway.

"You going to meet your lover?" He growled.

"What are you talking about? My lover? Who?" Her voice was shaking now.

"You know. Campbell. What's the attraction? His uniform?"

Willa was breathing hard, her lips quivered. She moved forward toward the door opening, trying to slip by her husband's thick body. "You're ridiculous. Get out of my way."

He seized her by her arms and shook her. "I saw you!" He screamed. His face was molten red. "I saw you all over Campbell like white on rice at the gas station. You've always had a thing about that puke. I won't stand for it. You're not leaving the house, by g ..."

His hand moved so fast the slap was indefensible. She reeled backward, her head spinning, and again struck the tall post at the foot of the bed, falling in a heap on the mattress. She looked into his demonic eyes as he closed the distance between them, hand upraised. The beefy hand struck her face again and addled her thinking, but not so much as to render her incapacitated. She timed a kick to his lower abdomen when he came within striking distance.

"Oof! You b—" The kick barely slowed him and served to enrage him further.

As he prepared for another strike, his hand balled into a fist, Willa heard another voice.

"No, Daddy! Don't hurt Momma!" A little hand appeared and grasped the angry man's wrist.

"Don't touch me!" he roared and slung the clinging girl away. Time stood still. Willa watched events unfold in slow motion. She saw her daughter desperately clinging to his arm. Then Violet, airborne, flew into the heavy oak dresser against the wall, face-first.

Violet's brief squeal ended when her face contacted the furniture. She crumpled and lay still.

A stunned look spread across her husband's now-sober face. "Oh, baby, baby."

He ran forward and sank beside his daughter, turning her tiny body over. The frame of her glasses had split in two, and they fell beside her head. Her eyes fluttered open. A gash on her forehead bled profusely.

Violet's confused whimper became full-fledged wailing. Her panicked eyes darted between mother and father.

"You're going to be okay. I'm sorry, so sorry." Her father pulled one of the drawers open on the dresser and grabbed at anything cloth inside. He found an old sweatshirt and started dabbing her bleeding forehead.

Willa regained some of her equilibrium and pulled herself up to a standing position. Seeing her baby girl on the floor sent a rage through her. Willa rushed forward, grabbed him from behind and began to rake his cheeks. "Don't touch her! Get away from her."

He seized her hands and peeled them off before they got to his eyes. "Stop it. We have to help Vi." He held her arms—but with a half-hearted grip. "Please," he pleaded.

Willa noticed with satisfaction the damage her nails had done to his face. An artificial nail was still stuck into his face where it had plowed a furrow. It was almost humorous as Bull stood there oblivious to the fashion statement.

She screwed up her courage. "I don't want you touching that child again. I am going to pack up and take Violet to the emergency room, and we will be leaving and not coming back."

"Please, we will get her care. Both of us."

"That's the way you care for her? Not to mention the way you care for me. Thanks, but no thanks." Willa spoke through gritted teeth.

Violet sat up—crying softly and touching her face, then looking around, presumably for her glasses.

Violet groped the floor until her fingers found her doll. She rose unsteadily, clutching Tinker to her breast. Her sobs were spasmodic.

Bull's words echoed in Willa's ears. The sting of his slap had given way to a greater pain in the back of her head where she had hit the bedpost. Maybe she had a concussion? She saw her daughter backing toward the doorway wearing a pained expression—pain from emotions more than the physical injury.

The child's shaky voice whimpered, "You're mean, Daddy. You're mean to Momma and me. I don't want you for a daddy anymore."

Violet clutched her doll tightly and spun around, walking unsteadily down the hallway, occasionally extending her arms to avoid running into things. They could hear her crying as she disappeared into the kitchen.

Willa turned to her husband. "I am going to get her checked out. She doesn't want you around, and I don't either. You've done enough damage."

He hung his head, wiping his bleeding cheeks, and finding the foreign nail, he pulled it from his face. He frowned as he examined the item.

"That's mine." Willa plucked the nail from Bull's hand and turned to walk out of the bedroom.

She heard him say belatedly, "All right," but did not acknowledge hearing it.

Vi was not in the kitchen. Willa combed the rest of the bottom floor and could not find her. She was about to search the second floor but paused to look out the window into the pool area. Her eyes swept the backyard. She then refocused on the part of the back fence—the gate. The gate was wide open.

Willa's heart leaped to her throat. She had a sinking feeling. Before she knew it, she called out to her husband. Softly first, then increasingly louder. "Bryce. Bryce." Now she screamed his name, "Bryce!"

Lamb stormed into the kitchen and roared, "What?"

"It's Violet. She's gone. The back gate is open. She never goes back there when she knows the cattle are working that pasture. She knows about the bull. She's terrified of him."

"Okay, okay. We'll find her."

Lamb rushed outside, and Willa followed, both calling her name repeatedly. Desperation and despair threatened to choke Willa as their calls were met with silence. Lamb shaded his eyes as he went out the gate and searched to fields in the back of the barn and sheds.

Willa was frantic now. "What are we going to do?"

"I'm getting the Gator." He spun around and ran to the shed. "We need to check the fields. That's the priority. Then we can search the house and the front yard."

"Please, God. Protect my baby." Willa sank to her knees in the tall grass, pausing her fervent prayer to scream out Violet's name. She heard the sound of the Gator's motor approaching. Seconds counted.

CHAPTER 37

Violet clutched her doll and pushed the gate open to the pool area. She had heard her parents have violent arguments before, but she had never seen Daddy strike Mommy. The arguments were mostly behind closed doors.

She cried as she ran into the field. The heavy grass tripped her, and she fell on top of her doll. "Oh, Tinker, are you hurt? I'm sorry."

Disoriented, she looked at her surroundings. Without her glasses, everything was a blur, made worse by the flood of tears. She could not discern the direction of her home. She looked left and right. Then, she saw something familiar.

A tree that was standing taller than the surrounding trees. Opposing large branches looked like a man with outstretched arms. "The Jesus tree! That's what Mr. Cecil called it. It marks a path to his house."

Violet sniffed and wiped at her tears. "Mr. Cecil will make me feel better. He will tell me stories about plants and animals and angels and Jesus."

She started walking, trying to keep the tree as her guide. "Ow, ow." A towering thistle with prickly needles hit her arm as she forged forward.

The heavy rains in the past week had encouraged wild growth in a one-time trim pasture that was grazed by her father's cattle. But the painful interaction with the thistle reminded her to slow her walk and pay attention to her immediate surroundings. Her heart pounded. What about snakes? She already couldn't see—now there was a new fear. Her father told her that copperheads were all over the place. Her brother, Cal, once brought home one he had killed. A big one. He had chased her with it, and she had screamed until her mother intervened.

She stopped trying to calm herself and looked around. Where was the Jesus tree? She didn't see it. Had she passed it?

Violet squinted and turned in circles to find the tree. She only succeeded in getting more confused. Something moved in the corner of her vision. What was that?

She leaned forward, trying to make sense of the movement. A dark mass that slowly pulsated. She fought hard to control her trembling. She realized that the dark group was a herd of cattle. One lone figure disengaged itself from the mass and slowly moved toward her. It was the bull.

She stifled a scream. All Daddy's warnings raced into her mind. Stay clear of the herd. Frantically, she looked for a direction to escape. She started running away from the herd, not knowing which direction she was going. She clutched Tinker in her hand and threw caution to the wind as she picked up speed.

Her heart pounding, she raced across the thick pasture until she tripped over a branch or piece of wood. She pitched forward, dropping Tinker as she sought to break her fall with her hands. Falling face down, she expected soft grass or rain-soaked soil to greet her. It was neither.

She sprawled onto boards, her face smacking onto them. For a split second, she smelled rotting wood—then she recognized where she was. A rising terror seized her. The well!

Violet fought to get off rotten boards and managed to get to her knees before her world collapsed. The boards snapped and she screamed in horror as she plunged into darkness. Violet ricocheted off the narrow rock walls. She lost consciousness before she hit the water.

Deke hurried up the stairs to the county sheriff's department. He glanced at his watch—it was almost noon. He pushed through the gate hinged to the complaint counter and entered the conference room. Tim sat on the heavy oak table, and Dan stood beside him. He noticed the state lab man was leaning on a cardboard box on the table with official state stamps and taped closed.

"Dan, I hope I didn't keep you waiting long. And I apologize profusely. The Page case took a sudden turn, and Burgess was acquitted. I clean forgot to advise you of the disposition."

Dan raised his hand in dismissal. "No problem. I did hear about the outcome, and I was waiting for some lab reports to come back. I had to go to Paducah anyway, so I thought I would drop the evidence on my way. No worries."

"You know how it is. You can't get good help anymore," Tim said in mock seriousness.

Tim shook his head. Dan guffawed.

"Like you never forgot something. I know what your wife says about your memory." Deke retorted.

All three chuckled in unison as a phone rang in Tim's office.

Tim hopped up. "Saved by the bell." He hurried out the door, grinning.

"Probably your wife is calling to remind you where you live," Deke yelled after him.

Dan laughed so hard he started coughing spasmodically. He finally got control. "Okay, now down to business."

He patted the cardboard box. "Here is the murder weapon, trace evidence. We got some prints and DNA off the ax. It turns out to be a partial print of yours. And it looks like the slight blood smear on the pick was yours."

"My blood?" Deke furrowed his brow in puzzlement. "Oh, oh. Yeah, I forgot about that. I had pricked my finger on a thorn, and I pulled on the ax before I realized what it was."

"Yeah, you told me that at the scene. We got a swab and prints from Burgess that you sent over to the lab. Then, of course, there was that on the ax." Dan walked around the table—his brows wrinkled in puzzlement.

Deke followed his movement. "What's bugging you?"

Dan rubbed his chin and seemed deep in thought. Then, finally, he closed the conference room door and turned toward Deke. "Sit down, Deke."

CHAPTER 38

Rita halted at the closed gate to the pasture road leading to Deke's barn and horses. She stepped out of her red convertible, a little uneasy about trying the sodden grassy roadway to the barn. She opened the gate and walked down the dirt and grass roadway, testing the firmness. It was surprisingly solid despite the heavy rainfall over the past few days. She guessed the gravel that had been laid on the roadway to Cecil's burned-out homeplace over thirty years ago had stood the test of time. The high water rushing under the bridge she had crossed reminded her of Deke's warning about the road. However, it looked all right.

She returned to her vehicle, stopping to open the gate wider. She drove slowly, watching for any sudden deterioration of the grassy lane. Zorro and Mandy watched her approach with curiosity. She made it safely to the corral, and only when she stepped from the car did the horses show recognition. They pushed their heads over the rails seeking a petting that they knew was coming.

"Yes, yes. I will pay attention to both of you. Just wait for your turns." She took turns stroking their necks and muzzles. Zorro nuzzled her shoulder.

"Leave it to you, Zorro, to smell treats." She had sliced some apples for them before she left home. Reaching in the pocket of her western shirt, she removed a plastic bag and selected a couple of apple slices. Zorro greedily grabbed the piece of apple and turned away to eat it. Mandy was gentle with the offered prize—slowly and delicately taking the apple and chewing it slowly. "Mandy, you are a lady, not like your little piggy friend." She chuckled about the human qualities she saw in the animals. "Your master cowboy will be here soon. What say we surprise him and get you brushed and tacked? He needs to know I can be a proper cowgirl. But you two have to help me by cooperating. That goes double for you, Zorro."

Rita entered the barn through the front door. The horses met her at the opening to the corral. She hummed a gospel song as she placed some feed into the trough attached to Zorro's stall. Then, she crossed over to the tack room and seized the two brushes with leather hand straps.

She turned around to see Zorro already at his trough. "Well, that didn't take much coaxing."

She proceeded to brush the muscular gelding while Mandy waited patiently for her turn. "Guys, Deke will be so surprised that I got you all ready to ride before he gets here."

She took her time brushing the horses as she looked out the open door and watched the lingering clouds disappear. She smiled—this should be a great day.

After Rita brushed both horses, she looked toward the tack room. "Here comes the hard part—getting your saddles and bridles on."

Rita had used a four-foot stepladder to reach the highest points on the horses for brushing. Getting the heavy saddles would be another story. She first got their bridles on. That proved easier than she expected. She followed up by tying their reins to the slats in their stalls. She then threw the blanket on Zorro's back. Zorro seemed to sense this was a new experience for Rita and tried to stand as still as possible.

Mandy, a couple of inches taller than Zorro, made for an interesting problem. Climbing the step ladder, Rita struggled to swing the saddle onto her back. It took three attempts before it was in place.

"There." Breathing hard, Rita examined her work. "Deke would be proud of me. I wonder where he is."

She pulled her watch from the pocket of her jeans, where she had placed it for safekeeping. *Wow! Have I really been tending the horses for almost an hour and a half? I wished I had called Deke before I left home and told him what I was up to. I know I can't get enough bars here on my phone to check on what's holding him up.*

"Zorro and Mandy, we are just going to have to be patient. Here, this is for your cooperation." Rita rewarded them with the last of her apple slices.

She led the two animals out to the front of the barn and tied them to the corral rail. Zorro snorted impatiently, but Mandy turned to her friend and extended her head, nibbling the top of his neck as though she was trying to calm him down.

Rita leaned against the corral and surveyed the farm in the afternoon sunshine. The woodlands that bordered the pasture were just beginning to show their changing colors. She would miss the warm summer. Especially this one, the summer of her new love—Deke.

She'd never met a man like Deke. He was funny, intelligent, and he had a soft side he tried to hide. Oh yes, he was stubborn, and backing down wasn't in his personality.

But she had seen the caring side of him that dueled with his need to see justice served. Was there a future for them?

Rita rechecked her watch and felt uneasiness stir within her. She pulled her cell phone out from her hip pocket. No bars. What good was it to have a cell phone that only seemed to work inside city limits?

Relief washed over her as the rumbling of Deke's truck sounded in the distance. The motor was winding out—going through the gears rapidly. Then the truck shot from the coverage of trees and braked for the turn into the drive. The truck fishtailed through the open gate and headed for the barn. Both horses were on the alert now. "Easy," Rita whispered more to herself than the horses.

The truck slid to a halt, and Deke opened the door and jumped to the ground. He took long strides toward Rita and the waiting horses. His face was intense.

"Is something wrong?"

He didn't seem to hear but walked between the two horses. He checked their saddles, bridles and tugged on their cinches. "You got them saddled. Good."

"Did I do it right?"

"I need to find Cecil. You can stay here."

"What? You invited me to ride, arrive so late I started to worry, and now tell me to wait for you without explanation?"

Deke walked over to Rita and took both her hands. "Honey, I'm sorry. I just have lots on my mind, and I need you to trust me until I get this sorted out." A glance at the waiting horses seemed to calm him. "On second thought, yes, ride with me, but I cannot explain things until I know how. Will you hang with me?"

Rita surveyed his face. "Of course."

"Thank you. I need to process something." Deke kissed her lightly on the lips and turned to Zorro. He stood still for a few seconds, then turned to her. "I need to process something, and I need you."

Rita felt an emotion she couldn't explain sweep through her. She didn't know what was going on, but she fought the urge to run to him and hold him. Instead, she copied his mounting style on Mandy. It was the first time he did not stand by until she was safely mounted. Instead, he just watched her with a distracted smile and a nod.

"Let's ride. I want to check on Cecil." Deke didn't wait for a reply but made a clucking sound with his mouth and neck-reined his steed to the corral exit. Rita followed his lead.

They crossed the pasture and entered the wooded shadows. The surefooted horses wended their way around the trees until they broke into the clearing at Cecil's cabin. Deke rode up to the front of the structure and called out. "Cecil, it's Deke. You here?"

Deke stood in the stirrups to get a better view. He sat back down in the creaking saddle. "He's not here. Plato is gone, too. Let's go back to the field and ride parallel to the woods."

They retraced their ride and rode toward the back of the property. Deke started whistling various tunes. Rita eyed him as he performed. Deke twisted in the saddle and gave her a serious nod. "I am not auditioning. I'm just trying to let him know I'm here."

"He's probably been driven into hiding."

"That's a good one," Deke mumbled.

As they approached the back of Cecil's place, the peaceful chirping of birds was interrupted by a blood-curdling scream. The startled horses jerked their heads up and danced a few steps. "Whoa, whoa. Easy," Deke's eyes scanned the horizon for the origin of the scream.

"What was that? Who was that?" Rita's voice quivered.

"Someone terrified, big-time. I hope it isn't *who* I think. Stay close."

CHAPTER 39

Deke urged his mount forward to the barbed wire fencing separating the properties, then dismounted. Rita remained in the saddle as Deke walked slowly beside the fence, leading Zorro behind him.

Rita's heart pounded. She rode as Deke walked. Her eyes combed the fields. Then something caught her eye. It was a red and white object that contrasted with the green grass of the pasture. From her elevated position, she rode closer to the fence, trying to focus, then she pointed.

"Deke, Deke. What's that?"

Deke froze in his steps at Rita's alert. He looked back at her. She was standing up in the stirrups, pointing an index finger to a spot he could not see from the ground.

"Where?" Deke's head swiveled back and forth.

"Right there. Something reddish with white," Rita responded with a touch of irritation in her voice.

Deke crossed the fence and moved slowly in the direction of the pointing finger, then stopped abruptly. He squatted down and picked up the item. "Tinker."

Rita called, "Tinker? What is that?"

Deke stood, holding the doll. He could now see the broken boards that had covered the old well. He dashed to the opening, fearing the worst. Then, dropping to his knees, he cleared some plant growth, rotted lumber away, and peered into the dark hole. There was enough light to see the small frame seated at the bottom and leaning against the side—water was up to her waist.

"Oh, God! It's Violet. She's fallen into the well. Violet! Can you hear me?"

Rita brought her hands prayerlike in front of her lips. "Is she—is she—alive?"

Deke's professional demeanor kicked in. He put a lid on his emotions and stood, ignoring her question. "Ride back to my truck. Our cell phones won't work here. Get on my radio and call dispatch. Tell them to get a rescue squad here along with an ambulance. Tell them to enter through Lamb's farm and come straight back to the back of the Burgess farm. Hurry."

Rita tugged Mandy's reins and spun her around in the direction of the barn and Deke's truck. Deke watched her ride off like a pro. *That's my girl.*

He jerked his head around to focus on the child, his mind racing. He could not see any movement. The well was too narrow for him to slide down. He noted that the base of the well swelled out. Reaching in, he tested the stones in the side of the well. Some rocks were loose. Any movement could discharge stones onto the unmoving child. He hoped she was unconscious, not dead. The sound of a high, winding motor broke into his rescue processing plans.

A utility vehicle was fast approaching. It was Lamb and Willa. Before it came to a complete halt, Willa had jumped from the vehicle and was running toward the well and Deke.

She spotted the doll lying by Deke as he knelt beside the well. Before she even got the well, she surmised the worst.

"My baby, oh my baby!" Willa dropped to her knees, and open-mouthed, she stared into the well.

Deke noticed the bruise and swelling on her cheek. Something for another time.

Her eyes widened as she saw her child's twisted form. She grabbed the edge of the stones, sending bits of them and debris into the well. "Vi, Vi! Answer me."

She jerked her head toward Deke. "Is she ... is she ...?"

Deke gently guided her back from the edge of the well. "Stay back. The sides are not stable. And I don't know what her condition is."

Deke's mind raced to formulate a rescue plan.

Bull was peering down the well now. "Oh no! We've got to get her out of there."

Deke rose and grabbed the agitated man's shoulders. "Bull, I need you to focus. We cannot waste time."

He half-expected Bull to shake him off and maybe swing at him. Instead, however, he only stared blankly.

"You have wire cutters in your vehicle?"

Bull nodded.

"Then get them. Willa, I need you to take the Gator and go back to wait for the rescue squad and ambulance and lead them here."

The couple seemed in a daze and stood immobile.

"Move, if you want to save your daughter's life!"

Bull grabbed his wife by the arm. "Come on. Do what he says."

As the couple raced to the side-by-side, Deke peered into the well—he thought he saw movement. Could it be? Wait! Something was different. He leaned over more. The water had been just below her waist. Now it was above her waist.

His mind raced. All the rain they had experienced the last few days made the underground caverns increase, filling the well. He was about to turn, then saw a little hand twitch and move ever so slightly in response to the cold water. "Vi, Vi," he called, but no response.

Bull had found some wire cutters and was returning. Deke intercepted him and snatched the cutters from him. "She's alive."

He raced to the barbed wire fence and cut all the wires. Each one spiraled up to the posts where they were stapled. He dropped the cutters and ran toward Zorro, untying him from the fence and leading him near the well. He retrieved his lasso from the saddle and paused a second, holding the muzzle of the horse. He whispered as he rubbed his ears. "Steady, old friend. I need you to be steady and listen."

Zorro stood erect and looked into Deke's eyes. Deke could see that the horse sensed the seriousness of the situation. Deke freed the lasso and approached the well, leaving Zorro to stand ground-tied. He had hoped maybe, just maybe, the girl would regain consciousness. Then she could help him get the rope around her. He dropped the rope into the well, flicking the loop near her hand.

He almost had it under her hand, but it slipped off when she moved slightly.

"She moved!" Bull shouted. "She's alive!"

"Yes, she's alive. But she has to come to for me to get her to put the rope around her."

"The rescue team. They will be here shortly. You said you called them?" Bull looked plaintively in his face.

"We can't wait. The water is rising."

"Oh my God. I gotta get down there." Panic rose in his voice.

"You cannot fit, and I cannot fit," Deke said.

There was silence for a few seconds. Then a squeaky voice spoke behind them as they stood by the well. "But I can."

Both men spun around. A surprised Deke greeted the voice. "Cecil!"

Deke looked at the opening and back at the rail-thin body. He shook his head. "Cecil, yes, you would fit, but you're not strong enough. I hate to be blunt. You would have to be lowered down and avoid the walls, then slip the rope off you, and get the rope around her in tight quarters. I would pull her back up then and send the rope back to you."

"Please, let him try," Lamb pleaded.

Cecil removed his hat and the canvas bag slung over his shoulder. "I'm ready."

Deke stepped closer, calling out to Bull over his shoulder, "Keep trying to wake her up." He placed his hands on Cecil's boney shoulders. "You can't do this. I know what your medical condition is. You could die in that well, or you could die of complications. Pastor Mike has told me of your condition. He did it only for me to understand and help him monitor you."

Cecil allowed a slight smile. "Pastor Mike needs to remember his clergy-flock confidentiality." He touched Deke's chest with long fingers. "We have to save our friend."

Deke nodded, and both neared the well. He slipped the lariat loop over Cecil's head and under his arms. Deke removed his leather gloves and handed them to Cecil. "Put them between the rope loop and armpits. It will help the discomfort."

He took a quick look down the well and estimated that the child was about sixteen to eighteen feet down.

"Stand here." Deke turned from Cecil and sprinted to Zorro. He backed the horse up to eighteen feet facing the well, added another four feet, and wrapped the rope around the saddle horn.

He returned to the men. Bull had been calling out to the girl to no avail. He shook his head at Deke.

"Okay, Cecil, I'm going to mount my horse, and we will lower you down. Bull, put those muscles to use—keep feeding the rope and Cecil down the well."

He turned to Bull. "Keep him clear of the sides. You are going to be my eyes. You have to tell me how close we are to Vi. You have to tell me if he is in trouble, and the critical part will be exchanging the rope from him to her. Can you do that?"

Bull's head bobbed up and down. "Yeah, yeah, I can do that."

"Ready, brother?" Deke smiled at Cecil.

Cecil turned his head from looking down the well. Deke thought he saw a puzzled countenance for a second, but it quickly was erased and replaced by a tight smile. "What do they say in the Marines? I got your 'stick'?"

"No, I've got *your* six."

"That's why I flunked out of airborne." Cecil snickered.

"By the way, can you swim, seriously?"

"Never learned. I always felt awkward in my speedo at public beaches."

Deke smiled. "As Rita always says to me, 'You're incorrigible.'"

Cecil returned the smile. "Then I am in good company."

"I'll take care of you." Deke's statement was sober.

"I know."

Deke mounted Zorro. "You both ready?"

The men nodded, and Cecil edged toward the opening of the well. Bull faced Cecil with the rope over his shoulder. Cecil stepped tentatively into the well with his feet pressed to the wall. Deke heard him praying softly.

Deke kneed Zorro with a light touch. "Easy."

Rider and the horse became one. Deke leaned forward and whispered in Zorro's ear. He pulled on the reins and alternately released them. Bull kept his shoulder into the lariat, and the rescuer descended slowly.

It seemed to Deke that Zorro understood the seriousness of this situation. This was not roping a calf—it was delicate, and it was essential to his rider.

CHAPTER 40

Cecil fought to breathe as the walls closed in around him. His brain screamed to his very soul to shout at the two men above to get him out.

"Lord, I know you are with me." The dank coolness surrounded him. His shoulders scraped the stone walls. Above him, Lamb leaned forward over him, inching the rope downward. His face was red—but this time it was strain, not anger.

Cecil looked downward, straining to make out the child's tiny form, but his body had blocked the sunlight.

He used his feet to give some relief to his chest, squeezed by the rope. He tried to ignore his racing heart and focus on his purpose. Then the sides widened, and his feet dangled.

Fighting through waves of panic, he realized this was good. The well bottom was widening. It opened into a chamber about four to five feet wide and six feet tall. He was clear of the tight stone walls. His toe bumped against a large rock. He stood on the rock trying to catch his breath. Freed from the tightness of the rope, he slipped it off and held it with one hand. His chest hurt, sharp pains raced across it and under his arm. *Lord, please don't let me die before I can get this child out of here.*

"I'm here!" Cecil shouted. The echo resounded from the walls startling him.

Lamb's voice rang out. "You get to her? Is she breathing?"

Cecil lay down on the jutting rock and looked the little girl over. "Checking."

The water was now up to the child's neck. Alarmed, Cecil attempted to pull her up with him. It took all his strength.

"Ahhh!" A pain-filled groan came from Violet's lips. One hand shot down to her leg. He could see her lower left leg was cut and bleeding. He felt her leg. There was a fracture.

Violet groaned and opened her eyes. "Mr. Cecil, I was looking for you." Her voice was weak and trailed off.

"I am here, Violet, and we are going to get you out of here."

Violet closed her eyes. "Yes."

He noticed a large bump on her forehead at the hairline. He stepped down off the jutting rock to the base of the well, and cold water covered his knees.

He called up to Lamb. "She is alive but hurt. Her left leg is fractured, and she has a possible concussion. I'm getting the rope around her. Better move fast—the water is rising."

When Cecil was satisfied the little girl was secure in the lasso, he called up again. "Okay. Start pulling her up but do it slowly."

He could see Lamb's head turn to talk to Deke in the sunlit opening. The slack in the rope tightened and Violet began to rise. Cecil guided the girl's unconscious body out of the chamber into the confines of the well walls. She rose slowly and entered the stone tube.

Pain wracked through Cecil's body. Even though he was no longer exerting himself, his breathing came in gasps.

The jutting rock he had stood on now became his seat as he fought against the dizziness that threatened to invade his mind. The water circled his waist. It was ironic: he'd never entered water deeper than a bathtub, yet now he was going to drown.

The pain under his arm was excruciating. He coughed, looked up, and saw open sky. Violet was safe! The white clouds gathering above formed what looked like an angel with wispy wings. So tired. He leaned against the stones in the chamber. The jutting rock was strangely comfortable. *Rock of ages. Yes, that's it. Like the old gospel song. This rock supported me to save Violet. Now it's supporting me while I wait on the Lord.*

Darkness took over and the pain was gone.

"Almost there." Lamb said.

Deke paused his horse, then reined him gently. "Zorro back, easy."

Lamb sank to his knees and reached into the well to pull his child up. He carried her to some soft grass, laid her down gently, and removed the lasso. "Baby, talk to me."

Deke jumped from the saddle like he was being timed on calf roping. He peered into the well. He saw Cecil's legs. "Cecil, Cecil, can you hear me?" There was no answer.

He heard hoofbeats coming fast. Rita was riding hard. Her long hair flowed out from under her hat. She pulled Mandy to a halt and dismounted, flipping the reins around a top wire of the fence. She pulled a flashlight from where she had shoved it in her belt and took in the scene as she ran through the opening in the fence.

"The ambulance is on the way. How is she?"

Lamb looked at Rita, his mouth opened and closed, but words did not come out. He shook his head.

Violet moved and moaned. Her eyes opened and immediately she started crying. "Daddy, Daddy. My leg hurts, hurts bad."

"We're going to fix it, honey. Fix it soon." Lamb kissed her forehead.

"Ow, my head hurts, too." She groaned, tears rolling down her cheeks.

Rita looked into Lamb's wet eyes. "She's going to be fine."

Rita smiled and the distraught father nodded. She turned her attention to Deke as he searched for any movement in the well. "Brought this flashlight from your truck. Thought you might need it."

"Great." He took the light and shined it down into the hole.

"The sun's dropping and it's getting darker. I can't get a response from Cecil. The water is still rising." Deke moved to another side of the well. "I see him. He looks unconscious or ... or ... Hold this." He handed the flashlight to Rita and ran to Zorro, detaching the rope from the saddle pommel and coiling the rope.

"Honey, move over here. Point your light at an angle. You see him?"

She moved to the point Deke indicated. "No. Yes. Yes, I see him. I cannot see his head, but I can see his body. The water is up to his waist or a little above."

"Keep the light on him. I am going to see if I can get a lasso over him."

Deke dropped the loop into the well. He started the loop spinning parallel to the floor of the well. He slowly raised it up where it was even with Cecil's head. The loop settled on his head and shoulder. His head leaned on the wall, preventing the loop from settling.

"I can't get a loop around his body. He is planted against the wall."

Deke chewed his lip. "If I can get his arm, and pull him away from the wall, then I may be able to get a loop around him."

He saw one arm beginning to float in the rising water. He spun the lasso again and then deftly made it spin horizontally, allowing the loop to settle into the water. Before it could float upward, he ran to the other side of the well and jerked the rope.

Rita shouted, "You got his arm!"

Without releasing the tension on the rope, he returned to the other side of the well beside Rita. He peered down at his work. The rope was solidly on Cecil's arm above the elbow.

"I can't lift him by one arm. I will tear his arm out of the socket."

"Maybe you don't have a choice," Rita said with tears in her eyes.

Deke studied his options, and the words were whispered softly. "Please, God."

Deke pulled on the rope around his arm. Cecil's body tilted forward, and his other arm floated up. He quickly whipped the rope and widened the circle. He dropped it around his body. A quick jerk and the rope closed about his body. It was under both arms.

"Thank you," Deke said with a sigh of relief.

Deke started pulling Cecil's body to the opening. "Bull, I need help."

Rita stood and yelled at Bull who was crouched over his daughter. "Help Deke get Cecil out of the well. I'll care for Violet."

The father rose from his sobbing daughter and stood across the opening from Deke. The two men worked together to pull Cecil up. No longer did they have the help of Zorro.

Both men had to extend their arms over the well and draw the rope upward hand over hand. Both men were powerful but found the awkward extension of the arms a challenge.

"I should have got my horse to help," Deke said.

"Too late now," grunted Lamb.

Cecil's head appeared, and both men walked sideways to extract him from the well. The men collapsed on the ground, breathing hard. Deke crawled to Cecil and checked his carotid artery. "He's alive."

Deke looked up at the sound of motors. An ambulance and a rescue truck were following Willa, who was bouncing across the field in the utility vehicle. Help had finally arrived.

CHAPTER 41

Deke glanced in his truck's rearview mirror and watched as Rita led his two horses into the barn. She looked so comfortable around them now. He was glad she had urged him to go on to the hospital to be with Cecil. He was thankful another ambulance had been dispatched upon the arrival of the first one. The EMT left an oxygen bottle and worked on Cecil as others loaded Violet into the first ambulance. He had stayed with his friend until the second one arrived. Now, he had to get to the hospital. Cecil couldn't die. He found himself asking God to help the man.

Deke slid into a parking place at the emergency entrance to the hospital and raced to the waiting room. Lamb sat alone on a straight-back chair. He stared at the floor, clutching a foam cup with both hands. He looked dejected, not like the powerful adversary that used to haunt Deke's life and dreams. For the first time, Deke pitied the man.

As Deke stood quietly in the doorway of the waiting room, Lamb lifted the cup to his lips and locked eyes with the deputy. He rose slowly but said nothing. Gone were the sneers and glowers that he usually had for Deke.

"How's she doing?" Deke asked.

"I guess pretty good, considering what she's been through. Her lower leg is fractured. They say she has a concussion, a few bumps and scrapes, but she will bounce back."

"That's wonderful news."

"Willa is with her now. They are putting a cast on her and will keep her overnight to monitor her concussion."

"Violet is a sweet little girl. She's special."

Pain filled Lamb's eyes and his lip quivered. Deke turned toward the nurse's station. "I'm going to try to see Cecil and find out what's going on with him."

Lamb's voice stopped him. "Deke, thanks for saving my daughter's life."

Bull had never called Deke by his first name. It took him off guard. "Well, Bull, the real thanks go to Cecil—the Waxman as you call him."

Bull nodded. "Yes, I will thank him. Mr. Burgess. It's a funny thing, I lose a son to the prison system over him, yet he saves my daughter. Confusing."

Deke spoke quietly with no emotion. "Cecil didn't have anything to do with Bobby's death. Your son intended to rob him, and your son, in a fit of rage, killed his friend. You need to come to grips with that. And yes, your daughter is alive tonight because of Cecil."

There was a flash of anger in Lamb's eyes, but it was momentary. He opened his arms in a gesture of surrender and nodded. He sat down and returned his gaze to the floor. Deke walked to the heavy door of the treatment room, which swung open. Out came a balding doctor in a lab coat.

He looked up in surprise. "Whups! Deputy, sorry if I hit you with the door."

"You didn't. Are you tending Cecil Burgess, Doctor Devlin?"

"Yes, in more ways than one. I happened to be on call as the emergency room doctor, and I am Cecil's regular physician."

"Can I see him?"

"Well, he's had a heart attack. You knew he had a heart condition, right?"

"Yeah, I didn't know how serious it was. Cecil never talks about his health."

The doctor paused and watched a medical assistant pass by, carrying a tray. He took Deke's elbow and guided him to a vacant office a few doors down. "Come with me, Deke."

The doctor sighed and scratched his chin. "You also probably know he has Werner syndrome. That complicates his recovery."

"I couldn't remember the technical term."

"People call it the aging disease. It's very rare, and usually, lives are cut short by cancer or heart attacks. And he has both."

"What? I didn't know."

"That doesn't surprise me. Pastor Mike usually brings him in for his appointments. I always try to see him discreetly after hours and provide any scans or lab work when I know folks will not be around. By the way, Mike doesn't know about the cancer either. The last scan shows it is spreading in his lungs. I am violating patient-doctor confidence by telling you this. But someone needs to know, and from what I hear from Mike, you and he are pretty tight. So, someone will have to take care of those end-of-life details."

"Are you saying he's dying?"

"I'm surprised he has lasted this long. Although I don't endorse his natural cures, I have to say I have seen results from his exotic concoctions on many of my patients. And I think his search for curing his condition has, at least in a small part, prolonged his survival."

"Can I see him?"

"He is being moved into an ICU room as we speak. Yes, you can see him, but he will be out for a while." Dr. Devlin patted Deke's shoulder.

He wheeled around and walked back toward the ER, leaving Deke to ponder what he had heard. Deke heard the whoosh of the automatic doors and looked down the hall. Rita walked toward him, still wearing her riding attire.

She stood on her tiptoes to briefly kiss him on his lips. "Have you seen him? What's the prognosis?"

Deke shook his head. "No, I haven't seen him yet. I was just on my way to ICU to be with him. By the way, when he comes to, he will be asking about his dog. I forgot all about Plato."

"Don't worry about Plato. He is taken care of. Shortly after you left, he showed up at the barn looking for his master while I was taking care of the horses. He let me take him home, and I saw the garbage can with his dog food in there."

"You walked him back through the dark woods?"

"Nah. Plato sat in my passenger seat, and I drove him to the cabin. I had your flashlight. He seemed to enjoy the ride. But he also seemed disappointed when it ended."

Deke had to laugh. "You allowed a mutt to ride in your immaculate toy car. You're reluctant even to let me ride in your car."

"Well, Plato is high-class. I draw the line with low-class mutts."

"Oh-oh, now I am a low-class mutt." Deke feigned hurt.

"But still, you are a cute one." She giggled and pinched his cheek.

Deke smiled, then glanced down the hall. "Look, babe, I need to get to Cecil. If he comes to and finds himself in a hospital, he might have a panic attack. You go home and get some sleep—I'll call you in the morning." He paused, then cleared his throat. "Cecil's doctor said he had a heart attack. Of course, I told you about his genetic disease that ages him quickly. I just learned he has cancer too." Deke tried to remain stoic, but his voice cracked.

"I am so sorry," she said. "Go, be with him."

"Okay. I will talk to you later—one more thing. You were tremendous in all this. Thank you."

She smiled and kissed him again. "Go."

He headed down the hallway, making multiple turns until he came to the door with protocols and rules spelled out below a small window. Easing the door open, he was greeted by beeping, clicking, and the sound of air movement from life-sustaining machines. The pungent odor of antiseptic assailed his olfactory sense. He did not like hospitals. Standing still, he gazed around at the dozen small rooms where patients were monitored around the clock. The smells and sounds surrounding him triggered a painful memory. The face of the homeless man flashed across his mind. The memory of the doctor turning to him and saying, "He's gone."

Deke jumped as a woman's voice spoke beside him. "Who are you looking for?"

He looked and saw a familiar face. Denise usually worked the ER area. "Oh, Denise—is Cecil Burgess here?"

Denise nodded. "Room Seven."

"Thanks."

Deke entered the room quietly. Cecil was clad in a hospital gown, his frail arms protruding from the short sleeves. One arm had several tubes hidden by bandages and tape. Wires attached to his chest registered his heart rhythm on a monitor on the wall. Deke walked closer to the bed. Cecil's scarred face was pale. Sparse wispy hair on his head floated on the pillow. An oxygen tube was softly guiding fresh air into his nostrils. His mouth gaped open, revealing small white teeth.

Deke dragged a black recliner closer to the bed and turned it so he could watch the thin man. He sat down to creaks and groans; the small recliner was not designed for his large frame.

"Hmm, so tired." He levered the footrest up and reclined, but his calves extended over the edge. "Oh well, any port in a storm."

His questions would have to wait. As he watched the placid man sleeping, he was struck by the courage Cecil had shown.

Had he expected to die?

Exhausted, Deke fell asleep.

CHAPTER 42

Deke awoke with a start in the recliner. It took him a few seconds to realize where he was. Hospital noises and smells kicked in and brought him into reality. He turned his head and saw Cecil facing him, eyes half-open. He smiled weakly and raised a limp hand in greeting.

Deke returned the recliner to a sitting position and rose stiffly. He stretched and smiled. "Not the most comfortable bed I have ever slept in. How are you doing?"

Cecil's mouth moved, but no words came out. He cleared his throat and tried again, managing a coarse whisper. "I slept well. I think. You should have gone home and slept in your bed." He squinted. "Plato? Have you seen him?"

"Don't worry about him. Rita is treating him like royalty. He came looking for you and then went back to your place with Rita. She fed him. He even got to ride in her fancy convertible."

"Miss Rita is a wonderful person. I don't know why she wants to hang around with you." Cecil grinned, then coughed spasmodically.

"You need water?"

Cecil shook his head. "I had enough water yesterday to last a long time."

Deke chuckled. "Still the stand-up comic of the county."

Deke looked down at the floor, then into Cecil's eyes. "Listen, I got a question to ask you. I have to know. I was trying to find you yesterday when Violet fell into the well."

"Go ahead. Ask. You know I will tell you the truth." Cecil nodded.

"That I do." Deke drew a deep breath, and stillness reigned as all the activity in the hospital seemed to be shut out."

Deke leaned forward. "How are we related?"

Cecil's chin quivered. "Why do you think that?"

"Don't play games. Tell me! Please." Deke pleaded.

He looked at the ceiling. "So much for Brother Mike's vow of silence."

"He didn't have anything to do with it. Yesterday morning, the lab tech from the state came by my office. He returned evidence examined relating to your case—including your rock hammer. He had found something strange on it. Your DNA was present, and mine was too. He had mine on file already, so he could eliminate any crime scenes I had accidentally contaminated." Deke paused. "He said my DNA indicated you're my relative."

Deke sucked in a breath. "I had to have answers. I raced to the nursing home and spoke to my aunt. Turns out she's not my blood aunt. I am not even a Campbell. I am a Burgess. Out with it, Cecil."

Dark eyes looked into dark eyes.

Deke broke the silence. "May cried and asked me to forgive her. She started to explain how this was so, but she faded into confusion before I could get all of her story ... but you knew all this, didn't you?" Emotion overtook him.

Cecil breathed heavily. "I didn't know until about a month ago. Pastor Mike and I were visiting Miss May. She was having one of her rare lucid moments. She seemed to sense her days were getting short and wanted to confess her secret.

"I was born the night our home went up in flames. Miss May had come over to check on mother and found her on the living room floor in labor. Then she heard screams from the bedroom, my screams. The bedroom was in flames, but she managed to get me out. I was already severely burned.

"Evidently the power had been knocked out by a storm. There was a kerosene lamp on the floor by the bed. May theorized mother had already had me and was trying to get to the living room to call for help. But she had knocked over the lamp and was overcome by smoke as she crawled into the other room."

Cecil stopped talking and coughed. Deke poured water for him out of a plastic pitcher on his nightstand. He raised his head and helped him drink a few sips.

"Thank you." Cecil seemed to be struggling for air.

"Do you want me to call the nurse?"

"No. I've got to get this out while I can."

He swallowed hard and began talking again. "May rushed me out to the fresh air on the porch. I'd stopped crying, and she thought I was gone. She then pulled mother out onto the porch. Mother stirred slightly, and then May saw another head appear. You."

Deke gasped. "Twins! You and I are twins?"

Cecil nodded. A single tear floated down his cheek.

Deke spread his arms and his voice quivered. "Why did you keep this hidden? Why didn't Mike tell me?"

"Because I made him and Miss May promise to keep this quiet. You were finally getting your life back on track. I didn't want to throw a wrench into it. It did not matter to me you did not know. The pastor urged me to tell you. I told him he could use his discretion after I was gone—whether or not to tell you. I guess I put Mike into a dilemma. Please don't be angry with him. Or May. Your adopted mother had several miscarriages and had had one a couple of days before. Joe and Wanda Campbell wanted children so bad. They loved you and thought of your as their own. As you grew up, I guess they never saw a need to tell you the truth."

Deke was numb. "That's why I don't favor the Campbells." He looked up. "So, how did she pull it off?"

"May said before the firetrucks arrived or anybody else, she wrapped you in a blanket and put you in the back of her station wagon. She returned to our mother, but she was gone, whether from smoke inhalation or just the injuries of birthing us—we'll never know."

Another round of coughing halted Cecil. Deke poured another glass of water, but the struggling man waved him off.

"I have to finish. I was transported to the burn unit in Evansville. The paramedics worked on me all the way to the hospital. She said she knew of one sister our mother had, but they were not close. Of course, our father had died from the accidental fall.

"May said her heart went out to you—and her sister's too. It seemed God wanted to join you with a new family. Ours was gone. She drove you to Fredonia and handed her sister something she always wanted—a child. After much discussion, your adopted parents made a pact to raise you as their own. No one would ever suspect. May was Mrs. Campbell's midwife too. Your adopted mother had undergone a recent miscarriage, gone into depression, and remained out of sight in her home. The timing was perfect. They obtained a birth certificate for a home birth. Nobody suspected anything. I was placed in the children's home, and although I was available for adoption, no one wanted to take me in." Cecil smiled. "Maybe they figured I was not too photogenic for family photos."

Deke dropped in the chair as memories swarmed his brain. He put his face into his hands, trying to make sense of all this. His voice was strained when he spoke. "My whole life is a lie."

Cecil's voice cracked. "That is why after I found out, I couldn't ruin your life. I did not want you ever to know. So you could live out your existence free of me."

Deke jerked his face from his hands. "Oh no, Cecil. Don't ever say that. I'm talking about all I missed out on. You and me! If I could have had a choice of brothers, I would have chosen you. You are the finest, most caring, and wisest man I have ever known." The corners of Deke's mouth twitched, and a tear rolled down his cheek.

He heard sobbing and looked at the doorway. Tears were streaming down Rita's face, and she stood with her hands clasped under her chin. "I ... I'm sorry. I didn't mean to interrupt anything. I couldn't help but hear ..."

She rushed into the room as Deke stood, wiping his eyes with the back of his hand. They embraced, and she cried into his chest.

"How long were you there? Did you hear everything?" Deke asked.

She stayed pressed to his chest and nodded.

Cecil watched the two embrace. "You two need each other."

His eyes were drooping. "Tell Violet to stay curious about the world. I expect big things from her."

Deke released Rita and moved to his bedside. He took both Cecil's hands in both of his. "Now that I've found you, brother, we have a lot to do and talk about. First, you can teach me natural cures, like your cure for my smoking. I will teach you how to ride. And, and ..."

Oh, God, please let him live. Please help me to forgive my adopted parents and May.

Cecil smiled with his eyes closed. "We can do that in glorified bodies on the other side of eternity." He turned toward Deke and clutched his hand. His eyes widened. "You need to talk to Pastor Mike." His breathing became labored, and the pain showed on his face. He strained to speak. "Brother."

Deke's hands shook. "Yes. Brother."

The heart graph monitor became erratic. In scant seconds, medical personnel were shooing the visitors out of the room. They closed the door, but Deke could see a crash cart and hear the word, "Clear!" shouted through the window.

He turned and looked at the nurse's station in the center of the room. The sign under the monitor that read "Room Seven" was now a straight line. Deke was vaguely aware of nurses around him who had stopped their activities and were watching him with tender expressions.

The door to the ICU was thrust open, and Dr. Devlin appeared, striding purposely to Cecil's room. He entered, and through the glass, Deke could see him conversing with the medical personnel.

The door opened again, and Pastor Mike appeared. "How is ...?" He stopped short, reading the expressions of everyone, then sat down hard on a nearby chair. "I wanted to say goodbye. Rita called me early this morning to tell me he was here."

Deke placed his hand on the pastor's shoulder. "Cecil knew you would come. You were a true friend."

Mike only nodded as he stared vacantly at the floor.

Dr. Devlin slowly left Cecil's room and removed his stethoscope from around his neck, placing it in the oversized pocket of his lab coat.

"I'm sorry. He is no longer in pain."

All three nodded.

"Uh. This is a little awkward, but since he has no family, are you aware of any arrangements that have been made?"

Mike cleared his throat. "Yes, he has shared his wishes with me. I will be taking care of the final details."

Deke cleared his throat and addressed the doctor, "You are wrong. He does have a family. I am his brother."

CHAPTER 43

The trees were now full of color as Deke plodded up the trail to Cecil's home. In one hand, he carried Cecil's Panama hat. Plato rose and stood stiff-legged with tail straight as he saw him coming. The dog sounded a short bark, then his tail wagged.

He bounded off the porch and ran to Deke.

"How ya doing, buddy? Today, we are going to lay your master to rest."

Deke knelt and stroked Plato's head with his free hand. The dog sniffed the hat in his other hand, then looked at him, his head cocked quizzically.

"I don't know if it's true, but the old-timers say a dog can smell death on their master's clothing. That they can get past grieving when they know they're not coming home. That true, boy?"

Deke rose and walked up the steps. He laid the hat down by the dog's makeshift bed and began to fill his food bowl from the galvanized garbage can. He checked to ensure his bowl still held water from the cabin's gutter runoff. It did. Deke did not want to go inside. He would have to soon enough.

He sniffed the fresh pine and cedar-scented air. The world around him was sunny but cool. It was hard to believe Cecil had died three days ago. Rita had been a gem—feeding Plato, helping Deke make funeral arrangements. She knew he was struggling. There had been women in his life, but none like Rita. God had certainly put her into his life.

He turned to see Plato watching him and gestured to his bowl. "Eat. You need to eat."

The dog turned and walked to his bed, picking up the hat along the way. He plopped down and laid his head on the ancient straw hat.

Deke's heart went out to him. "Okay, I understand. It'll just take time."

He moved to give the dog a final pat, then walked slowly back down the trail toward his truck. He had a funeral to attend.

The pastor and his wife were waiting at the door of the little white church when Rita arrived. A black hearse had backed up to the entrance, its rear door open. She parked beside Mike's car and went to the passenger side to lift a floral arrangement from the seat.

As she approached the church, the funeral home director was talking with Mike and Lois. Three of his boys, all dressed in suits, stood beside him.

Lois spotted Rita first. "Oh, Rita. We're glad to see you." She looked over her shoulder. "Where's Deke?"

"He's coming in his truck. He wanted to stop and check on things at Cecil's and feed his dog."

Mike smiled. "Good morning, Rita. Glad to hear it. We're going to need another strong back to carry Cecil inside."

"He wouldn't miss it. He'll be here shortly." Rita peered into the dark recess of the hearse. The wooden coffin was plain. Just hardware handles on the side. Rita whispered to Mike so that the men from the funeral home could not hear. "That coffin looks so, so ..."

"Cheap. Is that the word you were looking for?" The pastor gave a small smile.

"I guess so. I mean, didn't Cecil have any savings or insurance?"

"Cecil came to me with all his final wishes written down. He was very explicit about three things. No viewing, closed coffin, and the cheapest box he could get. Oh, he did add that if it was within a few days of Halloween, the coffin could remain open. When I gave him a funny look, he started laughing. Said, 'Gotcha.'"

Rita could only nod and blink back her tears. Mike patted her shoulder.

"Yes, he loved life and had a sharp wit." He stared at the coffin. "I'll miss him."

She sighed and regained her words. "Me too. He had no family, except Deke, and no other friends—that I know of. So do you expect many to show up?"

"Oh, a few. But most will assume it's going to be a closed casket, so the curious will not be here."

In the distance, the signature sound of Deke's truck grew louder. Before he appeared around the bend, Mike tilted his head upward. "Yep, he doth come. I've got to go to my car and get some programs."

Rita watched as Deke parked beside her vehicle and stepped from the truck. He wore a dark suit and a pale tie. He'd even donned black dress shoes. She didn't know he owned anything close to that attire.

He approached her slowly, without his usual jaunty walk. He seemed tired, but it did little to dim his handsome features. How incredible Cecil was his twin—even though they were not identical twins.

"Hi. How are you?" Rita kissed him tenderly.

"Doing fine. How about yourself?"

"Honey, you aren't a good liar."

"I've not had your courtroom experience," he said mischievously.

"You will pay for that, mister."

"I'm sorry. My humor attempts are not working on me or anybody else. I want to get this over." He took her hands and kissed her on the forehead. "I'm still trying to sort things out."

"I know you are. So, I will give you a pass on your dumb jokes." She shook her finger in his face. "But don't push it." Rita hooked his arm and walked back to the hearse. "C'mon, they need you to help carry."

Rita, Deke, and Lois took the front pew that was reserved for family. The pianist played several old hymns. The program listed Cecil's date of birth and death and place of birth—no pictures except an illustration of a dove. The nineteenth Psalm filled the inside front page, followed by parentheses and a note: "One of Cecil's favorites."

Strange, something missing? Rita saw no mention of Cecil being survived by Deke.

She heard movement toward the front of the church and turned to see a group of people quietly filing in. Then more. She looked at Deke as he sat, staring at the floor and fiddling with his program. He looked at her, and she nodded to the back of the church. He turned, and saw a

362

somber crowd had gathered and seated themselves. There were about twenty-five people. The sheriff and his family walked to the front and sat behind Rita and Deke. Tim leaned forward, squeezing his friend's arm.

A commotion arose at the doorway. Bryce Lamb appeared, pushing Violet in a wheelchair. Once the chair cleared the entry, Lamb stepped back outside and motioned Willa to take over.

Willa tugged on his arm, but he shook his head at her and looked to the very front as Deke sat watching. Then, expressionless, he nodded a curt greeting to Deke. He turned and walked out. Willa pushed Violet's chair down the window aisle, looking for a place to claim a seat. Vi's eyes lit up when she spotted Deke.

He rose and walked toward the mother and daughter and indicated the rest of the empty pew behind the three of them. Willa sat, leaving Vi in the aisle. Deke bent down next to Violet and touched the cast on her leg, then whispered something to her. Her smile widened, and she nodded. She adjusted the glasses on her nose, calling attention to the tape holding the broken frame together.

Rita turned and watched as more folks entered, including Deke's deputy friends, and found seats.

As Pastor Mike took the pulpit, Deke returned to his seat. Mike delivered a short, but powerful, eulogy and sermon. He told a few stories about how he and Cecil became friends and some humorous stories about Cecil that drew a spattering of laughter. He ended on a serious note. He talked about the character of Cecil—loving and kind. Moreover, he emphasized his wisdom about nature and his work developing cures for folks. Mike concluded by sharing Cecil's desire for all to know Christ.

"Before I pray and conclude this service, I want to allow anyone, I repeat anyone, to share your thoughts about Cecil Burgess."

Rita wanted to look around as Mike surveyed the congregation.

Deke rose slowly. "Pastor, I'd like to share some thoughts."

"Please, Deke, come up to the microphone so you can be heard."

Deke stepped to the raised dais and positioned himself behind the pulpit. Mike patted him on the back and moved aside.

Deke gripped the sides of the pulpit, cleared his throat, and spoke. "I know most of you folks here. Some of you knew me back in the days when I was a kid growing up. Lots of changes in your lives and my life since I returned and became a deputy."

He looked out on the crowd. "Most of you know Cecil let me stable my horses on his property. At no charge. I didn't know him long, only about five months. But I came to respect him as a kind and loving person. He was a model of what a Christian should be. He was wise and loved nature. He even got me to kick the cigarette habit. He knew people and loved strangers."

He paused, and his eyes looked sad. "But sometimes that love wasn't returned. Maybe in some cases, it was, but even those who benefited by his generous nature and remedies did not want to be seen with him. Cecil respected their wishes. He cared more about your feelings than his own and didn't want to be the source of your embarrassment."

Deke leaned forward. "I admit at first, I was repulsed by his looks. Said things that were not complimentary. He was the Waxman. I am ashamed I did that. I know by your presence here, maybe some of you share my regrets. Still, Cecil had nothing but love for everyone, and he was quick to forgive. I think we are a little better because of him. I know I learned a lot during the short time I knew him. Including the importance of faith." Deke paused and scanned the faces intently watching him.

He continued. "He often mentioned faith to me. He recognized I had not arrived. But I want to say I am working on it." His eyes met Rita's as she dabbed her eyes with a tissue.

Deke leaned back from the pulpit. "You all have your programs on this service, don't you?"

There was a shuffling of paper as they picked them up. Rita tensed and turned to look at the spectators.

"Okay. Now, take a pencil from the back of the pew. See where it gives the dates of death? What's missing? Usually, these programs read, 'Survived by son, daughter, grandson or some such.' Cecil was survived by someone too. Take your pencil and write in Deke Campbell."

People looked confused.

"Yes, I am his next of kin, his blood brother. You have heard the story about the Burgess homeplace fire. What you haven't heard was Cecil had a twin brother who survived and was raised by the Campbell family—me. I didn't find this out until about a week ago. Cecil knew it longer than I did, but he didn't tell me because he didn't want to 'mess my life up.'" Deke bit his lip and softened. "Cecil was my friend from the first. I never met a man so kind and wise."

He looked down at the pulpit. When he raised his head to the congregation, his dark eyes were moist. When he spoke again, his voice quivered. "I am proud to be Cecil's brother, and I will miss him. Thank all of you for being here. I am sincerely grateful. Cecil would be all smiles."

He looked down at the pulpit and took a long breath before raising his eyes back to the crowd. "That's all I have to say."

He stepped down from the dais and dropped into the seat next to Rita. He placed his hands on his knees and stared at them. Rita put her hand on top of his and squeezed. She was aware that she was having a full-on cry, but she didn't care.

Mike stepped back to the podium and sniffed. "Anyone else want to say something?"

Violet released her brakes and wheeled herself forward to the front. "Can I say something?" Her voice quivered.

Mike removed the microphone from its stand and took it to the girl. "You sure can."

Her small face scanned the crowd until it arrived at Deke and Rita. Rita smiled, assuming Deke was doing the same. Violet took a deep breath and began.

"Mr. Cecil taught me all about plants and animals. He showed me plants that could help me. He told me about Jesus, and he was always there to listen if I was having problems at home. But, most of all, he saved my life." Violet laid the mic in her lap and began to cry.

Pastor took the microphone and hugged her. Rita stood and whispered, "That was beautiful." She wheeled Violet back to Willa, whose eyes were wet.

"Anyone else?" Mike wielded the mic like a sword looking for another volunteer.

Rita watched as, one by one, people rose, timidly at first, but then boldly to express gratitude for Cecil and told of special times with him in private. Some even apologized for not inviting the medicine man into their homes. The testimonies to Cecil lasted longer than the pastor's sermon. Tears flowed freely.

SUMMER OF THE WAXMAN

Pastor Mike concluded the service with an emotional prayer. Deke, Rita, Mike, and Lois hung back after the service to shake hands with the attendees and thank them for coming. The folks waited for Cecil's coffin to be carried to the nearby grave site and lowered into the opening. Rita watched as the people went to their cars and left. How different they seemed now. It was as though Cecil's death had plunged each person into quiet introspection. They were never going to be the same.

CHAPTER 44

Deke's mind was a million miles away, reliving conversations with Cecil as he walked. Mike and Lois walked ahead of Deke and Rita. They were the last to leave. He glanced back to see the workmen had started filling the grave.

As they trudged toward their vehicles, Mike broke the silence. "I know this has been a hard day for you, Deke. But there are some things Cecil wanted me to tell you—hold on a second." Mike went to his car, opened the door for Lois, opened the back door, removed a box, and returned.

"Let's go sit down." Mike led the way to a picnic table near the church, where they held summer potlucks. Mike sat the box on the table and took a seat opposite Rita and Deke.

Deke recognized the chest. "That's Cecil's," he exclaimed.

"Yes. It is." Mike drew a deep breath. "Before I start, I want to tell you. What you did during the service was bold and cut to the chase. I think you have a future as a preacher." Mike grinned.

"Your job is not endangered," Deke answered.

"Look, you may not realize it, but you delivered Biblical truths."

"Thanks. I think. But it was Cecil influencing me. I saw what I was and what I could be. Both you and Cecil showed me what it is like to be forgiven by the Lord," Deke's mouth twitched at the corners, and his eyes moistened. "I also learned how to forgive myself. Thanks. I owe you a lot."

Rita stared at the table as Mike reached out and patted Deke's shoulder but said nothing. Seconds passed, and a slight breeze rustled through the leaves overhead.

Mike cleared his throat and spoke. "Now 'the rest of the story,' as Paul Harvey used to say. About a month ago, Cecil and I visited your Aunt May, er, your adopted Aunt May. She was very coherent at that time. May was a bit unsettled about the relationship between you and Cecil. She seemed eager to confess what she had done."

Mike scratched his head. "Deke, I know you discovered the relationship through other means. I hope you can forgive me for not revealing all this to you. I made a solemn oath to Cecil not to tell what May told us. He did not want to add more baggage to your life. He thought it would put your life in unnecessary turmoil. In addition, he'd just found out his life was moving into the terminal stage."

A sob caught in Deke's throat, and he turned away. He'd forever regret not having the chance to share Cecil's burden in those final weeks. Like a brother should. Mike's hand on his kept Deke from traveling too far down that road.

"Deke, he made me promise to guide you into salvation when he was gone. He liked you before he knew you were his brother. But he also did this."

Mike opened the little chest and took out a document packet.

"He had me set up a meeting with an attorney. I think you know him. Kressge, Bill Kressge. We met with him, and Cecil drew up his will. You now own Cecil's property. It would be yours anyway because you shared the same parents. You don't have to untangle things. It is all legal, and you can keep your name and family history."

Mike sat back and let what he said sink in. "Everything he owned is yours now. His cabin, personal items, two hundred acres, even this chest and its contents."

Deke reached inside the chest and drew out a black and white photo of his parents. "This is a lot to digest."

"By the way, you also inherited Plato."

"Hmph. That's not a problem. Plato and I are buds." Deke replaced the photo. "I'd rather have Cecil here than all the property." Deke studied the chest, aware the other two were watching him intently.

"I will miss him." He looked at them and smiled slightly. "I guess he was born first, so that makes him my *big* brother."

Mike and Rita nodded.

CHAPTER 45

Deke had spent two weeks after the funeral dealing with the legal aspects of Cecil's last will and testament. Rita had helped him with organizing Cecil's possessions and disposing of the plant life that had shared the company of his brother in his cabin. He knew he could not give the loving care to them their owner had.

Deke looked down at Plato, who was regarding him with curious eyes. "Well, my friend, it's you and me from here on out."

He smiled and rubbed Plato's head, which set the dog's tail in motion. Plato was getting used to staying with Deke. He slept at the foot of his bed. Each day, the canine looked forward to riding in Deke's truck to visit the place of his former master. Now Plato turned from the corral and barn, where they stood, and sniffed the breeze blowing from his old home, Cecil's cabin.

Plato's imploring look tugged at Deke's heart. "Yes, Plato, go check it out. Check out your memories. I do the same thing."

Plato didn't need any encouraging. He bounded off to the cabin. Deke watched his departure and returned to studying Zorro and Mandy as they finished eating. He glanced at his watch and saw he had about an hour before Rita arrived to join him for their Saturday afternoon ride. Although he loved to be with her, he found himself relieved he had some alone time.

He surveyed the land that was his inheritance, but his mind kept going down confusing trails. The sound of a motor rescued him from the foggy trails. *She is early. Wait, that's not Rita.*

A familiar vehicle appeared driving slowly through the gate. *Pastor Mike. He is probably here to chew me out for not being in church last Sunday. It's okay. In fact, it's more than okay.*

The car slowed, Mike exited, and grinned at Deke. "What a relief. I thought you had been raptured and then got scared that I was still here."

Mike walked up to Deke offered his hand, which Deke shook. The pastor squinted and inquired in low tones, "You all right, my friend?"

Deke rubbed his chin and smiled sheepishly at the preacher. "Oh, you mean because I missed church last Sunday? Yeah, I just had some time-critical evidence to process during that time slot."

Deke looked at the ground and leaned his back on the top rail of the fence. Neither man said anything for a few seconds as Mike joined Deke, imitating his fence-leaning by his side.

Both stared at the road as an Amish buggy clattered its way to town. The silence was loud. Finally, Deke cleared his throat and spoke, "You know, that's not the truth. Shouldn't lie to a pastor. They have a built-in polygraph."

Mike chuckled and bumped his arm with his elbow. "Glad you and lots of folks have that opinion. It makes my job easier—even though it is not factual."

"I'm not all right," Deke said flatly. "I feel like my whole world has come unraveled. First, to find out my mother and father were not my real parents. My aunt is not my aunt. My brother and only remaining relative is now gone ..." Deke felt a lump rising in his throat and fell quiet. He abruptly turned to stand facing the preacher. "Tell me, is God mad at me?"

"I think you know better than that." Mike's statement was kind and subdued. "You heard the gospel of salvation growing up. You have heard it preached in my church. And I know you have heard it from your brother, Cecil. He told me."

Deke felt his pulse increase, and his voice did not seem like his own. "I know that Jesus is in the business of forgiving sinners. But I cannot forgive myself. This is something I can't fix, and it haunts me."

"Forgiveness begins with the Lord. Only when you seek that will you be ready to forgive yourself," Mike said.

Deke bit his lip and scuffed the ground with one boot. He raised his head and looked at the concerned face of the pastor. Then he couldn't help himself—the tragic story of the homeless man who Deke had struck with his vehicle and killed all tumbled out.

Deke's breath was rapid, and he fought to control his eyes as moisture there threatened to dissolve full blown tears. "Mike, I came back to my roots to find peace, and it was not here. I was mistaken."

The pastor took Deke's shoulders in his hands. "You are ignoring the grace and forgiveness of the Lord. Let go and let him show you what he has for you. Do you want to do that?"

Deke could only nod.

Rita was looking forward to the afternoon riding time with Deke. He had been so stoic about the loss of Cecil. On top of that, she knew he was still recovering from the news of his real parents. *I can't push him. He is grieving, but he won't let me in. Please Lord, give him the peace only you can give him.*

She looked out on the fields and the barn that now belonged to Deke. *Yes, his truck is there. Whose car is that?*

She slowed the convertible down. *Oh, it's brother Mike.* However, neither Deke nor Mike were in sight. She eased into the opening of the driveway of the front gate, then stopped. They were kneeling—hands folded on the lower corral rail facing away from her. Zorro and Mandy were standing still a few feet away, watching them intently. *They were praying!*

She did not want to break the spell of the moment and shut her car's motor off. The scene was almost surreal. Two horses reverently watching—and now she could see Plato sitting on his haunches facing the same way as the men. Very still.

Rita was struck by the intimacy of nature and mankind, humbled by their Creator. Suddenly, tears coursed down her face as her hands folded on the steering wheel. "Oh, God, touch the heart of my Deke."

Rita blinked her eyes open and saw through a blurry veil of tears the silhouettes of the two men climbing to their feet. Deke paused to sweep his hat from the ground. Pastor Mike embraced Deke, and Deke returned the act, lifting him from the ground. Faintly, she could hear laughter from both men. Plato had stayed still enough and began to bark and dance around. *I don't want them to think I saw them.*

The attorney grabbed some tissue in the glove box and, looking into the mirror, dabbed her eyes. Her eyeliner was somewhat smudged. *Don't have time to do damage control.*

Satisfied she had minimized the streaking, she looked at the gathering of animals and men again. At this point, Deke was on one knee and petting Plato. Plato was energetically licking his face.

She started the engine and slowly drove toward the barn. As she drew closer, the two men turned to the sound of the engine and lifted their hands in greeting. Rita tried to be nonchalant as she stepped from the car. Plato rushed to her and made grunting noises as though he had something to tell her. She rubbed his head vigorously and said, "What's he trying to tell me?"

Deke nodded at him. "He does seem like he has something he wants to share."

Rita looked to Deke, ceased her petting, and walked toward Deke with a smile. He extended both hands and seized hers with a little more pressure than usual. She winced. He quickly released some of the pressure and reddened. "Oh, I am sorry, babe. Just got carried away at seeing you again." He kissed her on the cheek and stood there with a contented smile.

Rita knitted her brows and asked, "What's going on? I just saw you for coffee this morning."

Pastor Mike intervened. "Well, I got to make my rounds. See you all in church tomorrow. Deke, that means you too." The pastor affected a severe look at the deputy and pointed his finger at him. The stern look evaporated and was replaced by a smile. "Bless you, brother."

"Oh, one more thing." Pastor Mike took Rita by the hand and pulled her from Deke's grasp. A few steps away, he leaned down to Rita and conspiratorially said, "Ask your man about what's going on. And make him tell you."

"Pastor, you would never make a good criminal. I can still hear you," Deke warned.

Mike looked back at Deke, then winked at Rita. He continued to his car, whistling an old gospel song, and waved goodbye out the open window.

Deke and Rita watched as he disappeared down the country road. Rita turned to Deke and asked, "Now are you going to tell me what he is talking about?"

"All in good time, my princess. Let's saddle the horses and ride on this beautiful day."

"Can you at least give me a hint?" Rita pleaded.

Deke looked down, then up at Rita as he played with his hat. "Well, do they heat the water up before they baptize saints at the church?"

"Oh, oh, darling Deke." Rita was in his arms so quickly he almost lost his balance.

"Whoa," a surprised Deke exclaimed. "I just don't like cold water."

They both laughed and walked arm in arm to the waiting horses.

CHAPTER 46

Deke pulled into the driveway of Cecil's cabin, still unable to call it his. He jumped out of his truck and held the door while Plato jumped out of the truck to join him. Plato spun around and whimpered. "What's a matter, boy?" Then he saw Cecil's hat lying on the seat—

"Okay. We don't want to forget his lid." Deke grabbed the ancient straw hat and handed it to the dog.

Deke looked at the lonely cabin, half-expecting Cecil to open the door. Knowing his brother had gone to his reward, he smiled, feeling the happiest he had been in a long time. The events of yesterday were still vivid. He had accepted the Lord. But the event of making it public in church this morning was the apex. Yes, he had been nervous, but he wanted to tell others of his salvation. No, that was not quite right. He had to make that announcement.

Still holding the hat in his mouth, Plato directed his attention to the road. Deke smiled. "Yep, she is coming."

Plato, started down the path, wagging his tail. "No. Stay here. It's open." Plato heeded his command and sat waiting expectantly.

Rita pulled up in her convertible, and he stepped forward to open her door. Immediately, Rita clutched at his arms and kissed him deeply.

"I wanted to do that in church this morning but decided it would not be appropriate."

Deke cocked his head and frowned. "Well, I think it would have been all right. Didn't Jesus teach us to love each other?"

Rita punched him lightly in the stomach and suppressed a chuckle. She looked down at Plato observing the strange antics of this couple. "Isn't that Cecil's hat?"

"It's a long story. I just wanted to feed him again and pick up his dishes. It seems he doesn't like the new feed bowls I bought him. Persnickety mutt. And I want to look inside."

"I'll feed Plato— you go do what you need to do."

Deke climbed the stairs and opened the creaking door. He walked to the center of the room and looked around. The clock was still ticking, but he walked over to it and wound it. There was the other photo of his parents. His birth parents. It would take some time, but he'd straighten it all out. God and him. He liked the sound of that.

He opened the door and saw Rita petting and talking to Plato. She looked up and smiled. "He's grieving. I know you are taking care of him at your place, but he will miss it here. We have to convince him we are here for him."

"We." She said, "We."

Deke took her arm and stared into her bright blue eyes. "I know we have known each other for only five or six months. And our initial meeting was a little hostile."

Rita arched one eyebrow. "Indeed."

"I now have a farm and a dog. The only thing I'm lacking is a wife." Deke cocked his head to the side and gently squeezed her arm. "Will you take that position?"

She laughed. "You sound like you're giving me a job interview. I want to know how you feel about me."

"I've loved you almost from the start. And no, that will not change. I am too stubborn. I want to marry you."

"You sweet, insufferable, stubborn, man. I love you too."

They embraced and kissed a long-enduring kiss as Plato watched. When they parted, they walked down the steps and enthusiastically discussed a future homesite on the farm. Life was not perfect, but with Rita by his side, Deke could handle anything life handed him.

ABOUT THE AUTHOR

Dr. Brent Brantley has lived and worked in the South Pacific as a Community Development Specialist, taught internationally, worked a ten-year career in law enforcement, and served in missions twenty-eight years. He holds a doctorate in social research. His first novel, *You Cannot Grasp the River*, was published in 2021 by Elk Lake Publishing, Inc.

YOU CANNOT GRASP THE RIVER

Available at Amazon and other bookstore

www.ingramcontent.com/pod-product-compliance
Lightning Source LLC
Chambersburg PA
CBHW071149020726
47502CB00002B/338